Photograph © Justine Stoddart

# ZIZOU CORDER

is the not-so-secret identity of Louisa Young and her daughter
Isabel Adomakoh Young, who have been writing together since
Isabel was seven. They have previously written four books:
the LIONBOY trilogy and LEE RAVEN, BOY THIEF.
They wander the world in a gilded balloon, and have seventeen
pet ducks and twelve miniature grand pianos, as well as the
lizard and the dead tortoise.

# ZIZOU CORDER

# HALΘ

PUFFIN

PUFFIN BOOKS

Published by the Penguin Group
Penguin Books Ltd, 80 Strand, London WC2R 0RL, England
Penguin Group (USA) Inc., 375 Hudson Street, New York, New York 10014, USA
Penguin Group (Canada), 90 Eglinton Avenue East, Suite 700, Toronto, Ontario, Canada M4P 2Y3
(a division of Pearson Penguin Canada Inc.)
Penguin Ireland, 25 St Stephen's Green, Dublin 2, Ireland (a division of Penguin Books Ltd)
Penguin Group (Australia), 250 Camberwell Road, Camberwell, Victoria 3124, Australia
(a division of Pearson Australia Group Pty Ltd)
Penguin Books India Pvt Ltd, 11 Community Centre, Panchsheel Park, New Delhi – 110 017, India
Penguin Group (NZ), 67 Apollo Drive, Rosedale, North Shore 0632, New Zealand
(a division of Pearson New Zealand Ltd)
Penguin Books (South Africa) (Pty) Ltd, 24 Sturdee Avenue, Rosebank, Johannesburg 2196, South Africa

Penguin Books Ltd, Registered Offices: 80 Strand, London WC2R 0RL, England

puffinbooks.com

First published 2010
1

Text copyright © Zizou Corder, 2010
Map copyright © David Atkinson, 2010
All rights reserved

The moral right of the author has been asserted

Set in Perpetua 13.5/16pt
Typeset by Palimpsest Book Production Limited, Grangemouth, Stirlingshire
Made and printed in England by Clays Ltd, St Ives plc

British Library Cataloguing in Publication Data
A CIP catalogue record for this book is available from the British Library

ISBN: 978-0-141-32830-0

www.greenpenguin.co.uk

Penguin Books is committed to a sustainable future
for our business, our readers and our planet.
The book in your hands is made from paper
certified by the Forest Stewardship Council.

Mixed Sources
Product group from well-managed
forests and other controlled sources
www.fsc.org  Cert no. SA-COC-1592
© 1996 Forest Stewardship Council

*To Flora and Polly Docherty, heroines*

# Χαπτερ 1

S omething was crawling up the beach. It was a turtle, of course, because it was turtle-sized and turtle-shaped and turtles were the only things that ever crawled up this beach. Kyllarus squinted down at it from up on the cliff. The sun, pale golden in the pearly blue dawn sky out to sea, cast its shining path across the water, so smooth now after that wild stormy night. Already it was a little warm on his brown arms and bare chest.

He was meant to be looking for a goat that had wandered off during the night, and he knew his wife, Chariklo, would be waiting: for the goat, for the milk, for Arko to have for breakfast.

Well, who knows? Perhaps the goat had gone down there on to the beach. It was a mad little runaway, always jumping over things and climbing up them.

He peered over the rough cliff edge.

But it was — unlike a turtle. Its movements were wrong, and its shape. And it wasn't the season for turtles to crawl up the beach to lay their soft little eggs in the sand. Nor, for that matter, for baby turtles to crawl back down the beach once they'd hatched.

Plus it was too big to be a turtle.

He decided to go and look.

When he reached the beach, scrabbling slightly over the rocks for which his hooves were *not* designed, he cantered lightly towards where the turtle was still steadily crawling along.

He stopped and stared.

It was absolutely not a turtle.

For a start it was made of wood. And then, the four legs sticking out were not scaly turtle flippers. They were – well. He wasn't sure what they were. The front two were little arms, like his own, he recognized that – though they were soft and plump and very smooth and pale and very very small. The back two flummoxed him. He had never seen anything like them. They were like the arms, but stronger-looking, and bending differently. He stared and stared, and after a while he sighed deeply.

The not-turtle heard the sigh, and stopped its determined voyage up the sand.

Kyllarus, holding his breath, continued to watch.

The not-turtle pushed itself up on its arms, raised itself – and toppled, flopping over on to its back. As it did so, it let out a wail.

And that, even if he hadn't now seen inside the wooden turtle shell, Kyllarus recognized.

'It's a baby!' he gasped, and he trotted over to it. He picked it up, still in its shell, and began to cuddle it and sing the little song he always sang to his son, Arko, when he fell or bumped into something. He held it against his chest, and he could feel its little limbs moving and kicking against him. *Strong!* he thought with a smile. The baby kept on yelling.

He held it out at arm's length, and got his first look at its face: bright red, furious, howling, with thick black tufty curly hair flopping wetly over it. Cautiously with his thumb Kyllarus pushed the hair back. There was a small starfish stuck behind one tiny ear.

'By all the nymphs on this beautiful beach,' he said. 'If you are a human baby, then why are you wandering about all alone in a turtle shell?' So he laid it down on the beach and began to unravel it.

The shell, he decided, was some kind of cradle. The child had been strapped in, with a long cloth wrapped round it, which had come loose, and leather straps across the front, which hadn't. 'Well, that's probably saved your life, little turtle,' he murmured as he undid the straps and took out the child. The cloth, sodden, limp and dripping wet sand, fell away, and there it was: a cross little human baby with fish in its hair and a very very wet nappy.

Chariklo, when she saw the baby tucked under Kyllarus's arm, the goat under the other – he'd found it eating figs down by the spring – and the cradle on his head like a helmet as there was no other way to carry it, gave a little shriek and dropped the woollen blanket she had been folding.

'What is that?' she squawked.

'It's a baby!' he said cheerfully. 'I found it on the beach, sea-born like Aphrodite. What do you think?'

'I think it's a human,' said Chariklo, and she came closer to have a look.

Kyllarus dropped the goat (which ran off again, bleating) and took the cradle off his head.

'Here you are,' he said, and he handed the baby to Chariklo.

Chariklo held it in her hands and peered at it. It glared at her with its ferocious green eyes, kicked madly and yelled.

'How lovely!' cried Chariklo. 'Do you think we can keep it?'

'Of course,' said Kyllarus. 'What else? It's clearly clever, and lucky, because it managed to ride the stormy seas in its little cradleboat last night, and then, when it came to land, it turned over and clambered up the sand – so it's strong too. Maybe it's a new hero, like in the old days!'

'It can be a friend for Arko,' said Chariklo. 'It must be hungry, too. Bring some milk, sweetheart. Oh, Mama Demeter, where's that goat now?'

Kyllarus cantered over and grabbed it, just as it thought it had made good its escape. 'Oh no you don't,' he said. 'Come here and be milked for our new baby.'

Chariklo was unwrapping the infant. She took off its sea-sodden nappy. 'It's a girl!' she said. 'Hello, little girl. Oh! Kyllarus – look.'

'What is it?' said Kyllarus, turning to her and squirting a bit of warm smelly goat's milk on his leg as he did so.

Because of the sand and the cloth and the wet hair, Kyllarus had not noticed before what Chariklo now pointed out. Knotted on to a fine leather thong about the baby's neck was a tiny gold amulet.

'Look, it's a little owl.'

'So it is,' he said. 'Look at those big eyes. Well, maybe she belongs to Athena, not to Aphrodite after all.'

Chariklo was wiping the baby's damp, sandy face with a clean cloth.

She gasped. 'Oh – Kyllarus! Look at this!'

'What now?' said Kyllarus. 'This baby is full of surprises.'

Kyllarus looked, and gave a little gasp himself.

'What in all Hellas can that mean?' he asked.

It was not surprising that he hadn't seen it before, for her face had been very dirty and the mark was fine and delicately done. But it was unmistakable. Across her forehead was a small, feathery, blue-black symbol, right between her brows, looking almost as if it were part of them. A down stroke, and two semicircles crossing it, the lower, wider one cradling the smaller upper one, lying as it were on their backs, like two new moons speared to the ground by an arrow; or a tree with four wide, symmetrical branches; or a four-armed woman spinning in a dance, her hands held out and up in joy.

'It doesn't come off,' said Chariklo, wiping at it.

'How odd!' said Kyllarus. 'To tattoo a baby! It must mean something, but Zeus only knows what.'

Chariklo gazed at it a while longer. 'It's not a symbol I've ever seen,' she said. 'It doesn't even look Greek, does it?'

'Maybe our baby is foreign,' said Kyllarus.

'Maybe she is,' said Chariklo. 'She'll have a foreign mother somewhere, weeping and sighing because she has lost her baby . . .'

'Well, maybe,' said Kyllarus, and Chariklo bit her lip, and said, 'Oh – yes, I suppose . . . Well, wherever she's from, she still needs her breakfast.' Without thinking, Chariklo put the baby on the floor.

The baby promptly fell over, and squawked indignantly.

'Oh no!' cried Chariklo, who, being accustomed to

Centaur babies, hadn't realized that human babies couldn't walk. Centaur babies can stand up on their slender little foal legs soon after being born – though their human torsos are still quite soft and weak. They don't start galloping about until they are around a year old, and then they get into all sorts of trouble, because their horse legs are quick and strong to take them into situations their human toddler heads aren't wise enough to deal with.

'Oh, I'm so sorry!' she squeaked, and hurriedly scooped the baby up again. 'Are you all right? Oh dear . . . I wonder how you're meant to carry her,' she said to Kyllarus. 'It can't be like this,' she mused, holding the baby in both hands, 'or human parents would never get anything done . . . Oh! I know!' She had an idea, and slipped the baby on to her hip, just where her human torso met her horse flank. 'There. That's better,' she said, holding the baby in place with her left arm and feeling the little legs wrapping round her waist. She strolled across and filled a basin with water from their well. 'I wonder how old she is,' she said.

'Hard to tell with a human,' said Kyllarus.

The baby, meanwhile, had discovered Chariklo's hair, which was long and curly and dark red, and fell down her back in some rather untidy plaits, one of which the little one was now chewing. Chariklo disentangled her, put her in the basin and poured fresh water over her. She made sure there was no sand left in the creases of her knees and neck, and no more fish in her hair. Then she rubbed olive oil all over her, and poured some of the warm goat's milk into the little clay bottle she used for giving water to Arko. She put the cloth teat over its spout, and she cradled the little turtle-child in her arms to feed her. *How strange*, she thought, *to be able to hold your whole baby!* It was rather nice – cuddlier than a Centaur foal baby. *She's quite normal*, she thought, *if you don't look below her middle.* Chariklo peeked again at the funny little human legs, smooth and soft and pinky-gold. She started giggling.

'She's really nothing like a turtle,' she said. 'We could call her after one of the sea nymphs. Amphitrite, or Halosydne, or Amathea – Oh! Is that Arko?'

A cry had caught her ear. It was indeed Arko, waking up in the open vine-covered arbour where they all slept in the summer. 'Fetch him, darling, would you?' she asked, and Kyllarus brought him over, holding his hand, as he wobbled on his long baby legs.

'You feed him and I'll feed her,' said Kyllarus, and they folded their legs under them and sat in the shade together, the four of them, as the sun rose higher up the sky, and the babies gulped their milk.

## Χαπτερ 2

There are two tribes of Centaur: the Sons of Ixion, who were wild and bad, and the Sons of Cronus, who were wise and kind. In the dawn of time Ixion, who was a human, had a mad passion for Hera, the Queen of the Gods. Her husband, Zeus, the most powerful God of all, made a fake Hera out of clouds to trick him, and Ixion got the cloud-Hera pregnant, and the result was the wild Centaurs. They lived in Thessaly, in Greece, but after getting drunk and trying to steal the bride from a wedding they had to leave there. Those that weren't killed in the fight wandered off into the woods, and some of them died, and some, it is said, turned into bandits, and some, it is said, turned into horses.

One of them, though, was lucky enough to meet one of the wise Centaurs, a young daughter of Cronus, descendant of Chiron, the wisest Centaur of all, who trained Asclepius, the God of medicine, and the heroes Heracles and Jason and Achilles. Well, the two young Centaurs fell in love, and after a bit of fuss with her family they got married, and he came back to live with her herd. Soon after, the whole herd, in search of peace and quiet, emigrated, leaving Thessaly, crossing the forests and mountains, swimming the deep channel by moonlight to the beautiful and fairly empty island of Zakynthos – but that's another story.

Those two were the great-great-great-great-great-great-

great-grandparents of Kyllarus, and nobody in his herd ever forgot that his family had wild and naughty blood.

So when Arko's two big sisters, Pearl and Lucy, the lovely twins, came prancing into the *agora*,[1] chatting about their new human baby sister, a couple of old ladies said, 'If you'd asked me which family would adopt a human, I could have told you it would be that lot.' Pearl and Lucy didn't care. They carried on about how she was so sweet and lovely and they were going to teach her all the ancient stories and how to plait her hair and oil her skin and read and write and weave and dance and hunt and use the bow and arrow and make honey baklava[2] and perfume out of roses.

The leader of the herd, who was also called Chiron, sent Lucy and Pearl back to get their parents. The whole family came: Kyllarus, Chariklo, Lucy, Pearl, Arko and Grandma. And the baby.

'Chariklo,' asked Chiron. 'What is this?'

Chariklo said, keeping a straight face, 'It's a baby, Chiron.'

'Thank you, Chariklo,' he said. 'I know it's a baby. What is it doing here?'

'Dad thought it was a turtle!' said Pearl.

'It was all rolled up in a cloth with its legs sticking out!' said Lucy.

'We've been thinking probably it fell off a ship,' said Kyllarus, 'during the storm. But somebody loved it. Her, sorry. She had a very nice cloth wrapped round her, and a golden owl round her neck. She wasn't . . . you know . . .'

The Centaurs all went quiet. They knew what he meant. He meant — abandoned.

Sometimes, when humans had too many children, or when they didn't want a girl baby, or they thought the baby was too weak or had something wrong with it, they would just leave it outside, on the hillside, to die.

Several of the Centaurs shivered at the thought. They were kind creatures. In the old days, before the time of Homer the Poet, the Centaurs had quite often taken in abandoned human children. But most of the Centaurs of Zakynthos had never even seen an actual human, and if they had, it was safely far away, at sea, on a boat.

Chiron looked at the baby. She looked back at him – not the furious glare now, because she was clean and dry and full of goat's milk, and furthermore Pearl and Lucy had been tickling her tummy with their long hair, so she was happy. She gave Chiron a big smile with six little teeth in it, and waved her arms at him, and burped.

He smiled back.

'We should have a vote,' he said. 'Put the word out, and we'll vote tonight. And that means everyone!'

'But what's the vote between?' said Chariklo anxiously. 'I mean, what's the alternative? I mean, if the vote says we can't keep her, then . . .'

'We have to have a vote, you know that,' said Chiron. 'It's the law. No one can join the herd without being accepted.'

'But she's an orphan!' said Kyllarus. 'She has nowhere to go. And how would she get there if she did? We can't put her back in her turtle shell and send her back out to sea . . . What's the law on orphans?'

Chiron thought. 'I don't think we have one,' he said.

'Well, why don't we have a vote on that?' said Chariklo. 'A vote to have a law to say we have to look after orphans. And helpless babies.'

'It's our custom, traditionally, after all . . .' said Kyllarus.

That night all the adult Centaurs, after their dinner with their families, came back to the *agora*, and voted without exception to pass a law saying what they all felt in their hearts anyway – that they had to look after orphans and helpless babies.

Halosydne, they decided, would be her name. Pearl and Lucy chose it. It meant 'The Girl Who Was Fed by the Sea', but they thought of it more as 'Saved by the Sea'. 'With a name like that, the sea can never harm her,' they reasoned. Most people called her Halo, but Kyllarus always called her Chelonakimu – my little turtle – or Little Aphrodite, or some other affectionate nickname: Schnussy because that was the noise she made when she pulled at his earlobes; Owly-baby because of her amulet and her big round eyes; Captain Thumpy when she hit her fists against his chest in fury at being picked up and saved from some childhood peril; Dolly Dolphin when she started swimming underwater; Figling when she fell out of the fig tree.

Arko had lots of different names for her too. 'Pigling', at first, when he was jealous of her and was being mean, because she was pink like a pig, and had no proper glossy chestnut horsehide. But as soon as she could run about she was in the sun all day so she didn't stay pink and plump for long – soon she was a fine golden brown all over. Really all over, because she didn't wear clothes in the summer either

— why would she? Chariklo and the other Centaur women wove cloth for cloaks for the Centaurs to wrap around their shoulders when the north winds came, and for Halo they made a chiton[3] because, as Chariklo's mother said, 'She does seem a lot more naked than us, in that delicate skin. The fine, soft cloth that Halo had been wrapped in they put carefully away. 'It would last no time here,' Chariklo said, so she folded it with lavender flowers and wrapped it in another piece of cloth and put it in the stone barn where they stored their nuts and olives and dried grapes and wine. Only occasionally would Chariklo take it out and tell Halo the story of how she was found — a story which delighted all the young Centaurs. They would often ask for it round the fire on winter nights, along with the ancient stories of the Centaurs, and the tales of the Greeks and the Trojans, the heroes and the Gods.

And so it came about that Halo's first memory — one that stayed with her all her life — was of the deep, dark, star-spattered night sky above Zakynthos. It was so beautiful she could hardly bear to close her eyes to sleep. The night sky above her, cool and velvety, was the same deep blue as the deep sea by day. The stars and constellations hung against it so very bright that the patterns they made were printed on her eyes, and when she woke before dawn she saw them hanging on the other side of the sky. The air was cool and the ground beneath her was hard, but the woolly goatskin she lay on was warm and snug. The faint sweet scent of sea lilies rose up from the distant beach on the cool breeze. The quiet voices of the adults drifted over from the fire, where they sat late into the evening drinking the dark pink wine, which tasted of sunlight and dust. At her back, for her to curl against, was the warm chestnut flank of Arko, her dear friend, gently rising and falling, safe and warm, fast asleep. So her first memory was of something she felt almost every night of her childhood: that peaceful feeling of looking up at the stars, night and morn, warm and snug, with the cool fresh breeze on her nose and Arko beside her.

# Χαπτερ 3

One day, Halo was running and playing with Arko: he was teasing her, as usual, and she was trying to run as fast as him, still believing that if only she tried harder her human legs would be able to keep up with his horse legs.

She ran too fast and too bold. She tripped. She fell. She put her arm up to shield her face.

Her shriek of pain called the whole herd to attention and they came galloping up.

She had landed awkwardly. Her arm had hit a rock. The angle was wrong, her arm was . . . oh and the pain . . .

There was a bend where no bend should be. No blood. Just a strange bend in the middle of her forearm, and the skin misshapen over it. She could feel her hand and wrist dangling, wrong, agonizing, limp.

Chiron came. He knelt by her side, took hold of her arm.

'Watch,' he said to her. 'Watch through the pain and learn.'

She stared at his kind, ugly face and tried very very hard to do as he said. The others were standing around them, silent and attentive. Chariklo cantered up with a basket of equipment, including a jar of wine. Chiron gave Halo a cup to drink, unwatered. It was rich and strange.

'Watch!' said Chiron again. 'It will be all right. It's not all right now, but it will be all right.'

A fine sweat stood on her brow. A sweep of overwhelming pain overtook her, worse than anything, ever, ever . . . She shrieked again.

She forced her eyes open, and stared at Chiron's strong brown hands on her arm.

He was pulling her arm apart: one hand firm around her forearm just below her elbow, the other circling her wrist. The bend was between his two hands.

He was pulling her broken arm apart.

She howled but no sound came out.

A flaming blaze of pain.

Agony.

And within the agony, she felt a click. A clunk. A snap.

She looked at her arm. Chiron's hands were still in place. But the bend, the broken wrong bend, had disappeared.

Her bones were whole. It was all back in place. Tender, bruised, unbelievably painful still, but whole. It was as if he had slotted them back into place. He *had* slotted them back into place. Pulled them apart, and slotted them back.

She was shaking but she still tried to watch as he gently wrapped her arm in aromatic herbs, telling her their names as he did so, and bound it with a piece of soft cloth. She tried to repeat the names of the herbs, concentrating to keep the pain from overwhelming her. She stared as he laid a straight smooth length of wood under the soft inside of her forearm, and carefully, so kindly, bound it in place with strips. Chariklo had folded a third piece of cloth into a triangle: now they set her arm to rest in its fold, and tied it behind her neck in a sling. Another cup of wine; a cup of bitter herb tea, instruction to rest. She spent the time while she healed learning to read. Chiron came to see her.

'The ancient Chiron had to do that for Jason, you know, when he was a lad,' he said. 'And he taught Apollo's son, the God Asclepius, how to do it, and all the medicine the humans know. Do you think you could do it? Were you paying attention?'

'Maybe,' said Halo cautiously. She was only about seven. She was pretty sure she would never be able to do it. At least – she hoped she would be brave enough to do it. But she was far from sure.

'You can't go around breaking people's arms on purpose, to practise mending them,' said Chiron seriously. 'You've got to learn when you can. So what herbs did I use?'

She ran through the names of the herbs, and what they were for.

'Good girl,' he said. 'Remember the cures, and you'll always be able to help people. And animals.'

Within a month she could play her flute again; within two she started practising her archery again; within four her arm was as strong as ever, or stronger. Next time somebody broke a bone, Halo was at Chiron and Chariklo's side, helping and learning.

'All right, I'll never be as fast as you,' she said to Arko. 'I'll be a better shot instead. And better at curing people.'

'As if,' he said.

'You wait and see,' she said.

'Dad,' said Pearl, one evening some years after this, as they sat around admiring the rich red full moon rising over the sea. 'If that's the harvest moon, then it's ten years since Halo came. We should have a party for her.'

'What, with music and dancing and we'll invite all the boys?' said Kyllarus.

'Of course,' said Pearl.

She and Lucy were fifteen now, and would be getting married in a year or two. They loved music and dancing. And the boys.

'OK by me,' said Kyllarus. 'What do you think, Chariklo?'

Chariklo smiled. 'I'll tune my lyre,' she said, 'and make yoghurt. We'll need honey and wine.'

'Halo can go up a tree and find some honey,' said Lucy.

With her skinny brown legs, Halo could go all sorts of places that Centaurs couldn't reach: up trees, over rocks, down cliffs, right into the backs of caves. Arko would give her a leg-up, or she would climb up over his back, and he carried home her booty – figs, blackberries, sea urchins and octopuses for the grill, olives from the very tops of the silvery trees for oil, wild honeycombs.

Even though it was not really allowed, he would carry her on his back, and she would clutch him round his waist as he galloped about. Chiron had told them off for it: 'A Centaur carries only himself,' he said. 'He is not designed to carry any other person.' But Arko and Halo had just giggled about that as soon as he had gone. She could stand on his back, or his shoulders, and jump and do all sorts of tricks.

'And we'll go and get some figs,' said Arko innocently. There were reasons why Arko and Halo always volunteered to get the figs.

'I'll make baklava,' murmured Kyllarus.

'Tell us a story, sweetheart,' said Chariklo, leaning against her husband affectionately. 'Tell us . . . about the first Kyllarus, and Hylomene.'

Kyllarus went quiet for a moment.

'Are you sure?' he said to his wife.

'Tell us, tell us!' clamoured their children, but then Lucy saw that her father's face was serious, and she hushed the others.

'They're old enough to know,' Chariklo said. 'Tell them.'

'Well,' said Kyllarus. 'All right.' And he took a sip of wine, and cleared his throat, and sat up, and began.

'You have all heard about the night of the great shame of the Centaurs, when the Sons of Ixion betrayed their honour as guests. The daredevil human Pirithous, himself a son of Ixion, invited his Centaur brothers and sisters to his wedding. The feast was generous, and the guests cheerful. Kyllarus, my ancestor, was there with his wife, the beautiful Hylomene, who wore jasmine and rosemary in her hair . . . As the night grew late and the moon rose, too much strong wine was drunk, and in drink, bold Eurytus, the fiercest Centaur, stole Hippodamia, the bride of Pirithous, to his eternal shame. You have heard how the other Centaurs joined battle to defend Eurytus even though he was in the wrong; how Thereus, who could capture mountain bears and bring them home snarling, was killed, and Phaecomes dressed in six great lion skins laced together, and Dorylas in his wolf-skin cap with bull's horns . . . The hero Theseus was Pirithous's twin soul and fought magnificently for him . . . Enough of that, blood and shame.

'There was, that awful night, one moment of honour.

'That night Kyllarus, after whom I am named, tried to stop the fighting. But he was caught between his brother Centaurs and his human brothers, and in the heat of the violence his voice was not heard. Everyone was mad with bloodlust and drink.

'Peaceful Kyllarus, that night, was killed. A spear pierced his heart from behind, pierced right through him. And as he fell, Hylomene, seeing her husband bleeding to death, threw herself into his human arms, on to the blade of the spear that pierced him, so that she could die with him. Beautiful Hylomene, who wore jasmine in her hair, and loved her children . . .'

Kyllarus fell silent. There were tears in his eyes, and his children stared. Only the sound of crickets singing disturbed the night.

'Is that true?' whispered Pearl.

'True,' said Kyllarus.

'What happened to the children?' whispered Lucy, finally.

'The eldest son wandered the woods until he met his true love under the pomegranate tree, and the grandparents looked after the little ones,' said Chariklo softly. 'They grew up, they survived. They swore themselves to peace, and against fighting.'

'It was difficult for the boys, because in those days if you didn't fight you were nothing,' said Kyllarus. 'But my ancestor who combined with the Sons of Cronus learned that there are other roads to respect. He learned that if you have wisdom you don't need to shed blood.'

'I didn't know Centaurs had human brothers. I mean blood brothers, not like us and Halo,' said Arko.

'Nor did I,' said Pearl. 'Why weren't they Centaurs too?'

'Because their mother wasn't a cloud,' said Lucy.

'How can a cloud have a baby anyway?' asked Arko.

'It's because of Zeus,' said Pearl. 'He was always turning himself into different things to have babies – a swan, and a bull, and a cloud of gold . . .'

'It was the old days,' said Chariklo. 'All sorts of things went on in the old days that couldn't happen now.'

'So does a human have only one heart?' asked Halo. 'Because they were pierced through their human hearts, but they still died even though they still had their horse hearts.'

'That's right,' said Chariklo. 'We need both our hearts to live.'

Arko was about to tease Halo for only having one heart, when an idea occurred to him. 'So will Halo marry a Centaur or a human?' he asked, and suddenly a silence fell.

Chariklo and Kyllarus shot each other a look. They had, as their older daughters grew near to marriageable age, thought of this.

Well, the question had been asked, and so they had to answer it.

'A human,' said Chariklo, trying to make it sound as normal as possible.

'What?' Halo squawked. 'What?'

'*Eyurgh*,' said Arko.

'Shut up, Arko,' said Kyllarus.

'Must she really?' asked Lucy. 'Ooh. How odd.'

Halo was staring at them all.

'I can't marry a human,' she said, panicking. 'I've never even met a human. I've never even seen a human. I'm not a human . . .'

'Well, you are, darling,' said Chariklo. 'I'm afraid you are.'

Halo did not sleep well that night. She couldn't free her mind of the image of Kyllarus and Hylomene, torn between their human brothers and their Centaur brothers, lying speared and dead together. But alongside that was another, almost more frightening image. Herself, with humans.

On the day of the party, Halo and Arko, with a set of panniers across his back, set off to the big fig patch by the bay. The land was scrubby and dry with wild fennel and old hay, but it was cool beneath the ilex and hibiscus trees, and mostly downhill. Coming back up would be a different story – it would be hot.

At the fig patch, they unloaded the baskets, but they didn't start picking yet. They had another plan first, and the figs would only rot and get ants in them if they were left lying around.

The cool blue water twinkled in the sun ahead of them. Arko started heading across the smooth white sand, but Halo grabbed his tail, shouting, 'Oi! Wait!' Then she clambered up on to his broad chestnut back, and grabbed him round his waist. He cantered out into the shining shallow waters, kicking up froth and bubbles behind him until the cold bright sea was up to his human chest. He paused, and she stood up easily on his back, the friendly little waves breaking against her shins.

'Go on, before I buck you off!' he cried, and she stretched up in the hot sun against the blue blue sky and dived off, SPLASH, into the cavernous, luminous turquoise light of the sea.

When she came up Arko was laughing at her. 'You look like a mermaid when you dive,' he said. 'Like a sea nymph. I could see your flicky scaly tail.'

'Well, you look like a human!' she retorted.

He did – all his horse body was underwater. He glanced down. 'Ugh,' he said, 'human, how revolting,' so she splashed him, and he splashed her, and then they set off. Warm sunshine bounced all around them. Cephalonia drifted far off ahead, misty and pearly, and they swam round to the Caves.

Neither Arko nor Halo had seen anything of the world beyond Zakynthos, but they both knew for a fact that the Gods couldn't have made anything more beautiful than the Caves. Two Gods had come together to make them: Poseidon and Chronos, carving them out of the white cliffs, leaving arches and gateways, walls of rock and caves within, all the colour of clean bone. Inside the caves, in the morning, Phoebus threw his lancing rays through the water, filling it with clear, crystalline turquoise sunlight, which refracted and reflected until every movement you made left a trail of silvery-blue bubbles, and rainbows danced where the sea foamed on the rock.

They had two special caves. One was much further south, just where the high hills where the Centaurs lived met the flat, low plain where the humans lived. This cave's water was pale and milky and smelt of eggs, and strange bubbles rose in sparkly wobbly strings from the seabed. Halo and Arko could capture the bubbles in their hands and breathe their sweet other-worldly smell, and it would make them giggle and laugh and act foolishly. They argued a lot about where the bubbles came from. Halo thought maybe they came up from Hades, the underworld where the dead go; Arko said it was probably just invisible nymphs farting underwater. They talked a lot of nonsense when they had been breathing the bubbles.

But they didn't often go there. Although the humans didn't seem to know the cave, Halo and Arko didn't feel safe so near their territory.

The other was Arko and Halo's special beautiful cave, where you swam in through a low dark entrance with less than a metre to spare above the sea level, and inside all was turquoise dancing light and flashing bubbles when you splashed, and your whole body turned blue.

So Arko and Halo were playing and splashing about in there, and sitting on the friendly rock at the back to rest from their swim, and soothing their sun-weary eyes in the cool, refreshing sea shade. They were discussing sea nymphs, and regretting that there seemed to be none around there for them to be friends with, and perhaps get magical favours off.

'Perhaps they don't exist any more,' said Arko. 'Or they've gone somewhere else. It's not like the old days. The Gods aren't popping up all over the place, like they used to, getting mixed up in stuff. Just as well, probably. I think they've just sort of stopped, and it's all humans now.'

'Do you think there are any other Centaurs?' Halo asked. It had only just occurred to her that there might be.

'Dunno,' he said, making little silvery patterns in the water with his fingers. 'What, you mean elsewhere in Greece?'

'There could be,' she said.

He just grunted, and she left it, because at that moment, a dark shape crossed the water at the mouth of the cave.

Instinctively, they pulled back against the wall of the cave, into the shadows.

Dark shapes did not cross there. Nothing came there. The other Centaurs didn't come that way. Only Arko and Halo swam in the sea for fun – the others preferred to play in the fresh-water springs back up in the forest. The dolphins played further out to sea. The birds – the big birds – flew higher, and further from the cliff. The goats and foxes and porcupines – none of them swam, and there was no way to the Caves, except by swimming.

Or by boat.

At which thought Halo's throat dried up and her head began to quiver with fear.

She'd never seen a human. She knew about them. They looked like her, with black curly hair and smooth brown limbs. They lived on the south end of the island, and their king had a great white marble palace. They took over wild places and made animals move on. They kept animals for their own use. They built cities – Athens! Sparta! – and told stories. Some of them were noble, such as Homer the great poet who had recorded the stories of Gods and heroes from the old old days, and some of the heroes themselves: Odysseus and Achilles. But they were violent. They fought wars. They slashed each other with great iron swords, and speared each other with murderous iron spears, and shot each other with sharp, death-dealing arrows. They had never learned to be peaceful, as the Centaurs had. They took revenge on each other. They killed each other. And they left their little babies out to die.

Sometimes, from the clifftops, she had seen them sailing past – small boats fishing, or bigger boats heading off to Cephalonia or Ithaca. Once, standing on the clifftop with Kyllarus, she had seen a flock of long, low, swift ships heading north, dark and fast. 'Triremes,' Kyllarus had told her. 'Warships. Do you see all the oars?' They stuck out along each side, like an insect's legs, scudding across the water. They looked so determined. She had tried hard to make out the tiny figures on board, but she had seen nothing.

Now, she so desperately wanted to see nothing.

*Let whatever it was just pass by*, she thought, *and we will wait, and wait, and be late with the figs but we will be safe.*

But the dark shape had paused. They could see its shadow, just in the sunlight beyond the cave's mouth.

They heard movement. A cry, a splash.

Silently, glancing at each other with quiet desperation, they retreated to the very back of the cavern.

*Poseidon, don't let them see us*, she prayed silently. He might be listening. After all, hadn't she been blown safely on to the beach, and named 'Saved by the Sea'?

'Please, Poseidon,' she murmured.

A louder splash – bigger, nearer. Voices. Humans!

They were at the mouth of the cave.

She glanced at Arko. His chestnut eyes caught hers, and he gestured with his head. She knew what he meant. He knew what she meant.

Together, they breathed in deeply, and slowly, silently, sank down beneath the water.

## Χαπτερ 4

I t's a different world underwater. The sudden silence, the adaptation to different, underwater sounds. The stinging saltiness on the eyeballs. The clear heaviness of water all around you that you have to carve your way through.

Blue light shone down the underwater passage for about fifty metres, and after that they were in the dark. It didn't matter. They knew this passage as they knew all the caves and passages – for five years now they had been exploring and playing here.

Halo knew that if she kicked her legs gently and let her breath out bit by bit, she could make it to the Hole. Arko knew that the passage was deep enough to let him pass, and he knew where the rocks were so he could avoid skinning his knees and hooves – he'd skinned them often enough before. They both knew that they couldn't spend that long in the Hole, because there was no ledge wide enough for Arko to stand on.

Eyes alert, Halo spotted the light ahead, filtering through from the Hole. She speeded up towards the pale turquoise glow. In truth, she was scared, and as a result she went faster than she might have, and used too much breath, and it was with relief that she burst to the surface, salt on her face, the heat of the sun overhead, the blue sky at the top of the Hole, many metres up, and the joy of air flooding into her tight, empty lungs. Behind her, Arko burst up too, splashing and gasping. He swam straight to the wall with the jutting rock he could cling on to, and rested his hooves as best he could against the wall, trying to support his big body. Halo swam over to him and perched on the little rock shelf she always used.

'What do we do now?' she panted, as she got her breath back.

'Wait,' he said. 'We wait.'

'Do you think they saw us?' she said.

'No idea,' he replied, his breath returning. 'But I don't see how they could have. I think we went soon enough. If they saw movement in the water, bubbles and so on, they'd assume it was an octopus, wouldn't they?'

'Yes, or a big fish,' she said.

They were silent for a moment, as it occurred to each of them that the humans were almost certainly fishermen, and that a big octopus or a big fish was probably exactly the kind of thing they were after.

'How will we be able to tell that they've gone?' she asked after a while.

'Don't know,' said Arko, swapping arms and paddling his legs.

'Shall I go and look?' she said.

'No!' he said firmly.

'Or I could . . .' She glanced up the high rock walls of the Hole. Years ago, the Hole had been a cave like any other, but almost as many years ago the roof had caved in, leaving a deep shaft, about ten metres across, with deep water at the bottom, connected via the underwater tunnel to the sea.

The walls were mostly bare rock but there were plenty of ledges, and various small trees that clung on.

'Perhaps I could climb up,' she said.

Arko glanced at the almost sheer walls. 'Perhaps,' he said drily. 'Probably best to wait. You can't swim out again with a broken leg.'

'How long can you hold on for?' she asked.

'As long as it takes,' he said, with a cheerful grin, but she knew from the way he was shifting around that he was already uncomfortable. He couldn't tread water, or hang by his arms, forever. And nor could she stay in the water forever. The sun was already passing from overhead, and without it the sea was cold and the bottom of the shaft chilly even out of the water.

It was beginning to dawn on her that they were in a very tricky situation.

She climbed a little way up the wall, to be out of the water at least. It became apparent that she would not be able to climb to the top. The little plants she grabbed at came out in her hand; rocks tumbled down into the water below, and she scraped her knee quite badly before realizing that there just weren't enough things for her to hold on to. She couldn't get a grip.

'Halo,' he said, when they had been there for about twenty minutes. 'I'm going to swim back, and see if they're gone. I'll be very quiet . . .'

'No,' she said. 'How can you come up for air quietly after a swim like that?'

'But what's the alternative?' he said.

'I'll go,' she said. 'I'm smaller, and quieter. I'll just peek out of the darkness . . .'

'You can't,' he said. 'I can't let you.'

'I can't let *you*,' she said. And they stared at each other.

Then, in a swift movement, Arko hurled himself off the wall, and down under the water, heading in a stream of silver bubbles for the entrance to the tunnel.

'No!' shouted Halo, furiously, and she dived in after him, and snaked her way swiftly into the tunnel ahead of him, dodging his strong legs in the cool water, swimming too fast, but determined not to let him get there first.

*You fool, you're a Centaur!* she was thinking, as she kicked ahead into the darkness. *What would they do with you? They'd kill you like at the wedding, they'd put you in a muzzle on a cart, they'd send you away or sell you as a freak –* She turned suddenly, in the first blue light of the cave opening, and tried to shout to him, to mouth at him, to make it clear to him, that he must go back, and wait, and she would bring him news, and never desert him . . .

But she couldn't see him.

Could he have turned? Was the passage wide enough?

She couldn't see. All was dark.

She had to breathe. Her face was beginning to burst, and shoots of pain crossed her chest like acid in her lungs.

She kicked herself round, and thrust herself forward. The turquoise light was just ahead of her.

And she came up, gagging and gasping, spitting and aching.

And right there, two wet, hairy, bearded creatures were

sitting on her and Arko's ledge, short fishing spears raised, eyes wide with alarm.

They looked kind of like Centaurs, but they had human legs. Humans.

One had been so nearly about to hurl his spear that he dropped it at the sight of her. It clattered on the rock, and fell into the water beside her.

'What the . . .' said one.

'Sweet Aphrodite, it's a girl!' said the other.

'It's a nymph!' said the first.

Halo breathed hugely, turned again, and went under.

And as she sank down beneath the salty surface, she knew she couldn't make it. Physically, she couldn't make it back to the Hole. She was too tired, too short of air. And also – if she swam back, they would follow her. Or they would wait. Or they would send one of them to get help. They had seen her, and they wouldn't let her go. And that meant they would find Arko too.

Arko! Artemis helper of maidens where was he?

She couldn't let them find Arko.

So just as they were jumping in after her, she turned tail again, and with a hard strong push headed for the mouth of the cave, out to the sea, swimming crawl, as fast and clean as she could, breathing well, striking the water smoothly with her long capable arms, pulling ahead . . .

And she was quick. The fishermen in the cave, even though they were strong grown men and she was only a young girl, might not have caught her. But in the boat outside were two more fishermen, and the moment they saw her they leapt on her, and the others caught up, and she was a scramble of limbs and water and fighting and struggling to get away from them, though she knew she had no chance. They dragged her into the boat like a hooked fish, and rolled her up in a net because she wouldn't keep still.

She lay there, finally, panting, weeping, furious, with fish in her hair, cursing Poseidon. Once again, the sea had stolen her and thrown her up into a new life

## Χαπτερ 5

The wet salty ropes were horrible against her skin, and the bottom of the boat stank of fish. She badly wanted to rinse her mouth with fresh water. The fishermen had a water jar and were swigging from it. They were pleased with themselves, chatting away about their catch. She was too proud to ask for water, and they didn't offer her any.

At least, she thought, she had lured them away from Arko. He was safe, and the Centaurs were safe, and she would never give them away. In due course he would realize that she wasn't coming back, and he would guess that the coast was clear, and he would come out, and swim back to the bay, and go home, without the figs, and without her, and . . .

And tell everyone that she was gone, and lost.

She didn't know if the salt on her face was the sea or her tears.

She couldn't bear it. Chariklo! Kyllarus!

She wept silently all the time they were at sea. She was still weeping when they lifted her out of the boat on to a wooden jetty, an hour or so later. She stood, weeping, wrapped still in the fishing net, arms trapped at her side, on dry land at the dock of Zakynthos Town. She raised her weeping head, unable to dry her eyes, and looked for the first time on the world of men.

She saw buildings of mud and stone, with red-tiled roofs. She saw boats, with oars and sails. She saw a road, where the red earth had been packed down tight, with two big ruts to guide cartwheels. She saw carts and donkeys, stalls and crates, and land flatter than she had ever seen before. And she saw people. Men.

She flinched.

They saw her too. Zakynthos, large and strange as it seemed to Halo, was not a large town, and not much happened there. The arrival of a furious weeping girl rolled in a fishing net was of great interest to everybody, and soon half the town was gathered round, squawking and exclaiming and trying to touch her and poke her.

She stood silent, her head high and her teeth clenched. She was in shock. She should just be getting back home now, laden with figs and honey. She should be washing in the spring and oiling herself for her party. She should be laughing with Pearl and Lucy, and thanking Chariklo for the lovely new chiton she knew was being made for her but which she had been pretending not to know about. She shouldn't be here.

'Look at her!' the men were shouting, as if everybody wasn't looking at her already. 'Where's she from? What is she? Is she a nymph? What's that on her forehead? Where did you find her?'

How rude and stupid! Well, she wasn't going to answer their questions. She would never tell them where she was from. She would tell them nothing.

The fishermen were extremely pleased with themselves. No one had paid them so much attention for years. Catching a person was much more fun than catching a fish.

'It's a girl,' they said. 'We found her in a cave. She burst out of the water like a nymph! We thought she *was* a nymph – but she's too ugly. Anyway, she bites like an animal. She was just there, under the water!'

'A nymph! A nymph!' the people murmured, and Halo shook her head furiously to get her wet hair off her face. Stupid people! If they couldn't tell a nymph from a girl they really were stupid.

'But where's she from? Who's her family? Did she grow there?' they were crying now.

'What are you going to do with her?' called a man at the back of the crowd.

'We're going to ask Aristides!' said one of the fishermen, and everybody started nodding and agreeing that this was the right thing to do. Except that Aristides, whoever he was, didn't seem to be around, so they all just carried on standing about, staring at her.

Two hours later, she was still standing there, still wrapped in the fishing net, still furious, but colder and even more angry, when news came that the famous Aristides had returned from wherever he had been, and that the nymph was to be taken to his house to be explained. The fishermen picked her up and carried her between them like a rolled-up rug. It did nothing to improve her mood.

Aristides, when she was plonked down in front of him, turned out to be tall and fat, with an air of authority and impatience.

'What's going on?' he said, looking up wearily. 'What is all this fuss?'

Half the town had crowded into the courtyard of his house.

'Go away, you lot,' he said. 'Only stay if you've got something useful to say. Who's bringing this –' here he stopped to peer at her – 'this creature?'

'Us, Aristides,' yelped the fishermen, jumping up in their importance. 'We found her, in a cave. We don't know what she is . . .'

'She's a girl,' said Aristides. 'What's so extraordinary about that?'

The fishermen were not so easily deflated.

'She's all sun-burned and wild-looking,' said one. 'With that tattoo. And she had no clothes on.'

'And what was she doing up there?' asked another cunningly.

'Having a swim?' suggested Aristides.

'But why up there?' said another fisherman.

'Perhaps she lives up there,' said Aristides.

'But no one lives up there,' objected the fisherman. 'Well, no one except the –'

'If you were thinking of saying Centaurs, you old woman, then don't,' broke in Aristides. 'Centaurs don't exist.'

Halo blinked. Was this what humans were like, after all? Argumentative, rude, and completely ignorant? At least they didn't seem likely to get out their swords and start killing each other right now . . . But they were so rude! And – they were all men. Where were the females?

'But you're right, nobody does live up there,' Aristides was continuing. 'Well, leave her with me. If anyone's missing her, they can come and ask. Girl!' he snapped.

She stared at him.

'Who are you?'

She pressed her lips together and breathed through her nose.

He stared at her for a moment and then snapped, 'Oh, for Hera's sake, give her to the women so they can unwrap her from that fishing net, and put some clothes on her. She's not going to run away . . .'

'She might!' said the fisherman, and indeed Halo was thinking about it, but the door to the courtyard was closed, and she was shaking with exhaustion. She would run away later. After they had fed her. And she would look at the stars and see where north was[4] and Orion would smile down on her as she ran back to her family, and she wouldn't get there in time for the party but they wouldn't have held the party anyway, with her not being there – and how happy they would be when she ran into the *agora*, crying out, 'I'm back, I'm back!'

'She's practically fainting,' pointed out Aristides. 'Give her to the women till her father or her owner comes for her. Now off you go . . .'

Only after the fishermen had left did the women appear. They had been somewhere else in the house, but now they filed out. There were five of them. An old lady, a smarter young-ish lady, a girl, and two plainly dressed, tired-looking women who could have been any age. Halo tried to keep her nose in the air but she couldn't stop herself from staring at them. They were strange! She pursed her lips and looked away.

They were staring at her too.

'Get that net off her and take her to the bathroom,' said the youngish woman, who seemed to be in charge. 'Has she anything on? Get her an old chiton of Hypsipile's.'

The girl – Hypsipile, Halo guessed – was about to object, but then didn't. She was too busy looking at Halo as if she didn't like her.

'How old are you?' she demanded.

Halo didn't answer. She didn't like the girl's rude tone.

Hypsipile was annoyed by that.

'Can't you talk?' she said. 'Fish got your tongue? Or are you a barbarian? You look like a barbarian. You've got tattoos on your face like a barbarian. Can you not even talk Greek?'

Halo didn't even bother to snort. Of course she spoke Greek. She'd been educated by Centaurs, hadn't she? That's the best education you could get. Good enough for Asclepius and Heracles and Achilles and Jason of the Golden Fleece. She spoke better Greek than this girl, that was certain.

But – she didn't know if she *was* Greek.

If they were Centaurs, Halo thought, she'd say the woman was the mother, and Hypsipile the daughter, and the old woman the grandma. She didn't know what to make of the other two women though. Friends? But the mother was bossing them, which didn't seem right if they were friends visiting.

Anyway, the bossed women were now – finally – taking the net off her. She spun round a little as they pulled it this way and that to unwind it, and Hypsipile laughed. Then Halo stood there, damp and sandy, stiff and sore. One of the quiet women handed her a cloth, and she turned away from their stares and slowly, painfully, tried to ease and stretch her arms and legs, which had been bound for so long.

'What's that round her neck?' said Hypsipile suddenly. 'Mother! Can I have it?'

She was lunging at Halo's golden owl. Halo swiftly reached out and grabbed the girl's wrist, so tight that she squawked.

'Certainly not, Hypsipile,' the mother's voice cut through sharply, and the girl backed down. Halo let go, but she didn't take her eyes off her.

The mother herself reached out gently towards the owl. 'Gold!' she said, surprisedly. 'Well I never. Tempting people to steal!' she said, as if it was Halo's fault. Then she tired of the scene and wandered off.

The women relaxed when she had gone. 'Poor little thing's half dead,' said one, and, 'You'd think they'd give her a bite to eat,' said the other, but it wasn't until evening that Halo got a bowl of barley porridge and a corner of floor to lie down on in the quiet women's room.

'I'll sleep in the yard,' she said, but they just laughed at her.

She lay dry-eyed and angry in the dark room. She was glad to be warm again, glad to be fed. But she should be at her party, with her family! Not inside this stuffy little human building.

She would rest now, and she would leave in the morning.

In the early dawn light, Halo heard the women waking and rising. She rose with them, washed with them, and followed them into the kitchen. They smiled at her, and one said, 'You look a bit better today. What's your name? I'm Nimine. I'm from Sparta. Sparta's better than here. You look like a Spartan – strong. Here the girls all stay indoors and try to be pale and pretty. You'd do well in Sparta.'

Halo was taken aback. No human had so far spoken to her kindly.

Nimine handed her a fig. 'Have this while I make the porridge,' she said. 'So, who are you? Are you from round here? How come you were just in the sea with no clothes on? Maybe there was a wreck! Maybe you're a princess! Can you talk? Or maybe you're a slave?'

'I am not a slave!' said Halo, quickly and angrily, and forgetting in her crossness that she had not been going to talk to any human ever. Slave! No one was a slave in Centaurs' eyes – even people who thought of themselves as slaves. Someone calling you a slave doesn't make you one. She'd learned that when she was very young.

'Oh! You *can* talk!' said Nimine. 'No need to be sniffy. I'm a slave, thank you very much, so there's no need to be rude. Funny accent you've got though. Maybe you're from Kerkyra. I met a Kerkyran once and he spoke very funnily . . .'

Nimine handed her a mug of tea: mint with honey. It was delicious. And she was looking at her, waiting for an answer.

'I'm not from Kerkyra,' she said cautiously. It seemed an easier subject to approach than slavery. Though maybe not. The question 'Who are you?' had confused her. It had confused her yesterday too, when Aristides had asked it. She didn't want to think about it.

She drank her delicious tea, and ate her fig, and, when it

came, her dish of porridge. Then she said politely, 'Thank you. I'll go now.' And she headed for the door.

'Oh no!' said Nimine. 'Madam said you weren't to leave. Master said you're to stay till your father comes for you!'

'My –' Halo was about to speak but found she couldn't. What could she say? She had been about to say, 'My father can't come.' But she couldn't say that. They would want to know why, and then what would she say? Because he's a Centaur, and you don't believe in Centaurs? She couldn't say that. One thing she knew – she mustn't mention the Centaurs, or lead the humans to them in any way. It wasn't safe for them.

So should she make up a story? That was lying. She didn't want to lie. So should she say something about her human father? Something like, 'I don't know who my father is'? Or 'I haven't seen my father since I was a baby'?

What a choice.

So she didn't say anything about her father. She just said, 'No, I'll go on my own. He won't mind.'

And Nimine laughed as if that was *really* ridiculous, and replied, 'What father would let a young girl go off on her own? Now just sit down like a good girl and he'll be along soon, I'm sure.'

At that point the mistress looked in. 'Ah,' she said vaguely. 'Good. She can work with you till her father comes . . .' and then she wandered off to have her breakfast with Hypsipile.

'I'm leaving,' said Halo – and the mistress turned round in surprise.

'Of course you aren't,' she said. 'Don't be silly.' And Halo heard her call out, 'Nikos! Make sure that girl doesn't run away. We're responsible for her.' A gruff male voice replied, 'Yes, Madam,' and Nimine rolled her eyes and smiled and said 'Don't think about running away, Spartan Girl. Nikos'll catch you in minutes. Zeus only knows what they want with you, though . . .'

Halo didn't know either. Why wouldn't they just let her leave?

All that day and the next, Halo helped in the kitchen and eyed Nikos, a long-armed gangly man who seemed never to go out and never to sleep.

Nimine said, 'Your father should have come by now, if he cares about you. If your father doesn't come, well . . .'

Halo thought about what happened to human children whose parents didn't care about them. She thought about the babies lying out on the hillside, abandoned.

'Well what?' she asked, but Nimine wouldn't say.

It became clear soon enough.

Aristides strode into the kitchen one morning and said, in surprise, 'Are you still here?'

The next day she found herself leaving the house with Nikos clutching her arm so hard he left white marks on her tanned flesh. Hypsipile was laughing. Nikos dragged her down to the dock, where Aristides was saying to the Captain of a grubby-looking boat, 'We can't sell her here, in case some family or owner does turn up. Take her over to the mainland, and see if you can get anything for her.'

She was being sold as a slave.

'But I'm not a slave!' Halo cried in outrage. 'You can't sell me. I'm not a slave. I don't belong to you . . .'

'Then what are you?' said the Captain. 'Who do you belong to? What we hear is, you don't belong to anybody, so you're finders keepers.'

Finders keepers! That can't be right!

But she couldn't tell them who she belonged to. She didn't know who she belonged to. It was true, after all, that she wasn't a Centaur herself. Though she wished that she was – and the more she saw of humans, the more she wished it.

So the uncomfortable question had returned.

Who was she?

She had no idea.

The boat she was put on was heavy with sacks of currants and jars of wine and slabs of Zakynthos tar, for mainlanders to caulk their boats with. It smelt.

Halo sat miserably in the Captain's cabin, where she'd been put, wearing Hypsipile's old chiton and an even older cloak, which smelt of sheep. One of the sailors looked in at her: she spat at him and cursed him in the name of Artemis. After that the Captain locked the door, and the sailors left her alone.

'Artemis!' she called. Perhaps if she shouted loud enough the Goddess would hear her and take pity. 'Artemis! Protector of maidens! Help!! They're trying to steal me!' But Artemis didn't reply. She called on Athena too, but she knew Athena was very important and usually very busy with adult business, so she wasn't surprised when she didn't reply. Then she thought of Demeter, whose own daughter, Persephone, had been kidnapped – she'd be bound to help.

But she didn't.

Halo was a bit disappointed by their lack of interest.

For a while she stared. Then she dozed. Then she stared some more. Nobody bothered to feed her, but Nimine had passed her a piece of bread and some salty cheese as she left. She had tied it into the corner of her cloak, saving it up.

She stared some more. And she saw something: in the corner, by the Captain's pallet – something long and wooden

– a flute! She picked it up, and examined it, and longed to play it, but she stopped herself, because she didn't want anyone coming in and telling her not to. After three days in a human kitchen, she was fed up with people telling her what to do.

It wasn't a very good flute, but it was a flute. She held it, fiddling with it, covering its holes and remembering tunes. And she started to think. After a while, she thought up a plan. And as she thought it through, she ate the bread and cheese, and she began to smile.

After some time, she couldn't tell how long, Halo shouted that she was being sick. The message got through to the Captain, and he let her out. She followed him up on to the deck, and looked to stern. Where Zakynthos had been, green and smudgy, there was now nothing but sea.

'Too far to swim back now, eh?' the Captain said meanly.

Even as he said it she knew it was true. *OK*, she thought.

'You might as well be sick over the edge,' he was saying. 'Do it downwind.'

She said nothing; just went to the side and felt the clear breeze on her face. She hadn't been allowed beyond the courtyard in all the time she had been in Aristides's house. She hadn't breathed fresh clean air, or seen the open sky, or the beautiful sea. She glanced back at where Zakynthos had disappeared into the blue distance. And she looked ahead, at the nearing mainland of Greece. *That must be Elis, or Messenia*, she thought. She wasn't sure which.

They were about half as far from the coast as Zakynthos was from Cephalonia.

*I can do that*, she thought. She crossed the deck. She threw off her cloak. She dived almost silently overboard. The water closed over her head, cool and sleek.

One of the sailors noticed the tiny splash. 'Captain!' he cried out.

'Stupid girl!' the Captain cried, and glared overboard.

He could see nothing. Nothing at all. She had dived off the starboard side, which was facing west; the afternoon sun was shining in his eyes, and it dazzled him.

Then he spotted something. 'Get her!' he shouted, and a sailor dived in and grabbed – her cloak, floating empty on the surface.

'Where is she?' shouted the Captain, and the sailors crowded round the rail to see; and some ran to the other side to see if she had swum under the ship, and some to the stern, and some to the prow: nothing.

'She must be somewhere,' the Captain said angrily.

For half an hour they went in circles, looking for her. Nothing.

At last, in fury, he had to give up, and he directed the crew to continue on course. He had lost money and he had lost face. He would have to recompense Aristides for the cost of her. He swore.

Meanwhile, tucked under the stern, under the blue frothing water, Halo the sea-born girl streamed in the ship's wake. One arm held tight to one of the metal fixings of the boat's ladder. The other clutched the Captain's stolen flute. Its holes were caulked up with Zakynthine tar, and one end poked up through the foaming surface. The other she gripped between her teeth in her tightly closed mouth. She was breathing through it.

Only as the ship gave up on her, and picked up speed to make up for lost time, did she let go, drop behind, and set out with her steady strong front crawl for the mainland coast.

Strong as she was, Halo was exhausted when she finally came to shore in a small sandy cove. The coastline was all cliffs and precipices, but finally she had spotted this cove and carefully made her way in, avoiding spiky rocks underwater and treacherous swirling currents. Her limbs were so heavy she could not even stand. For a while she lay in the surf, catching her breath and feeling the sand shifting beneath her body as the flat waves curled in and crept away again. But then she feared she might fall asleep there, still in the water, and be washed away again, so she dragged herself up the beach and lay limp as a scrap of seaweed in the afternoon sun.

Gradually her breath settled, and slowly she smiled. 'Chelonakimu,' she whispered, hearing Kyllarus's voice. My little turtle. Spat up by the sea again – only this time, she had done it herself. She gave thanks to Poseidon, and promised him a sacrifice as soon as she was in a position to offer one. She sat up, her muscles trembling. The sun was still warm, so she took off her wet chiton and spread it on a rock to dry. Shaking out her tiredness, she went down to the black rocks lining her cove. On the way she picked up a flat, sharp shard of stone.

She was prodding around in the cracks and fissures just

under the water, searching among the froth and waving weed, and soon enough she spotted what she was looking for: the spiky little black topknots of sea urchins stuck tight to the rock surfaces. Taking care not to be stung by their poisonous little prickles, she prised them off with her sharp flat stone, and scooped out the rich orange eggs from their underside. They were delicious – salty and fresh – and she could feel the strength seeping back through her blood. She ate a little seaweed as well, and spread some of the flat wet leaves to dry on the rocks to take with her as supplies when she moved on.

She slept on the beach, still cold and damp, but the next morning the sun was up early, shining warm on her. She found a tiny stream and splashed herself all over to rinse off the salt, and let the sun dry her. Then, warm and full of urchin eggs, well watered from the stream, with dried seaweed tucked into the fold of her chiton, barefooted, suntanned and free, Halo clambered up behind the cove and set out to find her way home.

She walked north with the sea to her left, over rocks and dunes, along the top of the cliffs, her hair matted with sand and salt, eating grapes from the wild vines and blackberries from the brambles. She knew there was a town up that way. Sometimes on clear nights they had caught sight, across the water, of the great fires they burned during their festivals. In a town she would find a boat and get a lift home, and everything would be all right.

But the coast was very twisty, heading off in different directions, with deep little bays and long rocky promontories. She decided to cut across, heading due north, to pick up the coast again when she was past the promontory. But when she saw the sea again, it was at the bottom of a great cliff, so she carried on, heading north across country.

*If I keep left, I'll come back to the coast*, she thought. But things kept sending her right: first wide bays, then a rushing river mouth, and finally a set of deep, dark gorges, thick with pines and riven rock. Finally, she found herself in an ever-thickening forest. She tried to go downhill – the sea, after all, is always downhill. But downhill seemed always to lead to a precipice, or a rockfall. So she walked where she could.

She had been walking all day in the scrubby, rocky woodland when, towards evening, she came to the edge of it. Gladly she walked out into evening sunlight on an empty hillside.

But the sun was behind her.

The sun should be in front, or to the left – if she was going north, or north-west . . .

It was behind her. She had been heading east – away from the setting sun, and away from the sea, and away from Zakynthos.

The long shadows of the trees, stretching out, told her all she needed to know.

She ran out on to the dusty open hillside sloping down before her, tall dry grasses scratching at her knees and feet, and she stared back up the way she had come.

The sun was setting behind the slopes and shoulders of a massive mountain. There was a mountain between her and the sea. How had that happened? How had she got so lost?

And anyway – what mountain was it? Elis and Messenia are flat.

She had no idea where she was.

Gold and pink streaked the sky. The evening star hung behind her and the smell of warm late-summer figs lay on the air. Halo sat down on the dry prickly ground, hugged her knees to her, and wept. By all the Gods, by Artemis who protects young girls, and Athena the wise, by Hermes the traveller – how had this happened? How had she let it happen? And more to the point, what was she going to do now?

Dried seaweed and grapes and berries were all very well, but she was hungry for real food. Her feet, although tough from running around outside on Zakynthos, were battered and sore from walking all day over rough land. Her skin felt dry and burned for lack of oil. She could smell her own armpits and her limbs ached with fatigue. She needed a wash, a bed, a rest, a kind word, a hot meal . . .

She wept miserably.

A while passed, and her tears passed, as they do. She wiped her eyes and nose on her chiton, as she had nothing else.

She felt stupid, and hungry, and her head ached. She raised her head – and as she did, she became aware of something behind her.

She froze.

Humans?

No.

But . . .

Aware of her red face and puffy eyes, embarrassed, she

turned her head slowly. What she saw, inches from her and looking at her with kindly intelligence, filled her with the greatest amazement of her young life.

It was a face. A long, hairy, brown face with a white streak down its nose, big velvety lips and nostrils, huge brown eyes with eyelashes that stuck straight out sideways. Its nostrils were opening and closing, making snuffling noises. Its breath was warm and smelt of hay. It was attached to a great strong body with four legs and a full mane and a long swinging tail.

It nudged her, gently, with its soft nose.

She jumped to her feet, at which it took a step back in alarm.

'Don't be scared,' she said softly. She wasn't scared either. She knew what this wonderful strange beast was. She had never seen one, but she knew. A horse! What a miracle. It was like magic to her.

Smiling broadly, she looked the animal up and down and from side to side. It was just like a real Centaur! Only instead of the normal Centaur human torso, it had this beautiful, noble horse head, this strong fine neck with its elegant mane, and these funny velvety nibbling lips.

'Do you talk?' she asked eagerly. She thought it probably wouldn't – as goats and birds and octopuses don't talk – but you never know. Instinctively, she held her hand out flat to it.

The horse didn't talk. It whickered softly though, and it had a look in its eye, in the moment before it rubbed its forehead against her chest, that made her think it might understand.

Just being understood was welcome. She rubbed the horse's

forehead, patted its silky neck, laid her cheek against it. What a beautiful warm thing it was. It smelt clean and lovely and – yes – a little like a Centaur. They stood there together in the evening sun and, for a while, Halo was happy again.

Then the horse stirred, and shook its head, and turned, starting to amble across the plain. It was heading south – not the direction Halo wanted to take, but then neither did she want to part with this big friendly creature so soon. Soon it would be night. She wanted to sleep where it slept, to feel the great slow rise and fall of a horse's sleepy breathing, to feel safe. So she followed it.

It didn't mind. They just strolled along at an easy pace together, sniffing the evening.

After a while, Halo realized where they were heading. There was a big fig tree up ahead, and under it – she could almost make them out – yes. More horses. It was a small herd: a few mares, a stallion, a couple of young colts and fillies. *It's a family*, she thought, and her heart lifted.

The horses greeted them with a snicker, a little rustle of affection for her companion, a mild curiosity about her but nothing more. She stroked their noses, then they went back to picking in a leisurely way at the windfall figs. Halo was dreaming of barley soup, of yoghurt and honey, of grilled fish and salty cheese, but figs would do nicely – so she shinned up the tree and, while she was up there, threw down an extra supply for the horses to snuffle up.

She slept deeply that night, sandwiched between two big, warm, safe mares.

In the morning, there was a man there. She saw him before

he saw her because he was asleep – as she must have been when he had arrived the night before. He lay wrapped in his cloak, away from the horses, under the tree. He was short and bent, very brown, grubby. She had no idea how old he was. He had no shoes, and he was snoring. She peered at him.

*I should leave*, she thought, and it made her sad, because she had very much liked the quiet warmth of the horses. But men – well. She didn't know what to think about humans. True, they could feed you, and give you somewhere to sleep, and fresh water, and they could talk to you – but then they bossed you and wouldn't let you go where you wanted, and you couldn't tell them what you really wanted, and they didn't listen . . .

Were they all like that? She didn't know.

She didn't believe her human parents could have been like that. She brushed away the thought of her human parents. Now was not the time.

And Nimine had been kind, in a way. But no one listened to Nimine either. They only listened to Aristides, or the mistress. And they had gone on and on about her father, and then when she didn't seem to have one, they had decided to sell her, as if she belonged to them. She had always assumed that she belonged to herself, and with the Centaurs. Maybe she was wrong.

But who else could she belong to? Or with?

Her human father.

Her human mother.

Halo turned grumpily away from the man. She didn't understand humans.

Her eye fell on the horses. They were cropping quietly. She didn't really understand them either. Well – she understood them with her heart. But not with her mind. She knew that much as she liked them, and much as they had comforted her, she didn't belong with the horses.

The man started coughing.

Halo stood there, helpless. Run? Where to? Stay? The horses couldn't help her. And the man?

Her heart sank.

He rolled over, stretched himself, sat up and had a coughing fit. Then he saw her.

'Well,' he said. 'Who are you?'

*Here we go again*, she thought. She gathered herself together and stared him in the eye. He looked more like a fisherman than an Aristides. But what did she know of humans?

Silence had done her no good before.

'I am Halosydne, from Zakynthos,' she said. 'I got lost. Perhaps you could help me. I need a boat to get back home. I can work to pay my passage.'

He coughed again, and spat revoltingly, and patted the ground around him till he found his leather water flask.

'Oh yeah?' he said. 'You causing trouble? You a runaway? We've had enough trouble already this year.'

'I'm not a runaway,' she said. 'I got lost.'

'You talk funny,' he said. 'You'd better come with me.' He gave her a drink of water from his greasy flask, and a basket to put some figs in. Meanwhile he put a bridle on the lead stallion, and soon after they began to plod slowly eastwards across the plain, the man leading the horse so that the rest followed, single file, behind, and Halo going dispiritedly by his side. What else could she do?

Towards noon they found themselves in a river valley. The horses went to the waterside and drank and stood, ankle deep, in the shallows. The man rinsed his head and Halo tried to cool herself off. They rested awhile in the shade and he handed her a piece of disgusting sweaty cheese. Then he said, 'Come on,' and started off, heading up the valley.

'What about the horses?' she said in alarm.

'They stay here,' he replied, and strode off.

Halo ran swiftly to her horse, her friend. She put her hand on its cheek and looked in its beautiful liquid eyes.

'Goodbye,' she whispered. She kissed its nose quickly, and shut her eyes for a second. Then she turned and ran after the man. He hadn't hurt her. And horses don't have boats. Men have boats.

# Χαπτερ 7

Late in the afternoon, Halo was brought to a dirty little house, where the man handed her over to another man, short and skinny and not much less rough than himself. This man laughed out loud when she said she was lost.

He asked all the same questions. Where are you from, where's your family, oh, no family — so who do you belong to? She didn't say, *To myself. I belong to myself*. She had seen enough of humans now to know that he would just laugh even more.

'Well, you're mine then,' he said, and she clenched her teeth to stop herself from yelling at him.

'Here,' he said, and he threw a piece of bread at her. She had to jump to catch it before it fell on the grubby floor. That made him laugh even more. Then he said, 'What's that round your neck?' and grabbed her arm, and snatched at her gold owl.

'Pilo!' he cried. 'Come and get this off her.'

A woman appeared from the shadows. She looked scared and slow, but she cheered up at the sight of the owl, and took it off Halo with her onion-smelling hands, and put it round her own fat neck. Halo kicked her, but the man held her tightly by the elbows behind her back so there wasn't much she could do.

'Go and cook my dinner,' he said to the woman, who scurried off again, and then the man sat down and tried to make Halo sit on his lap, so she kicked him too, as hard as she could, on the shin with her bare tough little heel.

'You little snake,' he said, turning her round but not letting go of her, so she kicked him again and shouted and tried to scratch his face, so he dragged her outside and chucked her into what seemed to be an empty stable, throwing her on a pile of hay and locking the door behind him with a deadening thump.

Halo didn't bother to carry on shouting. She lay on the prickly hay, out of breath, furious, in the dim light. Humans! If this was what humans were, by all the Gods she did not want to be one! There was a hot sweep in the blood of her veins, and she wanted to kick him again, she wanted to be strong enough to bully him back, and hurt him, the disgusting thief, the bully . . .

She didn't know how long she was there. There was a small empty window up high in the wall – too high – and the light from it moved slowly across. She slept a little, and fumed, and plotted.

She thought a lot about where she was, and where she could go. She was going to run away, of course. But she didn't even know where she was. She could head back west, towards the sea – back through all the wild country she had already crossed. Yes, and get lost again, and starve to death. Maybe there was a better way. She tried to picture in her mind the map of the world: Zakynthos, between Sicily and Greece; Delphi, the centre of the world; and Athens, the great city towards the east. She recalled the great wild mountainous Peloponnese, in the middle of which she was now lost. She recited the names of the mountains of the Peloponnese, visualizing the map – and she realized what had happened. She must be far further south than she had thought. She must have come to shore not in Elis or Messenia but on the Mani, and come up to the east of Mount Taegetus.

Well, no wonder the people were so wild! Maniots were famously wild. Perhaps she could try to find a place where the people would be more reasonable. Maybe in a bigger city they wouldn't take so much notice of her. She tried to remember the cities of the Peloponnese: Argos and Corinth to the north – and Sparta.

Sparta was south. And east of Taegetus. And Nimine had said things were better for girls in Sparta. She would go there. People would be more helpful in a city. Less ignorant. She would find a reasonable person with a boat and she'd work her passage back to Zakynthos.

It felt good to have a plan.

Later, when the window had begun to show the dimness of evening, she heard the man and the woman laughing: a mean and scary echo of the Centaurs laughing in the night at home. She stared at the wall in the half-light, and then she gave a little snort as she had an idea. She stood up, took out the sharp stone from the beach which she still had in the fold of her chiton, and began to poke at the wall with it.

As she had thought. The wall was made of wood and twigs and mud. She easily poked a couple of holes big enough for a foothold, and just as easily clambered up the wall to the window. She peered out into the evening. It was warm and quiet and the cicadas rattled in the trees. Off to the west the sky was glowing.

Halo climbed back down and sat quietly on the pile of hay, thinking. After a while, long after the evening light had faded, the voices from the house died down and the moon moved round to shine in through the small high window. It was easy to boost herself up to it, and not very hard to jump lightly out of it. Easy, too, to pick her way across to the low house. Even easier to slip through the door to the little courtyard: it wasn't even locked.

The man was lying on a pallet in the main room, his head falling back and his knobbly throat visible. Beside him was the woman, curled up and snoring. Beside them was an empty jar – Halo sniffed at it. It smelt a bit like wine, but stronger. She wrinkled her nose, and put the jar down again. *Thank you, Dionysus, for knocking them out.*

Moonlight fell in through the open door to the courtyard, lighting up the woman's face. It was red, with broken little veins, and a bit of spittle had settled at the corner of her mouth. As Halo stared at her, she shifted and rolled over – and Halo saw that the woman had a black eye, bruised like an old plum.

Halo shivered with a sort of horror. What kind of creature was this man? She glanced over at him: fast asleep, snoring like a pig. And suddenly, looking at him, she wanted to slice his grubby throat. She was shocked by the feeling, and had to take hold of herself. She breathed out sharply through her nose, and shook herself. The urge passed quickly, but left her shaken, and her blood running fast. She made herself carry on staring at the man. She knew she didn't want to kill a man, no matter what kind of pig he was, no matter what he had done. Killing was for the Gods, not for her.

She calmed her breath, and waited for her heart to calm down. At last she was able to say to herself, *That was anger. That's what it's like. You know that.* Her teeth were still gritted though.

And after all, had he harmed her? No. Because there, lying on the woman's wrinkly neck, was her own golden owl. With a little hard smile, Halo leaned over the woman. The knot was under her neck, caught up in her tumbled hair. Halo slowly, delicately, took the leather thong between thumb and forefinger and gently pulled on it.

It shifted.

She pulled a little more. It shifted a little more.

The knot came into view. It hadn't had time to tighten and settle, and Halo was able to undo it quickly. She whisked the thong in one movement out from under the woman's neck, almost feeling the heat as it pulled across the woman's skin: then she froze.

The woman rolled over and made a little moan.

Would she wake?

Halo's heart seemed to be beating loud enough to wake them both.

But no – the strong booze had them both in its thrall, and they snored on.

Halo gave a little smile of triumph in the semi-darkness.

She glanced again at the woman. She thought of Nimine, who worked all day for these people. Of the mistress, rich and beautiful – but who never left the house. Of Hypsipile, the important man's daughter, who couldn't even read. Of all the women she hadn't seen in Zakynthos. Of this poor drunken beaten thing. Of the men she had met who had told her she didn't belong to herself. *No one has any respect for women, let alone girls*, she thought. And it occurred to her, there in the moonlight, tying her owl-thong back round her neck, that being a female human might not be all that great.

And at that exact moment an idea came to her.

She decided to be a boy.

Of course! It would be far better to be a boy. She had seen boys on the docks at Zakynthos, in the *agora* there, on the boats, in the distant fields as she walked here on the mainland. Boys and men were allowed to go about the place without being taken for a slave, or robbed, or laughed at.

She would be a boy. It couldn't be that difficult. She was tall, quite. She had a bony face and straight shoulders. She wasn't soft and pale and curvy like Hypsipile. She was skinny and suntanned and muscly. She just had to make herself look the part: dress like a boy, walk like a boy, think like a boy. Ha! It seemed she already did – thinking she could just go about the place and do what she wanted.

The man's chiton and cloak lay on the floor by the pallet.

She laughed softly. He had robbed her. So did that mean she could rob him? She thought about it for a moment and decided that yes, it did. He had broken that important law – so now that law didn't stand between them any more.

*Dike, Goddess of Justice*, she whispered silently, *please understand my situation and forgive me for robbing this disgusting pathetic horrible man.*

The clothes were a bit smelly but not much too big for her. She put his chiton on over hers, and wrapped her belt around it, to hitch it so it wasn't too long. She wasn't sure how a boy would fold his cloak, so she just slung it over her arm. As she lifted it, something fell from its fold. She flinched – but it made no noise on the hard mud floor. She bent and picked it up. A knife! Well, she'd have that too. She slid it through her belt, safely outside the thick chiton. Then she helped herself to the remains of their meal: more hard cheese and a lump of bread – and to the leather water flask that lay by them. Silently she filled it from the tall water jar by the door, and she slung it over her shoulder, and slung the cloak over that.

She had no idea if she looked like a boy or not, but for the first time since she had been separated from Arko she felt strong and well equipped.

She walked all night, following the stars, heading north. High clouds scudded across the moon, and she pulled the dirty cloak tight around her. She wanted to get far away from that man, but that wasn't the only reason for not resting. She was scared to lie down in the dark, alone, among the muttering noises and shifting shadows of the night. If only Arko were here . . .

As dawn came up and the stars faded, she saw the great mass of Mount Taegetus to the west, its flanks picked out by the silvery fingertips of sunrise. An eagle circled lazily against the crimson sky, appearing and disappearing behind the mountain. She stopped for a moment, shivering in the new sunlight, to watch the bird's elegant movement, the fluttered curve of its sharp wingtips. She was on the right path.

Not that she was *on* a path. There *was* no path, except the odd runnel made by wild goats, and the odd stream bed, full of rocks and tiny blue-black birds that roosted in holes in the cliffs above. She longed for fresh water – she wanted to wash these clothes, and herself – but it was late in the season and most of the riverbeds were dry, holding nothing but pebbles and cast-off porcupine quills.

In the heat of the day she rested, and ate a little, and drank a little, and in the cool of the afternoon she carried on. She didn't think the man would come after her – and if he did, he wouldn't find her. Centaurs have always been good at hiding and dodging.

In the evening, deep in the woods, she decided to stop for the night. She finished the cheese with some wild celery and a couple of figs she had found along the way. She was too tired to make any kind of shelter, so she just chose a decent-sized tree and folded herself up between its roots in the cloak to sleep. The cloak smelt disgustingly of sweat and old goat, and felt rough against her face, but she didn't want scorpions or spiders or biting ants to crawl on her in the night. She couldn't get comfortable, so she finally took off her small chiton and folded that into a pillow. At least it smelt of her, not of horrible man. 'Artemis, keep me from foul humans,' she murmured, and as she did she heard a wolf howl, far away. 'And from wolves,' she added quickly. 'And bears.'

Before she slept, she thought of home, and asked Demeter to bless the Centaurs' grape harvest. *And*, she said to the

Goddess in her mind, *please comfort them. They will be sad to have lost me, just as you were sad when your daughter, Persephone, was taken away from you to the underworld – please comfort them. Then, when I can, I will make a sacrifice to you – when I have food I will give you some. Even though it's yours anyway, as you're the Goddess of growing things . . .* She was still trying to work that one out when she fell asleep.

The next morning she was very very hungry. Figs and wild fennel were not going to keep her strong, she thought, as she munched on some. There was no point setting traps – she wouldn't be around to check on them.

She took out her knife and stared at it. What could she catch to eat with a knife?

Nothing. But –

She smiled.

The woods were generous to her. She found a long, strong, thin, flexible sapling of yew. She found a wild vine, strong and whippy late in the season, and cut a couple of lengths for twisting. She clattered through the dead sticks and twigs lying about underfoot, and chose a handful of the best – straight and strong. She sharpened her knife on a stone, and she set to work, whittling, twisting, cutting notches, threading.[5]

She sang as she worked.

By mid-morning, she had made a more than passable bow, and a set of sharpened arrows that, if not the best, were not half bad. She smiled at her work, and had another idea. She swiftly cut another length of twisty vine, and used it to strap her knife to the end of a long, strong shaft. A spear! Now she could hunt, and have meat.

But hunting meant slowing down – fast was too noisy, startling deer and birds as she went. Little animals heard her coming, and ran off. Deer were too big, anyway.

That evening she managed to shoot a small wild goat with her bow and arrow. She was proud. Not of the shot – it was an easy shot – but of the fact that her self-made arrow had flown more or less straight, and killed the goat cleanly.

But then: she had no way to cook it. She stared at it helplessly as its eyes filmed over. She had killed it, and now she couldn't eat it. What a fool she was. She so wished that she had some way of making fire to cook the meat, and burn some as an offering to the Gods, thanking them for keeping her safe so far. She could offer them raw meat, but it was the roasting smell they most liked. And fire would warm her; she could sit by it for comfort in the dark night. She imagined the delicious smell of grilling goat, the sputtering of oil on the embers of a family fire, a hot dinner . . . For a moment the pain of her loneliness was almost physical – a twist in her belly. She closed her eyes, screwed them up tight so that light and dark shot in sparks inside her eyelids – then she shook the feeling away, almost angrily.

She was *so* hungry. And she had killed the goat. She owed it the respect of not wasting it.

So she unstrapped her knife from its shaft. 'Artemis, Goddess of the hunt,' she said, 'I am sorry my offering is so pathetic, and not even cooked, but I thank you for keeping me safe from the wild beasts of the woods, and I thank you for this . . . er . . . meal . . .' and she cut strips of the tough meat from the animal, and she chewed them.

It was disgusting.

But it was food. And she got some nourishment, and nourishment was what she needed. She chewed the bloody meat, and she felt stronger. So she cut some strips and tied them in leaves to take with her.

On the second day she found a small stream at which to fill her water bottle, but on the third day she found no stream, and her water ran out. She spoke to Demeter again as she fell asleep. 'Please let me find food and water,' she said softly. 'Then I can give you some. Please let me be strong. I don't know who's in charge of the water here – let the nymphs lead me to it. Please, Artemis, protector of girls, make me brave. Athena, queen of wisdom, let me use my brain. Hera, queen of the family, and Apollo, friend to Centaurs, comfort my family . . .'

The fourth day was bad. She found no water, and ants had got into the last of the goat meat, which had in any case gone off and started to smell. Mosquitoes had bitten her – normally they didn't bother her, but these ones were different. The bites itched horribly. A couple had turned red and angry, but she hadn't been able to find the leaf to rub on them to stop them going septic. She was used to finding everything she needed growing nearby, but these woods were not generous the way Zakynthos was. But worse than all this, a great loneliness was building up inside her; a deep need for her own bed, her own home, her own friends and family. She wanted Chariklo. She wanted Arko.

She walked on, thinking about him, and how he would

encourage her if he were here, and how she wouldn't let him down. *I'll be the kind of boy he is*, she thought. That night she found some dank mushrooms and some bitter cornelian cherries. She ate them, along with a handful of last year's almonds that she found under a tree. She bashed open the shells with a stone on a rock. The white kernels were sweet and delicious, but the brown outer skins were dry and shrivelled her tongue. Even so, she could have eaten many more of them – but she saved some, because she didn't know what she would find to eat tomorrow in this dry country. If the worst came to the worst, she could eat asphodel tubers, or acorns . . . but she had no way to grind or prepare them, and uncooked they would make her ill. She slept badly, rolled in her lonely cloak, trying not to cry, listening to her stomach rumbling, and the wolves howling.

She woke hungry, and started out walking already tired. All was scrubby bits of bush, and rock: hot, dry, unforgiving. *I shall walk here forever*, she thought, *until I drop of weakness and just die, alone in the wilderness.*

Towards midday she longed for somewhere to rest. There was a gully ahead – perhaps there would be shade. She approached it – and through the dusty leaves, she heard a beautiful sound: the cool splashing noise of gushing, gurgling water. Even the noise of it seemed to clean her soul. New energy rose in her, and she rushed towards it. A bramble tripped her and she landed with a shock on her belly. Right below her face, a few metres down, dappled with sunlight and shadow, surrounded by thick undergrowth and long knobbly trees, was a slow-moving, shallow, narrow river, sliding towards a high, cool waterfall, and falling into a wide, dark pool.

She grabbed herself to her feet and scrabbled round, scratching herself and not caring, searching for a way down to the water. It took an unbearably long time to get to – maybe two minutes! – but then she stood on a rock at the edge, pulling off her sweat-stained, dusty clothes, desperate to dive in but stopping herself, making herself check the depth, making herself go slowly.

She slipped in, naked, from the rock, and let herself slide under the water, feeling the dust and heat lift off her, feeling her hair lift and spread, feeling the coolness spread across her scalp, behind her ears, all over her skin . . . Nothing had ever felt so good. She opened her hot eyes to the cool dim green of the underwater world, she laughed and gurgled out big silver bubbles of breath . . . and she shot out again on the surface, splashing, rubbing her fingernails on her grubby scalp, shaking out her head, happy happy happy. She floated on her back – and nearly sank again, for there was no salt to support her body here. But how sweet the water was! Even in the springs on Zakynthos the water had never been this sweet. She swam over to the waterfall and turned her face up to it, letting the silvery sweetness pour over her. She opened her mouth and drank, cautiously so as not to make herself sick. She kicked off, floating on her back again. Above her the sky was far away at the top of a tunnel of greenery, hot and blue and distant. All was silent.

She splashed.

Happy. And so hungry.

And – oh – there among the greenery, hanging over the bank, was a long branch dripping with feathery leaves and fat, heavy, dark berries, red and luscious-looking – mulberries.

Her favourite.

She kicked herself up out of the water and grabbed the branch. Hanging by one arm, she reached out with the other and plucked the berries, cramming them into her mouth, the sweetness bursting on her tongue and lips and filling her with joy. She kicked her feet in the water with delight. But the mulberries made her even hungrier for real food. She pulled herself out of the water and went upstream, where the fish had not all been frightened off by her splashing and laughing. It took a little while, but she caught four fish, tickling them with her fingers as Chiron had taught her. Using her knife, she cleaned out their trickly red guts. [6]

But before she ate, starving as she was, she laid one of the fish out carefully on a bed of fig leaves, with some of the almonds and a fig, on one particular high flat rock which she had spotted for the purpose. 'Demeter, Artemis, Poseidon and Dionysus,' she said, 'thank you. I will give you better as soon as I can.'

She sliced up the other three fish and ate them raw with some fronds of fennel she found growing by the river. They weren't as good as they would have been if Chariklo had put them on a spit and grilled them, but they were delicious because they were food, and she was hungry.

After she had eaten, she decided to wash her stolen cloak. The smell of the man's sweat still made her feel sick at night. She dropped it in the water and swirled it slowly about, and pulled it back up on the flat rocks to stamp on it. How heavy it was, full of water. It was hard work for her to lift it, all dripping and itchy. Several stamping sessions and rinsing sessions later, she hung it over a strong tree branch, and did her best to twist bits of it to get rid of the water. It didn't work very well – but the water was dripping down anyway, making little streams along the rock, and the sun was strong. She hoped the cloak would be dry by nightfall. Smelly or not, it made all the difference to sleeping out, and though the days were hot, the nights were getting colder all the time. It couldn't be too long now till the autumn equinox. She had to get home before winter, that was for sure.

She washed the little chiton as well, keeping the bigger one to wear. She would stay here a day or two, eating fish and getting her strength back. And she would wash the big one when the little one was dry.

It was a nice place to rest, with the water and the fish and the soft-growing grass on the river bank to sleep on, and the sun and the shade and the rock doves cooing. She swam and sang and slept and planned. Where exactly was Sparta? She couldn't just head north forever, hoping for the best. After all, she'd been walking for a while now.

Well. Rivers, she knew, flowed into bigger rivers. And cities are built on big rivers. She would follow this little river downstream, and she would see what big river it led to.

The cloak wasn't dry. The big chiton was, though, so she put that on and shivered herself to sleep with her toes tucked up behind her knees for warmth, and the waterfall gurgling a lullaby.

Halo was about to jump into the pool again early the next morning, before setting off, when she caught sight of her reflection in the calm, smooth water.

Her hair!

She couldn't be a boy with all that long wild black hair. Centaur boys and men wore their auburn hair long and curly, but the human boys in Zakynthos had their hair cropped short. She wondered how boys in Sparta wore their hair. All she knew about Spartan boys was that they had to leave their homes when they were only seven years old, to join the *agoge* – the Upbringing – to train as soldiers, and they grew up to be the toughest in the world. The adult warriors wore their hair long, she knew that . . . Well, she wouldn't be pretending to be a Spartan boy. She would be pretending to be a Zakynthos boy, because that was the only kind of boy she had ever seen. So she would have to cut off her curls. Just as well – they were horribly matted, and full of sand and twigs.

*I can always grow it again*, she thought, *when I go back to being a girl*. So she sat on the rock with her stolen knife, and prepared to hack.

'Apollo, lover of boys,' she murmured. 'Please make me a convincing boy. Please accept me as a boy for the time being, like when Achilles's mother dressed him as a girl to keep him safe – and Athena, queen of wisdom, you appeared to Odysseus dressed as a boy – and Dionysus, you were a girl for a while . . .'

Lifting the knife, she carved through her thick black curls ringlet by matted ringlet, and laid them in a pile on the rock beside her.

They looked like a dead animal.

Only then did she dare to look into the water again.

A worried-looking face stared back at her, with clutches of hair sticking up in all directions.

'I look like a girl with a horrible haircut!' she cried, and she sharpened her knife on a stone, and hacked again, making it shorter and shorter, checking each time, and each time being unsatisfied.

Finally she gave up. If she cut off any more she'd be as bald as a sheep after a bad shearing. She jumped into the water to rinse off. How cool and delicious the water was as it washed off the itchy shreds of cut hair. She dived down deep, moving fast this way and that through the murky green depths so that the bits of hair wouldn't stick to her again when she came up.

She moved too fast. She didn't see properly through the light and shade. She misjudged. One moment she was flicking and twisting like a fish. The next she had slammed her head, hard, full on, against an invisible rock under the water.

A dagger of pain, and then her mind was stunned, blank.

Her body curled back and went limp, hanging like a pale and mysterious flower in the dark water.

All was silence, but for the rock doves still cooing way above as if nothing had happened.

# Χαπτερ 8

The boy passing by should not have paid any attention
to the girl at the pool. He could see that she was there.
So what? He was busy. He had been busy all night. This
morning, he was going to sleep. He would have been asleep
by now if it hadn't been for her talking to herself and recit-
ing poetry and cutting her hair and splashing like a crazy
thing. But he didn't *have* to sleep. He was trained to go
without sleep as easily as he could go without food or water
or warmth. And she was showing no signs of going. Her
presence here changed his mood and distracted him from
his purpose. He would leave.

He had just made that decision when he became aware
that something was wrong. The splash as she had dived in
– there was no answering splash of surfacing, of swimming
or getting out again. The silence was too sudden.

He rolled across and looked over the crest down to the
pool. In the movement of light and shadow he saw the pale
shape in the water.

The boy didn't hesitate. He scanned the surface for rocks
or dangers, threw off his rough cloak and dived cleanly in.
He came up beside her and pulled her head backwards on
to his shoulder. Kicking his legs like a frog, on his back, he
dragged her to the edge and pulled her out on to the flat
rocks.

He laid her out in the sun, on her front, and pushed at

her back the way he'd been taught to rescue a drowning brother.

She was choking and gasping. There was blood in her spiky wet hair. He sat back on his heels. She was throwing up. She was conscious.

Halo raised her head. She saw a boy. Or a young man. Older than her, anyway. His hair was black like hers, short like hers, and his eyes were greenish-grey in a suntanned face.

A human.

She wiped her face on her arm. A little blood stained it.

Her blood was warm on her scalp, and she touched the wound tenderly with her fingers. Her head roared with pain. She laid it back down, feeling weak and woozy.

'Stay there,' said the boy. His accent was strange. 'I'll wash it.'

He scooped handfuls of water over her head, washing the blood from her hair. He too smelt of sweat and sheep, but on him it was a clean scent.

'The wound's small,' he said.

'Thank you,' she whispered. 'I might have . . .'

'But you didn't,' he said.

'Thanks to you,' she said. She pushed herself up, trying to turn towards him.

He stood up. He should just walk away now. If he walked away now, and left the area, he could carry on as if nothing had happened.

And then she passed out again: just toppled over like a piece of cut rope.

He jumped forward to catch her before her head bashed down on the rock. So then he was sitting there with her head practically in his lap. What was he meant to do now?

He looked down at her. He saw a girl of about twelve, with her cropped hair a mess and scratches all over her, wearing – strangely – a gold owl at her neck. She looked as if she had been living in the wild longer than he had. Her face was pale beneath the suntan, and she had a – what was it? A strange mark tattooed on her forehead, faded and indistinct.

Why wasn't she at home with her mother? Was she a runaway slave? She certainly wasn't a Helot, or any kind of Spartan . . .

The boy did not know what to do.

He knew what he *should* do. He should let down her head, leave her to her fate and return to his duty. There was no question about that. He was in the middle of one of the most important tests of his life. Soon he would be a full soldier of Sparta. Such a man does not get distracted by some runaway girl.

Her wound was bleeding again. He could see the thick dark scarlet blood seeping into her wet black hair. She was shivering.

He laid her head down, folding her chiton beneath it, and covered her with her cloak. It was as if he could not control what he was doing. He should leave, but some strong little part of his heart said, *Yes, yes, of course, but she's all alone and bleeding in the wild. Wolves might come. I'll just help her a little.*

Then his mind said, *Don't be so weak, so sentimental! She's not even Spartan — with her gold necklace . . . Do your duty!*

And his heart said, *Yes, of course, in a minute . . .*

He searched on the river bank until he found a clump of feverfew, the herb he wanted. He made a poultice out of it with some spider's web from a tree stump, and after washing the wound again he carefully applied the poultice, tying it into place with a strip he ripped from the bottom of her other chiton.

She was still shivering. The sun would move across soon to shine on her but in the meantime he pulled the cloak in around her.

'Wake up,' he said.

Her eyes opened and she stared at him.

'Hello,' she said.

'Don't go to sleep,' he said.

'All right,' she said. 'Where's Arko?'

'I don't know. Who is Arko?'

'My brother. Who are you?'

'Leonidas,' he said, and then shut his eyes swiftly. A Spartan soldier doesn't go round telling people his name! But then he had never met a stranger before . . . and she was only a girl. And likely to be eaten by wolves. But he didn't want her to be eaten by wolves. It didn't feel manly to leave a wounded girl to be eaten by wolves.

'Are you the King of Sparta?' she said.

'No. Named after him.'

'Thank you,' she said, very quietly.

'You already thanked me,' he said. 'Are you all right now?'

'Mmm,' she said.

'Sit up,' he said, and he propped her against a tree. His hands were strong. 'Don't go to sleep.'

'All right,' she said, and looked him straight in the eyes, to show him that she understood, that she was OK now. His eyes were very clear.

'I have to go,' he said.

'Goodbye,' she said.

'Goodbye,' he said.

He looked at her, unsmiling.

He was gone.

She stared around. Nobody, nothing. Silence and calm all around, but for the rock doves still cooing. All was just as it was before he had come, as if he had never been.

## Χαπτερ 9

Halo sat propped for a while before she felt able to stand. The boy had said she mustn't sleep. She wouldn't sleep. She wasn't at all sure what had happened.

After a while, she began to gather her things together, resting between movements. Her head was very, very painful. She couldn't remember how she had hurt it. She only remembered the green-eyed unsmiling boy who had helped her. Filling her water jar, she caught sight of herself – her hair! She touched her head, patting her shorn scalp, and the poultice tied on, and she tried to remember.

*I mustn't sleep.*

The best way not to sleep was to get moving.

Halo walked for hours. She didn't know where she was going. She finished her water, her head was aching and she was growing hungrier by the minute. She crested a low hill and saw farmland below her in the valley. The silver leaves of olive trees flashed and twinkled; a goatbell sounded, and in the distance was the red-tiled roof of a farm building. A mixed feeling of hope and fear twined in her empty belly.

She couldn't stop herself. Humans would have food.

'Gods forgive me,' she murmured. 'When I can I will give it all back.'

Circling and descending into the olive grove, she passed among the twisted and entangled trunks, and remembered the story of Baukis and Philemon, the old couple who loved each other so much that they asked the Gods to let them die at the same moment so they wouldn't have to be apart, and how the Gods turned them into olive trees, to grow together in a woody embrace forever. *I know someone like that*, she thought. But she couldn't think who it was. Her head felt light. She should look at her wound. How could she look at her own head? She would rest behind an olive tree until it was dark, and then she would go to the buildings and see what she could find. She wouldn't sleep.

She levered herself down on to the scrubby grass beneath the tree. The sun was warm. Insects buzzed. She spread her cloak beneath her, and curled up on it. She slept.

She was woken by children's voices.

Two small boys and a girl stood around her, staring down at her with big dark eyes. They were scruffy but clean, sunburnt like her. They didn't look unfriendly. They didn't look particularly friendly either. They were talking about her and then one of them shrieked at the top of its voice. 'Thanus! There's a boy here! There's a boy under one of the trees! He's got blood all over his head!'

An older boy's voice shouted back – a voice of alarm. 'Come away! Come away! Kids!' Its owner came pounding up: a strong stocky boy, sweaty from work, brown-faced, dark-eyed. Halo stood up as he approached. She didn't want to be down here while they were all up there. She was still half asleep and her head ached from the sun and her wound.

The boy grabbed at the children, and pulled them away from her. 'Who are you?' he said.

*Be a boy*, thought Halo. *They think you're a boy. Be a boy.* She put her weight on to one leg, as she thought a boy might, lifted her chin, and spoke in a low part of her voice.

'A traveller,' she said. 'Just travelling.'

The stocky boy looked reassured somehow by the sight of her – as if he had feared something, and she wasn't it.

'Where are you from?' he asked.

She had to think for a moment.

'Zakynthos,' she said.

Thanus exclaimed. 'I wouldn't go telling people that around here,' he said.

'Why?' said Halo.

'How long have you been travelling?'

She didn't know the answer to that either. A week? Two weeks? She had meant to count the days, but . . . 'Since after the harvest moon,' she said. She knew it was coming to full in the next night or two.

'So you don't know what's happening?' Thanus said.

'What's happening?' she asked, but then she started to feel woozy again, and Thanus said, 'You're bleeding!' and then he was helping her along, and she was inside a house, low and dark and cool, and sitting on a stool, and a woman was unwrapping her bandage and saying, 'Oh dear' at what she saw beneath it.

'I –' said Halo, but the woman said, 'Hush, let me tend to this.' As she peeled away the poultice the boy had put there, she gave a little frown. 'Thanus,' she called, and the boy came back. 'Look,' she said.

Thanus looked at the strips of torn chiton, the clump of spider's web and bloodied herbs that she held out.

'Someone has tended this wound before,' he said. 'Did you do it yourself?' he asked Halo.

'I —' said Halo, but the woman interrupted.

'Not just someone,' she said. 'The way it's tied. The fever-few. It's done the way they do it.'

Thanus turned fiercely to Halo. 'Who tied your wound?' he demanded. 'How were you wounded? Who are you?'

Halo closed her eyes. 'I don't know,' she murmured.

'I don't think he can answer anything now,' said the woman. 'Let me get him cleaned up. He's only a child —'

'And what does that mean, Mother, when their seven-year-olds are already training for the army?' Thanus said with a snort.

'He's not one of them,' the woman said. 'Look at him — he's too soft to be a Spartan. He doesn't speak like a Spartan. And look at that marking. God only knows what he is, but he's not one of them.'

She was dabbing at Halo's cut with a wet cloth. Halo winced with pain. The children were still just standing around, staring.

'You hungry?' the woman said, and Halo nodded.

'Thought so,' said the woman, and soon some black bread and a bowl of broth appeared.

Halo ate quickly.

'When you're a bit better you can work for that,' the woman said.

'Glad to,' said Halo.

Thanus and the children went back outside. The woman, once she had finished with Halo and washed and hung up her old bandages, sat down with a spindle in the little court-yard outside. Halo came too, and sat in the shade, resting.

The woman, whose name was Thalia, sang a little as she spun her thread. Outside, the sheep made low, comfortable noises.

'Thank you,' said Halo.

Thalia shrugged.

'When your son said things were happening . . . What is happening?'

'Ask him,' said the woman. 'He's the one who goes to market and hears the news.'

So later, after Thanus had locked the gates carefully and his mother had led the prayers at their little hearth, when the family gathered in the courtyard and sat down to eat, Halo asked.

'You say you are from Zakynthos,' he said.

Halo nodded.

'Zakynthos is allied with Athens, I believe,' he said, 'who the Corinthians have just denounced at the Spartan Assembly.'

Halo didn't know what he was talking about.

'Last year the Athenians sent their fleet – many triremes – to the north, to help the Kerkyrans.' He looked at her. She said nothing – what could she say? – so he continued. 'The Kerkyrans who are quarrelling with Corinth? Corinth which is allied to Sparta . . .?'

Halo knew the names of these human cities, but she had no idea who was allied with who, or why.

'The Athenians won the battle at Sybota,' said Thanus. 'Now the Megarans are up in arms about the decree and the

Potidaeans won't take it lying down either. The Corinthians are the angriest. They *will* involve the Spartans . . .' Her head was aching. '. . . The Spartans and the Athenians *will* be at war. The Spartans have already tried to have Pericles banished under the old law, because they know he's the most able leader the Athenians have . . . Anyway, they all love to go to war . . .'

Thanus glanced at her. 'All right, I'll keep it simple,' he said. 'Don't go wandering around the Spartan lands of Lacedaemonia telling people you are from Zakynthos. You might as well say I am an enemy spy.'

'I am not an enemy spy,' said Halo.

'Good,' said Thanus.

'But if everyone will think I am the enemy,' she said, 'why don't you?'

Thanus gave a big grin, showing all his teeth. 'I don't care about their wars,' he said. 'I am not a Spartan. I am not even a Lacedaemonian. I am not a Messenian . . .'

Halo was getting confused again. They were in Lacedaemonia, of which Sparta was the main city – who was he then? If she knew more about humans, she would know.

'Oh – what are you then?' asked Halo, as politely as she could. 'Are you Athenian? Or Corinthian?'

He laughed again, and the children grinned behind their hands, and the woman smiled too.

*What's so funny*, Halo thought, *about the fact that I can't tell which city they belong to just by looking at them? Why should I know all the details about who wears what or talks how or lives where or is enemies with who?*

'No,' said Thanus. 'We're Helots. We're slaves, didn't you know?'

'Oh,' said Halo. She thought to herself: *Better be careful what I say here. People are touchy* . . . 'Whose slaves?'

'We "belong",' said Thanus, in a way which made Halo think he didn't accept it, 'to Sparta itself. To all the citizens of Sparta. We grow all Sparta's food and in return Sparta lets us keep some. We work the land that Sparta stole from our ancestors –' at this his mother looked nervous, and seemed to want to shush him, but she didn't – 'and in return Sparta lets us live on a little bit of it. Spartan citizens are soldiers. They are too good to work the fields and make the wine and feed the pigs and pick the olives. They're not allowed to. By law. Didn't you know?' He said it in a blank but bitter way. Halo couldn't tell if he was being sarcastic or not.

'Thanus,' his mother said quietly, but he ignored her.

'They've got more important things to do,' he continued. 'What do they do all day? They have to train all the time, for war. Umm – yes, that's it. They train for war.' Then he stopped himself. 'Anyway,' he said. 'So who are you?'

'Halosydnus from Zakynthos, trying to get home,' she said. She'd nearly said Halosydne, not the male version. 'Need to earn some money to get passage on a boat home.' *That was close.*

He smiled again.

'What's so funny?' she said.

'There's no money here,' said Thanus. 'Spartans don't need money. They don't need things. They're so tough, they don't buy anything. Anyway – tell us your story.'

'I was taken by slave traders,' she said, 'from Zakynthos. I am not a slave, and I won't be made into one.'

Thanus snorted again at that. 'Good luck!' he said bitterly.

'I've been trying to get home,' Halo continued.

'No chance now,' said Thanus. 'No one will be sending boats across to Zakynthos. Not after last week. You'd have to try from Athenian lands, or from some Athenian ally. There's nowhere round here, and the season's drawing in. Too cold to travel soon. Where did you come from now?'

'I jumped off the boat – I don't know where. Somewhere off the Mani. I swam, and then I walked.'

'You walked, from the Mani?'

'Yes. I only wanted to get back to the coast . . . I lost my way in the forest. Then – circumstances overtook me.'

'Circumstances?'

'More slave traders . . .' she said.

'Is that how you got that bash on your head?' Thanus asked.

Thalia was clearing away the remains of the meal now, but she was listening.

Halo thought about it. How had she hurt her head?

'I . . .' she said, puzzled – and it came back to her. 'I dived into a pool and hit a rock,' she said.

'And who bandaged you up?'

'A boy,' she said. She remembered his clear eyes. 'His name was Leonidas.'

The effect of these words was quite extraordinary.

Thalia went white. Thanus went rigid. Thalia glanced at him.

'Children, go to bed,' he said.

'But . . .' ventured one.

'Now!' he thundered.

The children shuffled up the wooden steps to the upper room. Thalia went after them and carefully closed the door before coming back down and rejoining Halo and Thanus.

'Go up, Mother,' said Thanus.

'When your father returns I will leave you men alone,' she murmured. 'Until then I am at least an adult.'

Thanus humphed, but let her sit.

Thanus looked squarely at Halo and said, 'Was he alone?'

'Yes – I don't know,' she said. 'He said he had to go. He might have been meeting someone . . . Why?'

'Sweet Hera,' murmured Thalia.

'How old was he?' said Thanus.

'Older than me,' Halo said, 'but not a grown man. He had no beard.'

Thanus swallowed.

'What was he doing? Did he say?'

'We didn't really talk,' she said. 'He did have a knife. He was probably hunting or something.'

'Hunting,' said Thalia.

'Hunting,' said Thanus.

They both looked sick. Thalia's breathing grew short.

'The full moon is tomorrow,' she said. 'It won't be till full moon.'

'The pumpkins can stand another day in the field,' said Thanus. 'If we lock up everything now and stay inside tomorrow . . .'

'But Enus is travelling!' she wailed.

Thanus stood up.

'Don't go outside,' cried Thalia. 'Full moon is tomorrow . . .'

'They might have changed the rules,' said Thanus.

'What are you talking about?' asked Halo, full of dread.

'He's too young,' said Thalia.

'There's no such thing as too young with these people,' said Thanus forcefully.

'Hush,' said Thalia, but he took no notice of her. Then she murmured, 'And Enus out travelling . . .' and her eyes went panicky and hard. 'And what about Diomedes and his family? And Sattartes? Thanus, we must warn them . . .'

'Without going outside?' he said, with a bitter laugh.

'Warn them about *what*?' asked Halo, but they weren't listening to her.

'I'll make a fire,' said Thalia quickly. 'Outside. They'll see the smoke, and your father will see it . . .'

'They'll think you're burning leaves.'

'*What are you talking about?*' demanded Halo. They were so scared it was making her feel a little sick at her stomach.

Thanus turned on her. 'You know we were talking about war? About Sparta? Well, let me tell you something about this land you have wandered into.' He breathed deeply, angrily, as if he were trying to control himself, as if he wanted to be sick. 'Every year, every single year, they declare war on us again. Formally. Do you want to know why?'

Halo watched him.

'So that they can kill us,' he said. 'Without blood guilt.

They like to kill us. And if they call it war, they can kill us as much as they like!'

She breathed out, slowly. *Hunting*, she thought. *Hunting*.

Thanus gave her a weary, bitter look. 'It's part of their training,' he said. 'They call them the Krypteia. It makes a man out of a boy. Each year, they send their best boys out into the countryside to live off the land and toughen up and become men. By killing us.'

*Hunting.*

'And this year,' whispered Thalia, 'they have come here.'

## Χαπτερ 10

Halo had heard the phrase 'his blood ran cold'. Never before had she felt it in her own veins.

Surely the green-eyed boy was not going to come and kill these people? He had saved her life. Why would he save a life one moment and kill someone the next?

She didn't believe it. She had looked him in the eye.

But he was in the *agoge* with the other boys. They were all part of that harsh Spartan training. What did she know about what they could do?

'Don't make a fire now,' Thanus was saying to Thalia. 'We mustn't draw attention to ourselves or they'll come here. The children must stay in tomorrow, and for the next – oh, Lord Zeus, how long will it last? Oh, Zeus, Hera, if ever we made a sacrifice that was pleasing to you, protect our home now, protect us, protect us . . .'

Halo was shocked to see how the strong, bearish boy seemed to be crumpling.

Then he pulled himself together. 'Tomorrow morning,' he said, 'we'll make the warning fires, and no one will leave the house, and we will make sacrifices. Other than that it's in the hands of the Gods. Tonight you will all sleep together upstairs. Halosydnus, make your bed by the children. Mother, I will stay awake downstairs. Don't be afraid. And Halosydnus – we are in your debt. You have been a messenger to us, to bring warning. We thank you.'

No one slept well that night. Thalia insisted on dragging the children's pallets right close to hers, which woke them up.

'It's nothing, little ones. Nothing's the matter,' she said, in a cheerful voice that made them nervous. The small one began to cry, and Thalia was hugging him too hard.

Halo lay on her back on the hard wooden floor and looked up at the ceiling in the darkness; then she rolled over and covered her head in her cloak. 'Athena, queen of wisdom, owner of my gold owl, give me wisdom,' she whispered. She made her usual prayers for her Centaur family, and then she lay watching the moonlight hang in a shaft from the little high window, and listening to the sheep muttering in the enclosure below. The children had settled and Thalia's breath was low and regular as if she was sleeping. Halo hoped that she might sleep too. And perhaps she did sleep for a while.

And then she heard footsteps, and she came awake with a jolt.

Footsteps on the roof.

Silently she threw back her cloak, and silently she took her knife and crossed the room to the door to the stairs. It was easy to draw back the bolt. With the utmost stealth she crept up the wooden stairs to the roof, her knife ready in her hand, her breathing steady.

When her head came level with the roof, she stopped a moment, and then, keeping her head as low as possible, she peered over the edge.

It was Thanus, lying low on the roof in the moonlight.

Relief rolled over her. She hissed softly to alert him, and he looked round. Scurrying low, she crossed the roof to join him, and they spoke briefly in low tones.

'Anything?' whispered Halo.

'Nothing,' he said.

Together they scanned the moonlit landscape, spread out soft and strange in the silvery light. How beautiful and peaceful it looked. Mount Taegetus loomed black as ink to the west, a great silhouette against the sky. The moon shone so bright and spread its light so strong that there were no stars at all to be seen. Somewhere over there, she thought, looking to the right of Mount Taegetus, way over there, was the sea, and Zakynthos, and the Centaur village, and the little vine-covered shelter where her family would be sleeping. Perhaps Chariklo would be worrying about her right now, lying restless under the huge moon.

*Did I really walk all the way from beyond that great mountain?* It seemed hard to believe. She thought of the almond trees and the stream with the fish, the wild fennel and deer, the kind horses, the wild grapes, the blackberries. She thought of the rocks beneath her feet, the long days without water, the poor dead goat, the bears and the howling wolves and the wild boar; the snakes and the eagles and the scorpions. She thought of the gang of boys in their cloaks, looking for people to kill.

'Shall I keep watch for a while?' she murmured to Thanus. 'You'll be stronger tomorrow if you sleep awhile.'

'No,' said Thanus. His voice was tight. 'I can't sleep. But it's good to have another man here. My father is – well, I only hope he doesn't think of travelling home by night in the moonlight. He went to meet his brother. They're not due till tomorrow.'

Halo smiled to be thought of as 'another man'.

'I'll stay up here anyway,' she said. 'I'm used to sleeping outside. It's not so cold.'

She sneaked back downstairs and got her cloak, and lay down to sleep on the roof, dreaming of warm chestnut bodies lying around her, and scorpions climbing through her hair.

The next day was tense. Thalia and Halo were awake before the dawn, and Thanus had already prepared their little household hearth for the sacrifice. Being poor, all they could offer was a couple of barley cakes, but Thanus did it properly: washing first to purify himself, building the fire, calling on the Gods with such passion and intensity that Halo was sure they would hear him and grant his plea. Indeed, she prayed along with him in silence, even though she did not know the father and uncle for whose safety he prayed. Finally he burned the little cakes for the Gods, apologizing to them for the poverty of his offering.

The children slept on, and Thalia let them, though usually they would have been out in the fields working from daybreak. She and Thanus built a great fire in the courtyard, then as soon as it was burning well they put moss and water on it to make it smoke.

'I hope they see it,' Thalia murmured. 'I hope they understand it.' Halo was pretty sure everyone would see it from here to Asia Minor, it was so black and stinky.

Later Thalia and the children went to the storeroom, and worked quietly pulling the grapeskins from the surface of the new wine in its great jars. 'Might as well get something useful done,' she said. Thanus mostly strode up and down, looking nervous. Halo decided to help with the wine, as Thanus still would not let her take a turn at keeping watch.

*He's going to explode*, she thought. *I know he's worried about his family, but he's being foolish.*

In the afternoon, finally, Thanus slept.

Thalia and the children carried on working quietly in the house. Thalia was spinning and Halo was just about to say, 'Here, let me do that,' when she remembered, just in time, that no Greek boy would know how to spin. All afternoon they worked under the weight of silence, while Halo kept watch. Every now and then Thalia would look up suddenly as if she had heard something. The children grew fractious. It was as if they were all waiting for something dreadful to happen.

After dusk Thalia laid out the dinner: *kykeon* porridge, and olives and a little barley bread. Thanus woke up for the meal, but nobody ate very much.

After dinner, Thalia took the children upstairs. Tonight, she didn't argue with Thanus about staying down. Thanus, taking with him a big stick from the woodpile and the largest knife from the kitchen, went back up on to the roof, and without a word Halo followed him.

The moon was rising in the south: vast and golden, round and full. *How strange*, thought Halo, *that the beautiful moon, Selene, should allow such horrors.*

They lay on their stomachs on the roof, Thanus watching the north and east; Halo watching the south and west. The moon sailed higher, shrinking and growing paler as she rose. *Is Selene scared too?* Halo wondered. *Is that why she seems to be retreating and going white?*

The *agela* had prepared. They had met at sundown at the appointed place. They had eaten their little meal, said the prayers they had to say, and danced their ritual dance. They had sung their hunting songs, and sharpened their gleaming weapons. They had drunk their thin wine. They had grinned and laughed and clapped each other on the back, and as the moon rose higher they had run out from the forest, in a thin, flexible, unbreakable, invisible line, ducking and hiding, silent as the night, down towards the Helot land. This area was known to be full of people with rebellious notions. The Spartan mentors didn't send the boys just anywhere. They weren't hunting for the sake of it. They were hunting to warn off rebels, to protect Spartan citizens, Spartan families and the Spartan way.

The plan had been to skirt the houses, looking for movement, and whatever moved, to hunt it. Any house that was completely dark and silent they would leave. What is the honour in slaying the sleeping? But then they had had a stroke of good fortune – approaching the third settlement, they spotted two travellers on the track, trying no doubt to finish off a long journey and be home that night.

Concealed in the undergrowth alongside the track, the hunters, silent and concentrating, drew level with the travellers.

Two Helot men, in workmen's clothes, tired. And anyway, what were they doing out at this hour? Law-abiding men would be at home.

The hunters took pride in how long could they follow these two idiots, these bumpkins, without being spotted. These boys had known each other all their lives, had trained together, eaten together, rested together, prayed together, for ten years. They had learned the same things, shared the same bread, suffered the same punishments. They had done nothing else. Each youth knew how his fellows would react – they could move as one without speaking. They could dart and follow, knowing that they were protected. Each one put his comrades' lives before his own.

But they weren't even spotted. It was as if the bumpkins didn't even have ears.

The trees and thorn bushes thinned out as the track led into an olive grove, silvery with moonlight and black with the dark shade of night. The hunters, secure in their silence and invisibility, fell back a little. Soon their leader would give the signal to strike. They were well within reach. The Helots were as good as dead.

'Look!' hissed Halo. 'On the track in the olive grove! Two men!'

Thanus snaked over to where she lay, and squinted into the night.

'There,' whispered Halo.

'Hera, mother of all kindness, it's my father and my uncle,' Thanus gasped quietly.

'And look behind,' Halo hissed. 'Among the trees. Do you see?'

'It is them,' said Thanus, and his breath drew short. 'It is them. They have come. It is over.'

'Over?' asked Halo. 'Aren't we going to fight?'

'Oh, sweet Hera, what can we do?' Thanus whispered, quickly and oddly, his voice coming light and thin. 'What can we do? If we fight them we all die. If we don't fight them we all die. Even if — ha! — we fought them and beat them, others would come. And we'd die. Don't you understand? Spartans don't lose. Slaves don't win.'

He was gulping for air.

'Can we warn your father?' said Halo. She was staring at the figures. Was one of them Leonidas, whose kind hands had bound her wound?

'No,' said Thanus. He was shaking his head, and it wouldn't stop shaking.

'Shout?' asked Halo.

Thanus's face was white in the moonlight. 'If we shout,' he said, 'they will come here and slaughter my mother . . . and my little . . .'

Thanus turned away from her, and he threw up.

And at that moment a sound came from the olive grove — a blood-curdling shriek. Not the piercing call of a regimental trumpet, not the cold clang of metal on metal, or the dark clump of sword on leather shield, for this was no fair battle between soldiers — just that dreadful shriek, then cries, and grunts, and then the pounding of feet dull on the dust of the track in the dark.

Halo couldn't bear it — but she couldn't take her eyes away. She watched it as if it were some horrible perfor-mance, far from her, unchangeable, unstoppable, beyond her power. Ten or twelve dark figures had emerged from the shadows of the olive grove, and gathered round the two figures on the track. She heard shouts, and a thud. She saw one of the two breaking away and hurtling brokenly towards the house. Four of the hunters broke off to follow. She saw the flash of metal in the moonlight as a sword circled in the air. She saw the figure stagger and fall. She saw the further group dissolve and move apart, leaving a pile on the ground.

She heard laughter on the still night air, and the clapping of hands together above heads. She saw arms held aloft.

She too felt sick.

She saw one figure standing still, alone and black against the silver earth.

She heard Thanus weeping, and from downstairs she heard Thalia weeping too, and then the little children, one by one.

Leonidas spat and caught his breath.

What was wrong with him?

None of the others had noticed but he had noticed. He knew.

They had been so caught up in the glory of the hunt, the perfect availability of their prey, their joyful success at slaughtering them. But he, Leonidas, knew.

He had been the first to spot the prey. He had stalked them, with the others, brothers in arms. He had joined in the thrill of not being seen; a man's pure joy at his own skill and stealth. He had been ready to step out in front of the prey, challenge them, and kill them face to face as a man should kill his enemy. And the Helots *were* enemies! Pathetic enemies, for sure, but enemies all the same. Hadn't they tried to destroy Sparta at the time of the great earthquake, rising up and taking advantage of the chaos? Weren't they constantly scheming and plotting and looking for ways to destroy the state? Weren't there many thousands more of them than there were of the Spartans?

He would be happy to stand before any enemy and beat him in fair fight.

And he had given the signal for the kill.

But when the boys had leapt out, sleek and silent as a serpent, twelve of them on to two unarmed Helots, one of whom was almost an old man, and drawn their knives, and chased the old man and laughed . . . Leonidas had been unable to join in.

He had not killed a man. He was ashamed. What kind of Spartan was he? Was he a coward, after all?

He was the leader. If he could not kill a man, what use was he?

Thanus, in the fury of his grief, came rushing down from the roof and out into the olive grove to take his father's body in his arms. Leonidas stood before it with his knife drawn. Around him stood his boys, bloodstained and proud.

'Another one!' cried one of them. 'Take him, Leonidas!'

And Leonidas drew his knife up. Face to face, he had no problem with death.

But behind Thanus was someone else – a woman running up to them, desperate and shrieking. 'Thanus!' she cried, in a heart-shaking voice of fear. 'Thanus!' Behind her were two little children, and behind the children, trying to hold them back, clutching their wriggling, crying bodies and arms, there was someone else.

'What do you want from us?' cried the woman. 'What more?' Her voice rang across the valley and echoed back to them off the mountainside. 'What more? More? More?'

'Take them all!' cried another of the Spartan boys, and the cry went up: 'Take them all!'

Leonidas stood in the moonlight; his eye on the further figure, the one standing with the children.

'There's no honour to Sparta in killing babies and women,' he said harshly. 'We are blooded. Our business is done here.' He grinned, and Halo could see the moonlight flash on his teeth and on the blade he raised in the air as he turned to his boys. 'Leave these little animals to their little business,' he cried, and if the boys were disappointed they didn't show it, because they were Spartans, and Spartans always obey their leader.

Thalia fell to the ground. The children struggled from Halo's grip and ran to their mother. Thanus stepped up to where his father and his uncle lay on the dust track in the silver moonlight, and knelt by them, and holding his head in his arms whispered a prayer over their bodies.

And Leonidas, before he strode back up the road, pointed at Halo, and said, 'Just bring *that* one.'

# Χαπτερ 11

Halo knew there was no point in running, no point in trying to escape. Twelve Spartan boys? She wouldn't have a chance – plus she didn't want to get into a struggle with them. She was a boy now, and she did not want to be discovered.

She stepped forward when he spoke, her arms out to show she was unarmed, her head low to show she was giving in – *but only for now*, she told herself. *Inside, I'm not giving in to you.* Her mind was racing with what might happen to her. She didn't even have time to glance back at Thalia and the children, or at Thanus.

One of the boys quickly whipped a piece of rope round her wrists and tied them behind her back, leaving a tail of rope to lead her by. He prodded her to move along, back the way they had come. She seemed to be in some kind of dream, removed from reality in the silver and black night.

'What do you want this kid for, Leon?' said another of them.

'Look at him,' said Leonidas – and she glanced up quickly. 'He's no Helot.'

The boy who had tied her put his hand to her chin and tipped her face into the moonlight. Every muscle in her body clenched at the touch of his hand on her skin.

'Get your hands off me,' she hissed, staring at him defiantly. She could see the dark fuzz on his cheeks and lip.

'Ooo-ooh!' he sang, mockingly. But Leonidas glanced at

him and said, 'Leave him alone, Scitas,' and he let her go.

The boys gathered round.

'Look at that!' said one. He was pointing at her tattoo.

'What is it?' said another.

'He's a barbarian!' cried Scitas.

'No,' said Leonidas.

'How do you know?' asked one.

'I know,' said Leonidas. 'We're taking him back with us.'

And that was it. The Spartan boys set off, moving quickly and silently through the night. Halo was dragged along, tripping and stumbling, behind them. She put all her strength into keeping up and not falling. She was not going to shame herself in front of them. They didn't speak again for some hours, until Leonidas stopped them, and with a glance and hardly a word they rolled themselves in their cloaks and went to sleep.

Except for Leonidas. He didn't sleep. He sat, staring silently out into the darkness.

The night was cold by now, and the ground beneath her was rocky. Halo shivered as she huddled in her cloak. They had tied her feet as well, and tied the end of that rope to an ilex tree. There were stones beneath her back and she couldn't get comfortable enough even to rest.

Somewhere far off the wolves were howling.

*I am with the wolves now*, Halo thought, and shuddered. She closed her eyes, and looked into her own mind, trying to focus, to come round to herself after the dreadful dreadful things that had happened that night.

She felt cut off. It was as if the horror of it had severed her from her previous life. The innocent girl who had played with

Arko in the sea, who had picked figs and played the flute and never seen what slavery is, seemed a girl of long ago. The lost look in Thanus's eyes, Thalia's howl of sorrow, and bewilderment of the little children, the sound of the bodies dropping to the ground . . . those things had changed her.

Sparta was her enemy now.

And yet – the heartless Spartan, the sworn soldier, the cruel boy who thought nothing of life or death, was the same boy who had pulled her from the water, watched over her, and cleaned her wound.

'So,' she said quietly, in a hard voice, 'was that your initiation ceremony? Are you a man now?'

He said nothing.

'Now that you've murdered two innocent men, six to one . . .' she continued, in the same tone.

Nothing.

Then, 'How's your head?' he said quietly.

'Leonidas,' she said, and her voice was calmer. 'I don't understand. Why did they kill those people? Thanus – the Helot – told me you just go around killing them when you feel like it and it sounded true when he said it, but – Leonidas, you're not a bad person. Why would you do that?'

'They're only Helots,' he said. 'Don't get your chiton in twist.'

'What do you mean only Helots? They're human beings . . .'

'Hardly!' he said.

'Of course they are!' she said.

'They're the enemy,' he replied.

'Some enemy,' she said. 'What harm can they do you?

They're just conquered slaves on a farm. You're the warriors, the mighty Spartan Hoplites – or you will be soon.'

'There are ten of them to every one of us,' he said calmly. 'We have to keep them in line.'

'Who says?' asked Halo, and he turned to look at her curiously.

'Everybody knows that,' he said.

'And that makes it all right to kill those men, just run up on them in the night and kill them for nothing? What do the Gods think of that?'

'The Gods love Sparta,' he said gently, as if explaining the obvious. 'Those men were Helot rebels. Helots are the enemy and every man is honour-bound to kill his enemy. There is no blood guilt.'

Halo had been brought up to believe that if you were so unfortunate as to have got yourself an enemy you were honour-bound to make friends with them as soon as possible.

'Well, I suppose I should thank you,' she said sarcastically. 'For not killing *me* . . .'

He stood up suddenly, and stretched. His cloak fell back. For a moment she saw something gleaming on his muscular back in the moonlight – long pale marks, criss-crossing . . . scars. She wondered how he had got them. She wasn't going to ask him, that was for sure.

She lay in silence. She was thirsty, but she wasn't going to ask for water either.

One of the other boys snored suddenly. Leonidas glanced over and smiled. 'That's Dienikes,' he said. 'He's my cousin.'

'I thought you didn't have family,' she said. 'I thought you all just joined the army in your seventh year and had no family any more . . .'

'Oh no,' he said. 'It's the opposite to that. It's that we are all family.'

She was colder than ever. Soon it would be getting light again. She shivered into her cloak.

'Get some sleep,' he said.

She had one more question, which she was almost afraid to ask. But she had to.

'What are you going to do with me now?'

He was silent for so long that she thought he wasn't going to answer. Then he said, 'I'm taking you back to Sparta.'

A few days ago she would have been pleased. Now, Sparta was nothing but the home of this strange, mean, violent way of being.

'You could have just left me with the Helots,' she said.

He shook his head. 'No,' he said.

'Why not?' she asked.

He smiled and bit his lip. 'We are not the only band out in the woods tonight,' he said, very softly. And she understood. At least — she understood that another band might have killed her. But that didn't really answer her question.

She had to know. She was scared to ask him. But she did.

'Why are you protecting me?' she whispered.

He was quiet again. 'I really don't know,' he said. 'I suppose I must like you.' Then he turned and shot her a look which even in the dark went right through her.

She was staring at him, her eyes wide.

'You're a very odd . . . um . . . boy,' he said, with a little laugh. 'And you say very unusual things. I . . . would be interested in talking to you more.'

'Oh,' she said. 'Why?' she asked. Her belly was full of butterflies. Why had he hesitated before he said 'boy'? He must know she was a girl. After all, he had pulled her from the river . . . She couldn't take her eyes off his face.

'Because you question what I know to be true,' he said. 'That's interesting. Explaining why you're wrong makes my knowledge stronger.'

*Oh, sweet wise Athena*, she prayed silently, *guide my tongue*.

'And what if,' she said, 'I prove *you* wrong?'

'*If*,' he said, snorting softly with laughter at the idea.

*But you* are *wrong*, she thought. *You are so wrong.*

She could hardly keep up. Scitas was half-dragging her behind him. 'Come on, little Tattooboy!' he shouted. 'Keep up!' She was determined, but her knees were almost buckling, and her head still throbbed under the clean bandage Leonidas had put on it. These boys were unstoppable. Their dusty feet were even harder than hers; their sinewy legs longer as they strode their matching stride, their stomachs tougher, their needs fewer. Their voices lifted up ahead, a stupid song they kept singing:

> 'Why do you live, when all are dead?
> Are you a coward? You're not my son.'

Then: 'With it, or upon it; with it, or upon it . . .' That was the chorus. It was about a soldier's shield, his *hoplon*: how it was better to be dead and laid out on your *hoplon* than alive having lost it to the enemy. They kept shouting it out, keeping step with it once they were on a good enough road. It made Halo feel sick.

She was hungry, too. These boys hardly ate, and when they did the food was disgusting. They didn't seem to need water either – which was as well, because Halo couldn't exactly pee standing up, like them – and they weren't going to let her go off on her own to pee, were they? They seemed to need no privacy, and peed like animals, without even thinking about it.

Thinking about it made her want to go. She was *not* going to ask Scitas to stop. She held it as long as she could. Finally, when she was nearly wetting herself, she called out.

'Leonidas!'

'What?' he shouted back, not slowing down.

'I – need to stop.'

'What for?' Still no slowing down.

*OK then*, she thought. She gritted her teeth.

'I need to pee!' she yelled, in front of all them.

'So pee then,' cried Scitas. 'I don't see why you need to tell Leon about it.'

But Leonidas had stopped now. He looked back at her, and she stared him right in the face. He was almost, but not quite, grinning at her.

'Is it the custom of your people to pee in private, little one?' he said, with elaborate courtesy.

She narrowed her eyes at him. *You pig*, she thought. *You definitely know I'm a girl. You mocking pig.*

'Yes, Leonidas,' she said. 'It is.'

'Then let me accompany you behind a tree,' he said, 'where I can turn my back and hold the end of your rope and stop you running away without disturbing the peace of your . . . activities.' He took the rope off Scitas, who had doubled up laughing.

When they came back from behind the tree the whole troupe were singing a new song:

> 'Look and see!
> The little flea,
> has to go
> behind a tree
> too special to pee
> in companeee . . .'

'Unlike you,' she shouted back, 'happy to poo in your own stew . . .' It wasn't very good, but it was the best she could come up with. They shouted with laughter. She hated them.

As the day grew warm, they threw off their cloaks. She saw that all their strong backs carried the same shining white scars as Leonidas's, gleaming against their sun-brown flesh. Even their skin was tough, she thought. *Perhaps their minds are like that too — toughened.*

It took two days to get back to Sparta, by which time Halo was exhausted and hungry and thirsty and convinced that Spartans were different from any other kind of human she had seen so far. And far nastier.

# Χαπτερ 12

At first sight, Sparta was nothing special. It looked like Zakynthos Town, only bigger, and with a shining river instead of the sea. It was like a bundle of small country villages that had overlapped each other: thatched roofs on dry muddy-looking houses, a few red-tiled roofs. There were no city walls, no gates surrounded by guards. Rough rutted tracks. Some listless trees. Some dusty-looking training grounds on the outskirts, where she could see the tiny distant bodies of soldiers and cadets exercising. Tiny gleams of metal glinted across the valley, and she heard the distant sound of barked orders.

As they approached the town, they passed close by one of the training grounds. Halo peered and stared curiously as they passed. She knew nothing of military life, of training, of fighting. What she saw did nothing to dispel her ignorance: a small group of upright, muscular, long-haired men supervising as about twenty boys of her own age apparently attempted to push down a large, ancient-looking tree with their shields. The boys were piling on top of each other. Their muscles were tight with effort, their bodies wedged against each other, their shields each in the small of the boy in front's back. Their heads were lodged and buried in the backs of each other's necks, their bare feet struggled to find purchase on the dusty ground, and their sweating shoulders heaved. *The ones at the front must be completely squashed*, she thought. *And those shields are big. How can they breathe? Surely they must stop . . .*

But they didn't stop. They just continued to heave, to push, to push, to heave. The tree, it was clear, was not going to be pushed over. But the sweating, dusty boys continued to heave, and the men continued to observe. As Halo came closer, she could hear them shouting out.

'You girls!' one was yelling. 'You puppies! You little soft puppies! You're not even pushing as hard as your mothers did to get you out! You could hardly push a piece of meat across a plate at this rate! You think that's how Leonidas held Thermopylae? Pushing like a puppy? Get a move on, you babies, or the Athenians will use you to mop up their gravy!'

And the boys pushed, and pushed, and pushed.

Then as they drew level, Leonidas called out a greeting. The man who had been shouting turned. He had a broad, sun-reddened face, a big nose, and sweeping eyebrows.

'Leon!' he called cheerfully. 'Lads!' He called them in.

Halo hung back behind the others, horribly aware now of the rope at her wrists. It had been hard enough to bear out in the countryside, but here, with new people to see the shame of it, it hurt all over again.

'All well?' said the man to Leonidas. He was dressed like the boys: muscles, scars, a cloak flung back. Like them, he was strong, confident, relaxed, cheerful. He was clearly in charge, but no one behaved in the quiet, subservient way that she had seen in Zakynthos Town, when the fishermen or the slaves had spoken to Aristides.

'All well, Melesippus,' said Leonidas, and the smile he gave the man was fresh and clear.

'Come to the *syssition* tonight and tell us all about it over supper,' said Melesippus. 'But what's this?' He nodded towards Halo.

'Captive,' Leonidas said. 'Some foreign boy, lost. He's quite bright. I thought we might find a use for him.'

Melesippus looked her up and down, and Halo drew herself up straight. *I'm a boy, I'm a boy, I'm a boy*, she hissed silently, inside her head. It was very hard to maintain the idea in front of all these half-naked, very male people. How could she possibly get away with it? What if they made her run around with no chiton like the rest of them? What if they wanted her to push trees in a gang?

But she was pretty sure that was just for the born Spartans. Only they had to be soldiers.

Melesippus was peering at her forehead. 'Eastern,' he said. 'Funny, he doesn't look it. Tattoo's definitely eastern though.' But he wasn't that interested. 'Take him to Borgas,' he said. 'He'll do as a sparring partner for the Juniors.'

'Is he big enough?' said Leonidas idly.

'Show us your muscles, boy,' Melesippus said to her.

*I'm a boy I'm a boy I'm a boy.*

She held up her arm, and flexed her biceps, making it look as big as she could.

Melesippus looked at Leonidas. 'He'll do,' he said.

Leonidas gave her a nudge, and they moved on.

*Eastern!*

*Eastern?*

What did he mean by that? Was she not even Greek then?

'Leonidas,' she said quietly, as he moved her along. 'What would he mean by eastern?'

Leonidas shot her a look. 'From the east, at a guess,' he said drily.

She looked daggers at him.

'Now be quiet,' he said, 'and observe the glory that is Sparta.'

She looked around at the mud-clad buildings, the irregular roads and the dusty roofs. No one would think, to look at this scrappy town, that it was the mighty Sparta, second only to Athens itself for fame and glory.

She became aware of a kind of shuddering, though, a regular pounding, underfoot.

And then, from up ahead, she heard a sound. The shuddering became a firm step – or a thousand steps – there was a clashing, a hiss . . . and above it the harsh piercing note of a flute . . .

They turned a corner in the road, and what came into view she never forgot for the rest of her life.

At first, for a moment, her eyes tricked her and she thought an immense animal was advancing on her – a gigantic monster reptile, a dragon sent by the Titans, a gargantuan millipede armoured with bronze scales glinting in the evening sun – but it wasn't. It was more terrible. Gleaming and rippling before her marched row upon row, rank upon rank, of tall and mighty fully armed Spartan warriors. Hundreds of muscle-bulging left arms bore hundreds of great bronze shields, overlapping to form the unbreakable wall of the phalanx. Hundreds of proud and upright heads rose identical inside hundreds of brazen helmets, hundreds of human faces behind hundreds of masks of impassive metal anonymity. Hundreds of helmets bore hundreds of tall, cruel, curved crests, making giants of the men within. And hundreds of sunburnt right fists bore hundreds of tall spears, endless ranks of spears, pointed to the sky.

Just as Halo arrived, a shout of command went up on the summer air.

In one single swift hiss of movement, hundreds of Hoplites snapped their spears to the attack position – and every spear was pointing straight ahead, steady as if they were set in iron, held by the hundreds of mighty arms – and advancing.

Towards her.

She shrieked. She couldn't help it.

How Leonidas's friends laughed. Scitas actually fell over. 'Eeek!' he kept shouting, imitating her. 'Eeek! It's an army! Eeek!'

'The glory that is Sparta,' Leonidas said mildly. 'You didn't think I meant the buildings, did you?'

Halo gathered herself together. Her chest was heaving.

Of course they were just exercising – parading, training. They weren't going to hurt her.

*Not this time, anyway*, a little voice inside cautioned.

As the group moved on past the training ground, Leonidas whispered close in her ear, 'You're going to have to toughen up, little one . . .'

Was he teasing her or advising her? She couldn't tell. She bit her lip and kicked crossly at a stone. She *would* have to toughen up.

Leonidas was still talking: 'And over there, you can see our fine temples – Artemis Orthia, up there –' he was gesturing – 'and Athena of the Brazen House.'

Halo stared at the temples and offered up a heartfelt prayer as her heartbeat calmed down again: *Artemis, Athena, protect me, show me what to do in this strange place.*

Around the temples stood statues of the Gods – at those she peered interestedly. She had not seen statues before, though she had heard about them. She couldn't tell which God was meant to be which, though. In her own mind she had such clear images of them: golden Apollo, tall and strong with a laughing face; Dionysus with his black curls and wicked little smile – looking a bit like Leonidas, actually; Hera, with her strong white shoulders and serious look; Artemis, long-legged, clear-eyed and brown from the sun; Athena, with her grey eyes and and expression of quiet amusement at the follies of humanity; Demeter, who to Halo's mind just looked exactly like Chariklo.

But the Spartans, it seemed, did not see the Gods the same way that Halo saw them.

There was one she didn't recognize at all; blank-faced, male, tall. Leonidas caught her staring at it. He grinned at her.

'You don't recognize him?' he said mockingly.

'No,' she replied.

'That's Phobos,' he said.

The other boys turned and looked, smirking.

'*God of fear!*' hissed Leonidas, with a laugh.

God of fear!

'Why would you worship fear?' she blurted.

'Oh, you don't want to underestimate fear,' Leonidas mused. 'Fear can cut the strings in your knees so you fall weeping to the ground . . . or it can do that to your enemy . . . Fear can make you reckless, so put yourself and your brothers at risk by being macho . . . Fear spawns a loop of fear that only skill and practice can break – fear is only human. Why, little foreigner, do you want to study *phobologia*? Will you be training as a Hoplite? Do you want to know the secrets of esoteric harmony – how to release fear from your muscles, from your face, from your soul? And exoteric harmony? How to be united with your brothers like limbs on a beast? Will you undergo the Harrowing, and learn what Phobos can do for you?'

The other boys had gathered round him as he spoke. Even just standing there, laughing at the idea of this weedy little foreigner undergoing their training, they moved as one, like parts of a whole. *Limbs on a beast.*

She thought of the ferocious phalanx she had just seen, row upon row of Spartan warriors, crimson-cloaked, undefeatable, new ones rising up to replace the fallen. She imagined that phalanx grinding and grinding against their enemy as the little boys had been grinding against the tree.

'So what are *you* scared of?' she said.

There was a moment of icy serious silence as they all stared at her, amazed at her impudence. Then they all started laughing at her again. They laughed a lot.

The others went off, and Leonidas took Halo to the gymnasium to meet the man called Borgas.

'What's a sparring partner?' she asked him on the way.

'It means the little kids get to beat you up,' he said.

She squinted at him blankly.

'Boxing?' he said. 'Sweet Ares, where were you brought up? Fighting? You know what fighting is? Well, the little kids learn to fight by fighting you.'

'I don't fight,' she said. Even as she said it, she remembered the feeling that had flown through her back in the Mani, when she had wanted to kill the man who stole her owl and hit his wife. She squashed it firmly. 'I don't fight,' she repeated.

Leonidas glanced at her. 'You do now,' he said. 'Don't worry, they're only babies.'

Borgas was old, strong and hairy. He laughed like a donkey braying and smelt like an ox, and carried a small, vicious-looking whip. He squeezed her biceps, picked her up to check her weight, and made her punch him in the belly. The picking up and squeezing annoyed her so much she punched him as hard as she could.

He laughed like a donkey. 'Not bad,' he said. 'Bit of life in him. Do you know how to fight at all?'

'No,' she said irritatedly, rubbing her knuckles. His belly had been harder than it looked.

'Never mind, you'll soon learn,' he said cheerfully. 'All right, get rid of that girly chiton and you can start with the nine-year-olds.' He grabbed Halo's tunic and began to try and pull it over her head.

'Excuse me!' she shouted, wriggling out of his grip and leaping backwards. 'Where I come from we wear clothes and I am not going naked for you or anyone!'

'Quick on his feet too!' said Borgas.

Halo was glaring at him.

'Come on, take it off,' he said.

'No!' she shouted.

'My little friend is foreign,' said Leonidas, trying not to show his amusement. 'He's unusually modest. Let him keep his chiton. Titch!' he said.

'Don't called me that,' she scowled.

'Don't be a pain,' he said. 'Do as you're told. And don't try to run away. If you run away, they'll kill you.'

He said it so easily. Again she wondered, *Is he mocking me or warning me?*

'Good advice,' said Borgas, fingering his whip and showing his yellow teeth in a grin. 'Now come on. To work.'

Across the level grass of the field, bands of boys were engaged in various types of exercise. Runners flew down the track; at a safe distance a handful were throwing discuses, and measuring how far they had sent them. Borgas led her to where a group of boys was circled round something. Their shrill cries sounded almost like birdsong from a distance, but as Halo drew closer she realized that it was serious.

Two boys in the middle were fighting – it was that simple. Punching and kicking and scratching and slapping and grabbing and trying to gouge each other's eyes out. They were furious and they were trying to kill each other.

Borgas swore loudly and waded in.

'What are you doing, you twits?' he shouted. 'Calm down! Skill, you fools, not anger! You don't listen to a word you're told, do you . . .?' He grabbed each of them by the upper arm, pulled them apart, and held them up, dangling, still trying to throw punches at each other in mid-air. 'You little fools! Lesson number one! No anger!!'

Halo couldn't stifle her laughter. They looked so silly, hanging there like kites stuck up a tree.

The boys crowded round the fight all turned to look at her. Their eyes narrowed. Their mouths tightened.

*Oh.*

She realized her mistake.

*Now they all hate me. Fifty nine-year-old boys hate me. And until I find a way out of this madhouse, fifty nine-year-old boys who hate me are going to punch me and kick me and scratch me and slap me and try to gouge my eyes out, every day.*

Borgas was shaking his head at her in weary impatience.

'That's Titch,' he said. 'Someone teach him the basics of boxing, please, so he can be some use round here.'

A tiny, evil-eyed boy emerged from the crowd.

'I'll teach him, sir,' he said in a wheedly voice. He looked as if he'd like to teach her to fall on her face in the dust, spitting teeth.

Halo stared at him.

'OK,' she said. 'Here? Now?'

Borgas had turned to attend to a boy whose foot had been trampled.

'Yeah,' said the evil-eyed boy, his jaw hanging open and a nasty look of excitement appearing on his face. 'Here and now.'

Halo was ready. The boy launched himself on her before he'd even finished speaking – but she leapt out of the way.

'Oops,' she said, sarcastically, as he stumbled. He didn't like that, and turned, and grabbed at her neck – but not before she raised her fist and punched him, as hard as she could. He went down again.

'Titch!' shouted Borgas, who had realized what was going on. 'What are you doing?'

The boy had jumped up and had flung his arms around her waist, trying to bring her down. He was biting her arm too, and it hurt. And she could feel his spit on her skin, which was disgusting.

'Sparring, sir!' she shouted, trying to loosen the boy's armhold by digging her fingernails into him, and kicking him at the same time. She was furious. She hated this boy.

'That's not sparring!' Borgas yelled.

Halo gave up trying to get the boy off her waist, and elbowed him in the head instead. She caught him right in the temple. He fell to the ground.

Borgas swore again.

'Crenas, you twit,' he said. 'Get up.'

Crenas lay there, moaning.

Halo wiped his spit off her arm. She was breathing a little heavily. She was surprised. It seemed she did fight after all. When provoked.

'You head's bleeding,' Borgas said.

'Well, he didn't do that,' she said. 'That's my own wound – I brought it with me.'

Borgas sighed and swore and shook his head, as if those were the only things he knew how to do.

'OK, enough,' he said. 'You lot – you're sleeping in the

*agora* tonight. Go and get your dinners. Not you.' He gestured to Halo. 'You come with me.'

The sun was on its way down as they all headed into the city.

Borgas stopped beside a shack. 'There's your bed,' he said, gesturing inside, to a pile of straw. (Only later did she discover she'd be sharing it with a number of greasy little rats.) He reached into another shack, next door, and shouted to someone. A woman's voice replied.

'There's your dinner,' he said, passing Halo a dish of oats. (She suspected the rats had been there too.) 'Enjoy it. There'll be more tomorrow night. And remember – if you leave the city, or look as if you might leave the city, or even think about leaving the city, you'll be dead.' He gave her another yellow-toothed grin.

Later, lying on the straw, she heard the rats squeaking, the guards shouting to each other, and the bolt shooting into place on the other side of the shed door.

*So far so good*, she thought. *At least I've shown the nine-year-olds what a tough guy I am.*

The next morning, there was no breakfast. Instead there was a tiny boy with skin as black as the night sea and little muscles like knots in string asleep beside her in the straw. That was surprising enough, but then a handful of other lads emerged from the straw too. Three of them had black eyes; one had a badly mashed nose; one had stitches on his eyebrow. They all had scars. They greeted her with nods, and one said, 'Come on then,' as they filed out on to the street and along to the gymnasium.

*Well*, she thought. *I suppose some scars will make me look more like a boy, at least . . .*

The first two days she was banned from sparring because of her wound. Then she was put up against Crenas again. He gave her his evil grin, then ran up, grabbed her, and kneed her hard between the legs. Then he stood back, obviously expecting some big reaction. She just stared at him.

'What?' she said.

He did it again – so she did it back to him.

He doubled over and yelled blue murder. Borgas came running up and grabbed Halo by the ear.

'Listen,' he said. 'You little rat – don't do that. You're here to spar, not to destroy the future of Sparta. And Crenas, don't be pathetic. You think that the whole world fights with Spartan codes of honour? They do not. You need to be prepared for anything. This little rat is just the kind of thing you need to be prepared for. And next time you come moaning about pain, I'll whip you.'

As soon as Borgas's back was turned, Crenas kneed her again in the groin. This time she yelled and screeched like he had. It pained her to show weakness to him – particularly a weakness she didn't have – but she didn't want anyone noticing that she didn't hurt the way a boy did.

Soon after that, Borgas decided to put her up against the ten-year-olds.

Unfortunately, Crenas turned ten that same week.

Halo was not happy with the discovery that she did fight after all – and that she fought like a wildcat: scratching, spitting, gouging and kicking. She was ashamed of it. She remembered what the Centaurs had taught her. This was not the kind of boy she had wanted to be – a dirty-fighting filthy-tempered slave. She wanted to be like Arko would be – brave and strong, cool under pressure, with self-control.

But Borgas made her fight. He stood over her with his whip, and the boys insulted her the moment his back was turned, and she had no choice . . . So she took all the resentment she had built up against human beings and vented it on these Spartan boys. She thought of the Maniot, of Aristides, of the slave captain, of Hypsipile, of Scitas, of Crenas, of Borgas, and above all of Leonidas's band, attacking Thanus's father . . . If Thanus's father had been a fighter, would he still be alive now?

She fought.

She didn't, though, think of Leonidas when she was fighting. When she thought of him, she recalled how he had made Borgas let her wear her chiton, of how he turned up sometimes at the training and taught her the basic moves of boxing, and of how once he had given her a piece of cheese. None of the boys, Spartan or slave, ever had enough to eat, and the cold drawing in made it worse. The boys were kept hungry on purpose, to teach them to steal food. They weren't punished. They were meant to steal food – it was good training for times of war or shortage. They were only punished for being caught.

And for Halo it was a winter of constant fear. Every day, she was in danger of being discovered. She rolled her cloak tight round herself at night, and by day strapped her chiton against her so that none of the boys could see her body. Every time she had to wrestle, she could have been discovered.

The boys had all kinds of rough-housing games; she made it clear with a couple of sharp punches that she did not play. When she saw Spartan girls at the training ground she kept well away from them in case they might notice what the boys did not. And almost all the time, she needed to pee, because there was never any moment of privacy for her to relieve herself. Luckily, some of the other slaves also had the habit of privacy. The African boy, Nebo, and she looked out for each other as they slipped into the bushes. Otherwise, she was never alone. How could she be? She was a slave, and though she tried her best to seem obedient, Borgas seemed to smell that she was rebellious at heart.

The sky that winter was grey and heavy. Rain turned the training ground greasy with mud. The winds were chill and damp, the days short and gloomy. At night, on her smelly straw pallet, she cuddled up and dreamed of Arko, of picking figs and splashing in the caverns. Blue light filled her dreams, so that sometimes when she woke she wept because it was gone.

The worst thing of all was that she had no friends. She had had hopes of Nebo – but Nebo didn't speak. Sometimes he sang mysterious songs in his own language, but he knew no Greek of any sort. Halo smiled at him, and liked his singing, in a sad way, but she couldn't really be friends with him. In her rare free moments Halo would go out and visit the mules that shared the yard where the sparring boys stayed. She would stroke their long velvety ears, and stare into their big black eyes. She felt for them. She felt like them – alone, used and abused.

Often, the men would come down and watch the boys training, and she would sometimes overhear their conversations. She heard the same words Thanus had used: Kerkyra, Potidaea, what the Corinthians thought, what the Athenians did, how the Megarans had reacted. Melesippus, she heard, had gone away to Athens.

'Every Athenian assumes he knows best,' she heard him tell Leonidas, after he was back. 'They assume that only *they* can run Greece. Zeus knows Sparta wants peace, but the way things are going . . .'

Later that day Melesippus made a speech to the boys after training. 'The time will come,' he said, 'when *you* will fight; when *you* will make that wall of muscle and blood and loyalty, and battle side by side for Sparta. You will fight for family, for the Gods, for the ancestors, and for the man beside you.' The boys stood up a little straighter, and smiled. The older men, those who had seen war, looked on them approvingly. The warriors of Sparta would never fail, because there were always more young warriors coming up: the *agoge* continued. Leonidas's gang were nearly ready; and behind them were the fifteen-year-olds, the thirteen-year-olds, the eleven-year-olds, the nine-year-olds . . .

'Other cities,' Melesippus continued, 'pull farmers out of the field, fishermen from their boats, blacksmiths from their fires, and call them an army. Only we have real soldiers. We – Sparta – hatch out and train up from babyhood. Only Spartan warriors are really warriors.'

'We are warriors, you are scum!' shouted the ten-year-olds, as Halo turned up the next morning for another day of being beaten and abused. 'We are Sparta, you are no one!' She stretched and shook out her limbs and tried not to hear the insults. Using what Leonidas had taught her, she was getting pretty good now at dancing about and dodging their blows. The ten-year-olds were still nasty, but they were becoming more obedient. There was a word she had learned here: *oidos*. It meant a willingness to believe that someone else knows better than you. They all had it. Melesippus had told them that they would never be more free than when they freely gave obedience to the laws of Sparta – he'd said that choice was a stronger bond than being forced. They all agreed with him. Halo most certainly did *not* have *oidos*. *She* knew perfectly well that she, a kid, knew better than all these people. She felt a hundred million miles away from them.

Above all, she wondered why they lived like this, eating on their feet, sleeping in gangs just anywhere around the town, instead of at home with their families. She wanted to shout at them – 'You *have* families! Why don't you appreciate them? I don't even have my family!'

'You're no one,' Borgas said. 'You don't even know what city you're from!'

*So does having no family, no city, make me no one?* She rubbed her aching limbs as she lay on the straw that night. *Most of my bad fortune has been because I have lost my family. Perhaps – perhaps, if I knew who I was, perhaps I could turn my ill fortune to good. But at least*, she thought with a bitter little laugh – *at least I'm not a Spartan.*

*

One morning, there was no training. There was to be a festival. Halo was looking forward to it. The boys were nervy and excited: they were all going down to the temple of Artemis Orthia, their parents would be there, the priestesses too. Borgas said the slaves could go and watch. 'It'll teach you something about your betters,' he said.

She lined up on the side of the road. She didn't know what to expect – a procession perhaps. Beside her in the crowd was a tall fair boy not much older than her, with soft curly hair and pale creamy pink cheeks. His eyes were blue and dreamy, and his limbs gentle. He didn't look at all like the Spartan soldier boys. She had never seen him before.

Up by the temple a wooden statue of Artemis had been brought out. A crowd of older boys was up there – she saw Scitas among them – and Leonidas.

They had whips and wooden bars.

The younger boys appeared, marching in ranks up to the temple, cheering and singing, looking brave and bold.

As they passed, the older boys beat them.

The priestess cried out, singing a high and happy song.

The young boys bit their lips and blinked back tears and raised their heads and kept on singing. One or two cried out in pain and shock – men's voices in the crowd shouted, 'Shame on you! You're a disgrace!'

The pale boy beside Halo was smiling.

The older boys raised their whips higher, brought down their sticks harder.

Blood blossomed on the young boys' backs, welts coming up. Halo saw two boys holding hands, their fists gripping tightly, sharing their strength and their pain. A boy stumbled and fell. It was Silenas, a short quiet boy who was not quite as unpleasant as the others. Halo had sometimes wondered, as she held Silenas off in the ring, how he had escaped being left out on the hillside at birth, as a weakling.

The crowd – their parents, their teachers – booed him loudly.

She thought of the gleaming scars on Leonidas's back, and she looked at him now. For a moment, between the blows raining down on the boys, she saw his face, and saw that he saw her. Their eyes locked for a moment, and she felt a sudden sharp pang of pity for him, of tenderness.

*Is this how it works? They inflict such pain and hardship on each other that nothing can ever hurt them again? Poor poor Leonidas, to be brought up in pride and violence instead of love and kindness. She admired him for surviving all this, and still actually being kind.*

She wanted to turn away from it all, to leave, to run. She couldn't – Borgas was right there, She looked away in disgust, unable to watch any more. She stared at her feet and tried to block out the brutal, inhuman racket of weeping, booing, singing and the crack and thud of clubs and belts on young flesh.

Later, the boys who had not cried were crowned with wreaths of leaves, and marched around the city in triumph. The crowds shouted out to them, 'Bravo, well done, brave and noble sons of Sparta.' They laughed and grinned and waved, showing off their wounds and waving to their mothers in the crowd.

She didn't see what happened to the boys who had wept or fallen.

The next day, back at training, the triumphant boys bounced around, full of themselves. 'I was silent! I was silent!' they yelled.

'Well, be silent now,' said Borgas. 'There's no honour in vanity. We're feeding you too much, if you've got energy to spare to be vain.'

Each week there was a parade. Halo and the other slaves had to stand by and admire. She just turned her mind off as the boys marched up and down. One grubby evening, Borgas broke up the boys' half-hour relaxation. 'Parade!' he shouted, and they all leapt up and ran down to the *agora* to line up. Halo dragged her weary body off the straw and limped down there. Crenas had stamped on her foot in training. It wasn't broken, but it was very painful.

She never forgot this particular parade. All she saw was that after about an hour of standing in the cold, Silenas had fallen down, and that blood had seeped out from where he fell, and spread across the icy ground. Borgas told them all, the next day, what had happened. Silenas had trapped a fox, to eat. He'd had it in his cloak, ready to kill, when the parade had been called. He hadn't wanted to be shamed by revealing it. He had held it tightly against his belly, all through the parade. It had been biting him. All through the parade.

He died. But he had made no sound, so he was a hero now. His mother would be so proud.

Halo had thought she already hated Sparta completely, but after this, she hated it more.

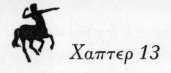

## Χαπτερ 13

Spring was coming. The sky was blue, and pale, and so high and big! There were little green buds of leaves on the trees – when had they come? The sun was shining. It was warm. And there was a smell on the air – a damp, sweet, lovely smell, like earth, and growing things . . . It was travelling season again. Halo had seen a group heading off to the north only that morning. Now she stood firm, thigh-high in the river while the seven-year-olds punched her belly, one after the other. She thought of Zakynthos, of anemones blooming, and blossom coming through on almond trees.

Sometime during the winter, Halo had stopped fighting like a wildcat. She had stopped answering back. She had stopped minding the insults, stopped responding to the abuse. After the festival of flogging, and Silenas's death, she had learned something: accept what is dealt you, and keep quiet. She started calling Borgas 'sir'. She fought only enough to keep from getting hurt. She grew as calm as she could be.

Borgas liked to think he was a good judge of character. He saw how the wildcat Titch had calmed down. Once the bravado had been knocked out of him, he'd turned out a coward like all foreigners. He hadn't even been able to *watch* the flogging. When it was time to choose the slaves to take the seven-year-olds into the countryside, Borgas didn't hesitate to choose Titch. Titch was no longer the type to try and run away.

Look at him now, standing there, being hit. Well, the littl'uns weren't going to learn anything that way.

'Titch!' he yelled. 'Give 'em something to do! Dodge! Duck! Splash! Keep them out of the current though.' She glanced towards the middle of the river. It was not so wide, but snowy spring meltwaters from the mountains surged swift and deep and cold.

So she dodged, and ducked, and splashed, feeling treacherous slimy pebbles under her feet, and swirling eddies of water on her legs and waist. Around her, the small boys slipped and slid, learning how to balance and move in water. One of them trod on a sharp stone, and squeaked in pain. For a second Halo felt a pang of pity for him – but this child already knew not to make a fuss. He shut his mouth tight, and looked around quickly to make sure no one had heard.

'Chase me!' she said, and dodged away from her group. Just beyond, Nebo was larking with his boys. They caught eyes for a moment, and smiled. Everyone was glad to be out of the city, in the spring sun.

Borgas and another instructor were on the bank, showing a group how to tie up their equipment to keep it dry when crossing a river. Borgas didn't really like water.

And then one of Halo's little boys slipped, and fell. She turned. He couldn't get his footing. He was too far out – Halo strode across to grab him. The current got him first. His yell was drowned by the rushing sound of water.

But Halo was almost there. Instinctively, she dived into the quick-flowing waters after him, the cold hitting her like a slap. She hurled herself at him with all her strength, and grabbed him, and kicked madly through the curling, hissing waters. Her blood pounded and the water was over her head, in her eyes, up her nose – but the strength of her dive took them across the danger zone. She kicked and kicked madly as they were tossed downstream – and suddenly they were in calm waters again. She shook the water from her head like a dog, panting and spitting. The little boy was in her arms. She looked around, trying to breathe. It was as if the pale icy green river had spat them out.

They were on the other side of the river.

Carefully, she picked her way to the bank, carrying the crying child. She put him down, kneeling beside him and holding him as he shivered and snivelled. She could see the group, not so far across the river: the boys standing in the water, staring; Borgas, staring.

He was really staring at Halo.

She felt her sodden chiton clinging to her. Quickly she pulled the wet folds away from her thighs.

Borgas was narrowing his eyes.

What he saw, modest, dressed, and cuddling a child, did not look to him like a boy.

What Halo saw was the end of her secret.

Or – and she quickly summed up the situation – an opportunity.

*It's now or never.*

*So it's now!*

She grinned, ruffled the child's hair, and she turned and ran.

She could hear Borgas yelling behind her. She knew he wouldn't brave the rushing river to come after her. She kept running. She doubted the other instructor would come either. Only a person acting on the instinct of life and death would jump into that icy crashing roaring stream. She kept running – away from the river, up the hillside, towards the woods, into the woods.

She was still running when she heard the thudding of feet behind her. For a second fear made her falter – and she heard again in her head what Leonidas had said about fear, about what it could do, about using it.

She used her fear to make herself run faster. Desperation clung to her. She dodged to where the trees were thicker.

Downhill now. A gully, a thicket.

A river. On the other side, a fallen tree, a pool. She could hear frogs croaking and hiccuping.

Footsteps behind. Her own breath tight in her ear.

Behind the tree, against the bank . . . a hiding place.

She flung herself flat on her belly, landing on ferns and mud, half in water, no breath left. Frogs plopped to left and right of her as she tried to get her breath back.

Her nose was practically in the pool. She smelt its damp greenness.

The footsteps stopped – somewhere above her. She heard voices shouting.

She could see across the water, right in front of her, level with her nose, a low dark gap, deep in the shadows. It lurked, almost invisible, overhung with new spring growth. River water stood deep and stagnant in there. Creepers overhung it.

It was a cave.

'Down here!' someone yelled, above.

There was no time to think. Silently, sleekly, she slid herself forward and slipped down beneath the oily dark surface of the pool. Gently, quietly, she propelled herself underwater towards the darkness of the cave. Into it. Eyes open, mouth shut, controlling her breath, repressing her fear, she followed the darkness.

Patches of sludge blopped at her face. She ignored them.

She needed to breathe.

She *had* to breathe.

She burst to the surface and flung her head back, gulping gratefully at the cold air, shivering as much with relief as with cold. She hadn't been sure there would even *be* a surface. If the water had filled the cave . . .

The relief did not last long. True, she had found air. But she found nothing else. She had followed the darkness all right. There was not a speck of light to show her where she had come from, or where she should go.

She had come up underground, cut off, in a pitch-black hole full of cold, cold water.

Halo doggy-paddled along desperately, reaching, seeing nothing. She was terrified, scared to reach out in the darkness, or put her feet down, for fear of what she might touch – or not touch, for there might be nothing beneath her feet but empty dark depth . . . but knowing she had to, because if she didn't find a solid surface and get out of this freezing water, she would die.

Her arms quivered.

*Keep going. Use your fear . . .*

She was so tired. She paddled tensely and frantically, as if trying to keep her body up, out of the water almost – what if there was thick, squelching mud full of water snakes, and rotten dead animals, or toxic, stinking gas bubbles . . . or dark, long, slimy weeds, their stalks disappearing down in the blackness deep below, reaching up to entangle and snare her . . . or quicksand to pull, sucking, at her legs and drag her down and swallow her up . . .

For all she knew there might be solid clean rock just beneath her feet but she daren't reach down . . .

Something trailed against her leg and she screamed. Her voice drifted out and echoed across an expanse.

*Ah!*

Her foot touched rock. She scrabbled towards it. The water was shallow there.

She pulled herself up, on to she could not see what. Some underground bank, or beach. She stretched her arms up, and stood. Too late she realized she might crack her head – but no. It was high enough to stand.

She could hear nothing. She could see nothing. She knew nothing.

Cold.

She called out again more softly, trying to judge how big the cave was.

The echo replied, hollow and lonely. The cave was huge!

She rubbed her arms, held her hands in her armpits, and jumped. She had no idea, no way of telling, which way she had come.

It occurred to her that she was a fool, and that she was in

great danger. Was this really better than being a slave? Better than Borgas knowing she was a girl?

Her teeth were chattering and her muscles were seizing up. She had to move. The air in the cave felt cool and fresh. It had to come from somewhere. The question was, where? How could she ever know if she was walking in the right direction?

This great dark cave could easily be her grave.

She put herself in the hands of the Gods, and started walking.

When she first saw the little twinkling lights, she thought that the cold and the hunger and the darkness were giving her hallucinations. When she bent down to look at them closer, she saw that they were real. Little blue-white lights. They seemed to be a fungus. She gathered a handful, and marvelled at it – a handful of light! She held it high. It showed her nothing much. But she could see, from the way it lay on the ground, that she was on a slight slope.

*I shall walk uphill, because uphill should lead away from water . . . and to the surface . . .*

The river was in a gully. The area round about was hilly. She had no idea where anything might be. For all she knew, she might come up under the temple in the middle of Sparta.

She walked on.

When she started knocking her head on long, firm strands of who-knew-what hanging from the ceiling, which seemed suddenly much closer, she was happy. She hadn't come across them before, so she was not going round in circles. It wasn't until she had walked far past them that she realized they must be the roots of trees. Should she turn back, and try to dig upwards into the ceiling? But would she find them again?

She walked on.

She would very much have liked a wall to walk along. It would have seemed safer, somehow. Then she felt, suddenly, by a change of air, that she *was* walking alongside something.

Not for a moment or two did she realize it was a precipice.

She had no idea how far it fell.

She gulped, and walked on.

She felt something rolling under her foot, something long and hard and thin. She picked it up. A porcupine quill. She smiled in the darkness. Porcupines wouldn't go very deep under-ground.

Bats. A sudden, massive, whispering flurry of bats, a shifting, rustling tube of bats swooping from behind her, peeping their high, high noise, catching her up in the movement of air from their fluttery, papery little wings . . .

Bats! They sleep by day in caves, and at dusk they go out into the open air . . .

Open air!

She began to run, following the bats.

Their exit was a one-metre hole high up in a sloping wall of rock. She could see the beautiful glow of the sky, blue and clear, as she scrambled up the rocks, breaking her nails and skinning her knees and elbows. She slithered out through cobwebs over a patch of wild thyme that smelt as sweet as the gates of heaven, and then she was lying on green grass in a wooded glade, practically on top of a little waterfall, as the last pink gleams of sunset were lighting on the under-sides of a few fluffy clouds.

## Χαπτερ 14

Halo washed under the waterfall, and then headed on, without food or water, or even a cloak to wrap round her. *If I travel by night I can keep myself warm and out of sight*, she told herself, *and then I can sleep in the day when it's warmer.* She was impatient. She was heading north and west, between the sunset's dying glow and the first pricking of the North Star. North and west, to Zakynthos. If necessary, she would *swim* across. She needed her home.

She could see dim flickering lights below her to the south. Sparta? If it was, she was already some distance in the right direction. She must have been going north underground. *So much the better*, she thought, as she strode on.

As the moon rose, she could make out the River Eurotas down below, with the road beside it leading from Sparta to the north. There was no traffic on it. Tomorrow, perhaps, she might be able to get a lift . . . she would have to be careful though. She turned her path downhill. Best to cross the river, and the road, by night.

She was tired, of course, and even though she had grown accustomed to the paltry Spartan rations she was very hungry. There were no nuts or fruit for her to eat. She was going along, parallel with the road, a little distance from it, thinking about how she would have to get back in the river to cross it. She dreaded it.

She sat down to rest. Sleep crept up swiftly.

It was the sharp toe of a travelling boot in her ribs that woke her an hour or so later. She was being kicked, or tipped over. She jumped up, confused, from a deep, deep sleep. A hand was twisted into the belt of her chiton, and a smooth arm snaked round her neck from behind, holding her captive. A voice she had never heard before hissed in her ear.

'You shouldn't be out here,' it said, and she was propelled, still blinking, down on to the road. She tried to struggle, to turn her head and see who her captor was – but each time she did she got a sharp jerk at her throat. *Well*, she thought, *I'll see soon enough.*

He threw her down at someone's feet, and she looked up. Firelight flickered, orange and black: two horses, a little wagon, a trio of faces in the dark.

Her captor was the silky blond boy from the crowd at the festival.

The feet belonged to Melesippus.

Beside him, sitting – Leonidas.

Splayed by the road beneath these three, she didn't know whether to laugh or cry. All that effort, all that danger, all for nothing.

'Hah!' said Melesippus, who was sitting on a tree stump, as if hardly surprised. 'It's your little friend, Leon. What are you doing out here? Can't bear to be parted from our handsome young cadet? Or are you running away?'

Immediately, Halo realized that they didn't know she had escaped. They must have left before Borgas got back from the river. She thought quickly.

'Yes, sir,' she said. 'No, sir.'

'What, sir?' said Melesippus. 'Yes or no?' He was having his dinner, and seemed in a good mood. She didn't feel that this was something she could rely on. *Think of something!* Her mind was a big, scared blank.

She glanced at Leonidas. She hadn't even seen him since the festival of flogging.

'No, sir,' she said.

'Tattooboy,' said Melesippus, a little more impatiently, 'tell us why you are here.'

'It's my fault,' said Leonidas suddenly.

Melesippus turned to him, looking a query.

'I offered him my protection, and then forgot to tell him I was leaving,' said Leonidas, as if it wasn't very important. 'He probably thought it his duty to follow me. In case I needed him.'

He stretched, and yawned. 'I suppose we'll have to take him along now,' he said.

Melesippus looked at him, as if weighing this up. He snorted.

'I suppose so,' he said. 'Do try and keep your responsibilities under proper control, Leon.'

Halo tried not to gasp with relief.

'Yes, sir,' said Leonidas. 'Come on, you, stand up.'

Halo stood up. Her knees were shaking. *If you even think about running away, they'll kill you ...* She could hardly believe her luck.

The blond boy was giving her a very clear look, from his round blue eyes. *It's as if he knows everything*, she thought. *He sees right through me.*

'Leonidas,' said Melesippus, as they turned in that night,

'don't let that slave of yours run away. Have him sleep by you.' And he threw a length of chain and two leather cuffs at Leonidas's feet.

Leonidas paused a moment, then said, 'Sir,' and gave a little bow.

As he laid out his cloak in the open by the wagon, she murmured, 'Thank you.'

In answer, Leonidas produced a length of rope and said, 'Give me your feet.'

She realized he was going to tie them together so she couldn't run away.

'Come and get them,' she couldn't help saying. Of course she was grateful not to be killed, but she had tasted a moment of freedom and she wanted more.

He glanced at her, and smiled. He recognized the quote: it was what King Leonidas has said to the Persian messengers before Thermopylae, when they demanded that he gave up his weapons.

'I see you've been picking up a bit of Spartan education,' he said. 'Which is just dandy, but no, I am not bending down to tie your feet.'

'Well, I am not sitting down to offer my feet to you,' she said, so he pushed her over, tied her feet together and said, 'Don't be such a day-old goat. I've done you enough favours. Stop moaning.' He clasped one cuff around her right wrist, and the other round his own left biceps. She watched, and raised her eyebrows as he chained them together. He smiled at her. He didn't even have to say, 'Don't even think about trying to run off.'

'You go there,' he said, throwing a cloak at her. She rolled herself up in it and lay down. He sat, leaning against the wagon.

*Chained like a naughty dog*, she thought bitterly. *How wonderful.* And then: *But not dead, killed as a runaway.*

The sky above them was liquid with beauty, and the ground beneath very hard. She could hear the horses' soft breathing as she rolled over on to her back.

'Is that all right by you, O master?' she asked sarcastically, as the chain pulled on his wrist. 'For me to roll over?'

'Do shut up,' he said.

The stars were very twinkly and bright.

'So, I'm *your* slave then,' she said at last.

'You know you are,' he said. 'Sorry.'

That made her laugh. The big boy with the big horse, the Spartan warrior, apologizing.

They lay silently. It was peculiar, lying there in the dark, looking up at the spring stars, lush and clear, way up high. Even though they were chained together, it reminded her of the many many nights she and Arko had lain under the night sky, whispering.

'Who's that boy?' she asked, after a while.

'"That boy" is Manticlas, the finest seer in Lacedaemonia,' said Leonidas, in an amused voice.

A seer! Well, that explained things. A bit. Kyllarus had told her about seers. They read omens and portents, look at the weather, and consider what animals pass by. They interpret dreams, and read the stars, and choose auspicious dates for great activities. They examine sacrifices, looking for good fortune or bad.

'Isn't he a bit young?' she asked.

'He has a great gift,' Leonidas said. 'His readings are true, and have been since he was a small child. It's not like normal wisdom that you get more of as you get older.'

'Can he read the future?' Halo asked curiously.

'Better than the rest of us, they say,' said Leonidas.

Halo wondered if she would be able to ask Manticlas about her parents. She felt probably not.

Silence fell again between them.

She grinned in the darkness.

'Why do you keep saving me?' she asked.

'Because –' he said. 'Because you're not a slave.'

'No one's a slave,' she said.

'Don't start that again,' he said. 'Slaves exist, all right? They're slaves, and that's the way things are . . .'

'So if you get caught in battle, you'd be a slave, is that it?'

He laughed out loud at that, and had to shut himself up.

'Yeah,' he said. '*If.*'

She had to laugh at that – at his cockiness and pride. Then they were both just trying to stifle their laughter in the still night.

An owl hooted above them.

'Athena's telling us to shut up,' he whispered.

'Very wise,' Halo replied.

It was so nice not to be alone. Even though her companion was Leonidas.

'Leonidas,' she whispered after a bit, 'if you agree I'm not a slave, why would you mind if I ran away?'

The silence was long, and she was afraid he had fallen

asleep, but finally he spoke. 'Because I'm responsible for you,' he said. 'You heard Melesippus. I couldn't cover for you again if you're caught –'

'*If* –' she murmured.

'But then, you weren't captured in battle, and you're not born to slavery, so in a way it isn't right for you to be enslaved.'

She didn't want to get him in trouble, she thought. But then, if the alternative to getting him in trouble was her being a slave all her life, well, grateful as she was, there was no contest.

'What you need to do,' he said, 'is find out who you are. Until you know who you are, you're no one.'

'I'm me!' she said crossly, but even she knew now that in this world of humans that just wasn't enough.

She rolled over again. She'd pull on the chain throughout the night, she decided, just to annoy him.


Travelling in company was so different from the long journey she had made alone. She knew that she was safe from wild animals at night. She knew that bandits would not come anywhere near a party of Spartans. She didn't even have to walk. Her supper was there in the baskets in the wagon. Dion the slave made the fire. Birds were singing. Tiny leaves uncurled on the knotty vines; baby mules and donkeys tottered in the fields; little white clouds danced in the sky and Phoebus the Sun shone down like a friend after a long journey. It seemed to Halo as if Demeter was having a party and had invited everyone. The world was beautiful. All of Greece and everything in it was beautiful.

Halo, sitting back in the wagon, her belly full of morning porridge, realized that things were much, much better than they might be. She would have felt almost peaceful as they trundled through the green valleys and rocky outcrops of Arcadia, up its lovely hills, alongside its rushing rivers, up into the high snowy mountains that sheltered them from the Gulf of Corinth. But she didn't. Her mind was on fire.

They were going to Delphi!

The centre of the world!

Apollo's home on earth – where his sacred Oracle, the Pythia, sat in the great temple, and answered any question, and always told the truth, no matter what.

Halo gazed up at the peaks as she passed beneath them. They looked like great piles of creamy yoghurt on which the Gods had poured golden honey. She looked down: striped buds on the beautiful asphodels, tiny blue wild hyacinths, crocuses and violets and scarlet windflowers. The sun warmed their backs. Leonidas, riding ahead, had thrown off his cloak in the sunshine and stuck a twig of almond blossom behind his ear.

It occurred to her, looking at his broad brown shoulders, that she would not be able to pass as a boy forever. The Pythia would know she was a girl . . .

They were plodding uphill. As they came to the highest point the air grew cold again. Everyone pulled their cloaks around them, and snow covered the road, sharp and gritty. Close up it looked nothing like cream and honey. She prayed they would make their way down the other side before nightfall.

An hour later she saw a gull wheeling overhead. Its sharp cry tugged at her heart.

She was trying to stand up on the wagon beside Dion, pulled down by her chain attached to the bench seat, gazing and staring, gazing and staring – and she was rewarded. An hour or so before sundown, the long hazy fingers of the evening sun lit up a gleaming streak way down before her: the Gulf of Corinth. The sea! She feasted her eyes as the water grew closer. More than once she thought she caught the scent of sea lilies on the breeze – but she didn't really. It was her imagination, because she wanted so much to smell them. *But the sea is real*, she thought. *Out there, where the sun is setting, is my beautiful Zakynthos.* She half thought that if she stared hard enough at the greeny gold sky perhaps she would even see Zakynthos on the horizon, floating like a memory of all that was happy.

The Pythia could tell her how to get home . . .

It was almost dark by the time they came into the little port from which the ferry crossed over to Delphi. She could see the two great mountains, Parnassus and Gion, on the other side, their snowy tops shining in the last rays of the evening sun. They seemed to be floating in the dusk, hardly any distance away. Her eyes rested too on the water, almost feeding on it. *I could dive into that water now, and swim, and swim, and swim, and wash up once again on my Zakynthine beach, and Kyllarus would come and find me and bring me home . . .*

Something of her thoughts must have shown on her face. Dion turned to her and said, 'It's the nature of the sea to give us longings.' That was all. She looked at him. He had already turned away again, to spit.

She stopped staring at the sea longingly. She didn't want Melesippus or Manticlas or Leonidas to notice that there were things on her mind. Instead she stared into the bottom of the wagon, and thought privately, deep inside herself.

The next day at dawn Halo leapt up bright and early and full of excitement and joy.

She had unfortunately forgotten that she was shackled to a young Spartan who was not quite so full of joy as she was, and who now barked at her to shut up and lie down and stop pulling his blinking arm off. She sat down next to him and played with the chain and began to hum. He could be as cross as he liked. She didn't care. She was excited.

Before they crossed over the gulf, Melesippus – who was rather a superstitious man, Halo thought – wanted Manticlas to read the omens for the crossing, and for whether it was good to approach the Oracle now. He wanted a sacrifice.

*A sacrifice to see if it is a good time to offer a sacrifice*, thought Halo. *Interesting. This could go on and on . . .*

Leonidas – with Halo still attached – was sent along to the small market to find a lamb.

The spring lambs were too pretty, with their clean curling fur, like Dion's beard, their bright dark eyes, and their little noses. They clustered round her hand, licking her with rough little tongues. Halo couldn't bear to choose one, knowing it would die.

Leonidas said, 'You do know they're all going to die, in the end.'

'Well so are you and I,' she said. 'That doesn't mean we want to race towards it.'

'I'm happy to die any time it's required,' he said, matter-of-factly.

She looked up at him. She could see from his face that he meant it.

'What do you mean?' she said. 'That's a dreadful thing to say – how can you want to die?'

'I mean,' he said, 'if it helped save Sparta in battle, say. Or to save my brothers in arms. When it's right for me to die, I'll die. The Gods give you your spirit, and you give it back with a glad heart when the time comes.'

'You're crazy,' she said. 'How can you say that? Look, the sun is shining and the light is golden, and the market is full of cherries and we're off on an adventure – how could you turn your back on this beautiful world, and go down to the underworld where it's all dark and cold?'

'My body is not mine to do what I want with,' he said. 'I belong to Sparta. My life's purpose is to defend Sparta. So we fight until we win, or until we're all dead. There's no point living with dishonour.'

'What's so honourable about dying?' she said – but by then the stallholder wanted them to buy a blinking lamb or get out of the way of decent people who would, so Leonidas grabbed the nearest one, and slung it, bleating, round Halo's shoulders while she handed over the iron coin the seer had given her. Spartan money was so heavy. *It's not surprising*, she thought, *that no one is rich there. They wouldn't be able to carry their own purses.*

She held the lamb's feet to her chest as they walked back to the port slowly, thoughtfully.

'I don't expect you to understand this,' he said, 'because you are a girl and a foreigner. But look – do you know why a Spartan can give up his helmet, or his armour, but never his shield?'

'Is this to do with that horrible song?' she asked.

'What song?'

'About coming back with your shield or on it?'

'Yes. It's because your helmet and your armour protect only you, but your shield protects the line. You, and your brothers in arms. Each man protects his brother to the left.'

She was quiet.

'If you lose your shield, you leave a gap in the line, and you put all the men in danger.'

She could understand that. She recalled how she and Arko had each tried to protect the other when they had been stuck in the Hole.

It gave her a pang of pain. Without Arko, she had no line. No brothers in arms. Nobody to fight alongside; nobody to protect her; nobody to protect. Not that she wanted to fight. Lying under the stars, walking among green leaves and birdsong, chewing on hard cheese, remembering the blue light of her beautiful caves, she was in love with life not just for herself but for everybody. She thought it tragic that the Spartan boys were bred for blood and gore and death; that they whipped each other to harden them to pain; that they could laugh as they killed people . . . But she was a human, and almost as much as they like being alive, humans like to have some other humans to belong with.

'Do you understand?' he said.

'I understand about the loyalty,' she said. 'But I don't understand why humans are always attacking each other.'

'Most of the time,' he said, 'we're not. We're defending each other.'

'But what from?' she demanded. 'Somebody must be attacking in the first place.'

'The enemy,' he said mildly.

'The enemy probably think they're defending against *you*,' she said.

'That's not my problem,' he said. 'I'm a soldier, not a politician.'

Halo didn't know about politicians. She just knew that the Centaurs didn't fight. 'If you have wisdom,' she said, 'you don't need to shed blood.' She remembered the look on Kyllarus's face as he had said that. She was glad Kyllarus had never seen her trying to tear Crenas's head off.

'Listen,' Leonidas said. 'Listen. You don't know what you're talking about. You have never been attacked. You have never seen an enemy. There's an old saying: "My grandfather was a soldier, so my father could be a farmer, so I could be a poet." Well, maybe you're like the poet or the farmer. But I'm the soldier. My duty is to keep things safe. Things aren't safe — that's just a fact — so I have to be ready in case I'm needed. Wouldn't you like us to be on your side when the bandits came down on *your* city? Though of course they wouldn't come if they knew we were on your side. They'd be too scared.'

She knew that was true. She knew too that she always wanted Leonidas, with his broad shoulders and his honesty, on her side. But – but –

'I have no side,' she said. 'I have no city.'

'You *must* have a city,' he said. 'Who are you? Who are your parents?'

His eyes were clear and not unkind, and to her own surprise, she told him the truth.

'I don't know,' she said. 'I was lost at sea, and found again – but not by my own people. They probably think I'm dead.'

She was so used to it by now that she just said it simply, as a fact. But when she looked up at him, to her amazement, there was kindness in his eyes.

'I didn't realize,' he said.

'I've got used to it,' she said mildly.

'Well, get unused to it again,' he said urgently. 'You mustn't be used to it. You should find them, and how are you going to find them if you're not hungry for it?'

Hungry for them? For her parents, her family, her blood, her people?

Hungry.

So that was the word. That word he used explained everything she had been feeling, everything that she hadn't understood. She *was* hungry for them. Desperately hungry.

'But who brought you up?' he was asking.

'Kind people, in the countryside,' she said.

'In times of peace,' he said. 'Poets and farmers.'

'In times of peace,' she agreed.

'Lucky for you,' he said. 'But you're not a little kid any more. And peace doesn't last forever. You need to know who you are.'

'I'll ask the Oracle at Delphi,' she said suddenly. She was joking when she said it, but as the words came out she thought, *Why not?*

'Apollo won't mind that I don't have much to offer,' she said. 'I'll give what I can.' She wondered if she was right. *I could give my owl*, she thought. If Apollo could really tell her who she was through the Oracle, she would be happy to give him her owl. It would make sense. The owl her parents had put on her to look after her when she was a baby could now help her to find her parents.

*Is that what I'm doing? Trying to find my parents?* she thought.

*Yes*, she thought. *I am.*

Halo had to help with the sacrifice. She didn't like it. It wasn't the same as killing an animal by hunting, to eat it. Then the animal had a chance to get away, and it was her skill that shot it down, and it was fair. She offered the animal to the Gods afterwards out of gratitude for having been given the food. But just buying an animal, and it sitting there with its nice eyes . . . she didn't like the lamb looking at her.

She helped Manticlas to wash and purify himself, and to put on his ritual sash. She listened as he murmured his prayers. And she stared at the ground, clenching her jaw, when he lifted the knife, invoked the Gods, and whipped the sharp blade across the lamb's white throat.

It was peculiar to see a young boy performing these actions. All the floppiness had gone from him, and he seemed inspired. His hands were firm and his movements strong. He seemed to enjoy it.

The animal died quickly and silently.

Halo looked at Manticlas's face, lit up and excited. She watched while he sliced the lamb open and looked at its dribbly, bloody entrails.

*He's revolting*, she thought.

'This is the heart,' he said, pointing to a small yellowish-red object with many tubes coming out of it. 'Either side, the lungs.' These were purple and spongy. Despite herself, she was interested. She knew the names of the parts, of course, because Kyllarus and Chariklo had taught her long ago, as they cleaned their prey for dinner. But she had never seen a liver taken out and read to tell you what was going to happen. How could Manticlas know what it meant? She would be interested, actually, to learn about that.

Manticlas carefully cut the lamb's liver away from its veins and arteries, and held it up, shiny wet and purply-red. It bled a lot. 'Good, good,' he murmured. 'The liver is a good shape, clean and firm . . . no extra lobes, nothing missing or misshapen . . . the colour is fine and lively . . .' He poured water over it to wash it, then paused for a moment, looking thoughtful. 'Still bleeding,' he said. 'Hmm.'

'What does that mean?' asked Melesippus. He didn't look anxious, but he looked as if he might look anxious if looking anxious was something he did, which it wasn't.

'Nothing much,' said Manticlas. 'It's good. Flowing is a

good omen for a journey. If the blood wasn't moving, then neither should we.'

Halo watched as the thin red blood dripped down. *Perhaps it is an omen for me*, she thought. *Perhaps it is telling me to keep moving. Perhaps it is telling me to run away again.*

And risk a Spartan death sentence?

*Living as a slave is a death sentence.*

# Χαπτερ 15

They crossed the Gulf of Corinth on a wooden ferryboat, which danced on the sprightly waves of spring. Gulls wheeled and cawed. The air was clean and sparkling with promise, and the sun turned the gulf into a long streak of silver and rose.

Halo was so happy to be with the sea that for a moment she almost forgot that she was a captive. She lifted her head and closed her eyes and felt salt and sun on her face and lips. She breathed deeply – among the smells of salt and rope and fish and tar was the distant, delicious scent of sea lilies. Finally, when she had to breathe out, there was a sharp sweet tear of joy and loneliness in her eye: joy for how much she loved her Zakynthos family; loneliness for how far she was from them and from . . . from the other thing. The other thing she needed.

And ahead lay Delphi, the centre of west and east, of the world – of the Universe. Even the orbit of the stars and the heavenly spheres circled round Delphi, and there the mysterious airs and mists rose to inspire the priestess, the sacred Pythia, with the words of Apollo.

There Halo, like thousands of others before her, would find an answer.

Even as they got off the boat, Halo found herself grinning at the bustle and the noise. She saw tall fair people from the north, sun-blackened people from the south, fat people, skinny people, sick people, poor people, muscled rowers for hire carrying their cushions and oars. Striding along the dusty winding road up through the rippling silvery olive groves to Delphi, she saw a man with a withered leg; a girl with a white monkey on a leash; and merchants in fine coloured cloaks, come to ask if their ships had sunk, or if their plans would be blessed. In the little town of Delphi itself she saw food vendors offering smelly fried fish and honey cakes; scrawny dogs trying to make off with bits of kebab; cheerful hawkers trying to sell amulets, crying out, 'Kind sir, good luck for you, protection from sickness and harm, good luck in love and money, very cheap, very good!'

Halo smiled. She knew everyone needed the protection of the Gods, but she knew, too, that a little piece of metal wouldn't make you rich, or keep you healthy. That said . . . she touched her little owl, at her neck. It did seem sometimes as if the owl protected her.

She struggled to keep up with her party, who were still marching like Spartans: quickly and easily, determined yet with a relaxed look, and expecting everyone to get out of their way. Which, when they saw Melesippus's crimson cloak and Leonidas's black one, they did. Pilgrims, priests and poets all made way when the Spartans came through.

They went straight to the lodgings the Spartans always used, to prepare for the following day, the seventh of March. The Oracle only operated on the seventh of each month, and then only if the augurs were good. And even then, not everybody got to put their question – they would have to draw lots for a place.

In the morning, they all put on clean clothes – even the Spartans, who usually thought such things frivolous. Stars were still fading from the sky as they left their lodgings, breathing again the pure air of early morning. The silvery-green slope of Mount Parnassus swooped up to the left. Two great wings of marble cliff, the Phaedriades, the Shining Ones, hung behind. The terraced gorge dropped away to the right, and across the dim valley Mount Kirphis lay long and low. And they came round a bend, and she saw it. Rising from the terraced slopes, lit up by the pale early-morning sun, was the glorious sanctuary of Apollo – row upon row of marble columns, ranks of statues in bronze and gold, strange creatures carved from stone, mighty and mysterious rocks, and temple upon temple upon temple. Stone maidens supported pediments on their heads. A winged sphinx perched on a column taller than she had ever seen. Broad staircases were interspersed with almond trees spattered with blossom, dark cypresses and flickering silver-green olives, and the endless statues of beautiful boys and beautiful girls. Every surface was carved with writing, with images of heroes and beasts and Gods and nymphs, and above it all paraded the great temple of Apollo itself, its immense columns lined up, white and perfect, and its gigantic statue of Apollo – ten metres high, with blue eyes and golden hair.

Before they could enter, they had to go to the Castalian Spring, to be purified. Petitioners, quieter and more sober than they had been the day before, were queueing up outside the stone court where the sacred water gushed from the row of eight lion-head fountains.

Melesippus, Leonidas and Manticlas went up together to the row of fountains. Halo, still shackled to Leonidas, stepped forward with him. *What would it feel like, to be purified for Apollo?* she wondered. Would she feel it in her body, or in her soul? She breathed deeply, spoke to the God as she so often did, and stuck her head into the flow of water.

Agh but it was cold! She pulled her head out, and shook it like a dog. She drank. How delicious it was. Sweet and pure. Even the water from the spring on Mount Taegetus, when she hadn't drunk for two days, had not been so delicious.

Leonidas was looking at her, amused. 'So you are going to do it?' he said.

'Well,' she said. 'There's a slight problem – I'm chained to you.' She gave him a huge smile.

He laughed, and shook his head. 'And how do I explain to Melesippus that I have to let you loose because you want to talk to Apollo?'

'Find a way?' she asked hopefully. *You have to. You wouldn't stop me doing this. Would you? I told you my secret.*

As they came up to the temple, loose crowds were gathering. A young man with a broom of bay and laurel leaves was sweeping the steps, and sprinkling them with holy water. The Spartans greeted him, and he directed them round to the north of the temple, where they could drink from the sacred spring of Kassotis, which gathered in a basin there before it dived down underneath the temple itself. There the most sacred chambers lay, the *kella* and the *adyton*, where Dionysus was buried, where Zeus's two eagles stood, with the great stone that Apollo had cast there, and where the Pythia sat on her three-legged throne over the sacred chasm, from which the holy vapours rose.

Not that any of them would be allowed in *there*.

Halo was breathing deeply, speaking to Apollo already in her mind. She had saved her last barley cake from yesterday's lunch to offer as sacrifice along with her golden owl.

Leonidas ambled round to the west end of the temple. There, the pediment held a great frieze of Athena defeating a giant.

*Why do they treat girls as if we were nothing?* she thought. *Is Athena nothing? Look at her!*

Inside, there was another frieze: she glanced up, curious. Centaurs! For a moment she was delighted – and then as she saw what it was she felt a chill of shame. It was the wedding feast of the Lapiths. There was Eurytas, carrying off Hippodamia. There were humans and Centaurs fighting and killing each other. The sons of Ixion. She pressed her lips together very tight and blinked. *Why couldn't they have a frieze of Chiron up there, teaching medicine to Asclepius? Why have the bad Centaurs?*

Leonidas glanced up, and back at her.

They turned back to the steps at the eastern end of the temple, where the main sacrifice would take place, and stood with the petitioners queueing up. It was almost time to draw lots.

Melesippus and Manticlas had lingered by the pool. By the time they returned Leonidas and Halo were at the front of the queue.

'Here, Melesippus,' Leonidas called. 'I have held your place.'

'You pick out our bean, Leon,' Melesippus said. 'Be lucky for us.'

Side by side, Halo and Leonidas took their beans from the pot.

'You're going to do it?' he murmured.

'Yes,' she said. 'Yes, I am.'

Halo closed her eyes, clutching the hard little bean in her palm. She was begging Apollo to choose her to put her question.

The priest called that all those with dark beans should come forward for the sacrifice.

She could hardly bear to look at her bean.

*Well, if it's pale I'll just come back . . . somehow . . .*

She opened her hand.

It was dark.

She smiled, and a roll of thanks poured from her heart to Apollo. She didn't even care now what the Spartans were doing, if their bean had been dark or not. But Melesippus came up and clasped Leonidas's shoulder, and a bright smile passed between them. They too had won their draw.

She wondered what their question was.

A respectful quiet fell over the crowd when the priests brought out the goat, the cold water, the knife. The creature's thin splayed legs wobbled on the flat stone beneath the columns; the priests sang, and the morning for a moment hung silent about them.

Everyone could hear the splash of cold water on the little beast.

It shivered at the shock – from its head down to its hairy feet.

A shout of joy went up. The goat had shivered. The Oracle would speak today.

*Χαπτερ 16*

When their turn came, and the Spartans made to enter the temple, a priest stopped them gently.

'Only two,' he said.

Leonidas shrugged, gestured to Halo, still trailing behind him from the chain like a dinghy from a ship. 'I might as well stay outside,' he said.

The moment the others had gone in, she smiled up at him, a smile of pure excited joy, and dragged him across to the altar before the temple, under the shade of the great portico, to offer up her little barley cake to the priest there.

The priest glanced at the chain attaching her to Leonidas.

'Release him, please,' he said. 'No one goes bound into the temple.'

Leonidas gave a little laugh, and raised his eyebrow at her as he unlocked the shackle at his wrist. She grinned at him. She had known he'd do the right thing for her. Hadn't he always when it came to it? The chain fell, heavy, by her side.

'Have you your fee?' the priest asked kindly, and she nodded, silently putting her finger on the little golden owl lying at her throat.

'Question ready?' asked the priest, and she nodded again. She couldn't speak. He seemed used to that.

'And is this your *proxenos*?'

*My what?* she thought.

'I don't . . .' she said nervously.

'The representative of your city, who will accompany you,' he said firmly.

'I don't know my city,' she whispered miserably. Even here, did she have to belong to a city? Even though she had come here specially to find out where she belonged?

'No city!' the priest murmured, with concern.

He glanced up at Leonidas, who said drily, 'Well, he's definitely not from *my* city.'

Helplessly, Halo looked up at the priest. Behind him was the entrance to the *kella*, the inner chamber. There were words carved massively across the entrance:

*ΓΝΩΘΙ ΣΕ ΑΥΤΟΝ*

which means

KNOW THYSELF

Halo almost laughed, and almost cried. That was what she was trying to do. To know herself.

*Please, Apollo*, she begged silently.

'That is my question for the Oracle,' she said to the priest, pointing up. 'Who am I?'

She gazed at him, her eyes pleading.

'Then you are following the God's instructions,' he said, and he whistled, and a boy came running over – the one who had been sweeping the steps earlier. 'Ion,' he said to the boy. 'Play *proxenos* for this pilgrim' – and she was through.

Clumsily she tried to unfasten the leather thong, so she

would have the owl ready to give to Apollo. He was being so kind to her today. She wanted to be able to give it up without a second thought. But it was her little owl. It was the only thing her human parents had left with her. The only thing her mother had touched . . .

'Nonsense,' she whispered to herself fiercely. 'They left me myself! My body! My hands and my brain and my heart and my thoughts! My mother fed me and my father gave me life – why, I *am* them! I don't need any bit of gold to prove anything!'

As she entered the cool, shady chamber within the temple, another priest held out his hand, and she dropped the owl into it.

'Where is your *proxenos*?' he asked, looking round.

'Here,' said the boy.

'And have you the final sacrifice?' he asked quietly.

*What?*

'That is my final sacrifice,' she said, through dry lips. 'I have nothing else. Should I have more? I'm sorry . . .'

The priest peered at her, and at the little owl. 'There is a third sacrifice to be offered within,' he murmured.

Feeling foolish, she held out the thong the owl had hung from. But maybe Apollo wanted a sheep, or money . . . Tears stood in her eyes. She had come so far. Was she now, at the last moment, to be turned away?

She fell to her knees. 'Sweet Apollo,' she murmured. 'Sweet Apollo, who has been so kind to me, help me, please – my owl is all I have . . .'

The priest watched her through tired eyes, and then

sleepily turned away. 'Go through, child,' he said, as if it didn't matter so much either way.

She went in. *Thank you Apollo thank you thank you thank you . . .*

How dark it was! A great dim cave. Fire flickered, and shadows jumped. She could see an altar, statues, dim figures. At the end a tall shape and a slender one stood out against a glow: it was Melesippus and the seer. It was only when she saw them that she realized Leonidas was not with her.

She moved through the shadow, close to the wall, and came up by them. They didn't notice her.

Beyond them was an entrance. She stared at it. *That's the entrance to the* adyton, *she thought. In there is the Pythia on her tripod, the* omphalos, *the sacred laurel tree, and grave of Dionysus, the chasm* . . . From there, she realized, emanated the eerie calm of the place. She heard a quiet, echoey, hollow sound of splashing water, like a slow fall into a pool, and there was that delicious smell again . . . She closed her eyes and breathed deeply. How cool it was, and refreshing. It reminded her of . . .

As the sweet air coming from the *adyton* filled her lungs and spread through her blood, she knew the smell. She felt again Arko's hand in hers, and the fresh salty spray of the sea, and the cool blue light of the caves of Zakynthos – it was the same funny air that bubbled up from the seabed near the tar lakes, that made them laugh and talk and sing – it was the air of her childhood, her brother, her home.

A great smile spread across her face. Apollo was welcoming her. His sacred vapours were her own sweet memories.

She squatted down by the wall, and breathed, and waited. She would know herself, as Apollo wanted.

The Spartans, standing stiff like puppets strung tight with anticipation, had asked their question. They stood attentive and firm like sentries, waiting. And now she could hear their answer. A woman's voice, as if from far away, yet somehow within her head, echoing yet clear, musical yet frightening, cried out, 'It is coming, and there is no way to avoid it. If you fight with all your might, victory will be yours. Apollo himself will be on your side, whether you invoke him or not.'

When they heard the words, a great sigh burst from Melesippus like a gasping wind. Manticlas turned, and began to move his hands, to and fro, in an odd way.

She flattened herself against the wall as the Spartans turned and left the *kella*. They strode determinedly, emerging from the darkness, heading for the light. *It is coming, and there is no way to avoid it . . . Victory will be yours.*

She hadn't heard them ask their question, but she remembered the conversations of the long winter. She knew they had asked about war.

*War is coming.*

But now it was her turn. She almost crept towards the entrance. Ion stood by her.

'Go to the doorway,' he said quietly, with a smile. 'And speak to her.'

And she approached the door.

Another powerful burst of the beautiful smell wafted out. She breathed it deeply, and took courage from it.

'Blessed Pythia,' she said, and her voice was clear. Within, she saw a glimpse of green leaves, a flash of bronze. The water gurgled. She knew that the Pythia was in there.

'Blessed Pythia, blessings on you for hearing me, my thanks forever to Apollo and all the Gods and to you – blessed Pythia . . .' She had been going to ask so formally and nicely, but now she feared she was just gabbling . . .

'I'm sorry to come like this, as a boy, not as myself,' she whispered hurriedly, 'but Pythia, that is my problem – I don't know who I am – please, ask Apollo – who am I, and who are my parents?'

It was a plaintive cry. Such a small question, and yet so big.

And from within she heard a deep sigh, and a rustling, and then a light laugh, and then a woman's voice called out: 'You are the child of Aiella from the east, and Megacles of the Family of the Accursed of Athens. Go there and they will tell you.'

And that was it.

'Aiella and Megacles,' whispered Halo. They had names. Her human mother and father were Aiella and Megacles.

'Thank you,' she called softly. 'Thank you, Pythia, and thank you, Apollo . . .'

She left as if in a trance.

Aiella, and Megacles. Megacles, and Aiella.

Aiella might bake bread, and sleep on a low bed. Megacles might laugh, and come home with fruit from an orchard. Perhaps Aiella was beautiful and wise. Perhaps Megacles was strong and kind. They might hug her, or tell her off, talk to her, listen to her. They might look like her.

They existed. She thought of Kyllarus and Chariklo. She thought of Aiella and Megacles.

Perhaps they had loved her.

Tears were streaming down her face as she came out, reeling, into the shock of the hot sun.

Leonidas was there. She ran almost into his arms. He took hold of her, and sat her on a smooth white step under an almond tree.

'So?' he said, and sat down beside her on the step.

'Aiella and Megacles,' she said.

'What about them?' he asked.

'My parents,' she said. 'Megacles, my father. Aiella, my mother.' She smiled enormously at him. 'There you are! I have parents.'

He grinned back. 'Congratulations!' he said. 'Good news. And do you have a city?'

*Ah*. Her face fell.

She didn't want to tell Leonidas that she was from Sparta's enemy city. Or that her family was cursed.

In fact, as she started to think about it, the Pythia's pronouncement just led to more questions. Wonderful to have parents, but she didn't know if they were alive or dead, where they were, how she could find them – if she could find them – or anything, really . . . other than that they were cursed.

And did that mean she was cursed too? And who by? And why? And . . .?

She couldn't talk to Leonidas about that. Could she? She glanced up at him. He was looking at her encouragingly, his green eyes friendly, waiting for the answer to his question.

She wanted to tell him. Despite all the things that separated them – two more now! – she wanted to talk to him.

*No*, she thought.

'Well,' she said. 'She told me where to go to find out!'

'Where?' he said, with a smile.

*No!* If he knew, he would never let her go there. He had already snapped the chain back on to the cuff on his arm, and Melesippus and Manticlas had reappeared. They were very taken up with their own business, and didn't seem to have noticed that she had also spoken to the Oracle. She was grateful for that.

'Where have you been?' Melesippus was saying. 'We must get on the road. Our news can't wait.'

Leonidas rose to follow him, and Halo was dragged along as usual. She was utterly perplexed. She must go to Athens to find her parents; Sparta was about to declare war on Athens, Apollo was on Sparta's side, and the Oracle said Sparta would win!

She was more than ever among the enemy. She must go straight to Athens and tell them. There mustn't be a war! The mighty Spartan army would destroy Athens, the city she had only just discovered was hers.

She trotted along behind Leonidas, too many thoughts spinning. She pinned down the most urgent: *How can I escape before we get on the ferry, which will only carry me in the wrong direction?* She didn't notice that something was going on on the broad marble steps of the Sacred Way. A crowd was bustling and pushing. Some were tutting, some stumbling, some telling the others to calm down. They were all trying to see something, at the centre of the jostling. Cries of amazement rose up. Grinning boys followed on. 'Dear Gods! Dear Gods!' Halo heard someone cry in disbelief.

Melesippus was trying to get through, his mouth set firm with impatience. The Spartan cloak and air of casual determination were not having their usual effect. Manticlas was glancing into the crowd with idle curiosity as they tried to squeeze past.

In the chaos, several people had come between them and Halo and Leonidas.

A loud, authoritative voice called out, 'Stand back please, make way!'

Halo found herself pushed to the front of the crush. She looked up to see what was amazing everybody.

The sight stunned her, delighted her, and cast her into terror all at once.

An unmistakable, beautiful, bright-eyed, red-haired, four-legged, chestnut-flanked sight.

Arko!

But Arko in chains.

'Arko!' she cried out, before she could stop herself.
He turned and saw her, and his face lit up like the
morning sky.

She longed to rush to him. He longed to rush to her. But
he had shackles on his legs and arms, and he wore a broad
leather belt, from which several heavy chains ran to the
hands of a couple of men on either side of him.

Arko was a prisoner, just like her.

'Arko?' murmured Leonidas, right behind her. He
remembered that name. 'Arko! Well, my little slave, you are
a creature of mystery.' He meant to say it almost silently.
How could he know that Centaurs have exceptionally good
hearing? Arko picked up the sound of his own name, and
flicked Leonidas a narrow look. Even narrower when he
heard the word 'slave', and saw the chain hanging from
Halo's narrow wrist.

'Now, now,' said an authoritative voice. Halo looked over.
It was a priest; a tall man with a dry brown face like a dead
vine leaf. 'Calm down, everyone, or none of you will be
coming in. This is the sanctuary of Apollo, not a Dionysian
revel. Now who is with this . . . er . . .'

He stumbled to a halt. He didn't know how to describe
Arko. So Arko helped him out.

'I'm with myself!' he called out firmly. 'I'm a free creature. I am here to ask Lord Apollo of the Silver Bow,

Far-shooting Apollo, to remind these villains that they have no right whatsoever to put chains on me and attempt to drag me around!'

His voice was clear and strong, and shut everybody up.

'It can talk!' squeaked a bystander.

'Of course I can talk,' said Arko kindly. 'Why shouldn't I?'

One of the men to whom he was shackled, a low-browed rapscallion with a long bushy beard and a fur cap, started to shout. 'He's our captive!' he said. 'He's our animal! We're here to get Apollo to tell him so! He won't shut up!'

'Sweet Zeus and Athena,' said Arko. 'How many times do I have to tell you I'm not an animal? Do animals talk? Or play the flute? Or pray to the Gods? Honoured priest,' he continued, 'do I look like an animal? Am I behaving like an animal? You all know what I am! I'm a Centaur!'

'That's an animal!' shouted someone in the crowd.

'No it ain't!' shouted someone else.

Everybody decided to shout out their own opinion. There were quite a few opinions, and a cake-seller's tray of cakes got knocked over, and a skinny yellow dog ate some of them, and a small fight broke out.

'Desist!' thundered the priest. 'All of you!'

Silence fell.

'The Oracle will tell us,' he said calmly. 'Is that not why you are here?'

There was a mumbling of agreement.

'Everybody not connected to the question, stand back,' he said, and beckoned Arko and his captors up the Sacred Way.

Leonidas had his hand still firmly on Halo's shoulder. Halo glanced around at him. She couldn't see Melesippus or Manticlas at all.

Leonidas was grinning at her. 'Don't you want to go and see what happens to your brother?' he said. 'Come on.' And he grabbed her by the elbow like a naughty child, and propelled her through the crowd, towards the temple.

When they got there, the priest was deciding that he himself would put the question to the Oracle. He wasn't sure a Centaur was allowed in the temple at all, and the slave dealers who had captured Arko were horribly squabblesome. More sacrifices had to be made. Arko had to stand on his own, up on the temple steps by the columns, still chained. Pain rose in her throat at the sight. How dare they! *Apollo!* she prayed, angrily – then stopped herself, and breathed slowly for a moment or two, and started again. *Sweet Apollo, you have given me so much today; you are so kind. I know you know Arko is not an animal. Please make them let him be free.*

That was better. It made no sense to be rude to the Gods.

At that moment, a hand touched hers – a gentle touch, almost as if by mistake.

She turned her head. It was Ion, the temple boy.

'Glad I found you,' he whispered. 'Here.'

He pressed something into her hand. She took it quickly, instinctively. She couldn't tell if Leonidas had noticed what was going on.

She glanced quickly down to see what it was – and filled up with joy.

It was her little gold owl.

Quickly she closed her hand around it again, and looked up at Ion with joy all over her face.

'What's that then?' came Leonidas's calm voice. He nodded a greeting to Ion.

'Spartan,' Ion greeted him in return.

'It's my owl!' Halo said. 'Look!' She showed it to Leonidas.

'She wanted you to have it back,' said Ion.

'She?' Halo asked.

Ion nodded. 'The Pythia. She said, "The owl is a great gift, not to be given up lightly",' he said.

Halo smiled. 'What does that mean?' she asked.

Ion laughed softly. 'Ah, you'll have to ask one of the interpreters of the Oracle,' he said. 'I never understand what she says. But I do know,' he went on, and he shot her a look, 'that the owl means Athena, and wisdom.'

Halo shut her mouth firmly. *And it means Athens*, she thought – but she couldn't say anything about Athens in front of Leonidas. He stood quietly, looking at Arko, as if not interested at all in what she and Ion were saying. But his strong brown hand was still tight on her upper arm, and she knew perfectly well that he was taking it all in and storing it up.

Ion bent and whispered quickly in her ear, 'I know you heard the Spartans' oracle. Don't be afraid. Apollo cares for all the Greeks. But he can't stop them from doing what they're going to do anyway. And after all – he has given you back your owl.'

Apollo had given her back her owl. She swallowed, and she smiled hugely, feeling it spread across her face.

'Say to them thank you,' she said to the boy. 'From me.'

He grinned, and slipped away through the crowd. She smiled. Here she was, a slave, and there was Arko, a captive, and war was coming, yet she felt happy! How rich she felt! From friendless orphan to girl with parents and her best friend – and her owl back – in about ten minutes. Now, she thought, she had her line. She had something to fight for. Yet there were tears in her eyes. *Unless I suddenly grow giant teeth to bite through this chain, it's all pointless.*

'So many unexpected friends you have,' Leonidas said. 'Whatever next? Are a couple of nymphs going to appear, perhaps, bringing a message? Or Dionysus, greeting you as his long-lost daughter? Apollo himself, perhaps, might come down and offer you a cup of wine.'

'Don't be silly,' she said, but she laughed anyway.

She was trying, and failing, to fasten the owl round her neck. Leonidas brushed her hands away and did it for her, quickly and easily. She glanced back at him to thank him.

'Halo,' he said. He held her eyes.

'What?'

'Halo, look at me,' he said. 'Halo – do you understand?'

'What?' she said.

'Halo, if you are an Athenian, we are enemies now.'

*I should have known you'd notice that . . . Enemies.* The word in his mouth pulled her up sharp. She turned and stared at him.

'We are *enemies*,' he said softly.

A voice deep in Halo's heart said, *I don't want to be your enemy. How can we be enemies?*

She didn't say it out loud. Instead she said, 'Leonidas?'

'Gentlemen!' the priest called out. The announcement!

Leonidas squeezed her upper arm even tighter, looking at her intensely. 'Enemies,' he said, with a grim little smile, and he took his hand off her arm, raised it as if in surrender, or farewell, and he turned and he walked away from her through the crowd.

She could see the leather cuff still strapped to his sunburnt arm.

The chain dangled, empty, at her side.

*Leonidas?*

'Gentleman, the God has spoken, and desired that his words be made public.'

She looked up to where Arko stood, still wearing a bold face and a proud demeanour, but Halo could see he was pale. She looked back to Leonidas – but he was gone, melted into the crowd.

'Far-shooting Apollo, the Just God, speaking through his most honoured Oracle the Pythia, has said, "Dishonour is upon any who takes the Centaur to be a slave; as it is upon any who makes a slave of a free person illegally . . ."'

*Yes! Arko!*

The priest said more, but it was lost in the hubbub. The captors were complaining, but they soon shut up. The temple staff were calling for order and decorum. Halo stood motionless and alone in the crowd, her mouth open. Everyone else was crowding up the steps to Arko, undoing his chains and at the same time poking him, talking to him and pulling hairs out of his tail as souvenirs and lucky charms. He was trying to be polite, trying to shake them off. They wouldn't go. Suddenly he reared up on his hind legs, a magnificent and noble sight beneath the gleaming portico, the sun shining on his flanks.

The people scattered, shrieking in alarm.

Arko nodded to Halo – a nod of *Are you ready?* She came back to her senses, in a flood of reality.

And then – Arko leapt. He bounded right over the heads of the people below him on the temple steps, his hair flying behind him, and landed by her. He scooped her up in his arms and she flung her arms around him, forgetting everything else in a flood of affection and relief such as she had never felt in her life before. He was hugging her and she was hugging him and he was picking her up and rearing up on his hind legs with joy, and everyone started yelling even louder, and her legs were flying out behind her as he swung her and his tail was swirling and never, ever, had brother and sister been more delighted to be reunited. Then he flung her over his shoulder. He swerved, and skidded to a halt for a second, and then he was galloping off down the Sacred Way, his angry hooves sending chips of marble flying, and crying out, 'Blessings on you, Apollo, and the gratitude of all Centaurs!'

The crowd went mad.

'What in the name of all Gods was that?' cried Melesippus, muscling through with Manticlas to where Leonidas was standing silently at the back of the crowd. 'Has that creature just stolen your boy?'

'Just taken back his own,' said Leonidas.

'Leonidas?'

'Well, he wasn't really a slave, Melesippus,' he said. 'Couldn't you tell?'

'So who was he?'

'I have no idea,' said Leonidas. He knew he was in trouble. Sparta doesn't let slaves run away.

'Extraordinary,' breathed Manticlas. His huge pale eyes were glowing as he took everything in.

'I gave you a chance to control him, Leonidas, and you failed,' Melesippus said coldly. 'I don't have time to go and kill him now – and I don't trust you to do it.'

Leonidas forced his face to stay rigid. He hated to hear these words from Melesippus. He knew Melesippus was right. But how could he have not let her go?

'How did he escape his chain?'

'I unchained him, sir,' Leonidas said. He held his chin high. He didn't blink. He wouldn't lie.

Melesippus stared at him for a long moment, and then he gave a little snort, and said, 'Then his death is your fault. Is that punishment enough?'

'Sir,' said Leonidas, and gave his mentor a swift soldier's bow. He knew well enough how not to betray his feelings. He didn't betray them now.

'But now, if you remember, we have things to do.' Melesippus was angry. 'Manticlas, what does it mean? Is the Centaur an omen for us?'

'Oh, I should think so,' said Manticlas thoughtfully. 'It could well be. But the Oracle spoke so clearly in our favour. It is most unusual . . . We have been told that we can win this war if we fight our hardest.'

'True,' said Melesippus.

'Are we to take that to mean using all weapons available to us?'

'Of course,' said Melesippus.

'Including more . . . esoteric weapons?'

'Esoteric?' asked Melesippus.

'Unusual,' said the pale-haired boy, with a distant look in his eye.

'I know what it means, thank you,' said Melesippus. 'I just don't know what *you* mean.'

'I will tell you in due course. But thank you for your words. You put my mind at rest. One last question – the Oracle, did she say "*the* Centaur" or "*a* Centaur"?'

'"The",' said Melesippus. 'Why?'

Manticlas stared at him dreamily. 'Don't you know?' he said. 'A Centaur's heart can win any battle . . . *This* Centaur may be forbidden, but perhaps . . . We have assumed that there were no Centaurs any more, but as there are, well . . . we might as well, don't you think? Melesippus, I won't be coming back to Sparta just yet. I have something to investigate. I'll return before –' and here he breathed a great sigh – 'before the black blood starts to drip from the highest roofs.'

Melesippus, the stalwart soldier, gave a little shiver as Manticlas turned away. Clearly, the strange pale boy saw things which others didn't see. *Or want to see*, thought Melesippus.

As for Leonidas, he felt the cold claw of Phobos touch his heart. *Now one of them will kill her*, he thought, *and the other will kill her Centaur brother, and I, who have already betrayed my duty, for her . . . I can't help her any more.*

'East!' shouted Halo into Arko's ear, as they reached the road outside the sanctuary. 'Go east!'

He was running like the wind, like a free strong creature who had been shackled and imprisoned and now felt the spring breeze in his wild hair and the open road beneath his hooves. She was dangling and bouncing over his shoulder, and felt only extreme pain in her stomach, and in her arm where he was grabbing it to keep her from flying off.

'And let me sit properly!' she yelled.

He couldn't make out what she was saying.

In the end she had to pull his hair.

'Let me get round!' she shouted.

He glanced over his shoulder. If anyone was after them, they were not in view.

He slowed down a little, and she was able to pull herself up, and slip round on to his back.

'Phew,' she said, shaking out her body, then wrapping her arms round his waist and leaning against his broad back. 'That's better. We're not being followed, by the way.'

He slowed some more. 'Well, you were in a good position to see . . .' he panted cheerfully.

They both looked round. No one.

'Well, thank the Gods for that,' said Arko, and slowed to a walk. 'Let's get off the road, anyway, and get our breath back.'

They had put a few miles between themselves and Delphi.

Within moments, they were lying by a stream, hidden from the road by a clump of ilex and almond trees, and the high flower-spattered spring grass of an olive grove. They both drank, and stretched, and then grinned at each other in delight.

'So what happened?' they said, in unison.

By the end Arko knew all Halo's adventures, including her visit to the Oracle, and Halo knew that Arko had not, in fact, been caught when she had.

He had given himself up.

'Why?' she demanded.

'The humans came back,' he said. 'Many more of them. They wanted to capture all of us, to fight us. I saw them coming, and I persuaded them to take me and leave the others. And I warned the others, before I left, that they could not stay in Zakynthos any longer.'

It took a moment for this to sink in.

'Do you mean – they left the island?' she asked.

'Yes,' he said.

'So – the village . . .'

'Is empty,' he said.

'And – our home . . .'

'Doesn't exist any more,' he said, and he tightened his mouth a little as he said it.

She was silent a moment. A big tear appeared in her eye and hung on the edge of it.

'Oh,' she said softly.

'It's not your fault,' he said. 'They would have come anyway. The grown-ups had been discussing it for a while. No one could have prevented it.'

'And is everyone . . . did they . . .'

'They swam to the mainland,' he said. 'Went back the way they came.'

Halo pictured the scene: the whole herd, swimming the channel by moonlight, their human torsos gleaming pale and their hooves thrashing beneath the wine-dark sea, throwing up phosphorescence and the streaming white lace of sea foam in their wake. She smiled.

'Where have they gone?' she asked.

'Back to Thessaly was the plan, up into the deep forest beyond the Ixion lands,' he said.

'So are you going to go and join them now?'

'Yes. Are you coming?'

'Of course – but I must go to Athens first.'

'I'll come with you. It's on the way. And that Spartan toad might come after you.'

For a moment she didn't know what he meant. 'What Spartan toad?'

'The Spartan toad who called you his slave,' said Arko.

'Oh – Leonidas.' She frowned. 'He's not a toad.'

Arko raised an eyebrow.

'Well, I *was* his slave,' she said. 'And he could have held on to me, tried to fight you off – but even before you grabbed me he unchained me, and – kind of said goodbye, and walked away. He *let* me come with you . . . I don't know why. He'll get into trouble for it when Melesippus finds out.'

'Then why didn't Melesippus follow us?'

'They've got better things to do. They have to report their oracle, back in Sparta. That they should declare war on

Athens, and they will win it if they fight with all their might,' she said. A silence hung on the air after she said it.

'War,' said Arko. 'I've heard all sorts of rumours. So it's really going to happen.'

'Looks like it,' she said.

'And you want to stop it.'

She laughed.

'I have to go to Athens,' she said. 'That's all I know. My fate is there.' *And isn't it strange*, she thought, *how saying something out loud makes it more true?* 'Athens!' she yelled cheerfully.

Only four or five trees away, pale blond Manticlas sat in the crook of an olive branch, hidden by dappled leaves. He, at least, knew that Centaurs have good hearing. Much though he wanted to eavesdrop, he dared go no closer.

When they left, he jumped silently from the tree and followed them. Though he knew now where they were going. That bit he *had* heard.

'Oh, and Arko,' Halo said, as she tramped alongside him. 'I don't know if you've noticed, but I'm not a girl any more. By the way.'

Arko said, 'Oh, you are *such* a girl . . .'

'No, really,' she said. 'Humans are horrible to girls. I'm living as a boy. Can't you tell?'

When he had stopped laughing, Arko said, 'I suppose that explains the ridiculous haircut.'

She gave out a little warm snort of laughter. She was so happy to be with him again.

'Well, *boy*, before we go to Athens,' said Arko, 'there is something I must do. I can't stand all that attention. If I'm to live in the human world for a while, I have to get them to leave me alone . . .'

An hour later, Halo and Arko were standing behind a stall in the market at Thebes. Halo was failing to keep back the gawking crowds, and a long-haired Oriental tattooist in knee boots was sitting astride Arko's chestnut back, carefully inking into the flesh across his tanned shoulders, in large black letters, the following words:

*ΚΕΝΤΑΥΡΟΣ ΤΟΥ ΑΠΟΛΛΩΝΑ*
*ΔΕΛΦΟΙ*

which means

## CENTAUR OF APOLLO
## AT DELPHI

'Now,' Arko was saying, in between little winces at the pain of the needles sticking into him, 'I just have to tie my hair up and everyone can get the message, and they'll leave me alone.'

'Yes, it's really working already,' said Halo, scowling at a pair of small boys who were actually trying to climb Arko's hind legs, looking for a better view. 'You two! Down!'

'It will work,' Arko insisted, wriggling his horse-back to get rid of the children – which made the tattooist shout 'Oi!' and complain about being jogged. 'You children,' Arko said, and he made his voice larger and more important. 'I am protected by Apollo. Leave me in peace!'

The children, it is true, scampered off immediately.

'You're finished,' said the tattooist brusquely, leaning over Arko's shoulder. 'I just need to dress it now. Keep it clean, and oil it every day till the scabs come off, and then for another week or two.'

Halo stared at the new tattoo – not that she could make it out clearly. Arko's whole upper back was a big mess of drying blood and ink.

'Ugh,' she said.

Was that what her forehead had looked like when she was a baby?

Well, of course not, as her tattoo was much smaller. Still, she hadn't known a tattoo made so much mess. Arko, she realized, was pretty brave not to have made more fuss.

The tattooist, who had jumped down from Arko's horse-back, returned with a flask of wine, which he poured across the inky wounds to clean them. He followed on with a dark fragrant oil, and a clean cloth poultice to cover the tattoo, strapped with linen strips round Arko's chest. Halo, fascinated, interrogated him about the ingredients of his oil, and made note of his bandaging technique, which was quite different from the Spartans'. She would take care of the new tattoo till it healed up.

'First time I ever done a Centaur,' the tattooist observed as he expertly tucked in the straps. 'Been an honour. Change the bandage when you can. You only need it a few days. And no need to worry about scarring – ha ha ha. That'll be an *obol*.'

Arko had one small coin. Now they were penniless.

'Never mind,' said Arko. 'Athens, here we come!'

\*

Neither of them had noticed, when they arrived, a big-eyed pale boy leaning against a tree by the fountain, across the *agora*. He had noticed them – he had been watching out for them. As they settled in with the tattooist, this boy had lazily pushed himself upright, and ambled off towards the Athens road. Beyond Thebes, somewhere quiet, up on Mount Kithaera, perhaps, as the evening drew in, he would have a word . . .

## Χαπτερ 19

On the road, Arko and Halo fell to chatting with five brothers herding a pack of mules over the mountain. Manticlas, sitting in a tree, watched them pass beneath him, and cursed.

They slept the night surrounded by thirty-five warm smelly animals.

Manticlas wrapped his cloak around him, thinking evil thoughts, and carried on. In the farmlands, down the other side . . . his moment would come.

The next morning, Halo, Arko, five muleteers and thirty-five mules emerged from the snowy mists of the mountain. Starting to come down Mount Kithaera, they stopped short to stare.

Halo halted Arko with a touch. 'What is *that*?' she said, her eyes shining.

'I think it's Athens,' said Arko.

Before them lay the great flat plain of Attica, rippled with a blanket of olive trees as far as they could see, and dotted with straight deep black cypresses. To the east and north were high embracing mountains, and stretching out to the south was a gleaming sliver of sea. Right in the middle of it, far away, stood a mighty rocky outcrop, a tiny mountain almost, rising above a scattering of red roofs and white buildings, and on top of the outcrop they could clearly see racks of rosy-white columns glowing in the bright sunshine, miles away.

Halo smiled.

'Athens,' she said. 'Arko, that's my city. If I have family – human family, I mean – they are there. Aiella and Megacles. Arko, I'm scared.'

He put his arm around her shoulder.

'It's your city,' he said. 'It will love you. Plus, even if it doesn't, Athens loves visitors. It's not like Sparta. In Athens, everybody likes things. Even if they complain about them, it's because they like complaining.'

'How do you know?' Halo asked. 'Have you spent many years in Athens, O wise one?'

'Centaurs know everything,' he replied, with his nose in the air. 'You know that.'

She made a face at him, and started running down the hill. 'Come on!' she cried. 'Let's get there then!'

Unfortunately, she wasn't looking where she was going, and she ran straight into the back of a wagon. The wagon's owner, once he had stopped yelling at her for a billowing fool and a troublesome frog-child, said he quite understood she was keen to get to Athens, but the festival didn't start for two days, so there was plenty of time, assuming that time would continue to pass in the normal way, which of course it was a risk to assume, but not a risk one could do anything about.

Halo thought about this for a moment, then decided that 'What festival?' was the simplest response. And he rolled his eyes at their ignorance, and said, 'The Great Dionysia, you turnip. Dionysus's festival. When the Dionysus from here gets paraded round Athens.'

'Why's the Dionysus from here in Athens?' asked Halo.

'The Eleutherians gave him as a gift years ago,' said the wagoner. 'And us stupid Athenians rejected him, so he sent the plague on us, so now we give him a big festival every year so he won't do it again. Excuse me for mentioning it, but aren't you a Centaur?'

'Well spotted,' said Arko. 'And are you perhaps an Athenian?'

'None other,' said the wagoner. 'You can always tell us by our superior wit.'

'Is it really Dionysus?' Halo asked curiously.

'Ah, well,' said the wagoner. 'A very Heracleitan question. What, after all, is reality?'

'There's no need to get philosophical,' said Arko.

'Interesting point,' said the wagoner. 'Why not? If being philosophical is my nature, then surely it is my duty to be true to my nature, i.e. to be philosophical at all times?'

'I don't agree,' said Halo. 'Someone might be a horrible liar by nature – that doesn't mean it's his duty to be a horrible liar. And also, if you were philosophical at all times you would get very annoying.'

'It might be my duty to be annoying some of the time, if that was an unavoidable by-product of my being philosophical at all times,' he replied.

'OK,' said Halo. 'But first, you haven't answered my first point and second, what if your being so annoying, through being so philosophical, led someone to punch you on the nose, and they got arrested – could they say it was your fault?'

'Aha!' cried the wagoner. 'I see you are a true Sophist . . .'

'Am I?' said Halo. 'Is that good?'

The wagoner was delighted. '"Is that good?"' he cried. 'Another splendidly Sophistical question! What's that on your forehead?'

'It's my tattoo,' said Halo. 'We're going to Athens now.'

'Well, I'd give you a lift,' said the wagoner. 'But I'm not going there. See you around!'

He waved, and clicked to his mule, and moved on.

'Do you think they're all like that?' Halo asked, when she and Arko had stopped laughing.

A few hundred metres ahead, Manticlas smiled as he saw the wagon turn off. The road was empty, but for the boy and the Centaur walking towards him, giggling, coming under the tree . . .

*Now*, he thought.

He sprang from the tree like a leopard, his sinews tight and his knife in his hand. He landed just as he had planned, on Halo's back, pulling her backwards with his arm across her mouth and the knife at her throat. She gasped and stumbled. He steadied his feet, held her firm, and yanked her head.

The Centaur turned. His face changed to horror. Instinctively he reared up on his strong hind legs, his hooves high in the air –

'I'll kill him!' shouted Manticlas. 'Step back or I'll kill him now!'

Halo couldn't breathe. She was gasping and coughing. She tried to bite the arm across her mouth, but all she got was a mouthful of rough dusty cloak. Whose voice was that? She recognized it . . .

Arko came down. His hooves clopped on the road and his horse flanks were quivering. His tail twitched. 'What do you want?' he said.

'Just information,' said Manticlas.

Arko was circling him, moving around. Manticlas turned, moving Halo with him, so that they were always facing each other. 'Stay still,' he said. He jabbed the knife.

Halo gasped. 'Don't tell him anything!' she squeaked.

'What information?' said Arko. He was much bigger than this little human. He could just give him a powerful kick, kick him right off the road, break his leg, if he could get the right angle . . . but his knife was right against Halo's throat . . .

'Tell me where your people are,' said Manticlas, with a soft little smile that made Arko feel sick.

'What people?' he said, stalling for time. 'I don't even know who you are.'

'This little runaway does, though,' whispered Manticlas. 'Don't you, you little runt? Your Leonidas is in big trouble now – betraying Sparta, for a pretty boy. If I drag your corpse back to Melesippus I'll be the hero of the day . . .'

She recognized him now. That slimy cruel dreamy boy, Manticlas. She craned her neck away from the knife, but he followed her movement.

He wasn't big. He wasn't even stronger than her. She was a good fighter. The wildcat rose in her. How dare he!

She felt the sharp chill of the blade nestling at her throat. She felt the weight of Leonidas's chain, still hanging from her wrist. She smiled. *Thank you, Leon.*

In a swift, strong movement she flicked the chain out and

swung it back. She jumped her feet to avoid it, and with a horrible crack it snapped against Manticlas's legs. Yes!

As he collapsed to the ground, crying out in pain, she turned to hit him again. She could hear hooves – *Arko*, she thought, but it wasn't. There were too many – galloping, and drawing up. A young male voice shouted out, 'Hold that right there!'

She turned and saw three tall, muscular young men sat bareback astride three tall, muscular horses. They wore silk breeches and leather knee-boots, dogskin caps and long moustaches. Thick silver chains hung round their necks, and each had several belts slung around his lean hips, and each belt had several blades stuck through it. Curved bows hung from their bare, broad shoulders. Their eyes were narrow and flinty, their skin tanned, their cheekbones high and wide. Beside each horse panted a huge brown hound, jaw hanging, teeth gleaming, silent, alert, ready at any moment to leap to his master's bidding.

Once again, Halo felt very much a girl.

She stood there like a fool. The chain she had been about to thwack Manticlas with dangled uselessly from her hand. Arko, too, was frozen.

'A Centaur!' shouted one of the riders.

Then before they knew it ropes flew out. With deft, matching movements the horsemen had lassoed Halo and Arko, catching their arms and holding them tight.

She started to cry out – but it was too late. Manticlas was gone. She and Arko were captive again.

'But he was attacking us!' she yelled.

'That's not what it looked like,' said the one who had spoken. His accent was thick and strange.

'But he was – I was fighting back!' She could have wept with frustration.

'It's true,' said Arko. 'He had a knife to her neck – why else did he run away?'

The man glanced at Arko. 'You can tell the Captain when we get back.'

Halo allowed herself to be hoisted up in front of her lassoer, and dumped across his legs. What else could she do?

## Χαπτερ 20

It was not the glorious entrance to her native city of which Halo had dreamed. She, flopped across a horse like a sack of potatoes; Arko, bound like a criminal; and a crowd of people gathering around them, amazed at the sight of a Centaur, wondering what was going on, making stupid comments. Her first view of the gates of Athens was from an unlikely and ignominious angle, as her head dangled over the side of the horse. She was furious at the indignity of it.

As they approached, the rider pulled her up and set her upright. Before her, guarding the gates, were another ten or twelve silk-trousered, high-cheekboned, multi-belted men on horseback.

'Captain,' called the rider.

One of the men turned. At the sight of his face, Halo gasped.

He was handsome – or had been. He would be still – but his face and neck were riven with shining scars, like white wax crawling across the skin. A bright midnight-blue silk cloth was bound tightly around his head, covering one eye. Suddenly, looking at him, Halo got a strong feeling that under the silk there was no eye, just a gaping empty socket. The man's good eye, as pale, green and icy as Spartan melt-water, seemed to dare her to mention it.

'What's this, Gyges?' he said. His voice was low, slightly husky, with the same curious accent.

'This one was trying to beat up a boy with his chain,' said the man who had brought them in. 'Two against one. Out on the Eleuthera road.'

'He attacked *us*!' Halo burst out. 'He had a knife to my throat!'

The Captain glanced at Halo, and at Arko. His look was cool. He seemed utterly unsurprised at the sight of a Centaur. 'Unlikely bandits,' he said. 'Where's the victim?'

'I'm the victim,' said Halo angrily. 'The attacker ran away.'

The Captain glanced at Arko.

'It's true,' Arko said. 'Look at his throat.'

And there was, on her throat, a tiny nick, a smudge of blood.

The Captain glanced at Gyges. Gyges hung his head.

It was about then that Halo noticed that the rest of the silk-trousered riders were staring at her. She was surprised – after all, Arko was much more extraordinary. Why weren't they staring at him?

It was time to be brave.

'I am Halo, from Zakynthos,' she said. 'This is my friend Arko. We are peaceful visitors with honest business. We have news for Pericles.'

The Captain stared at Arko with his one cool green eye, as if soaking him up. Then he turned his gaze again on Halo. It was unnerving. He didn't blink. He had no expression at all. She supposed he was thinking, but there was no way of telling *what* he was thinking.

'That's not all,' she said. 'He was threatening our family – Arko's family. We have to get a message to them, to warn them.'

The Captain sniffed. 'Follow me,' he said, and he wheeled his horse round.

Someone in the crowd called out, 'It's the Centaur! Take it to Pericles!'

Arko rolled his eyes. '*Him*,' he said. 'Please, I'm a *him*, not an *it*.'

The other horsemen didn't take their eyes off Halo as she passed. *Who are they?* she thought.

The Captain led them the short distance into the *agora*, the central marketplace of Athens. As they went, people turned and whispered, stared, and followed. Word had spread about Arko. The Gods had sent a mythical beast to Athens for the Grand Dionysia!

Halo gazed around at the city. There was the Acropolis – so close! So high! So huge! Building after building was finer and larger than anything she had seen before. There was another temple, and another on a small hill, there an arcade, with fine-dressed Athenians walking beneath it. She began to to feel small. Here were shops, barbers, animals, fountains, wells, houses, marble benches, cypress trees, grassy glades, stone pavements, children running, slaves carrying shopping, musicians playing, bathhouses – oh, it was fine. And huge. *My city*, she thought. *My people*. So many of them.

*Yes, and you are accursed in this city.*

She breathed in deeply. Deep calm breathing. She didn't know where the horseman was taking her. Suddenly, she felt very stupid to have come here, to have just arrived, unprepared, so small and insignificant. She had no idea what would happen, what to do. She was helpless. At least Arko had Apollo's protection, and it was written on his body. She had nothing, and *her* tattoo meant nothing.

She wondered if she could ask the one-eyed Captain where they were going. But even if he had been the kind of person you could just talk to, his horse was so high she doubted if he would even hear her up there. She did *not* want to run alongside him tugging at his silk trouser legs, crying, 'Please, sir!' like a beggar child.

*I'm a boy I'm a boy, and I've done no wrong. I'm bringing important news from Delphi. And accursed or not, I need to know my parents. Megacles and Aiella.*

It occurred to her that it might be an idea to find out about them before telling anybody that she was their child.

The Captain pulled up his lean horse, and stopped. With a curt nod, he summoned a youth nearby and exchanged a few words with him. A group of men ahead turned, noticing the commotion around Arko. Among them was a tall man, well built, with curling grey-white hair, which reminded Halo of the way sea foam curls flat as it runs up a sandy beach. Though older, he was strong. She liked him on sight, and smiled at him. He glanced at her, and at Arko, and raised his eyebrows. The Captain, at a nod from him, bowed his head and retreated.

*A powerful man*, she thought. *But a kind man.*

'Welcome to Athens!' he said, striding forward and holding out his hand, first to Arko, then to her. 'I confess I have never met a Centaur before, and always thought you mythical. Forgive my rudeness. I am delighted to be proved wrong.' He looked as if whatever he met, whoever turned up, he would greet them with the same aplomb. 'Are you tired from your journey? I would like to speak with you at length – I am curious. But today and the days that follow we are all busy with our Dionysia. Do you stay long?'

*He seems to rule the world*, she thought. *Such confidence, such manners.* He was the kind of man who would bring out your best behaviour. She had no idea what was best behaviour to an Athenian. She really, really wanted him to like her.

'Hello,' she said. 'I am Halosydnus. This is Arko.'

'How rude of me,' he said. 'I am Pericles. Perhaps you would wait for me?'

Of course they knew he was Pericles. Everyone knew the great leader, the wise man, the father of Athens, the greatest city.

He gestured a bench. Halo sat. A small boy brought them a flask of water. They waited while Pericles talked seriously with man after man who approached him.

'Arko,' she said after a while, 'why would Manticlas want to know where the Centaurs are?'

'I don't know,' he said. 'But I can't imagine it's for any good reason.'

'No,' she murmured, thinking of the times he had jumped her from behind, and of his cruel look of excitement when he had slaughtered the lamb and taken out its liver. 'Nothing good.'

They had to get a message to the Centaurs, telling them to beware of the pale boy. But how?

'As soon as you've found out about your parents, we'll

go up to Thessaly,' said Arko. 'There's time. Manticlas doesn't know where they are.'

'So, Centaur,' Pericles said as he joined them on the stone bench half an hour later, 'tell us everything. Start at the beginning, continue till the end, and include why your back is bandaged up, and who your friend is, and why he was beating off an assailant with a chain.'

Pericles inspired trust immediately. So Arko told him: about the Centaurs of Zakynthos, about being discovered by humans, about the herd leaving, about what had happened at Delphi. But there are things no Centaur would ever tell a human being – where the Centaurs lived was one.

Pericles was delighted. 'Sons of Chiron,' he mused happily. 'Well, son of Chiron, humans and Centaurs have been estranged too long.' He stared at Arko, his eyes shrewd. 'I am in favour of friendship between us. What do you say?'

Arko replied, 'I'm not the leader of my herd, but I am the one who is here, and I say yes to friendship with you.'

Pericles smiled softly. He could see that Arko was not saying yes to friendship with all humans.

*He's treating Arko like an adult*, Halo thought. She looked at him again. He was, almost, like an adult – even though he was not much older than her.

But Pericles had turned now.

'And you, boy?' he asked. 'Why are you running around with a Centaur, and a tattoo on your face, beating people up? Who are you?'

Halo stared at him. Perhaps the intensity of her feeling

showed on her face at that moment, because Pericles looked at her with particular attention.

*If I tell you I am accursed, you won't be so welcoming . . .*

'The Centaurs brought me up,' she said. 'They found me washed up on the beach. They called me Halosydnus and taught me and loved me. I was stolen by fishermen and brought to Sparta –'

'Are you Spartan?' he said. 'You don't look it.'

'No, sir, certainly not. I don't know what I am. But the Delphic Oracle told me to come to Athens, to find out. But sir, I was with the Spartans in Delphi, I heard what the Pythia said to them –'

When she said this, the group of men standing around Pericles tautened, froze for a moment. Then: 'Oh yes?' Pericles said mildly. 'And what did the Pythia say to our Spartan friends?'

'I was with Melesippus, sir –'

'Melesippus, eh?' he murmured.

'– and they were told – It is coming, and cannot be avoided, and if they fight with all their might, victory will be theirs. Apollo himself will be on their side, whether they invoke him or not . . .'

Halo's voice trailed away. This was really not a very good thing to have to say to Pericles, but he didn't look too alarmed.

'Hmm,' he said. 'Interesting. If they fight with all their might . . .'

And he started laughing.

Everyone was surprised at that.

'No, no, it's all right,' he said. 'It's more than all right. I have a plan, and this confirms it to be a good one. It's all fine. Really! And thank you, young fellow, for bringing us this news. And how was Melesippus, when you last saw him?'

'Returning to Sparta, sir, to prepare for war.'

The word hung heavy, like a thud, a footprint, a fallen rock.

Pericles sighed. 'Well, and so must we.' He stood up. 'And if the threat of war does not incline you to leave immediately, will you stay and be our guests? Aspasia will look after you . . . Our friend Arko can't wander around the town with no shelter, at the mercy of the unruly folk of Athens. They'll never leave him alone. After all, the Pythia told you to come here . . . and we must all listen to the Pythia, mustn't we?'

He started chuckling again.

Halo wondered what he was planning. It must be something stupendous, to chuckle at the might of the Spartans and the word of the Pythia. If it had been anyone else, she would have feared that he had lost his senses. But not this man. This man clearly had a firm hold of senses she'd never even heard of.

Pericles's house was not far off. A shy, smiling slave boy, Tiki, accompanied them to show them the way, and admitted them to a paved courtyard. Jasmine and pomegranate trees grew in tubs, and the scent of the blossom was sweet on the air. A well at the centre gave water for them to rinse off the dust of the journey. There were seats and benches, with soft cushions and fine cloths covering them. Everything was clean. It looked like heaven.

Halo sat nervously on a low stool, her bottom unaccus-
tomed to the comfort of the cushion. She was very aware
of how grubby she must be. And it was so strange to be in
a human building with Arko. Normally if they were relaxed
they would sprawl on the ground together, or she would lie
on his back, or on a branch of a tree to be at the same height
as him. But here, if she sat, he was too tall, and he could not
lie down – even with his front legs neatly folded in, it would
be too informal. So he stood, and she sat, and then stood
again, and then sat again.

After a few minutes, a woman came out. Aspasia, Halo
assumed.

If Aspasia wanted to stare at Arko, she courteously
concealed it. Halo, however, could not stop herself from
staring at Aspasia. It had been so long since she had seen a
female at home. And she had never seen a human female in
her own home. At least not one she liked.

Aspasia was tall. She was beautiful. She was not young.
She was well dressed, in a long belted chiton and a cloak of
soft white cloth pinned with a gold brooch. She had gold
earrings. Her hair was clean and curly, held up with a kind
of comb. She was graceful. She smelt lovely. She was smiling.

Halo could hardly believe her eyes.

'Do sit down,' Aspasia was saying. 'Please!' Then: 'Oh!'
she cried, as she realized the situation with Arko – that
Centaurs, of course, do not sit as humans do. 'Hmm,' she
said. 'Samis! Ask Evangelus to bring a nice rug. And some
honey tea.'

A nice rug appeared. Aspasia invited Arko to lie on it. He

lowered himself elegantly, and tucked his front legs under. Halo pulled her stool over to be near him. Aspasia lowered herself just as elegantly on to a cushioned bench, leaning against one arm. Halo thought perhaps she was lounging on purpose to make Arko feel less . . . horizontal. More at home.

'Tiki says I am not allowed to ask you any questions until Pericles comes back,' Aspasia said. 'I hope he comes soon! I don't think I can contain myself.'

Halo couldn't think of anything to say to that. If they were forbidden to talk —

Well, they were forbidden to talk about themselves.

'Is Pericles your husband, madam?' she asked politely.

Aspasia laughed. 'Not quite,' she said. 'I'm not a wife kind of woman.' She looked quite relaxed about it. Halo had understood that marriage was very important to humans. Now she was confused.

'You may know that wives have to stay at home and weave all day, and have no fun,' Aspasia said quietly, leaning forward, with a twinkle in her eye.

Halo tried to look as if she wouldn't know anything about that.

'I don't,' whispered Aspasia. 'I get to do a bit more of what I want . . . but look, this is no good. Let's get rid of that chain on your wrist, and Samis will show you where to bathe, and rest, and that way I won't be tempted to ask questions . . . I *do* want to know about that strange tattoo —' She reached out her hand and gently rubbed her thumb across Halo's forehead, and its peculiar marking.

The touch brought tears suddenly to Halo's eyes. It was the

gentleness. Arko caught the look, and registered it. How lucky they were, they both thought. And again, after Pericles returned and they had told as much of their story as they dared, all was kindness. They had been brought to the house of the most powerful man in Athens, and they had found kindness.

The next day, Arko and Halo found themselves garlanded in leaves and flowers, and Arko's tail plaited with colourful ribbons, at the heart of the *pompe*, a massive procession through the city. In front of them were seven beautiful white bulls with flowers round their necks and little ring-shaped loaves of bread hanging from their wide flyaway yellow horns. They, too, stared at Arko with their huge long-lashed eyes. One of them nudged Halo with his wet, smooth muzzle, and slurped at her with his long pink tongue. It made her squeak – and trying to turn the squeak into a boyish grunt of laughter gave her a coughing fit.

Behind them was a high wagon containing a big wooden phallus.

'What's that meant to be?' Arko asked.

Halo, who had seen plenty of them among the Spartans, had to explain it was the human male's private parts.

'Really?' said Arko. 'Hmm!' And he glanced down at where his own human belly met his horse chest. 'So that's what I would have if I were human. How odd . . . And why are they parading it about in a festival procession?'

'Fertility!' said Halo. 'Because it makes babies!'

'Fair enough,' murmured Arko.

Then they were to go to the theatre.

Tiki came running up to them and said, 'Come on, you're sitting with Aspasia.'

She had kept them good seats on a wooden bench – Arko lay down in the aisle, to the delight of all around. Then the performers came out, singing and dancing and playing on flutes and lyres. Arko and Halo sat entranced as team after team of boys or men came out – fifty at a time – and did their piece in honour of Dionysus. They had never seen such a thing.

They didn't like it so much when the seven beautiful bulls were sacrificed to Dionysus.

'If I were a God I don't think I'd want my beautiful animals killed,' Halo murmured to Arko.

'It's the humans' way of doing it,' said Arko. 'You'd better get used to it, if you want to be one of them.'

'Apparently,' said Halo, 'there's a philosopher here who thinks that men created the Gods. Because our Gods look like us, and the Gods in Africa are black-skinned, like the people there, he says a horse's God would be a horse, and therefore we must all have invented our own Gods that look like us!'

'When did you hear about that?' said Arko.

'Talking to Aspasia at breakfast,' she replied.

'At breakfast! Good Gods, what a city,' Arko murmured.

The feast was laid out on long wooden tables in the street. All the Athenians joined in the magnificent party for Dionysus. Once they realized they were allowed to, Halo and Arko ate like demons. Vine leaves stuffed with meat, honey cakes and cheeses, soups and vegetables, warm bread and good oil, meat and chicken, fish . . . and so much of it. Halo's teeth sank into mouthful after mouthful, and soon she could feel her little belly sticking out of her skinny frame. She hadn't had so much to eat since . . . well, ever. She thought of those raw fish on Mount Taegetus, of the long days of wild figs and fennel, and of the black soup of Sparta. *Thank you, all you kind and loving Gods, for this wonderful food . . .*

'Come on,' said Aspasia. 'The *komos* will be starting soon. We'd better get home.'

'What's the *komos*?' Halo wanted to know.

'It's when the young men drink far too much of Dionysus's lovely wine, and go completely mad carousing all over the town in a Dionysian frenzy. All the laws turn upside down, and the donkeys are king for the night. Even the Skythians give up trying to keep order . . .'

'Skythians!' cried Halo. 'There are Skythians here!'

She had heard about Skythians. They came from beyond the Euxine Sea. They were the finest archers and horsemen in the world, but they sacrificed humans, and gilded their skulls for drinking cups, and hung the dried-out scalps of their enemies from the bridles of their horses, and had giant Molossian hounds with them everywhere they went, and . . . oh yes . . .

'The City Guard,' said Aspasia. 'You'll have seen them. Terrifying-looking men on horseback, with those alarming big dogs. Of course – the ones who brought you in.'

'Those men are Skythians?' she gasped. 'But – is it safe?'

'Not everything you hear is entirely true,' Aspasia said. 'You can see for yourself there are no scalps hanging from the bridles of the City Guard. And none of the Athenian Skythians are bald. And certainly the ones here don't chop up their dead and eat them in sausages along with the sacrificial meat . . .'

'I suppose not,' Halo said.

'But you're right,' Aspasia said. 'It is good to be wary of them. They are not like us. And they don't see the point of worshipping a God who drives you out of your mind, so they all go back to their barracks during the Dionysia. That's another reason why it gets so very chaotic out there . . .'

'It sounds interesting though,' said Halo.

'Yes, well,' said Aspasia, with a little sniff. 'In a few years no doubt you'll be doing it yourself, but tonight we are going home and closing the doors. And anyway, I think you'll like tomorrow.'

## Χαπτερ 21

Every day for the next three days, Halo and Arko found themselves back in the Theatre of Dionysus, watching the tragedies – three a day – of the Grand Dionysia. Only one of them made Halo cry.

Later that night, she sat with Aspasia in her little sitting room, drinking honeyed tea.

'So, Halosydnus,' Aspasia said. 'Why did you weep so much at the story of Medea? Have you not heard it before?'

'Of course, I have,' said Halo. 'But I haven't seen it acted.'

'And what was it touched you so? I was watching you, and it looked personal.'

Halo grinned at her feet, embarrassed. 'Well, according to the play, it's better to die than to lose your homeland,' she said, and she tried to laugh, but it was hard. 'And I have lost my homeland twice . . .'

'Tell me about that,' said Aspasia kindly.

Of course Halo and Arko had told Pericles and Aspasia their stories already – but Aspasia was so gentle, so perceptive and so interested that now Halo told her things she had told no human but Leonidas. She told her about the shipwreck, she showed her the little owl, she told her about the Centaurs, about the Spartans, about going to Delphi. She did *not* tell her she was a girl. But she did tell her what the Oracle had said to her – at least, some of it.

'Aspasia,' she said. 'The Pythia told me my father is

Athenian. My mother is foreign, but then you are not a citizen either and you lead a good life . . . Aspasia,' she burst out, 'do you know anyone of the name of Megacles?'

'Of course. Many men are called Megacles. It is a fine Athenian name, and a noble one.'

Halo took this in. She was trying to find out as much as she could without admitting what she must not, could not, admit. Many men called Megacles. Well, that didn't help much.

'And,' she said, 'um, are people in Athens, um, cursed, very much?'

'Cursed?' Aspasia said. 'Well, there are always people who cast around superstitious curses, which mean nothing.'

Halo didn't think the Pythia would have bothered to mention it if it was something like that.

Her heart was thumping.

*Do not reveal it, you will be banished, you will lose your home-land a third time . . .*

She had to know. The curse was the only clue she had. Aspasia was kind. She had to ask.

'But is there, perhaps,' she said, trying to make it sound like it wasn't at all important, 'I mean I just heard about it, a *family* in Athens, which is cursed?'

'A family?' said Aspasia. Then she cried out, 'A family!' Then she sat up suddenly straight, and looked at Halo quite differently, and Halo knew that Aspasia had seen through her, had worked it out, and that it was all over.

'Halosydnus,' Aspasia said. 'Did the Pythia tell you that your father is of the Family of the Accursed?'

Halo couldn't speak. *What shame does it mean? Megacles – if I am your child, as I must be, I submit to any shame.*

Her mouth had gone very small and tight, and tears were in her eyes, but she held her chin up and clenched her teeth and tried to be proud as she nodded, shortly, 'Yes'.

'Halosydnus!' Aspasia cried.

Halo's eyes were clenched as tight as her mouth. She had to control herself, not make a fool of herself. Her heart was breaking. She would have to leave Athens at least; or be punished, or – oh, but she didn't want to leave beautiful, interesting, exciting Athens!

'Halo, calm down,' Aspasia was saying. 'Halo?'

*Why is she using my short name, which only Arko uses?*

'My dear . . .'

*My dear?*

'Did the Pythia tell you who the Accursed are?'

Halo shook her head quickly.

'Halo – the Accursed are the Alcmaeonids.'

*The whats?*

'Halo – it's Pericles's family.'

Halo's eyes flew open.

She stared at Aspasia.

'You couldn't belong to a better family,' Aspasia was saying. 'Really. You are cousin to Pericles. You are cousin to my son. Come here, my child. Come here.' Aspasia held open her arms, and like a bolt from a bow Halo shot into them, and hugged her like a mother. It felt unspeakably wonderful. She hugged her and hugged her, and she cried and cried, and Aspasia stroked her hair and murmured little

soft bits of nothing – and also, after a while, bits of important information, about why the Alcmaeonids were known
as the Accursed,[7] and how it means nothing now, except
when enemies tried to make an issue of it. Why, only this
year the Spartans tried make the Athenians denounce and
reject Pericles because he was an Alcmaeonid – and it only
made the Athenians love him more, because it showed how
scared the Spartans were of him. In Athens, to be associated
with the Accursed was a blessing.

And that was when Pericles came in. Halo jumped up
nervously. He was tired, but friendly.

'I'll go to bed,' said Halo. 'It's late –' but Aspasia cut in.

'No, wait – Pericles, we are starting to solve the mystery
of this boy,' she said excitedly. 'Guess what?' Aspasia paused
for effect, her eyes sparkling, excited at the news she had
to impart. 'The Pythia told him his father is Megacles, and
an Alcmaeonid. What do you think of that?'

The tiredness fell off Pericles's face, replaced in that
instant by a look of wonder and keen intent that he fixed on
Halo.

'How old are you, boy?' he said urgently.

'I don't know, sir,' said Halo. 'I think perhaps twelve or
thirteen or so.'

'And found on Zakynthos, you said?'

'Yes.'

'Eleven years ago, come the end of summer,' said Pericles,
stating it as a fact.

'Yes,' said Halo. 'How do you know?'

Pericles ignored her question. 'And the Pythia told you?'

'Yes, sir,' she said.

'I might ask for guarantees and witnesses,' he said, his voice full of emotion, 'but to look at your face and your eyes I don't think I will.'

He put his hand over his mouth, and blinked.

'Sweet Hera, by Zeus and all the Gods, Apollo, sweet Apollo,' he said, and he fell to his knees. The great Pericles was weeping on his knees. Aspasia's eyes were wide.

Halo just stood there. What else could she do?

'My child,' he said. 'My child, my cousin's child returned to me – oh, the kindness of the Gods, your kindness to me . . . Come here, child.'

Halo went to him. He stood up again, a little sheepishly. He stared at her face, clasped her, and said, 'Am I deceiving myself? Do you look like him? I swear, I think you do. Skinnier than he ever was, but his clever eyes look back at me. Megacles's son, brought back to me, looking like him, and guaranteed by the Pythia . . .'

His eyes . . . she had her father's eyes. She was skinnier than him, and she had his eyes, and Pericles had loved him. Megacles began to take shape in her mind.

'I have this, sir,' she said, and she pulled her little owl on its thong out of the neck of her chiton.

He bent to look at it. He took it between thumb and finger. 'Hmm!' he said. He seemed to be finding it hard to speak. 'Hmm. Well. And you were wearing this when you were found?'

'Yes, sir,' she said.

He was blinking quite a lot.

'My mother gave it to him,' he said shortly. 'Before he went away. Superstitious fools, the pair of them. As if an amulet can help anything. She said, "Never forget you're an Athenian. May Athena bring you home safely." That was the day he left. He said he'd always wear it. Big fool . . .' He blew his nose.

Halo was holding her little owl, feeling it so small and smooth between her fingers. Her father's owl that he had worn, that he had given to her.

Pericles sat down. Aspasia poured him tea. Halo sat on a stool at his feet. Her heart was so full of feelings that she didn't know where to begin. Everywhere she looked she saw a thousand questions, and each answer might lead to a thousand more questions.

*I'll start with a simple one.*

'Sir,' she said, 'are you my uncle?'

'As good as, child,' he said. 'Your own flesh and blood. You have many relatives here, you know.'

But Halo knew in her heart that none of those other relatives could make her happier than this, her first relative, her Uncle Pericles.

*Except, of course, if . . . if . . .*

Well, now she could learn the truth. Here – she had come all this way, and now she could know.

She was strangely reluctant to ask. Knowing meant the end of possibilities . . .

'Uncle Pericles,' she whispered. 'What happened to my parents?'

He took her hand in his and she leaned against his knee.

'Well,' said Pericles, and he looked her in the eye and she knew in that moment that there was no good news coming. 'Fifteen years ago, my brave and amusing cousin Megacles, the kindest man you could hope to meet, with no sense of money and a dreadful singing voice, then twenty-five years old, took it into his head to visit another cousin, in Ionia, who had stayed on after one of our family banishments. While he was there, he met a woman, whose name we never knew. He married her, and travelled with her, and had a child, whose birth we heard about. You, Halosydnus — though actually that's not your name . . .'

'It's not? — Oh! No, of course not . . . um, what is my name?'

'I don't know,' said Pericles. 'Cleisthenes, probably, after your father's father.'

Cleisthenes the father of democracy. 'Was Cleisthenes my grandfather?' she exclaimed.

'He was your grandfather's grandfather,' he said. 'So his name is yours.'

*I am descended from Cleisthenes!* But even that was just an interruption to the story she wanted — needed — to hear.

'Carry on, Uncle,' she said.

'Well. We heard that Megacles was travelling to Graecia Minor, that he might come via Athens, and I for one was very excited at the idea of seeing him again . . . and they didn't come.' Pericles paused for a moment. 'Instead, news came that the ship was lost, and . . . we mourned them as dead.'

*Dead.*

*That doesn't mean they* are *dead. After all, I'm not dead.*

*But how could they be alive? If they were alive, Pericles would know.*

'Her name was Aiella,' said Halo softly. 'My mother.'

'Aiella,' said Pericles.

Halo felt peculiar rivulets stirring inside her, to hear him say the name.

'Are they dead, Uncle?' she asked.

He had a faraway look in his eye. Memory was enfolding him.

'I believe that they are dead, my child. But without a body, how can one be sure? Halo – listen. I do not expect to see my dear cousin again in this life. I would be a liar if I said otherwise. Believe him to be dead, my dear. Do not spend your life seeking *his* life. Honour him as one does the dead. I will show you the monument.'

'There's a monument?'

'Of course. At Kerameikos . . . Halo, he is *ataphoi*,[8] and there is nothing we can do about that, but only the superstitious still believe that would affect his chances in the afterlife. All care has been taken for him – he was much loved. You will want to perform your own rites, as his first-born son. I will speak of him with you at length, as best I can, though the coming months will be busy for me . . . I would like to help you to know him as he was. But you will know him as an orphan, my dear, not as a son to a living father.'

*As an orphan.*

'But Halo – I will be your father now, if you will have me.'

*If I will have him? By all the Gods yes, I will have you for my father.*

'Sir,' she said. 'Uncle. I have lost a father and gained a father within two minutes . . . I don't know what to say . . .'

'Will you not have me?' he said.

'Oh, I *will*,' said Halo, nodding a lot, and then she started crying, and after a while Aspasia said that there would be plenty of time for talk later, and that she should go to bed now, and took her through, and laid her down.

Halo curled up with Arko, still weeping, and whispered to him until he woke.

'Arko,' she whispered, 'Arko, I'm an orphan. Arko, they're dead. Arko, they're dead . . .'

He shifted so she could curl up to him. 'You knew that already,' he said softly. 'Didn't you?'

'Yes,' she said. 'But now I know it more.'

## Χαπτερ 22

Pericles was so delighted with Halo that he took her everywhere with him, introducing her, laughing at her jokes, clapping her on the back. He showed her the city walls, fed her from his plate, and admired her intelligence. She liked him very much, and imagined that her father might be a bit like him. 'Oh, he was much younger than me,' Pericles said. 'And much sillier . . .' Halo was happy to hear stories of her father. They made him real.

'Aren't you forgetting something?' asked Arko.

'What?' said Halo, slipping on a clean chiton to go up to the Assembly with Pericles.

'You're a girl, and you're lying to him,' said Arko bluntly.

Halo stopped in mid-movement. 'And if I tell him, he won't like me any more because I'm just a girl . . . and he'll be angry that I lied . . .'

'Yes,' said Arko.

'I know,' she said. 'I know. I just don't know what to do about it . . . He'll be angry either way . . .'

'Yes,' said Arko.

'I know I should tell him the truth . . .' she said.

'Well, we'll be leaving soon,' said Arko.

This too was proving complex. Pericles had plans for them, and it seemed ungrateful just to leave. But they *had* to warn the Centaurs about Manticlas. They decided just to leave quietly, with a promise of a quick return.

'After all,' said Halo, 'Pericles and Aspasia are not just hosts. They're my family . . .'

But the day they planned to leave, the house and the city fell into uproar.

News came in at dawn: Halo was woken by a ruckus in the yard, as a messenger arrived from the north, soaked, mud-streaked, and pale with exhaustion.

'Thebes has attacked Plataea,' he panted to Pericles. 'Plataean traitors let them in during the storm last night – everyone surrendered and we retreated inside our houses, but we tricked the Thebans – we dug through the mud walls and all joined up and we came out fighting – we've taken hostages. But we need help, Pericles. We need Athens's help. Thebes will send more men. They'll besiege us . . .'

'The Thebans?' said Halo, confused, looking down. 'Plataea? I thought the war was to be between Sparta and Athens . . .'

Aspasia was behind her, looking out too. 'It's not going to be that simple,' she said softly. 'There are many alliances, and also many old grudges, which people will take up under the pretence of war. The Thebans have always wanted Plataea for themselves, though how they can attack a city promised safety forever by all the Greeks after the great battle there fifty years ago, when we beat the Persians . . .'

'Who beat the Persians? The Athenians?'

'Well,' said Aspasia. 'All the Greeks.'

'Including the Spartans?'

'Yes – and the Thebans!' said Aspasia. 'So for them to attack now, while we are still in negotiation with the Spartans . . . well, the peace is well and truly broken.'

The only bit Halo understood was that fifty years ago at Thermopylae and Plataea all the Greeks had fought together against the Persians, and now they were all fighting against each other. She would have asked Pericles about it, but he was very busy now.

She remembered Thanus talking about these things. She hoped he and his family were all right. The thought of Leonidas skittered across her mind.

'So will Athens send Hoplites?' Halo asked. She recalled so clearly the Spartan phalanx marching out, so fine, so terrifying. Would the Spartan Hoplites come to Plataea to support the Thebans? Imagine them in battle. Two phalanges, face to face across the battlefield. Imagine them colliding.

Leonidas would not be a Hoplite yet. She pictured him for a moment, two and a half metres tall in his crested helmet, dealing death at close quarters from behind his great bronze shield. Another image flew into her mind: a small boy being beaten and cheered outside the temple of Artemis. And another: a strong arm pulling her from deep water. A strong young man standing up for her over and over again. A friendly warm voice under a starlit sky. A cry of 'Good luck.' A pair of green eyes, laughing.

And now, war.

All human men killed people, it seemed. Pericles had killed men. That's how it is among the humans.

*When war comes*, she thought, *everyone will be a killer.*

Aspasia was talking. 'I don't know,' she was saying. 'We will see . . . but war or no war, Pericles wants you to be educated. You'll start school tomorrow. Arko too.'

School? But — 'Aspasia, we can't. We have to go to — to visit the Centaurs . . .'

'You can't go now,' she said, 'Halo, not possibly. It's far too dangerous. There'll be no travelling without permits — even if it were OK for a child to wander around the country.'

Halo was silent.

'And Halo, you're not just any child any more,' she continued. 'You're a son of Pericles. His enemies will know that . . . You have to take care. You'll go to school. Aides will take you.'

So the next morning they set off with Aides, their own *pedagogue*, a grumpy old slave whose job it was to look after them.

'It's quite funny,' murmured Arko, 'given what we've been through before on our own.'

Actually they both rather liked being looked after for a change, and being told to watch out not to be knocked down by wagons. But soon it grew annoying.

And school had its own risks for Halo. *With any luck*, she thought, *everyone at school will be so busy staring at Arko they won't see anything odd about me.*

But she had no such luck. After that first morning of reading and writing and learning poetry with a bunch of boys who did indeed stare at Arko and ignore Halo, they were sent out to the gymnasium, to exercise.

The boys all stripped cheerfully, leaving their chitons in a pile, and ran off to stretch and warm up. Arko cantered up and down, beating them at races. Halo stood like a fool.

She couldn't take her chiton off.

'Come on,' said the teacher, Martes. 'Chiton off.'

'I can't,' she said, fiddling with Leonidas's leather cuff, which she still wore on her wrist.

'What's wrong?' he said.

'Medical reasons,' she said. It was the first thing that came into her head.

He frowned. She refused. She was not going to reveal herself as a girl.

'Do as you're told, child.'

'No.'

'Do you want to be beaten?'

'No.'

'Then get ready for gym.'

'No.'

Martes didn't want to beat Pericles's adopted son on the first day. In the end he called for Aides, and sent her home.

'What's the matter?' said Aspasia.

'He wouldn't strip for gym,' said Aides. 'Point blank refused. Won't say why.' He stomped off.

Aspasia looked at her. 'Why?' she said.

Halo stared at the ground.

'Halo,' said Aspasia firmly.

Halo was going hot and cold under her skin. She knew the lie would catch up with her, but not yet. And she had never meant it to be a lie to *them*. And if she admitted it now, she'd be in trouble for lying, she wouldn't be able to go to school, she'd be kept in the house, and made to marry and do housework for the rest of her life . . . no more swimming in caves, or running with Arko, no more adventures, no hope of ever going to Thessaly to find Chariklo and Kyllarus, and find out what Manticlas was really up to . . .

Halo had lost so much already. She wasn't going to lose being a boy. She couldn't . . . she couldn't . . . but she couldn't think of any way out . . .

She wrapped her arms tight around her torso, as if she were holding herself close.

Aspasia sighed.

'Halo,' she said. 'Is there something you want to tell me?'

Halo shook her head angrily.

'Really?' said Aspasia, looking down at her.

Halo blinked. She wasn't going to cry. She didn't know what to do.

Aspasia made a little shape with her mouth, as if to say, *Well, I think there is something.*

'Halo,' she said, and her voice was not unkind, '*I think you're a girl.*'

Halo jumped. Across the room.

'Oh!' gasped Aspasia. 'You are! Aren't you?'

Halo nodded, dumbstruck. *There goes all my freedom, all my hope . . .* 'Are you going to reveal me?' she asked in a very small voice.

'No,' said Aspasia. 'I mean – I don't think so . . . Except . . .'

'You can't lie to Pericles,' Halo said. 'You know you can't.'

Aspasia was silent for a moment. She was thinking about how life would be for Halo, as a girl, not a citizen, even in the family . . . How she would have to be washed and tamed and set to weaving and laundry, instead of running about the country with

Spartans and Centaurs. She would have to be married off – but who would want her, with that tattoo, and her wild history? She was thinking about how Pericles, for all his virtues, still thought that the best thing a woman could achieve in life was never to come up in conversation among men.

Yet he loved *her*, Aspasia, and people talked about *her* all the time . . .

'You're right, I can't,' she said. 'I have to think about this . . .'

'Please don't tell him,' Halo blurted, but then she stopped herself – she couldn't ask that.

Aspasia gazed at her, sympathy and impatience mixed in her expression. 'You can't possibly . . .' she said. 'Halo – the family – listen. I understand. Often, *often* I have wanted a man's freedoms. But – how long could you get away with it? You're fine for now, but soon you will start looking like a girl. You're pretty; the men will look at you. It's too late to make you respectable, but in a few years . . . What are you going to do, grow a beard? And you'll start to bleed . . .'

'Why would I start to bleed?' said Halo, confused.

'Why . . .? Your periods,' said Aspasia. 'Ah. Yes, I suppose it's different for Centaurs.'

Halo did not like this talk. It sounded womanly. She did *not* want to be womanly. Nor did she want to be manly. Pictures sprang up in her mind. Leonidas's strong, scarred back. The Skythians with their long moustaches and wiry muscles. The Spartan phalanx, those giant men, with spears and swords and massive shields . . . deep harsh voices, and the smell of sweat.

But she was only twelve, or thirteen . . . there was plenty of time . . .

'We can think about all that later,' said Halo. 'Can't we? Can't I just go to school . . . and . . .?'

'No,' said Aspasia. 'Here in Athens girls marry at fifteen.'

'That's two years,' said Halo pleadingly. 'Plenty of time.'

'So, what, in two years we turn to Pericles and say, "Oh, your adopted son is a girl, by the way"?' Aspasia said. 'No. No. I'll tell – no, you tell him. For your honour. Tonight.'

Halo lowered her head. 'I'll tell him,' she said. 'But I won't tell anyone else.'

'Well, that will be up to him,' Aspasia said.

Halo smiled bitterly. *Of course it would.*

As Halo was about to leave to find Arko, Aspasia said, 'By the way. Your father – you know he recorded your birth, wrote to his family about you.'

'Yes,' said Halo.

'You know, normally they only do that for a boy.'

Halo didn't think that was very nice.

'So he must have loved you,' Aspasia said, and looked at her.

Halo took that thought away with her, and in moments of darkness for the rest of her life she would take it out and stroke it.

That afternoon Arko and she talked it over, tussling the question to and fro and still coming up with no answer, as they took the road out to Kerameikos, the cemetery beyond the city walls. Gyges the Skythian was manning the gate. He checked their permits – 'cemetery only' – and waved them through. The big dogs stared and drooled in the shade.

'Don't think about it now,' Arko said. After all, they had something else on their minds.

The guardian at the cemetery pointed out the *periboloi* of the Alcmaeonids: an area of soft green grass surrounded by a fine stone wall. Plaques gave the names of the people buried within. She found several with the name Megacles. Her father's was easy to identify. It was the newest. It said, simply:

*ΜΕΓΑΚΛΗΣ, ΧΑΙΡΕ*
MEGACLES, FAREWELL

She stared at it for a long time. She couldn't help thinking of bodies at sea, floating, lifting and falling, in the waves, in the foam, so cold. She thought of her own little baby body washed up on the beach in Zakynthos in its turtle shell. She thought of her older body, diving from the Zakynthine ship, hanging from the stern of the ship, swimming and swimming and washing up on the shore of the Mani. She thought of her body floating unconscious in the Lacedaemonian pool, and of Leonidas dragging it out. She thought of when she was lost in the icy waters of the underground cavern. All the times she didn't drown.

Her mother was of course not mentioned on the plaque. Halo traced the shapes of the letters of her name with her finger, under her father's name:

*ΑΙΕΛΛΑ*

There was enough room. She would ask Pericles if a mason could come and carve it in.

But how would she be able to ask Pericles anything, now she had to tell him she had lied to him?

She laid a bunch of wild celery at the base of the wall, and propped a flask of oil with it: traditional mourning offerings. She sat quietly there for the rest of the afternoon, crying for her dear parents, and for herself, remembering nothing about them. Arko sat with her, and wouldn't let anyone disturb her.

Afterwards, feeling purified, she went back to face Pericles. But he didn't come home that night till after she was asleep, and he was gone early in the morning.

'I told him you have something important to say to him, in private,' said Aspasia. 'He said could you tell him tomorrow.'

But that day too he was in meetings and discussions and negotiations till after midnight, and Halo didn't see him.

The morning of the third day, Pericles swept out of the courtyard at dawn. Halo gathered all her courage together and ran after him.

'Dear boy,' he said. 'Not now.'

He was away from the house for days on end, preparing for war. He was always surrounded by advisers and colleagues. Halo remained ready at all times to tell him.

The moment didn't arrive.


Aspasia told Martes that Halo could not go to the gym as she had other studies in the afternoons – which she did. She had music. She and Arko sat in a glade below the hill of the

Areopagus with a nice old man called Philoctetes, who taught them song after song, and they taught him Centaur songs in exchange, which he was very interested in. They got into the habit of bringing fruit with them, and Philoctetes's slave Bokes would prepare it, and his grandson Alexis would drop by, so it often turned into more of a musical picnic than a class. Arko started to learn the lyre, which he felt was appropriate for a Centaur of Apollo.

'You can't do music every day,' said Aspasia.

'Medicine then,' Halo said, surprising herself.

Pericles had told Aspasia that as Halo would be in the army in a few years, she should concentrate on military training. Aspasia decided to understand that Pericles meant medical training would be useful for the army, and sent Halo two afternoons a week to see a young man called Hippias, who had studied at the new medical school in Cos, under the famous Hippocrates.

The first time Halo went to Hippias's little house, it was full of people who had come to consult him. A boy with tufty brown hair and a mouth like a straight line, his apprentice, Halo thought, let her in, and told her to sit quietly in the corner. She did so, eyes and ears wide open as Hippias, a sleek brown-eyed person rather like an otter, dealt with a woman with a vastly distended tummy. She had a high squeaky voice, in which she complained a lot about feeling exhausted and having no bleeding.

'Has it occurred to you, madam, that you might be having a child?' Hippias asked patiently, after taking her pulse and prodding her gently.

'Oh no, I can't be,' she said. 'My husband's away.'

'Well, when was he here?'

'He's been gone seven moons, at least,' she squeaked.

'Then after two moons, expect a baby,' said Hippias. 'They take nine moons to grow, you know.'

'Do they?' squeaked the woman.

'Have you not had one before?' he asked, and she agreed that no, she hadn't.

'Go and talk to your mother,' he said very kindly, and not laughing at all. 'You're not ill. Send for the midwife when your time comes.'

'How will I know?' she said, alarmed.

'You'll know,' he said ominously, and, clucking with excitement, she went on her way.

Hippias looked up. 'Next!' he called, and when Halo went over first he asked her what seemed to be the matter.

'Oh no, I'm all right,' she said. 'I'm Halo. I'm here to learn.'

He stared at her for a moment as if he had no idea what she was doing there, but then remembered, and smiled, and said, 'Well good. Have some cake.' He handed her a piece of syrupy baklava from a dish on the table. 'Good, now, so – what do you want to learn? How to set broken limbs and sew wounds? Or what herbs to use to lift a fever, how to clean a pustule, or rebalance the humours of the constitution? Magic spells to move on a dropsy? Or do you want to know if it is true to say that goats breathe through their ears? Or do you want to know whether a disease comes from the air or from the individual? Or do you want to know the nature of the human soul?'

His expression was completely serious.

Halo looked at him, and she couldn't help laughing through her cake. 'Yes please,' she said.

His eyes brightened. 'Well good,' he said again, amiably. 'And do you know anything yet?'

Halo swallowed and licked her lips.

'I can set an arm. Well, I've never done it, but I know how, and I can clean a pustule, I could probably sew a wound . . . I know that if many people get the same disease then the disease is in the air, or maybe the food, if they ate bad meat – but if only one gets it then the disease is in the person – or in the person's reaction to the air, or the food, like those people who if they eat a nut come out in a rash . . .'

He was grinning at her. 'And what don't you know?'

'I don't know . . . I don't know so many things! How to pull the bones of the leg apart to reposition them for setting. How babies get inside the mother. How to bring an unconscious person back to the world . . . How to cure people . . .'

He raised his hand to hush her. 'And what will you do with your knowledge?' he asked.

'Help people,' she said. 'And animals.'

'Then I'll take you on,' Hippias said. 'Follow what I do with my patients, watch and listen. Soak up everything I do and say, like a dry sponge. Keep an open mind. And read – start with Alcmaeon. Though I can't agree with him about the goats. Now – extending the leg for setting, you said. Come with me . . .'

Ten minutes later, she was cranking a heavy winch, which was attached to thick leather straps, which were attached to the ankle and knee of a poor builder who had fallen from scaffolding and snapped his thigh bone. He in turn was strapped to a chair, which was nailed in place to the floor. Even before she started the stretching and pulling and rack-ing of the leg, he was howling pathetically in pain. Like Chiron when he had set her arm all those years before, Hippias explained what he was doing.

'Pull it hard!' he cried. 'Hard as you like! We don't want to leave him lame with a shortened thigh. You can't pull it too hard. A little bit of pain now, but the bone-ends will meet cleanly, and his leg will be good as new. Don't be scared . . .'

Like all those years ago, Halo gritted her teeth and refused to allow pain to prevent the doing of what had to be done.

Hippias pressed the snapped bone back into position.

The man shrieked in agony.

It was a lot easier now that the pain was not hers.

That night, Arko said, 'We can't do what can't be done. We can't go to Thessaly yet. You're doing your best to confess to Pericles. We can't do more.'

'I could write to him,' Halo said.

Arko thought for a moment, and said, 'But Halo – you don't want him to know. Do you?'

'No . . .'

'So don't write to him. Let things be.'

It was a very appealing idea.

## Χαπτερ 23

Arko admitted easily that he had no talent for medicine, and no interest in it, so he didn't go along – also, the patients might think they were having hallucinations if they saw him. After a few attempts at training with the boys at the gymnasium he had to give that up too: he won all the races and got in trouble for kicking during the wrestling, even though he wasn't trying to kick.

Their other class was archery.

Halo and Arko turned up at the field where the archers practised. There were no Athenian boys there – just a few foreigners and public slaves. The instructor was a bored-looking Cretan. An even more bored-looking Skythian with thin clean scars down each cheek sat on his horse beside him, casting his bored look over the trainees, and not thinking much of them.

Halo glanced at him. Did they never get off their horses? Wherever she went, there seemed to be a Skythian, astride horse, chewing and watching and looking dangerous, daggers hanging off him, hound at his heel. Whatever Aspasia said, they made Halo nervous. This one was no different.

The bows were the Cretan type, which neither Halo nor Arko had used before – sleek and well made. She liked the look of them. The targets, though, were so big that she thought someone must have drawn the line in the wrong place, and went to take her first shot from another line, twenty metres further back.

'Get back here,' shouted the Cretan. 'That's the border of the discus course.'

So Halo went back to where he indicated, even though clearly even a five-year-old could hit the target from that distance.

'OK,' said the Cretan wearily. 'Let's see what you can do.'

Halo strapped on a belt with a pouch of arrows, picked up the bow, felt its weight, tried the strength of its string. She strung her arrow (socketed, with a bronze head – *nice*, she thought), fitting the string neatly into the nock. She raised the bow, holding the string to her ear with three fingers, the way Kyllarus had taught her, her sightline running straight and true along the arrow.

She hardly had to glance at the target: she hit it dead centre, re-arrowed, hit it dead centre, re-arrowed, hit it dead centre again, re-arrowed – she did it eight times in two minutes, and only stopped because she had no arrows left in her pouch, and there was no room left on the target. She looked up. The Cretan was frowning. The Skythian was smiling softly. His hound panted quietly, watching the action.

She hadn't seen a Skythian smile before. It was unnerving. She was afraid she might miss her shots.

'OK, OK,' said the Cretan. 'Try from twenty metres back.'

Halo collected her arrows, estimated twenty metres

again, strung her arrow, tried to ignore the Skythian, and did the same thing.

The Cretan sighed.

The Skythian smiled again.

Arko was finding it hard not to snort with laughter.

'OK, OK,' said the Cretan. 'Shoot from where you like.'

Halo was finding this very easy. After all, the targets stood still and let you take your time. She wasn't being given the chance to show her skill at all. But she collected her arrows, went further back into the discus course, steadied her eye and began to shoot. Every one of them hit the bullseye. Then, as she raised her last arrow, from the corner of her eye she saw a duck flying by, quick-flapping up from the river, flying low. She couldn't resist it. She'd show that silly Cretan. She swerved, glanced, and loosed the arrow just far enough ahead, just where the duck would be by the time the arrow arrived and – yes. The bird plummeted. Shot through the heart. She ran across the field to fetch it.

The Cretan was shouting at her when she got back. 'This is not a hunting trip! This is target practice on a sports training field! That was extremely dangerous! What if you had hit someone! I will be informing your schoolmaster of your lack of discipline. Stupid boy! You will be punished!'

Halo narrowed her eyes. He was really beginning to annoy her.

'Tell you what,' said the Skythian mildly, not looking at her. 'Why don't you join us tomorrow, see what the Skythians can teach you.'

Halo was so very surprised that for a moment she forgot

to be alarmed. No one trained with the Skythians. They hardly even spoke to other people, except to arrest them or put the fear of the Gods into them. They were the tightest of all the bands of foreigners in Athens. Partly because they were guards and police, living in their special barracks; partly because of their strong accents, partly because technically they were slaves, they kept together and weren't interested in anyone else. They even had their own doctor, an old man called Taures – she'd seen him by the barracks, coughing and drunk. (Hippias had pointed him out. 'That is the kind of doctor who doesn't deserve the name,' he'd said. 'He only knows how to bind battle wounds, and he's no good at that anyway.')

Halo looked up at the Skythian.

'Really?' she said – because alongside alarm and surprise came curiosity. Skythians were the best archers in the world, everyone knew that. They could shoot backwards, on horseback, while pretending to retreat. They had the best bows, the best techniques. She would *very* much like to see what they could teach her.

'Really,' he said.

She glanced at Arko.

'Could he come too?' she asked.

'You two are as one person,' the Skythian said courteously. 'He comes too.' His hound lifted its head, letting its long pink tongue show a little between its white teeth. Its ears perked up.

She looked at the man, and at the dog, and back to the man. She was scared.

She grinned. She'd trained with Centaurs, Spartans and now Skythians. Leonidas would be proud of her.

'OK,' she said.

Halo and Arko joined the Skythians the following evening, as the air was growing cool, in their field, outside the walls. If anybody passing by stopped to watch them, the Skythians shot arrows at their feet to send them away. Everybody knew this by now, and they didn't linger.

'Are we mad?' Halo murmured to Arko, as they approached for the first time.

'Utterly,' he said. 'Oh, sweet Ares, there's old One-Eye.'

The Captain rode swiftly up to them as they arrived, reining in his long, sand-coloured horse. Unlike the others, he wore a tight jacket. The deep-blue cloth was still bound round his missing eye. His scars were livid, but his face beneath them was almost delicate. It made him all the more frightening.

'You are welcome,' he said briefly.

'Thank you,' said Halo.

Then, much to her amazement, he swung his leg over and slipped off his horse. She had never seen a Skythian standing. He was still pretty tall.

'Show me how you ride,' he said.

He was offering her his horse!

'I have only ever ridden Arko,' she said. 'Er, this is Arko. I am Halo.'

'We know who you are,' he said. His voice was soft, but lined with steel. 'Arko, do you wish to be ridden?'

'Only in emergency,' said Arko. 'Or play.'

'So mount,' said the Captain, turning to Halo.

She looked. How on earth? There was a bridle. She eyed it, sideways – there didn't seem to be any scalps or blood-stains on it. There was the huge horse. There was an audience of tough unsmiling Skythians, and their tough unsmiling dogs. There was nothing that could help her. So she smiled gamely, took the reins in her right hand, and jumped. The Gods knew she'd jumped on to Arko's back before – and sometimes he'd just galloped off, as perhaps this horse would do now . . .

She flung herself across the horse, on her belly. She swung herself round, to get her left leg over, to pull herself upright. She had no idea what to do with the reins, but she knew to grip with her knees.

She gripped tight. The horse took it as a signal – and took off.

It ran faster, purer, cleaner that Arko ever could. It lowered its head into the wind created by its own speed, and it galloped like a ghost, searing across the field, running, running, running . . .

She held the reins loosely, and her knees tight. She kept her weight forward and her head down. She felt so exposed – no human back in front of her, no waist to hold on around, no shoulders, no russet head of hair flying in her face – just a horse head, pulling, pulling, horse ears flattened back, horse mane flying from strong horse neck, and the wind . . . It was fantastic.

It was over too soon. The horse, perhaps sensing that all

was not going to plan, slackened, and returned to the Captain as if obedient to a silent call.

Halo sat, smiling shakily.

'Well,' the Captain said. 'We have something to work with. Akinakes, teach him.'

Akinakes – the rider who had invited them – appeared and took the horse's bridle. He offered Halo his big silver-ringed hand to help her down from the horse. He even had a ring on his thumb. The courtesy surprised her. She had expected their training to be brutal.

'Thank you, Akinakes,' she said, and turned to the Captain. 'And please, what is your name?'

'Arimaspou,' he said.

'An unusual name,' she said politely. 'What does it mean?'

'One-Eye,' he said, staring at her calmly. Out of his one eye.

Zeus only knew what gave her the stupidity, or the stupid courage to say it – but before she knew it . . . 'It suits you,' she said, deadpan. And then flung both hands over her face in horrified shock at what she had said – surely now, her cropped black curls would soon be hanging from that very bridle . . .

But vengeance did not immediately slice her in half with its sharp Skythian dagger. Instead a strange sound greeted her ears.

Arimaspou was laughing. He was laughing a lot. They were all laughing. In fact, for a moment she thought Arimaspou might reach out and rumple her hair.

Anyway, she laughed too. So did Arko. And something was released by them all laughing together.

In the following weeks Akinakes trained her, and sometimes Arimaspou himself. Their bows were far more advanced than the wooden Centaur bows she had been used to. These were backed with sinew for flexibility and strengthened with horn, and their bronze arrowheads were tiny and deadly sharp. Before she was even allowed to shoot the first time, she had to learn to restring the big bow and refix an arrowhead. They corrected her technique in riding and archery, making her practise over and over. They nodded unconcernedly at her blisters, and approvingly as her hands toughened up. It was hard work. She took it without complaint. They would never, *never* know that she was a girl, or think that she was soft. Her muscles grew stronger, her skin grew tough, and she was bruised every day from falling off the horses.

As she got to know the Skythians a little she took to greeting them when she saw them around town, instead of glancing nervously at them. In return she would get a grave nod, or the laconic lift of a finger in greeting. It was easier though to get to know their Molossian dogs, and she discovered the great pleasure of being on affectionate terms with a big fierce animal that everyone else was scared of. It turned out these great fanged, drooly-mouthed creatures very much liked to play with balls. Except for one laughing young rider called Nephiles, the Skythians were not the game-playing type, but Halo loved throwing the balls for the Molossians, and having them bring them back, and rest their heads against her knees, and squabble with each other for the place of luxury, sitting across her lap, when they all gathered round in the evening after training to drink *askhu*, the cherry-syrup in milk that was the Skythians' favourite.

One night, as they sat around the evening fire, Arimaspou gave her a present of a metal thumb-ring, like the silver ones they all wore. He had showed her before how it was used to hold the bowstring in place, and to protect the flesh of the inside of the thumb from the rubbing of the string.

'Your thumb is tough enough now,' he said. 'Tender thumbs cannot wear this ring. Maybe you'll earn a silver one one day . . .'

She was incredibly pleased. It was almost praise.

'. . . if we survive the war long enough to train you up,' he said drily.

A strange, tense mood had criss-crossed the city ever since the Plataean messenger had arrived. The leaders were finalizing alliances, captains were preparing their troops. The watchtowers along the Long Walls to Piraeus, the port of Athens, were fully manned; storerooms were full, weapons were in tip-top condition. Halo watched the Athenian Hoplites perfecting their manoeuvres out in the training field. She couldn't help comparing them to the Spartans – and yes, they looked good, but . . . The Spartans looked like one creature made up of hundreds of men, and the Athenians looked like hundreds of men. That was the best way she could find to describe it.

Rumours of war with the Spartans rippled to and fro, and Halo heard plenty: Corinth had changed sides, Potidaea had fallen, Kerkyra had been invaded, one of the two Spartan kings, Archidamus, was mustering the Spartan army at the Isthmus.

It was beginning.

When Halo heard this she made her way to the Assembly, to hear what was being said by those who really knew. As she entered, everyone was sitting hushed and attentive, because Pericles was speaking. It made her proud – and ashamed too, because she still had not told him the truth. He was in the middle of a sentence, speaking quietly but firmly.

'. . . the Spartans invade, as they will any time now, and start to ravage our beautiful land of Attica, I have a feeling that they will try to trick you. They might think it clever to ravage everybody's lands but mine, which lies right on their route to Athens. I think they will leave my land untouched, to make you suspicious of me. Well – if that happens, I will give that land up, and declare it public property. But more importantly – my advice, as the General who has had the honour of serving the people of Athens for so many years, is this. We will prepare for war. We are wealthy and well equipped. We have strong walls protecting the city and Piraeus, our food supplies by sea are safe. We have twenty-nine thousand Hoplites. We have one thousand and two hundred cavalry, including mounted bowmen; we have one thousand and six hundred unmounted bowmen, and three hundred triremes ready for active service. We will bring into the city all the property we can from the countryside. We – all of us, country dwellers included – will come inside the city and guard it. We will *not* go out and offer battle.'

A wave of surprise and incomprehension circled the gathered Athenians. But Halo understood. So that was his idea!

That was why he had laughed at the Oracle about the Spartans winning if they fought their hardest. They couldn't fight their hardest, because he wasn't going to fight them!

It was brilliant. Bring everyone inside the city walls, and leave the Spartans running around outside with no one to bash their big shields against. She started laughing. Her uncle was a genius.

At that moment, a youth hurtled past her, stepping on her toe in his hurry to get into the Assembly.

Pericles looked round. 'Yes?' he said.

'Citizens!' panted the boy. '. . . Spartan envoy is at the gates now . . . wants to discuss coming to terms . . . Do we let him in?'

A hubbub of discussion welled up.

'Who is it?' called someone.

'Melesippus, sir,' said the boy.

Melesippus! Halo's heart clenched. Where Melesippus was, Leonidas was.

'Tell Melesippus,' cried out Pericles, his voice suddenly stronger and louder, 'that the time for coming to terms was *before* the army of Sparta marched out of its own lands. Tell him, let the Spartan army return to Sparta, and then send an embassy, and *then* we will think about receiving him. Tell him to be beyond the frontier today.' And then, with withering scorn, he said, 'Offer him an escort.'

His voice was still ringing as Halo wheeled round and raced from the Assembly. She hurtled down the Sacred Way towards the main gate, and was there before the messenger made it, joining the throng which had gathered to stare at the Spartan who dared to come asking for negotiations. She wriggled quickly through the crowd and clambered breathlessly up on the wall by the gate. Boosting herself up, she sat on top, and looked down to where the Spartans waited outside, on the road just by Kerameikos.

She saw Melesippus, looking just the same, strong and dark and broad-faced, standing straight and patient, waiting for his answer. She saw Dion, the slave, sitting with his pack, taking a rest. And she saw Leonidas, and her heart leapt.

His name was in her mouth on a big bubble of air that almost burst out. Stopping it choked her, making her cough. She put her hand over her mouth, and her eyes fixed on him – on the angle of his neck, his curly hair, the movement of his cloak. How familiar he looked! She really wanted to run over and talk to him – to thank him for letting her go free at Delphi, to ask if he'd got into trouble over it, to ask had they made him a Hoplite yet, would he be coming here again, soon, to fight . . .

How could he be her enemy?

It hurt her heart to see him there, so close, and yet separated from her by so much.

She was still up on her perch as the messenger returned. He went over to Melesippus and spoke to him. She watched as Melesippus heard the answer; saw his shoulders set and his head nod slightly as he listened, and saw his little snort of derision at the notion of being 'escorted' across the boundary. She watched Leonidas watching his mentor. She saw his face harden.

She saw Melesippus raise his head and heard him cry out,

in a great voice, for everyone to hear: 'This day will be the beginning of great misfortunes to all Greece.'

She heard the crack of sorrow in his voice. She thought, *Melesippus has seen war. He is a decent man.* She thought, *I could run after them and tell them it's pointless coming anyway because Pericles will not bring the army out to fight you; you might as well go home . . .*

Halo did not want them to come to Athens, in their unstoppable ranks, with their swords and their trumpets and their scarlet cloaks and their long hair, and their ranks of deadly spears. She did not want Leonidas and Athens to be enemies on the field of blood. They were both too close to her heart. Imagine if a Trojan girl, Cassandra or Polyxena, had been in love with Achilles or Odysseus and then the Siege of Troy had started . . . She stopped herself. She wasn't in love with Leonidas.

Was she?

*I don't know what being in love is*, she thought.

In her urgency clambering up the wall, she hadn't noticed that she had grazed her knee. Now the blood was hot and red against her dusty brown skin. She touched it gently as she watched Leonidas, a small figure on the road, walking away to the west.

# Χαπτερ 24

A few days later, on a beautiful May morning, the Spartans invaded Attica.

The word came through, zigzagging down the street and across the *agora*: they've mobilized! They've crossed the border into Attica! They're marching across our land! On their way to *our* city! If you go up the Acropolis you can see their shields flashing in the mountains! They're stopping at Decelea; no, they're havering on the border . . .

As soon as word went round, another invasion began: the invasion of the country Athenians coming inside the city walls, obedient to Pericles's strategy.

Halo first noticed it when out at the training field with the Skythians. She was practising the Parthian shot: trying to get the timing just right, so you let your arrow loose at the exact moment when all four of your horse's galloping hooves are off the ground – if you pace it wrong, you get jarred and cannot aim, but if you aim swift enough and shoot swift enough in mid-air, you can get as pure a shot as if you were standing with your own two feet on firm ground. If you carry a fistful of arrows in your right hand, you can just about do it – reaching back to the quiver takes too long.

She was riding forward, controlling the horse with her knees as Akinakes had taught her, her bow and arrow in her hands, bowstring by her ear, ground thundering along beneath her – many was the time she had fallen off just trying to ride without hands – listening and feeling the rhythm of her steed's movement – judging her moment, *thudderderNOW thudderderNOW thudderderNOW* and on the fourth NOW she unloosed her shot – she missed her target by a *stadion*, but at least she was getting the moment right now. She was satisfied – for the time being.

Jumping down to collect her arrows, Halo noticed the people on the road. Many more than usual – a slow, ever-increasing trickle of creaking wagons and musty donkeys and heavy-laden people ambling in from the countryside. She stared at them and felt a pang of pity. She knew how it felt to leave your home, and she could understand why they were bringing everything they could carry – pots and pans, tools and looms, food supplies, beds, chickens, wooden doorposts and fireplaces even, clanking on the backs of their wagons. The only thing they didn't bring were their animals – all the farm livestock, she knew, was being sent to the big island of Euboea, for safety.

Halo had had to leave with nothing. Suddenly she remembered the soft cloth she had been wrapped in as a baby. She wondered if Chariklo had been able to take it with her when they left Zakynthos. *Of course not*, she told herself. *She had quite enough to worry about . . .*

Halo hadn't realized there were so many people living on the plain. They kept coming, hundreds, thousands of them. Every day more would arrive, and the early arrivals would bless their luck for getting there first, for where was everyone to go? Those who had relatives in town went to their houses; those who didn't camped out. Gradually, bit by bit, the open spaces of the city filled up with people, with temporary roofs, with little shacks, with country wagons and country wives, country habits and country dogs, country slaves and country dialects. Some people built bivouacs up against the Long Walls, some slept in glades and parks and the *agora* even, some in temple grounds or even the temples themselves. Soon, everywhere Halo went she was tripping over some country children, or a pile of bedding. Many of the farmer families had never been to Athens before. The Athenians stared at them.

The country people were not happy. It was spring; their vines were sprouting and their olive trees flourishing, their grain was nearly ripe, and they weren't there to protect and tend and harvest their crops. And Archidamus with his army still sat outside Oenoe, near the border, waiting there, expecting Athens to send heralds to declare battle in response to the outrage.

But the Spartans heard nothing.

Athens made no move at all.

People gathered in the street to laugh. Poor old Archidamus, what a fool! Waiting and waiting, giving the Athenians plenty of time to bring everything inside the city. Stuck out there with all his soldiers, wanting a fight, and no one to fight with! It was unheard of! No city – let alone a mighty empire like Athens – would let an army invade its countryside and just ignore it! Pericles went daily to the *agora* to hear what people had to say, and there among the stalls and the shops and the shady benches and the yapping of the dogs everyone told him his idea was brilliant, and he was brilliant, and Athens was brilliant, though it was a bit damn crowded.

He reassured them. 'The Spartans are trying to provoke Athens, not destroy it,' he said. 'They want to strike fear into us, so that we come out and fight, or come to terms. They are using our land as a hostage, but they will not harm it much. Your vines will grow again; olive trees are strong.'

The farmers from around Oenoe were the most doubtful, knowing that it was their farms being trampled by Spartan feet; their vines being cut, their olive trees with fires being built around the base.

But Athens held firm. Small parties went out to harass the ravagers, but no grand battle was declared.

At midsummer, when the corn was ripe, Archidamus moved on. Clearly he felt he must provoke Athens more, and harder, in order to get the response he wanted. The Spartan army moved through to Eleusis, camped there and started to ravage the land thereabouts.

When Halo and Arko went down to train with the Skythians as usual, Captain Arimaspou said to them, 'No more, my children. We are busy. We have Spartans to harry and though each of you could pierce them easily and from a long distance, in Athens they do not send children to fight. Do not come again.'

Halo didn't like it, but there was no point protesting. Arimaspou was not a persuadable man.

Then, one hot hot evening, while she was doing her homework for Hippias (1: learn the different kinds of pus that could come out of a wound, and whether they were good or bad; and 2: learn the names of the surgical implements in the leather roll Hippias had given her), Tiki told her that a detachment of the Athenian cavalry, out harassing the ravagers, had been put to flight at Eleusis. Some of the Skythians had gone down to give support. There had been fighting.

Halo stuffed her homework into the fold of her chiton, and raced down to the compound. Banned or not, she wanted to check if the Skythians were all right. The more she learned from Hippias, the less she trusted their doctor, Taures.

Their horses came thundering in in the dusk, overtaking her and almost knocking her down, just as she arrived. 'Stretcher!' someone shouted, the voice hoarse and breathless. 'Two dead, Arimaspou is bringing them. Ando and Lotess, the Gods rest them.'

She heard a deadened thud.

A handsome black mare, Ivy – Gyges's mare – was skittering nervously in the yard, her hooves dancing about. In her shadow, a body lay splayed in the dust. A long, cruel arrowshaft was sticking out of his leg. Blood showed on his leather boot, dark and fearful.

The sight of the blood had always affected Halo. It didn't make her want to be sick, or faint, as it would some people. It made her want to clean it up, and put things right. It was a very strong urge. Without even thinking about what she was saying, she looked Akinakes in the eye – amazed at her own boldness – and said, 'Two dead, and Gyges is wounded. Taures might need an assistant.'

'The Captain said you were to stay away,' Akinakes replied,

wheeling his own horse round, trying to calm it. He was sweating, and dust-smeared from the fight and the road.

Gyges moaned softly.

'That's true,' Halo said, 'but – is Taures here?'

The weary, blood-smeared Skythians, reining in their horses, glanced at each other. Akinakes coughed, and took a swig from a water flask. 'He's drunk,' he said at last. 'He's drunk in a ditch in Kerameikos. His manhood has deserted him.'

Halo could see how it hurt him to say the words.

'Then why don't I use my skills?' she said gently. 'Before he loses consciousness . . .' She was tense with impatience.

Akinakes and the others were still reluctant – nervous, even. But helpless.

'I can wait for the Captain to return,' she offered. 'Just let me clean the wound. Please. I studied with Centaurs and also I know some Spartan ways. And I am learning the new ways from my teacher Hippias of Cos . . . but if there's any special way you want me to do it I can try . . .' She kept talking, as she approached the wounded rider. 'Come, let's lift him, at least, and get him comfortable. We must raise his foot to stop the bleeding . . .'

Nephiles and another lifted Gyges, and laid him on a rope-cot in the yard.

Akinakes looked Halo in the eye, nodded, and turned away.

The arrow had pierced right through the boot, and into the flesh of Gyges's calf. The arrow-shaft was sticking right out, bouncing slightly as they moved him. It was nasty.

Carefully, Halo untied the boot and cut it away, peeling

the blood-soaked leather back. 'I need hot water and cold water,' she said, 'and give him strong wine to drink.'

She wondered if Hippias had chosen surgery as her first topic on purpose, knowing than the war would need surgeons. She hadn't planned on using her new skills on her own quite so soon.

'How did he get the wound?' she asked, just to steady her own nerves as she washed her hands and took out her probing tools from the roll. She looked for the first time at the wound, and felt gently around it. She could feel the arrowhead – still attached to the shaft, good. Not stuck into the bone, very good. The bleeding had slowed. Good.

*I'm going to do this*, she thought. *Dear Asclepius, I'm going to take out this arrow. I can do it.*

It was as if she couldn't stop herself.

She washed away the worst of the encrusted blood, then she took the medium probe – she didn't know its name, she hadn't done her homework yet – and gently slid it into the wound.

Gyges gasped. *Don't go into spasm*, she prayed. *If your muscles seize up in pain they will lock around the arrowhead and I won't be able to get it out.*

'It was a Cretan mercenary,' said Akinakes. 'The arrowheads were big, but not barbed, don't worry.'

She felt around gently, the probe inside the wound and her careful fingers outside. Akinakes was right: no barbs to catch and do more damage if you pull the arrow out.

Which method of arrowhead removal should she use? She ran through the options to reassure herself. *Ektome*, cutting the arrowhead out? Or *ephelkysmos*, pulling it out, back the way it went in? Or *diosmos*, cutting a new wound on the other side and pushing the arrowhead through? *Well, ephelkysmos, of course,* she thought. *Pull it out the way it went in. The shaft is still attached, and the arrowhead isn't too deep in the flesh.*

Halo removed her probe. She wasn't scared. She knew she could do it. As long as the arrowhead didn't come off the shaft. Arimaspou had told her how some tribes designed their arrows specially to fall apart – to make the wound harder to heal, and to stop the enemy from reusing the arrows.

'One-fingered archers,' she said. 'Centaurs use three.'

'We all do in the north-east,' said Akinakes, watching her quietly. 'Centaurs, Skythians, Saurians, Thracians, Amazons . . .' Halo smiled at the mention of Amazons. She had heard about the legendary tribe of women warriors.

'But Amazons aren't real,' she said. She took her pot of pitch cerate – waxy ointment made antiseptic with pine resin – and smeared a dollop on to a cloth compress. She put that to one side, then cleaned her little pincers. *Might the arrow be poisoned? Perhaps I should give Gyges some peplis or galbanum just in case.*

'Nor are Centaurs,' said Akinakes drily.

'True, true,' she said, 'though Arko might disagree . . . Do Cretans use poison on their arrows?'

'No,' he said. He was watching her closely.

*I think I can do this without cutting the wound open more . . .* and she whispered, 'Hold on, Gyges.'

She took a sharp breath. She held his flesh firm and the

wound wide with one hand. With the other, she neatly and swiftly tucked her pincers into the wound, either side of the wooden shaft. Blood flowed faster. She dug deep, quickly, and grabbed the arrowhead. She couldn't risk pulling by the shaft, and having the head come off inside. She had to catch it first time – he had already bled enough.

It felt solid between the prongs of the tool, slippery with blood.

She pulled. She yanked it out.

Gyges made no sound – just a tiny silent gasp. She poured clean water over the wound, then warm wine, then she patted it dry, and firmly held the sides of the wound together, pressing on the ends of the blood vessels. No large one had been severed. Good. The bleeding slowed. Good.

'Needle and thread,' she requested, and Akinakes passed them to her. Swiftly, she stitched up the wound – only three little stitches. It was like sewing soft soft leather. Still Gyges didn't cry or moan. *How very brave they are.* She tied up the thread, oiled the wound, and put the soft compress of pitch cerate over it. *Asclepius, please heal this wound*, she breathed. *Please make me a good surgeon and don't let his blood be poisoned and don't make the Skythians hate me by letting him die . . .*

'There you go,' she cried. 'Keep the foot up high, Gyges.' She had done it! She felt fantastic. She felt like the doctor Homer talked of: 'A man worth many others, for cutting out arrows and applying soothing remedies . . .'

Gyges, his breathing shallow, reached out his hand, and touched hers. She smiled. Akinakes inclined his head to her. Someone passed her a jar of wine. She fed it to her patient.

*Thank you, Asclepius.*

Now, he just had to heal.


She went back the following evening. This time Captain Arimaspou was there. He stared at her and she stared at him, and she was very nervous as she asked, 'How is Gyges?'

Arimaspou was silent for a moment, and then he said, 'Why don't you ask him?'

Horrible images ran through her mind: Gyges, writhing in agony; Gyges's wound pouring out all the different types of pus the names and badnesses of which she couldn't remember; Gyges, poisoned or sick; Gyges dead.

But Gyges was well and comfortable. He lay back on a cot in the cool shade of the barrackhouse. He had his foot up, resting on a stool. He was drinking a cup of the tea she had left.

She changed the dressing. The wound was raw and red and ugly and the stitching rough, but there was no pus. Gyges thanked her.

'If you like,' she said to Arimaspou, 'I could ask Hippias my teacher to come and tend to your wounded . . .'

'No,' said Arimaspou. 'You are our doctor now.'

*Oh*, she thought. *That's not quite what I meant* . . . But Arimaspou had already left.

What had she let herself in for?

The Spartan army crossed the Thriasian plain, ravaging as they went. Bit by bit, they neared Athens.

As soon as she heard they were in view, Halo, like many other Athenians, raced to the city walls to see them.

And when she saw them, her heart sank.

Bronze and crimson and terrifying, calm and determined and unstoppable, they marched across the calm, beautiful, deserted plain of Attica. She remembered the phalanx in training, the boys trying to push down trees, the boys of the Krypteia, on their way back from the Helot lands, how they had just walked lightly over everything, through everything, never hungry, never tired, never scared, always united, perpetually strong . . .

This was it. Thousands, tens of thousands of them. So many . . . a great snaking mass, gleaming, silent, a single creature in the distance, a flat bronze dragon, spreading out across the empty countryside of olives and vines and deserted farms. Aiming for Athens.

Were they just going to march on the city?

What would Pericles do if they just came up to the gates, the thousands of them?

What would *she* do? What is a kid meant to do when her city is invaded?

She scrambled down the wall and rushed home. *Phobos can unstring your legs*, she heard in her mind. She understood now what Leonidas had meant. And that was just at the *sight* of the army! She *was* scared. Her lovely new home had been safe for so short a time, and now yet again everything was under threat, and not just *her*, and *her* safety, but everyone, the whole of Athens and all the people in it, Pericles and Aspasia, Arko, the Skythians, Tiki and Samis, Philoctetes and Martes and the boys at school, the singers and the actors and the men in the market and the women who never left their houses, the girls in the *pompe*, the priests, the philosophical wagoner . . .

Pericles, unusually, was at home – though he was about to go out. He looked up as she hurtled in. She tried to hide her face. She didn't want him to see that she had been crying. Boys don't cry.

*Must she tell him now? Didn't he have enough on his plate?*

He stopped her with a hand to her shoulder. 'Halo,' he said. 'What's the matter?'

How cool he was! *Thousands of Spartans on his doorstep, and him the General, the head* strategos *of the city, and he asks what's the matter?* She looked up at him but couldn't think of a thing to say. If he didn't think anything was the matter, who was she to worry?

He was smiling.

'Dear boy,' he said, and he pulled her to him. 'Don't be ashamed. Fear is natural. Feel it, acknowledge it, then let it go. It doesn't serve you. Did you see them?'

She nodded.

'Are you afraid?'

She nodded.

'What of?'

'If they come into the city . . .' she muttered.

'They won't even try,' he said. 'They just want us to come out and fight their famous Hoplites in pitched battle because that is the only way they might be able to beat us. And we won't do it. That's all. Come with me now – I am going up to the Acropolis to see how close they're coming – see how cheeky old Archidamus is prepared to be.'

Walking up through the mighty Propylaeia gate – built by Pericles; past the beautiful temple of Athena – built by Pericles; and along to the north end of the Acropolis – built by Pericles, with Pericles at her side, Halo no longer felt like a little animal staked out for a vulture to descend on. She began to feel like part of a team that was taking a calculated risk but knew it could win.

They looked out to the north across the plain. There was the Spartan army, clearly visible, only about ten kilometres away, outside Acharnae. They were making camp.

'They hope to provoke the Acharnaean young men into coming out to fight,' murmured Pericles. 'Pray all the Gods that they have sense enough not to do it. Pray all the Gods that they see the whole war, and not just the heated pride of today. Tomorrow, no doubt, the ravaging will start again.'

With Pericles by her side, Halo found herself thinking differently about the Spartans.

'I wonder who is there,' she said. 'Would Melesippus be there?'

Pericles said yes, he probably would. Halo knew that he knew many of the Spartans personally. Archidamus was a friend of his. That's why he had made the point about giving up his estate, if Archidamus spared it. He didn't want anyone making accusations.

Halo listened, but she was thinking of who might be with Melesippus.

'Did you like them, Halo, when you lived among them?' Pericles asked.

'I was their slave,' she said. 'They used me as a punchbag for their young boys. But yes, I liked some of them . . .'

'Who did you like?' he asked curiously. 'Melesippus?'

'I liked a boy called Leonidas, Uncle,' she said – and as she said it she wondered why she had. Was it because one day he might be taken prisoner and brought before Pericles in chains and he might remember the name and say ah, yes, my boy Halo liked you, I will spare your life . . .

Actually, yes. That, foolish as it sounds, was what she was thinking. And that was not all.

*We're alone. Tell him.*

'Ah, those Spartan Leonidases,' he said. 'True, the one they are named after was a great man, a great warrior, a great king. If we still had kings, we'd want one like that. So, did you want to be a Spartan? Did you fall for their legend?' He smiled.

'No, Uncle,' she said. 'I only ever wanted to be a Centaur. Or an Athenian,' she added quickly. *And a boy* . . . she didn't say.

He laughed at that.

'Perhaps Manticlas is making their sacrifices for them,' she said, gazing out over the evening. 'Telling them yes, tomorrow is a good day for mighty Hoplites to dig up a cornfield and try to burn down a barn built of mud.'

Pericles laughed again, and rested his arm on her shoulder in a friendly way. 'Don't worry, boy – you'll have your chance to fight them yet.'

'Pericles,' she said. Her arms suddenly got the heavy feeling and her stomach seemed to be collapsing. '*Phobos leave me!*' she hissed to herself. She was going to tell him. She had to.

'Pericles.' She gulped. He was looking at her in concern. Perhaps that was the last kind look she would ever have from him.

'It'll be all right!' he said cheerfully, and then – he was striding off, due at the Assembly, calling that he would see her soon.

He, and the moment, were gone.

From then, Spartan fires, fed with Attic crops, burned daily. Their smoke spiralled on the hot summer air, and in the crowded city, everyone could see them, like taunting exclamation marks pointing out this farm or that. They could smell the scent of destruction. Even during those windless summer days, particles of smoky, oily ash fell on the streets and monuments of Athens. And the Athenians could see too when the fires went out – because new green corn is too alive, too full of sap and fresh growth, to make good fuel.

Pericles still went each day to the *agora* to hear what the people were saying. Now, they told him he was a fool, a suicidal fool, and he must lead them out against the brazen, arrogant Spartans at once, and punish them, beat them, send them packing. The young men, those who had seen little enough of war to find it attractive, were furious at the offence to their dignity and that of Athens. Pericles was called a coward in the street. Some even talked of taking matters into their own hands. But Pericles held firm and calm.

'Our ships will be ravaging their coasts as soon as this army leaves,' he said. 'The Spartans will pay, have no fear. But we must hold firm to our strategy.'

With every gust of smoke the city grew tenser. Out in the *agora* with Arko, Halo overheard a commotion between a wagoner and a farmer.

'We have no choice,' the farmer was saying. 'Give us somewhere else to go and we'll gladly go there. But it's not physically possible to have a body and keep it nowhere. If you like we will come and lie in your courtyard –'

'I already have nine of my cousins lying in my courtyard,' said the wagoner. 'You may lie on top of them, if you like, I don't mind. My point is just that you shouldn't have built on the Pelagian Quarter, because it is sacred ground and you are bringing great bad fortune just when we rather need good fortune – or hadn't you noticed?'

'What do you want me to do? Go to Delphi and ask the Oracle's permission?'

'Oh please – the entire Spartan army is standing between here and Delphi . . .'

'I know! It's my farm they are standing on! My corn they're uprooting – my vines they're slashing to bits as we speak! That's my point! In desperate times you can't follow every old superstition . . .'

'Oh! So the Oracle is an old superstition now, is it . . .?'

'If we survive this, I'll go to Delphi myself and make amends, but I still can't leave my babies sitting in the middle of the road until the Spartans decide to go home . . .'

It was not what Halo had expected of war at all. Where were the martial glory, the discipline, the honour of Thermopylae and all the strength and loyalty and blood and guts? All those little boys trying to push down a tree – and here were the warriors, actually trying to push down actual trees. So much for self-sacrifice and each man's shield protecting his brother to the left. What were they protecting them from? A left-behind chicken on some Acharnaean homestead?

*This isn't the noble Hoplite warfare that I saw them training for*, she thought. *You don't need to spend days in the wilderness, living off the land and murdering Helots, to hack at olive trees and destroy vineyards.*

She wondered how they felt about it, all those proud young men.

Down in the *agora*, Pericles told the Athenians, yet again, as often as they challenged him, 'Sooner or later, the Spartans will get bored, and go away, and then everyone can go out again and rebuild and get back to normal.'

Over at Acharnae, Archidamus told his young men, yet again, 'Sooner or later the Acharnaeans will lose their patience, they will burst out to fight us, and we will beat them.'

'It's like a staring match, isn't it?' Halo said to Arko.

'I just wish they'd give up and go home,' he said.

And, after two months of siege, of not telling Pericles, of

wondering where Manticlas was, and whether he had found the Centaurs, two months of Halo and Arko not being about to do anything – the Spartans did give up and go home. Archidamus lost patience and Pericles won this match.

'Is that it?' asked Halo. 'Is it over?'

'Oh no,' said Aspasia. 'They'll be back. It's just beginning.'

*We'd better go quickly to Thessaly then.*

It certainly seemed over.

The very day the Spartans left, Halo and Arko raced out into the countryside, laughing and happy after months of being stuck in the smelly overcrowded city. The roads were already clogged with country people going home. The air was festive – everyone was glad.

They were stopped in shock by the sight of the ruined farms – vegetable fields dried out, vines ripped out, trees burned. The land that had been so sweet and green and fruitful in the spring, full of blossom and new growth, was now desiccated and trashed. The farming families stood among the ruins of their homes, blank with disbelief. What would they do now? Some of them, stalwart and brave, started immediately trying to tidy up, digging their fields again, wondering if there was anything they could plant so late in the season. Halo and Arko walked and walked, watching as the country people tried their best to make good the damage.

They went down to the port at Piraeus. Pericles was keeping his promise, and a hundred ferocious Athenian triremes were leaving to head round the coast of the Peloponnese to ravage Sparta and its allies. Halo and Arko saw them in the harbour, and remembered when they were small and Kyllarus had pointed out triremes from the clifftop. Then, the triple ranks of oars had looked like insect legs. Now, close up, they could see clearly the heft of the snub, dangerous battering ram at each prow, lying like a shark on the water-line, ready to plunge into the flank of an enemy ship, holing it and sinking it.

Halo stared out at the sea, and the ships, and the distant islands. She saw dolphins leaping, and fresh white frills on waves far out to sea. She thought of deep, deep water, and of drowning.

It was time to make her peace.

'Let's go to Cape Sounion!' she said suddenly. 'Let's go now.'

'Sure,' said Arko.

They walked, ran, and thumbed lifts from passing wagons on their way to the silver mines at Laurium. The road was busy with everybody making up for all the time they hadn't been able to get anything done, during the Spartan invasion.

They were about halfway there before Arko said, 'By the way, why are we going?'

'I want to talk to Poseidon,' Halo replied. 'We're going to his new temple.'

The great Cape of Sounion faced south and east over the restless sea. Halo had never seen the Aegean before, and her heart lifted in delight at the sight of the changing colours of the shining water, the unspeakable beauty of the many islands, the late-afternoon sun dimpling the waves with silver, the rocks and the fish and the glory of the world.

Without pausing, reinvigorated by the beauty, the pair trudged up the hill to the immense shining new temple. Halo stared up at it, dramatic on its hilltop, glowing golden in the evening sun. From that rock, King Aegeus had stood to watch for his son Theseus's ship, and if the sails were white the prince would be alive, and if they were black he would know that his son was dead . . . only the sails were not changed, and he saw the black, and cast himself down from that great rock and died, and never learned that his son, Theseus, great king of Athens, slayer of the Minotaur, had been so excited about coming home that he had just forgotten to change the sails.

Looking up, Halo felt shy. She didn't want to have to talk to priests. She didn't want to have to walk up to this great building . . . she wanted to speak to Poseidon herself, privately. Her heart was as restless as a ghost.

'Let's go down there,' she said, pointing to a rocky route down to the beach below. 'Let's do it the old-fashioned way . . .'

*Do what?* thought Arko, as he scrambled down behind her. She had a determined, sad look in her eye, and he was not going to leave her alone.

He was slower than her, with his hooves and his delicate legs. When he got to the beach, she was sitting hunched over, carving something into a thick piece of driftwood. Two pieces. He watched, without disturbing her.

When she was done, she unfolded herself, and handed him the two salty bone-like slabs of wood – sections of plank from an old wreck, he thought, worn smooth and strange by many years in the sea, and bleached by salt and sunshine.

They were wet with tears, and on each one, Halo had carved a name.

On the wet, smooth sand, she was scurrying to and fro, poking among rocks above the tideline, collecting twigs and dried-out seaweed and gnarled, pale driftwood. She piled it up, like a tiny pyre for a funeral.

She held out her hands and Arko handed her the two named slabs. She laid them on top. Then she went and washed, carefully, in the scudding, mild wavelets, the damp sand sucking at her feet.

Finally, she took out the ember-bearing fennel stalk[9] she always carried and carefully, steadily, brought a handful of dead leaves to leaping flame from its slow-burning heart.

'Poseidon,' she called, into the rising breeze of the evening. 'Lord Poseidon, all these years my parents have floated unburied in your waters, my father Megacles and my mother Aiella – Poseidon, please . . .'

She and Arko stood, heads bowed; the only mourners at this strange funeral.

As the flames died down, and the smoke drifted away over the sea, Halo went to the edge of the rocks and looked out.

It didn't feel enough.

And suddenly, on the spur of that moment, she yanked her golden owl, pulled it off her neck, and cast it into the waters. The leather thong fell at her feet.

'Halo!' cried Arko.

'It is all I have to offer, Poseidon, please recognize my sacrifice, Poseidon, please help the souls of my parents, who gave me this . . .'

'Halo, your owl!'

She was crying. 'I want them to be all right,' she said, tears running down her face, staring out to sea. 'Please, Poseidon, let me know they are all right . . .'

And at that moment, she heard a strange and wild call, out to sea.

'What's that?' she cried.

Arko was looking out, searching the darkening water.

'Look!' he shouted.

She stared where he was pointing.

There was a fringe of light – a scattering of diamonds, thrown and spattered against the wine-dark sea. It arched, and fell . . . and reappeared, three metres ahead.

A smooth dark form led the crystal chain – or trailed it. A nymph?

No. It was dolphin, leaping before them, twisting and jumping in the waves, throwing beautiful arcs of phosphorescent sea-droplets out into the evening air. And crying out – as if to them.

'Is it talking to us?' Halo asked, amazed.

'I think it is,' said Arko.

The dark, shining creature danced on its tail, flicking sideways along the crest of a long rolling wave, its tail twitching brilliant diadems of light. It was smiling, nodding its head, singing. Arko and Halo gazed at it in amazed delight.

'It's Poseidon's messenger,' said Arko. 'He has taken pity on you . . .'

'It's a miracle,' said Halo, and she sat down as if her legs had been unstrung.

'I think it is,' said Arko.

The dolphin spun, and dived, and reappeared again and again, until the night overtook it: its dark shape faded into the darkness of the night, and only the eerie sprinklings of phosphorescence told them where it was. And then that too flew, and dropped, and faded, for the last time.

Halo put her hand over mouth, and whispered thank you, thank you, thank you, over and over.

'But your owl!' said Arko, as they walked back to Athens the next morning, stiff and dazzled after their night on the beach.

'My owl doesn't matter,' Halo said. 'I feel peaceful about them now. I know that they're all right.'

'I suppose,' said Arko. 'Still, it's a pity.'

'No, it's not,' she said stoutly. She still wore the leather thong, worn smooth by the many years round her neck. She was sad about the owl. Of course she was. But there – it had to be done. Giving the owl had shown Poseidon the depth of Halo's need. And Poseidon had noticed, and responded.

'And now,' she said, 'isn't it time we went north?'

'Will you come with me?' he asked. 'Aren't you Athenian now, with your family and everything?'

'Half Athenian,' she said. 'Half Centaur, half whatever my mother was . . .'

'That makes you one and a half people . . .' Arko said.

'That's me,' she said with a grin.

'You can't go,' said Aspasia. 'It's still dangerous out there. You can't just go off. You're a child. You're – Halo you're a *girl*!'

'So what?' said Halo. 'Isn't that the whole point? I came to Athens to find who my parents are. I've found them and honoured them and now I must go and . . . there are reasons I must go. I'll be with Arko. We'll be fine.'

'What will I tell Pericles?' whispered Aspasia.

'Tell him I'll be back,' Halo said, and she kissed her, and she left.

After all her previous adventures, Halo expected trouble and hardship – but the journey was easy. Aspasia gave them food and blankets and water and money and soap and a map, plus travelling boots for Halo and a new cloak for Arko. 'It gets cold in the north,' she said.

Halo packed them up, and Arko slung the bags across his back. They were well equipped. They knew where they were going. Strangers did not try to kidnap them, once they had read Arko's tattoo, or observed the size of his biceps and his hooves. They walked in the cool of morning and evening, slept in the heat of day, talked for hours, swam in the sea, padded along in companionable silence. When Halo was tired, Arko let her ride on his back. She felt like a child again. And when they slept, they slept as they had when they were little, curled up under the stars.

They passed country families renewing their farms; they saw the animals returning to Attica from Euboea; they passed the battlefield of Thermopylae, and saw the monument there to the fallen Spartans. They stopped to read the inscription:

Go, tell the Spartans, stranger passing by,
That here, according to their laws, we lie.

Three hundred Spartan Hoplites had held off the entire Persian army here, for two days and nights, long enough to save Greece from invasion. They had all died.

'Do you still think of your Spartan toad?' Arko asked, later that night.

'I do,' she said. She couldn't say anything else. And that night, Halo dreamed of Leonidas.

Soon they were in Thessaly, walking the dim woods that seemed to go on forever. *How easy it is to be brave*, she thought, *with your friend at your side, your brother.* The wolves and the shadows and the scorpions didn't bother her at all.

The villages of men were easy to find; those of Centaurs much harder.

At the end of their third day, they settled by a small lake, deep in the forest, made a fire and caught some fish. So far, they had seen nothing, no sign.

'Don't worry,' said Arko. 'We're in the right area, and we're making plenty of noise. They'll find us.'

Halo tried to feel convinced. But she had been lost and hungry in a forest before, and she didn't like it. *It's different now, I have Arko . . .*

And she heard a quick rustle . . . *Wolves? Spartans?*

And a sudden vast racket, shrieking and yelling . . . Female voices!

'Sweet Apollo, it's Arko! It's Halo! It's Arko and Halo!! Arko and Halo!!!'

A tumble of flesh and flanks and tails and hooves and long red hair fell out into the glade – Pearl and Lucy.

'We saw your smoke so we came down to see who . . . Oh Apollo, it's really you – well, look at you so grown up – oh, and you're all right – oh, Arko, dearest Arko . . . oh, Halo . . .'

Without ceremony Halo was lifted on to Arko's back. A massive galloping rushed them through the woods. She was utterly out of breath and almost in tears when she slid to the ground at the Centaur village.

They were all there. Chariklo, tears pouring down her face. Kyllarus, hugging Arko, hugging Halo. Chiron, opening and closing his mouth like a shocked codfish. Pearl and Lucy, jumping up and down, so proud and happy to have been the ones to find them.

'And look, look!' cried Pearl. 'Look at my baby!' She had a foal. A long-legged, smooth-flanked, milky-skinned, curly-headed, freckle-faced little Centaur baby, who had been sitting with Grandma, until Pearl pushed him forward.

'Pearl! Are you a grown-up?' asked Halo, smiling.

'Sort of,' she replied with a grin.

Halo was so happy. Her breath was short and she didn't know whose arms to throw herself into first. So they all came round, a big circle of red curls and loving arms, and they all hugged her at once.

'There's something else,' Halo said, carefully, after they had eaten and drunk and told their stories and been hugged half to death, and everything had quietened down. 'We came to warn you. There's – there's a human, a young human, a seer, blond and pale and strange-looking . . .'

Chariklo gasped softly. 'How do you know about him?' she said.

'How do *you* know about him?' said Arko.

'All the Centaurs know about him,' said Chiron bitterly. 'The evil little worm . . .'

Halo was surprised. Chiron was normally so moderate. 'Was he up here?' she asked.

'He was,' said Kyllarus. The adult Centaurs were glancing at each other, as if wondering how much to say.

'He was after Arko, at Delphi,' said Halo.

More glances.

'Tell us,' said Arko. 'You must tell us. We need to know what we're dealing with.'

Chiron told the story. 'He appeared in the woods a few weeks ago. He tried to shoot at a hunting party of ours. We concealed ourselves, and he wandered on into the Ixion lands. We had sent them a message, of course, to warn them, so they were aware, and concealed themselves too. He must have waited there, hiding, for days – but he found their grave-yard. The Ixions' gravedigger was there, and this human –'

Chiron's face twisted with disgust – 'this person tried to buy a dead Centaur from him. Offered him money. He said he'd rather have a recent one, but an old one would do, if it could be dug up for him, or a living one, if the gravedigger could hand one over. Any age, he said . . .'

Halo and Arko could hardly believe what they were hearing.

'What did the gravedigger say?'

'He told the human he'd think about it, and he reported it to their chief, Ixionas. So both tribes put guards on our graveyards, and we held a council, of the Sons of Cronus and the Sons of Ixion. We decided that he was a mortal threat. We voted to run him off the land; the Ixions voted to kill him. In the end we were too late to do either. He must have realized that the gravedigger was not playing his game, and we haven't seen him since. It appears he has left the woods.'

They pondered this for a moment.

'But what does he want?' asked Halo after a while.

'There is an old story,' said Kyllarus. 'A stupid legend based on nothing. It says . . . it says that a Centaur's heart can win any battle.'

For a moment, she was silent, as she thought this through. Some of the Centaurs stamped their hooves, others pursed their lips.

*That's disgusting*, thought Halo. *That is disgusting.* 'So no Centaur is safe,' she said, 'when he is around. Arko – you should stay here. It would be safer for you to be with the others. I can go back to Athens alone –'

'If you go back alone, he could capture you, and hold you

hostage knowing we must rescue you,' Arko replied thoughtfully. 'Plus, I really am not going to live my life in fear. If he wants a Centaur, he'll have to fight for it.'

'He's not a fighter. He's a trickster,' she said.

'Then he'll have to trick a Centaur, and that's not easy either,' Arko said. 'We know who he is, we know what he is and what he wants. We're prepared.'

Halo and Arko kept that thought in their mind the next day, on their journey back to Athens. They took the main road, travelled swiftly, and stayed at inns, not in the dark of the countryside. She had her bow at the ready, and they kept their eyes open, and their senses alert. They were not going to be tricked again.

It was a relief to get back inside the city walls. Halo was happy to see Aspasia, and to get back to school. It felt nice to know that both her families knew where she was. Even when one was threatened by a mad seer who wanted to kill someone and take out their heart, and the other was at war with Sparta . . . Still, everyone knew what they were up against, and that helped.

While they were away Pericles had led the entire Athenian army into Megara, the city on the Isthmus that had allowed the Spartan army through, giving them access to Attica. With every axe-blow into the trunk of a Megaran olive tree, the young men found it easier to forgive Pericles for keeping them inside the walls during the spring and summer. Halo heard that the Athenians did more damage in Megara than the Spartans had done during their invasion of Attica.

'Is *that* it then?' Halo asked Aspasia, as winter drew in and the sailors and soldiers of the fleet and the army returned – Pericles included.

Everyone was so glad to see him, so happy. *I'll tell him soon*, Halo told herself. *I don't want to spoil this moment though*.

'No,' Aspasia replied. 'It's over for the season, but it'll start up again next spring.'

Halo had watched Pericles go to war. She had watched Aspasia sit and wait for him to come back. She didn't want to be a man *or* a woman. She didn't want to be a grown-up at all.

Not everyone came home. Even a strange, suspended war like this one killed men, and there were mothers and wives and children whose family tables had an empty seat. As the weather grew colder, the Athenians held their great public funeral for the war dead. Halo and Arko saw the huge tent going up, and couldn't help staring sadly at the families bringing in the bones of the dead, and making their offerings. Then two days later came the funeral itself.

*It looks almost like the* pompe *of the Dionysia*, she thought as she stood by the road, watching the procession, *but the other way round – instead of coming into town celebrating fertility, it's heading out to Kerameikos and it's all about death*.

Wagon after wagon left the living city for the graveyard, bearing coffins of cypress wood filled with the bones of the men of each tribe, and followed by their relatives, mourning and lamenting. As the Skythians passed, she prayed for Lotess and Ando, the two who had been killed the day she helped Gyges. Then came an empty wagon: it was decorated as finely as the rest, and carried with as much honour. But there was no coffin, and no bones. This was for the men whose bodies had not been found. Later, when the coffins were laid in the tombs at the cemetery, she went and stood with those families, and listened as the women shrieked and wailed their formal and heartfelt laments. Part of her wanted to join in – but she was a boy, and boys did not shriek and wail at funerals.

Pericles had been chosen to make the oration to the dead. Halo watched him proudly as he came forward from the tomb and climbed up on to a high platform so that everybody could see and hear him. The sky was very blue behind his head, and though he had aged even in this past six months, to her he looked like a God would look, with his white beard and his wise eyes.

His voice was clear and true, and his words were too. She didn't understand a lot of what he said, but it made her heart fill up over and over. When he spoke of the courage and virtue of their ancestors, who had handed over the land, a free country; and when he spoke of everyone being equal, and free and tolerant before the law, because the law commands respect, she felt proud. When he said, 'Each of our citizens is able to show himself the rightful lord and owner of his own person,' she thought, *I am the lord and master of my own person* – but then she realized that actually, no, she wasn't, of course she wasn't. She was a girl, and half foreign. Then he was saying, 'Happiness depends on being free, and freedom depends on being courageous . . .' *Well, that's true*, she thought, and she laughed softly. For her, free-

dom depended on being a boy, and that took some courage
– more and more every day.

*I will have to stay a boy forever then*, she thought, *if I want
Pericles's good opinion*.

But she knew by now that Centaurs were pretty much
the only creatures in the world who didn't think that females
were less important than males. And she knew why – she
had worked it all out with Arko. It was because of War –
men were physically stronger, and made better soldiers. And
War was because of Fear – all the men were afraid of their
land and their women being taken away from them, so they
fought to protect them. And the women had to stay at home.
She'd talked about it with Aspasia. Aspasia had laughed, and
said, 'I'd like to see a man strong enough to have a baby.'

Her head was reeling from all the ideas which Pericles's
speech brought up in her.

'I wonder,' she said quietly to Arko as they walked home
afterwards, 'if anyone will ever say to Pericles, and the Athenians, that all that fine talk is wonderful and inspiring, but
it's not really true . . .'

'What, because of the slaves?' Arko replied.

'Yes! And the women! All that he was saying about every
Athenian being master of himself, and not being ruled by a
minority is only true if you're a grown-up, an Athenian
citizen, a man, and free. Even if I *was* a boy, I'd never be
master of my own self the way he means, because my mother
was a foreigner.'

Arko paced on, slowly, his hooves clopping on the stone
road.

'They're a lot freer here than anywhere else though,' he said mildly.

'I suppose,' she said. 'But a lot of that is because they've conquered everywhere else and get money off them. The people they've conquered aren't exactly free, are they?'

Arko laughed. 'Don't say that too loud,' he said. 'People will think you're a Spartan sympathizer.'

'Well I'm not!' she exclaimed, walloping his flank – one of the good things about Arko was you could hit him as hard as you liked and he hardly noticed. 'I just wish they could be a bit freer with their freedom, that's all.'

Still, she was reassured that the funeral without the body was all right for the lost soldiers. It comforted her to see how much care and attention was paid to the dead.

'Halo,' Aspasia asked one wintry night, though she knew the answer. 'Have you spoken to Pericles?'

'No,' Halo replied. She was ashamed. 'You know I haven't.'

'Will you ever?'

'I don't know how I can now.'

Aspasia was quiet. 'Circumstances have not helped you,' she said. She looked at her fondly. 'My dear,' she said, 'are you sure you want to continue like this?'

Halo looked up. She knew what Aspasia was talking about.

'Aspasia,' she said, 'I know of no women who heal the sick, who set bones and remove arrowheads. When a woman can be a doctor, then I will be a girl again.'

Aspasia made a little face, as if to say, *Well, of course you have a point*, then she sighed, and then she said, carefully,

'When you came here, my dear, you wanted to know who you are. You *are* a girl, Halo, whatever you may think about it. Younger girls than you are married, are mothers . . . What of your future? I could find you a husband, you could grow your hair, change your name, nobody need know . . .'

*I can't think about that . . .*

Aspasia kept watching her.

Finally she said, 'In the meantime, you may want to bind your chest.' She handed her a roll of bandage. 'You're growing.'

## Χαπτερ 28

One morning in May, two days after Archidamus and the Spartans returned to ravage Attica again, Gyges the Skythian woke with a filthy headache. He rolled over on his straw pallet, got up anyway, poured a jar of cold water over his head and hoped the pain would go once he had eaten.

The country folk were already filing back into Athens. Halo stared at the clanking wagons and worried faces, at the distant columns of smoke rising against the clear blue sky. As she walked down to the Skythians' compound, she saw how swiftly the city was filling up again. Already, shacks had been rebuilt along the walls, lean-tos and makeshift roofs had appeared almost overnight alongside the temples and shrines, tents and little piles of bedding were beginning to fill the arcades and the grounds and gardens. Again, the sections of land between the walls towards Piraeus, the Pelagian Quarter and the marketplaces had become camps for the refugees. She thought of the ravaged farms she had seen the previous summer, and she felt sorry for them. How lucky she was, having a home.

And strange, she thought, that a whole year had passed – more than a year. Here she was, a year older, a year wiser. A year taller. *A year more Athenian*, she thought, smiling, as she strode easily down streets that she now knew as well as she used to know the fig groves of northern Zakynthos. *With a year's more experience of doctoring. Yes, and a year more female*

… She might be fourteen by now, a tall girl, stronger through the good Athenian food, but still skinny and rangy. Her breasts were small, but even so she bound a cloth round her chest every day beneath her chiton. When her periods had started, Aspasia had helped her. Without Aspasia, she could not have kept the secret. Even the slaves in the house did not know. She no longer told herself she was a boy though. How could she be a boy now? Other people would see her as a boy, she would make sure of that. But inside, she told herself she was a warrior girl, an Amazon. A secret Amazon. It made her feel better about lying to everybody. One day she would be able to tell Pericles that she was a secret Amazon, and he would respect that. He would understand why she had to do it. Surely . . .

She felt almost cheerful. It wasn't that she didn't mind about the war. It was just – she felt at home now. She felt capable. If the war this year was the same as it had been last time, well, it would not be too bad. Well, of course it was bad. But you could live with it. Pericles would reassure the city. Everybody knew it couldn't last too long. It had been all right last year. Again, the Athenians would grit their teeth and get on with it.

Arimaspou and Akinakes greeted her.

'Any Spartans today?' she said, with dark cheerfulness.

'No,' said Arimaspou. 'We rode out at dawn, and patrolled all day, but there's nothing going on within reach of Athens. It's been quiet so far. But have a look at Gyges,' he added. 'He's not well . . .'

Gyges was on his pallet inside. Dusk was drawing in, so

Halo lit a lamp. Even before its flame steadied so Halo could see him properly, she could sense his illness. There was a sour smell in the room, and his eyes when she drew close to him were red and painful-looking. She was sorry to see it. Gyges was special to her – the Skythian who had brought them into Athens (there had been many jokes about that) and the first patient she had ever helped. She liked him to be well and healthy.

'What are you feeling, friend?' she said gently. She had learned a lot from Hippias over the past year. There were many things she could do to make a sick man comfortable while his humours realigned themselves, and nature ran her course.

'That my head is on fire,' said Gyges. His voice shocked her – it was gravelly and rasping.

'Since when?' she asked.

'This morning,' he said. 'And my throat too.'

'Open your mouth,' she said. 'Let me look . . .'

The youth let his jaw drop. Halo peered in – and had to hold herself very firm not to reel back in dismay.

His mouth in the dim lamplight was dark and red with blood.

'Have you bitten your tongue?' she asked, steadying her voice.

'No,' he said. He was blinking as if his eyes hurt. 'But I know my throat is bleeding. I have been wiping blood from my mouth since noon . . .'

'I have never seen or heard of anything like this,' she said quietly. 'I will go to Hippias and ask him. Rest, and remember to eat, even though it must be difficult. I'll come back as soon as I have found out what to do.'

He smiled his thanks, and she went back outside.

'Well?' asked Arimaspou, who was sewing a tear in his arrow bag with a leather thong.

'He is sick,' said Halo. 'I don't know what it is. I'm going to ask Hippias about it.'

Arimaspou grunted. 'Let's hope it passes quickly,' he said.


It did pass quickly. Within a week, Gyges was dead.

He had bled, and sneezed and coughed, he had vomited every kind of bile, his body had been racked by spasms and retching, his skin had turned red, and erupted in pustules and ulcers, he had been unable to bear even the lightest cloth to cover him. By the fifth day, he was unable to sleep, or even to lie still, and he had been consumed and burned up by a terrible terrible thirst, which all the water his brothers brought him could not quench. Finally, with a kind of mad strength, he had torn himself from his bed in the middle of the night, run into the street and down to the canal, where he had drowned himself in his desperate need for water.

But within that week, Athens had become a different city.

Halo had gone straight to Hippias's house after seeing Gyges on his sickbed for the first time. The house was unusually crowded.

'Halo!' the doctor called. He looked pale and intent. 'How useful you should turn up. Come, help me.' He didn't offer her cake.

'I come only with a question,' she said. 'It's late, and Aspasia will wonder where I am.'

'Does your question concern a burning head and a bleeding throat?' he asked.

'It does,' she said, surprised.

'Tell me it is not *your* head and *your* throat,' he said, turning to her, fear in his eyes.

'It is not,' she replied.

'Thank the Gods,' he said. 'I'm glad of it. Though I think it's the only thing I *am* glad of. Who is it?'

'Gyges the Skythian,' she said. She knew Hippias didn't approve of her tending the Skythians – he thought she hadn't enough experience and knowledge to take the responsibility – but he knew too that they wouldn't see any other doctor.

'The Skythians too,' he murmured.

'Only one of them,' she said.

'The day before yesterday, my child,' Hippias said, turning his dark eyes on her, 'only one person came to me, speaking of a relative very weak with a burning head and foul-smelling blood in his mouth. Yesterday, six. Today, twelve. How many tomorrow?'

'What can we do for them?' she cried.

He didn't answer for a moment, then he said, 'I was going to spend this evening reading every treatise I can find, to see what is recommended. But as you see –'

The courtyard was full of supplicants. They were not ill – they wanted Hippias to visit the sick person, who was elsewhere. He could not possibly visit them all.

'You're lucky to have caught me,' he said. 'Please, go

inside and look through my library – see what you can find that will help us to treat these symptoms.'

'Can I send your boy to Aspasia, to tell her why I am late?' she asked.

He smiled at her, nodded, and turned to leave with the next supplicant.

She spent that whole night reading, and finding little of any use. Comfrey and plantain might help with the bleeding; a tea of terebinthine to cleanse the mouth, feverfew for the heat . . . nothing new. She fell asleep at Hippias's desk. That was where he found her, returning from a house call, about to go out again on another.

'Go home,' he said. 'Go on.' She heard his voice in her dream.

'No,' she murmured. 'Haven't finished yet . . .' The lamp had burned out, and a slight moon shone from the doorway. Outside, all was dark and strangely quiet. In the distance she heard someone weeping.

'Halo,' he said. She blinked, and tried to be awake. 'Go home. You will need to be strong, to take good care of yourself. Something very harsh has come among us . . .'

She looked at him, his face tired and pale. 'What is it?' she asked.

'I don't know,' he said sadly. 'It is like everything at once. I have seen more than twenty people now, twenty people with red inflamed eyes and bloody throats and mouths, vomiting, coughing, with stomach aches, aches in their chests, spasms . . . all in such pain . . . yet days ago I hadn't seen one.'

Halo tried to make sense of it. How could so many people

suddenly be sick like this? Where did a sickness come from, that it could fall so strongly on so many people, just like that? Oh.

There was a name for a sickness like that.

It was not a name she wanted to utter.

'Hippias?' she asked. She looked up at him, and her eyes were solemn. 'I heard there was a plague, in Lemnos,' she said carefully. 'Hippias – is this the plague?'

The doctor had tears in his eyes. 'I don't know,' he said. 'I am lucky, I have never seen the plague. But I fear . . . I fear that if I saw the plague, it would look like this. I fear that this is the plague.'

'Will they die?' Halo asked. Her mouth was trembling. She locked her teeth together to hold her strength. *Phobos.*

'Yes,' he said. 'They will die. Dark Hades will grow rich. The Gods have mercy on us all.'

The school had closed. Three of the masters were sick, and one dead already. How many of the students, they didn't know.

'It's worst among the country people,' Hippias said. He had a big plate of baklava before him, and he was stuffing pieces of it methodically into his mouth as he talked. 'They all live so close together in their camps, and they have no way to be clean even if they want to . . . They have no clean water supply, and nowhere to relieve themselves, and the sickness has gathered in the air around them . . .'

Halo knew it was true. She and Arko had seen a country slave lying in the street, his eyes red. *He shouldn't be here*, she thought. They had spoken to him – he had said he wasn't ill, he was fine, he was just going home, he was staying with his owners by the Long Walls, he was all right. He didn't look all right. But what could they do?

Hippias had found nothing that could help – just the usual herbs and diets. Nothing new. Nothing special. 'So do you mean that people will just have to suffer this illness, like any other?' she asked him.

'Yes,' Hippias said. He stopped munching, and put his hands over his face. 'We can try to make them comfortable – but they won't be. We can try to keep them strong so they survive – but perhaps that will only prolong their suffering. Perhaps,'. he said, and he gave her the saddest look she had ever seen, 'the best we can do for them is to let them die quickly.'

She could hardly believe that kind, good Hippias was saying something so terrible.

It all happened so fast. Gyges was dead within the first week, and after he died, Arimaspou said she was no longer to come. 'If there is no cure, and no help, then there is no need for the doctor,' he said. His face was as hard when he said it as it had been the first time she had seen him. It was as if there had been no friendship between them, no teaching and learning, no joking and growing fond.

'You should stay at home,' he said harshly. 'Children should be at home. Don't come here again.'

Children! She was fourteen now. If she'd been a real girl her family would have been marrying her off . . . She was no child. But she didn't argue with Arimaspou. He wouldn't even look at her.

'Let me at least mourn for Gyges with you,' she said, and

she was biting back tears as she said it, but Arimaspou was relentless.

'No,' he said. 'Go home, and stay home. We don't want you here.'

She knew why he said it. He didn't want her get the plague too. It still hurt, though, to be sent away.

She strode home with her lips clenched and her teeth aching. Poor sweet Gyges, whose leg she had saved, and all for nothing. She had her head down, barging along, so angry and upset.

She barged straight into somebody.

'Sorry,' she muttered, and glanced up. Shock grabbed her. It was Manticlas.

Without pausing, instinctively, she dropped her head again and scurried swiftly on.

Had he seen her? Recognized her? *What's he doing in Athens?* That was the last place she expected to see him. He was a Spartan! They were at war! And who would come here, now the plague is blossoming? She must warn Arko – she must find Arko NOW.

She rushed home, calling for Arko as she ran into the courtyard.

'He's not back yet,' Tiki called.

*He'll be coming from the gym – I'll go and meet him*, she was thinking – but at that moment Aspasia, pale and fretted, grabbed her arm.

'You're not to go out any more,' she said, without preamble. 'It's not safe.'

'I have to find Arko!' Halo said. 'I have to go now –'

'Arko is on his way home,' said Aspasia. 'He'll be here soon. You have to stay in now, Halo.'

She was deadly serious. And Evangelus had locked the courtyard gate.

*Arko's on his way . . . He'll be here soon. It'll be all right.*

'You're not to go anywhere,' Aspasia was saying. 'Not to the Skythians, not to school, not to Hippias . . .'

'Not to Hippias!' Halo exclaimed.

'Most of all not to Hippias,' said Aspasia. 'Halo – my dear – let me tell you . . . Doctors, since they are most in contact with the sick, are among the first to die. We will all stay in the house now. Pericles has said. We will not let the plague feed on us.'

Halo desperately wanted – needed – to go to Hippias. She wanted to discuss with him how they could find a way of treating these poor people, or a way of making them comfortable at least, or a way of stopping the miasmas[10] of the plague from attaching the sickness to you, or a way of preventing it coming into a city . . . Why did plague behave as it did? It didn't care who it took – true, the refugees from the countryside were suffering most, but some rich people had caught it now, as well – rich people, poor people, old people, young people, healthy people like Gyges, weak people like that country slave in the street. People who worshipped the Gods, and people who neglected their duty. She wanted to find out all about the plague. They couldn't just let it stalk the city, casting people down, and nothing to be done – there must be something they could do.

'But . . .!' she protested . . . But she knew she would do

as Aspasia asked. As Pericles asked. Though it felt like deserting the city, and ignoring her heartfelt desire, she and Arko would stay home, and stay healthy.

Only it didn't work out like that. That night, even before Arko came home, before she could warn him that Manticlas was in Athens, Halo developed a headache.

There had never been such pain. A hundred broken arms could be stretched and reset, a thousand skulls could break on a thousand underwater rocks . . . Her head was burning. Her throat was burning. Wet, and burning, and tasting of old, wet metal.

Her arms were shivering. Someone was trying to feed her. Foul coughing tore her burning throat. She was sick – blood and vomit.

'I have the plague!' she shouted. 'Do I? Am I to die? I won't die! I won't die!' She shouted a lot. Someone was trying to soothe her. 'Go away!' she shouted. 'Go away . . .' She couldn't eat – there was nothing in her stomach to puke, but she kept puking. Her chest was burning, her lungs, her heart, her stomach. Someone was wiping her mouth, giving her water. Her body was stiff, stiff with spasm, but coughing and puking still. She was hot, her skin burning, she wanted to tear it off. Someone was bathing it with cool wet cloths; she felt the skin would come off in strips, washed off with the water, long tender red strips. She was horribly, horribly thirsty.

Her mind was not her own. Her mind was . . . she had no mind to know where her mind was. Asclepius, Apollo, she called, in her mind, perhaps in reality too. Her body was not her own. A million insects owned it, twitched it, crawled in it. She just burned, and wailed with fear, and it never ended.

And then it did. She woke. The room was dark and cool. Someone was in the room.

'Come,' it said. It was a woman, dark-haired, dark-eyed, with a face that didn't care. 'Come, and it will be over.'

Halo didn't want to go with her. 'No!' she cried loudly, and the sound of her voice, strong now, woke the other person in the room – she hadn't known there was another person. He was lying asleep, his head on his arms, across the end of her bed. She wailed, 'No!' to the woman, and he lifted his head. His green eyes were clear.

'Go away,' Halo wailed. 'I don't want you to die. Go away, Leonidas . . .'

'I'm not going,' he said. 'I'm staying with you.'

'Come on,' said the woman, gently, to Halo, and at that Leonidas jumped up lightly, and grinned, and laughed at the woman, saying, 'Come and get her. If you dare.'

And the woman glared at him, and he laughed again, and came back and sat by Halo. He took her hand, wiped her face with a cool cloth, and gave her water to drink.

When Halo looked up, the woman was waiting, looking bored.

'She's not coming,' Leonidas said. 'You can stand there as long as you want.'

The woman stood.

Leonidas was stroking Halo's hair.

She slept.

She woke.

The woman was still there in the doorway.

Leonidas was still there by her bed.

'You're not going, are you?' he said to her, and Halo smiled and said, 'No.'

Leonidas turned to the woman. She seemed to be fading.

'See you next time,' he said cheerfully. 'Bye!'

'Bye!' Halo called.

Then she was asleep again. The next time she woke she was being held over a pot, her bowels lurching. For three days and nights every waking moment she was propped up on the pot. Someone fed her water, and emptied the pot and coaxed chicken broth into her poor bashed-up mouth.

It was no longer bleeding.

She was no longer puking.

She lay in bed another week, not speaking. Then one morning she said, 'Where's Leonidas?'

'Out in the olive groves in Paralia, hacking down good Attic trees,' said Arko. 'No doubt.'

Her eyes were still closed. So were Arko's. He was so tired, so very tired. He had been at her side throughout her illness. He didn't know if she was properly conscious now or not. She'd talked all kinds of chaotic nonsense over the past few weeks. Who knew what was real to her or what was not?

'No, he was here,' she said.

'They didn't come near Athens,' he said. 'They saw the smoke from our funeral pyres; they heard the stories told by runaways more scared of the plague than of the Spartans.

They're ravaging round Laurium instead – cleaner, healthier air, down by the sea. They didn't have to come and scare us – the Gods have got us half dead already – why should the Spartans bother?'

'He was here,' she murmured. 'Who are you?'

'Arko!' he said – but he jumped up at this question, and paid attention. 'Halo? Halo!'

'Halo?' she said. 'Hmm. I don't know. Are you a friend of Leonidas?'

'I'm *your* friend,' he said. 'Are you awake?'

'Oh yes,' she said. 'Mmm. Awake. Hungry.'

Arko fed her three bowls of *kykeon*. She was too weak to feed herself.

'Leonidas *was* here,' she said. 'Death was here. She asked for me. Leonidas told her to come and get me, if she could.'

'Death is a woman?' Arko asked.

'Yes.'

'And you saw her?'

'Yes,' said Halo.

'But you didn't die . . .'

'Leonidas wouldn't let me,' she said.

L ater, when she was better, she thought it very strange
that Death had waited so long for her before giving up.
As far as Halo could remember, Death had been there by
her bed for a while. Arko said, judging by what Halo had
been saying, it had been most of one night.

'You'd think, wouldn't you,' Halo said, 'that she'd be busy
elsewhere. With all the other people dying.'

'You'd think,' said Arko.

Many, many people had died while Halo was sick. All the
schoolmasters had died. The man from whom the cook
bought vegetables had died. Two slaves next door but one
had died. More than a thousand of the four thousand Hoplites
sent to Potidaea had died. Pericles's sister had died.

'But I have not died,' said Halo.

'No,' said Arko.

'And you have not caught it,' Halo said to Arko sharply.
'Even though you were nursing me.'

'No,' he said with a shrug.

'Though you could have.'

'I suppose,' he said, looking embarrassed.

'You risked your life,' she said.

'Yes, well . . .' he said. 'We didn't want anyone else changing your chiton, did we? And actually, I think Centaurs don't
get it. I've never heard of a plague among Centaurs. And it
doesn't affect horses.'

'Interesting,' she said. 'But you don't know for sure. So you're a fool – unless – have the doctors found any way of treating it? What did you do to care for me?' she asked, suddenly eager.

'No, they have found nothing,' he said. 'Hippocrates himself has come from Cos – he is recommending sea water, and burning fragrant smoke, with pitch and resin – but nothing is changing.'

'Smoke!' said Halo. 'Interesting. Where is he? I want to hear him speak . . .'

'When you're stronger,' said Arko.

'I feel strong!' Halo said. 'I feel . . . how long have I been ill?'

'Two weeks,' said Arko.

'Hm,' she said. 'And how are Pericles and Aspasia?'

'He's leaving soon,' said Arko. 'He's taking the fleet round the Peloponnesian coast: Epidaurus, Troezen, Hermione, Prasiae. He'll be off as soon as the Spartans leave. There are some things to be grateful for.'

As soon as Halo was well enough, Arko took her out. They went to see Hippias. The city, as they walked across, was as strange to her as the weak legs she walked on. The sky was still blue, the sun was still bright, the air was still clear . . . but it was very different. The streets of the city, normally so noisy and lively, were quiet, almost empty. Such people as they did see were sad and subdued. Passing houses, through the open windows they heard not the usual laughter or conversation or the busy sounds of everyday work, but sighs, and muffled footsteps, and bursts of wailing from women and children, wails of pain, or of loss and mourning. They passed three funeral processions, the women crying, the men stern-faced. In the *agora*, a few knots of people were gathered. One was shouting – what was Pericles going to do about it? The Gods were angry! Athens was polluted! Something must be done.

Some of the country people, it seemed, had left already, heading back home now that the Spartans had retreated. Scraps of their makeshift houses stood forlorn by the walls of the temples, dirty and neglected in the hot sun. A small girl sat by one of them, her face tear-stained. By another, a dog ran to and fro, sniffing, lost. But most of the shacks were still occupied – the country refugees sat in the shade by the walls, very still, very quiet. They looked as if they feared attracting attention – as if, if they made any noise or moved too fast, the plague would notice them, and come and get them. The angry voices from the *agora* were still audible, but these people took no notice.

Out in the town that day, Halo did not see a single person smile.

'This is terrible,' she whispered to Arko. 'This is so terrible.'

'Nobody knows what to do,' Arko replied. 'Nobody knows what has caused it. One of the market boys is telling everyone he saw Spartans poisoning the reservoirs down at Piraeus . . .'

'Is it true?' she gasped.

'No one knows,' he said. 'The priests are saying that Apollo is offended, because the Pythia told the Athenians never to occupy that bit of land – you know the Pelagian

Quarter? By the Acropolis? They are reminding everyone of the plague at Thebes, caused by the blood-pollution of Oedipus, when he murdered his father, and married his mother – and of how Apollo sent a plague on Agamemnon's army at Troy, when Agamemnon disrespected his priest . . .'

Halo remembered Homer's description of Apollo's piercing silver arrows, raining down on Agamemnon's men for nine days and nights, slaughtering them. Was that what had happened to her? Had Apollo shot her down?

She couldn't believe it. After all, Apollo had been kind to her – he'd told her who her parents were, and given her back her owl. And why would he be *so* angry with Athens, to send such a curse on them, when they were already at war? Or was it the truth of what the Pythia had told Melesippus and Leonidas – that Apollo really was on the Spartans' side?

She thought about the sharp, hard arrowhead she had removed from Gyges's calf. She thought about flesh and blood and the four humours, and the Hippocratic books Hippias had given her to read. She thought about mosquito bites, and how they can fill with pus if you scratch too much, and how doctors who are clean have better results than doctors who are dirty. She remembered: 'Do not concern yourself with plausible theories, but with experience combined with reason.'

She thought it far more likely that, as Hippocrates had said, a miasma had blown into the city on the wind, and people had breathed it in, and that was how the sickness entered.

'Teacher,' she said to Hippias the next day, 'is it

disrespectful of me to believe that the plague has a physical cause, and is not caused by the wrath of the Gods?'

'It is reasonable of you,' he said. 'You are a reasonable boy in a city that was beginning to be reasonable, but seems now to be going backwards.' He was happy to see her, but it was a tiny happiness in the face of the amount of grief he was seeing every day.

He told her he was not visiting the sick any more. 'There is no point,' he said. 'There's nothing I can do, and the more I see, the more likely I will take the plague myself, and then I cannot heal anybody, of anything. Where is the justice in that? Apollo would not inflict such injustice. This is not the work of the Gods.'

'So what are you saying to those who come to you?'

'I am telling them that there is nothing I or anyone can do,' he said, and he looked ashamed. 'And then they go and waste their money on witchdoctors and all kinds of superstitious rubbish instead.'

'It's not your fault,' she said softly.

'All I want to do is heal people,' he said, so sadly, and she reached out and touched his hand.

'Tell me,' she asked. 'Has anybody else survived? Or is everybody dying?'

'Some are living through it,' he said. 'One is blind, I heard of yesterday. One has lost his memory completely; he is like a mad man, he knows nobody. Several have lost fingers and toes, it's not known why.'

He looked queryingly at Halo.

'I am whole,' she said thoughtfully. 'Thin and weak, but

every part of me is working. How can I show my gratitude for that?'

Hippias was looking at her, smiling.

'What?' she said.

'Everyone in Athens is cursing fortune and the Gods, distraught at the misery, the war, the plague, the horrors – and you speak of gratitude.'

Halo laughed. He was quite right. And yet she did feel grateful. She wasn't dead!

Halo was up on the Acropolis one morning, getting some clean air, as Hippias had advised her, when a thought struck her: *Why haven't I caught the plague again? If I had it before, and you catch it from being near it, or near to people who have it, why didn't I catch it again – even from myself?* She ran to Hippias's to talk to him about it.

'If we're agreed it's not from the water, and not from the Gods, but it's the same plague that came from Libya, and was at Lemnos, and arrived first at Piraeus, so it has travelled in the air, or through the people . . . So why haven't I caught it from myself again?'

Hippias gave her a very straight look. 'You will make a good doctor,' he said. 'I haven't told you before, because I didn't want to give you an unprovable hope, but so far nobody who has taken the plague has taken it twice. People die on the seventh day, or the eleventh. Nobody, that I have heard of, has taken it twice.'

Halo immediately understood.

'Then I am safe,' she said.

'It looks that way,' said Hippias.

'Then I can help the sufferers,' she said.

'There is no help,' he started to say, but she interrupted him.

'I cannot cure them,' she said. 'But I can give them cool water during the time of the great thirst. I can go and talk to them, when their family can't, without risk of death. Nobody was ever made worse by a bowl of soup, or a cool cloth on the forehead. I can relieve suffering, and I can take notes, and I can observe, and apply reason to my observations, and – can I?' She was pleading with him.

'I can't stop you,' he said.

So she did. But first, she went down to the Skythian barracks and shouted into their compound, 'Hey, Arimaspou! I'm immune! I've had the plague and I can't get it again – so do you still reject me, or can I come in?'

And Arimaspou, when he came out, hugged her. Of course she jumped back in alarm. No one could hug her. It was too risky, now she had a girl's figure. But she was very glad, all the same, that Arimaspou had welcomed her back.

Walking home that evening, Halo and Arko could smell the smoke from the funeral pyres. She flared her nostrils against it, swallowing and trying not to breathe. It smelt like meat cooking. She didn't want that smell inside her.

In the *agora*, as they crossed, she heard a man shouting. 'Who brought this war on us? Pericles! Who didn't listen to the Delphic Oracle? Pericles! Who has let the Spartans ruin our land and destroy our farms? Pericles! Who brought all the country people into the city, where there is no room for them? Pericles! Who let them occupy the Pelagian Quarter, and brought down Apollo's wrath on us? Pericles! The Oracle said we can't win. And how can we win, when this man won't even let us fight but keeps us locked up inside the walls like a bunch of girls! And how can we fight now anyway, now that we are dying, dropping in the street? You all know who is to blame for this . . .'

The group of men around him were nodding and agreeing. Halo glanced at Arko. They hurried on through the slackening light.

As they passed the corner a dirty-looking man called out softly to them, 'Plague cure! Best plague cure! Magic medicine from Persia, it costs but it works, and what price life, eh?'

It was the rabbit-foot amulet man – they had seen him around.

He put his hand on Halo's arm to stop her, and she turned on him, hissing, 'You should be ashamed of yourself!'

'Just offering a little hope, in dark times,' the man said, offended.

'Just making a little money out of human misery,' Halo spat, and marched on.

'Loosen up, sweetheart!' the man shouted after her. 'Cheer yourself up! Buy a new dress!'

Halo froze in her tracks.

He thought she was a girl.

'Bound to happen,' muttered Arko, alongside her.

'I know,' she said. 'But . . .'

'You have to tell Pericles,' he said. 'You've been really lucky to get away with it so long.'

Arko had said nothing about this for months.

Halo cursed.

At home, Aspasia was weeping in her chamber, Pericles was striding up and down the courtyard, and Tiki and Samis were hiding. Pericles glanced at Halo and Arko, and they quickly removed themselves too. Even so, they couldn't help hearing what was being said, as Pericles tried to persuade Aspasia to come out and talk to him.

'My dear,' he called softly, at her door.

Halo was embarrassed to hear what was not meant for her ears, and Arko was looking at his hands and pretending he *couldn't* hear.

'My dear – my son Xanthippus is angry with me because I wouldn't pay his debts. That is why he is telling these lies. You know that. He calls me stingy because I won't let him be extravagant . . .'

'That's not all he says . . .' cried Aspasia angrily.

Halo winced to hear the kind voice sounding so hurt.

'I know what is being said. I know he says I waste my time talking about philosophy when I should be fighting . . . Aspasia, you can't believe that is true . . .'

'Of course I don't believe it!' she says. 'That's not why I am upset! I am upset because . . . because you let people say these things. You are blamed for everything, and you are slandered, and I hate it! Not just for you, but because who will lead Athens when you are cast out? What will become of us without you? They'll elect some fool like Cleon, and then what? They have already sent ambassadors to Sparta, asking for peace . . .'

'My dear, they won't reject me to make Cleon leader . . .'

'Anything can happen now,' she said, her voice falling. 'Athens is full of fear and panic and death and blame. Anything can happen.'

*Dear Gods*, Halo thought. *The world has changed completely in the few weeks I was ill.*

Pericles spoke to the Athenians the next day. Halo went down to the Assembly to listen. He told them he understood their anger; that bad things happened and that was all the more reason to stick to thought-out plans rather than panic; he told them that they had known there would be suffering, he told them that they were stronger than they knew, and that the reason Athens has the greatest name in the world is because she has never given in to adversity. He was full of strength and determination, and Halo's heart was full of pride for him and for Athens.

Then, a few days later, 'They're prosecuting me,' he announced, after dinner. 'I am to leave office, and pay a fine.'

'What for?' Halo asked, aghast.

'For not being superhuman, I think,' he said. 'For not being able to make everything all right. But do you know what?'

'What?' she asked.

'That is the least of anyone's problems.'

He looked so tired. Later, she brought him a cup of wine, and laid her arm across his shoulders.

'I'm glad you didn't die,' he said, looking round at her with a little smile. 'My extra son.'

When he said that, smiling up at her like she was his one comfort in the wicked world, a panicky feeling came over her.

She had to tell him.

She felt as if she were going to vomit, choking on the words.

*Say it.*

Arms prickling.

'I'm a girl,' she said.

He didn't take it in. How could he?

'Uncle, I'm a girl,' she repeated.

He stared at her, blank-faced.

'I'm a girl. A kind of Amazon. I had to pretend to be a boy. I never meant to lie to you.'

'What nonsense . . .?' he said.

'I'm a girl,' she said again, and she kneeled in front of him. Whatever he said now, she had to accept it.

He said nothing, just staring at her. She did her best to explain, in fumbling words. She didn't know if he was understanding her.

Aspasia came in, with a soft rustle of the folds of her dress.

Pericles asked, 'Did you know?'

She lowered her head.

'I see I am made a fool in my own house. So, I lose a second son. And is that your only lie? Or have you been lying about other things too? Are you Megacles's child at all?'

'Yes!' she shouted. Then: 'I'm sorry. I deserve anything you say. But I am his child. At least, the Pythia said so.'

'A girl,' he said. 'Well, Aspasia,' he said, standing up, 'find her some girls' clothes, and some girls' activities, and tell the school – whatever you like. That my son is dead. Tell the household we have a female cousin. Keep her out of my sight. Get a husband for her. If anyone will have her.'

'But, sir,' Halo said.

'But what?' Pericles turned. His voice was furious.

'My schooling, sir,' she said. 'My studies with Hippias . . .'

'What, are you mad as well as female? Learn to sew, girl, and to be quiet.'

'I can sew, sir,' she said quietly. 'I sew the wounds of the Skythian Guard . . .' but he cut her off.

'Mad,' he said. 'Or stupid or ridiculous.'

'No,' she replied, and she never knew where she found the courage, the determination. 'Just female. And determined.'

'Determined on what?'

'To continue and become a doctor, sir,' she said quietly.

A silence fell.

'Not from this house,' he said.

Silence fell all around, like impossibility. He would not listen. He could not allow it.

Halo felt it closing in around her.

'Then from somewhere else, sir,' she said, her voice smaller than ever. It was all she could say. She knew who she was now, and she could not give it up.


Halo left right then. If Pericles was determined to make a conventional girl of her, there was no point in drawing it out. She left in the clothes she was wearing, and walked through the night down to Piraeus, where she lay on her back on the dock wall and listened to the sea crunch and pound, staring at the black sky, watching the familiar stars, listening to the last shouts and rustles of the port at night, and the first comings and goings in the morning. The stone was hard and uncomfortable beneath her.

*I am doing the right thing. I am doing what I have to do.*

As soon as the sun was up, she walked back up to the *agora*, to the barber who cut her hair.

'Shave my head,' she said.

The barber feared that she, like so many others, had lost her mind in the weirdness of the times. But she hadn't. She was purely sane.

Shaven-headed and sleek, with her tattoo more than ever like wings across her forehead, she returned to Aspasia's house and gathered her few possessions together. Quickly and determinedly, she hugged Aspasia.

'Don't go,' said Aspasia, with tears in her eyes. 'We can sort this out.'

But Halo didn't let herself stop to be affected. She shouldered her bag, said, 'Thank you for everything. I won't forget you,' and swung out of the courtyard.

It seemed the familiar road to the Skythian barracks already had her footsteps marked out for her to follow.

'Pericles has thrown me out,' she said to Arimaspou, in a voice that brooked no discussion. 'I know you've got room for me.' She marched into the men's sleeping quarters, and pointed to Gyges's old cell. 'Is that still empty?' She flung her bag down on Gyges's bare pallet bed, and then sat down, suddenly. She looked up at Arimaspou. Her eyes were huge, the shadows under them deep. But there was a new light in her face.

'Why?' asked Arimaspou.

'He doesn't think I should be a doctor,' she said, 'and I do . . .'

Even as she said it, she knew she was being unfair. But everything else was unfair – why shouldn't she be too?

'No more family, Arimaspou,' she said, with a tight grin. 'Just duty now.'

Arimaspou's face was very thoughtful, as he moved away to tell the cook there was one more for dinner. And when Arko arrived, Arimaspou was not surprised.


Halo would not go back to Aspasia's house. She couldn't bear to witness the hurt she had caused. It was Arko who over the next days visited Aspasia, and brought news.

'Aspasia says to tell you that Pericles has not told anyone your secret. She asked him if he would, and he just shook his head angrily. She thinks he will calm down, and that you will be able to come home . . . but not yet . . .'

'Aspasia says, if you need soap, they are making a new batch tomorrow, and shall she send you some?'

'Aspasia says, did you hear, Pericles is back in office again? They didn't last long without him, did they?'

And then, 'Aspasia says to tell you that Pericles's son Paralus has taken the plague.'

Halo went to Paralus's funeral. She stood in the weeping crowd. Half of Athens – those who were not sick and dying themselves – were there, weeping for their own dead as much as for Paralus. They watched with hollow eyes as Pericles, the strong, steady, safe and wise Pericles, broke down and wept when the wreath was laid. Pericles, who never broke down. Pericles, on whom Athens depended as if he were the city's foundation stone.

Halo watched him from a distance, and her arms ached to go to him, to hug him. She wished she could say, 'I am a boy, I am your son, you still have me . . .'

But he did not want her. She was only a girl.

# Χαπτερ 30

'You've done the right thing,' Arko said. 'You had to tell him, and if he doesn't accept it, there's nothing you can do.'

Halo knew he was talking about wanting to be a doctor, not about wanting to be a boy. She didn't want to be a boy. She just wanted to be free. Why did it have to be so complicated? All she wanted to do was follow her instinct. And being a doctor was good and useful. Why would anyone object?

But they would – if they knew. And Pericles could tell anyone, any time.

'You know, don't you,' said Arko, 'that he's upset about being lied to as much as he is upset about you being a girl?'

She knew. And she realized what that meant.

Dragging her heart behind her like a reluctant dog on a chain through the fearful empty streets, she went to Hippias. Round his house a small crowd was gathered as usual, people desperate for help even though they knew there was nothing to be done. He was there, with his books and his dish of cakes, as usual. He looked up as she entered, glad as always to see her.

*You won't be so glad in a moment*, she thought.

'Hippias,' she said, as firmly as she could, though her heart was fluttering. *Perhaps I could go to Cos, and start again as a boy there, with a new name, a new life* … 'Hippias, I am no longer the adopted son of Pericles …'

'What are you talking about?' he said, smoothing down his already sleek hair, looking at her uncomprehendingly.

'I'm nobody,' she said bitterly.

He stared.

'I'm a girl.'

'You're a girl,' he repeated.

'I'm a girl.'

'You're raving,' he said. 'From the plague. You're still raving . . .'

'No. I'm a girl.'

'I am astonished,' he said. 'But you're such a quick learner –'

'Maybe all girls are,' she said. 'How would anyone know?'

More than anything, Hippias was puzzled. 'Why are you a girl?' he asked.

'I was born that way,' she said drily. 'I have had to pretend to be a boy, in order to be allowed to learn anything *at all*.'

Hippias put down his piece of baklava. 'So have you come to tell me you can no longer work with me?' he asked.

She laughed a little. 'No, I've come to hear you say you no longer want me.'

He rubbed his nose thoughtfully. 'Is it still secret?' he asked.

'You are the first I have told, other than Aspasia and . . . Pericles . . .'

'Will they keep your secret?'

'I hope so . . .' she murmured.

He was thinking.

'Then don't tell anyone else,' he said at last, urgently.

'Please, Halo, don't panic. Stay a boy. I need your help. So I need you to be a boy.'

The ground seemed to stabilize beneath her feet. 'Really?' she said.

'Oh yes, really,' he replied. 'Very, very really. But seriously – it mustn't get out. Not just for your personal reasons. You are doing such good and useful work, but . . . I fear the people would not let you help them if they knew you were female.'

She had been thinking about telling Arimaspou. She wanted to, now – telling the truth at last felt good, even when it hurt. Confiding in people she trusted. And if Hippias could accept her for what she was, then maybe . . .

But would the Skythians really accept a female doctor? Living among them?

No, she couldn't imagine that they would. And for that reason she couldn't risk it.

Living with the Skythians, Halo wanted to earn her keep. And she hated staying inside the city, cooped up with every-body else. *What would a boy do? Or an Amazon?* she thought. *They'd fight, that's what . . . They'd ride out with the Skythians and Arko to protect Athens and the Attic lands.*

'You're too young,' Arimaspou said.

Halo glared at him.

The next morning, she and Arko were up and ready in the cool black early morning, the rosy fingers of dawn splin-tering the eastern sky. She waited at the compound gate with Gyges's brave and clever black mare, Ivy, and when Arimaspou and the others came silently out, their hooves muffled and their cloaks across their faces, she just silently joined the line. The Captain said nothing. Arko fell in at her side. Silently, they slipped out of the city gates, heading towards the sea and the east.

The Spartan ravagers were early risers too. Not even during war do people want to work in the heat of the day.

Arimaspou had a good idea where the Spartans would be that day – and he was right. A few kilometres along the coast, the Skythians gathered in a knot behind a group of cypresses, while Akinakes rode out to confirm the Spartan position.

'They're in the olive grove beyond the farmhouse,' he called, low, as he returned. 'Forty or fifty with axes, trying to chop trees down, and a few Cretan archers protecting them. No one on horseback.'

It was easy to kick Ivy into motion with her heels, to gain speed and rattle up to pace, to gallop past the party in the olive grove, riding so fast, so furiously, shooting a rain of arrows at the Spartan men: *thudderderNOW thudderderNOW thudderderNOW thudderderNOW!*

Halo's blood was singing in her ears, her thighs tight around the horse's strong round body, her bowstring taut on her thumb-ring, arrows clutched in her fist, letting them off one and two and three and four –

She found she could, after all, shoot arrows into other human beings. She glanced across. Arko too was fighting to protect Athens.

The band of Skythians didn't stop – they just galloped on. They were shooting as they went in; they were still shooting as they rode out. The Spartans were left reeling – but the

Skythians never knew. They never knew how many they had hit; who had hit, what damage had been done, what limbs pierced or lives taken.

Halo preferred it that way. She only aimed at their arms. She wasn't going to kill anyone. Death was still her enemy, whatever form it took, whoever it approached. That dark woman who had stood in her bedchamber, who Leonidas had laughed at – however or whenever she appeared, Halo was against her. Seeing so much of Death sharpened her aim, but it hadn't dulled her mind. When Halo pulled her bowstring taut, loosed her swift arrows, and galloped away as distant Spartans clutched their arms and fell to the ground, she wasn't trying to kill them. She just wanted them to go away.

A kilometre or so on the Skythians wheeled round, dust flying from under their hooves. They circled and took stock of where they were. They checked that no one was wounded; they threw water down their throats from the leather water bottles; laughed and clapped each other's shoulders. Then they rode on to the next place, and did it again. In the evenings, they ate, stretched out their muscles, treated any wounds, and slept.

So for a few weeks, Halo shot Athenian arrows at Spartans, and in the evenings, she took Cretan arrows out of Skythians. Messages still came from Aspasia, but no message came saying, 'Pericles says come home, everything is all right, he's agreed to let you study.'

Halo was becoming a Skythian: living, eating, sleeping, guarding, training, fighting. She even asked Arimaspou if she could have her own Molossian puppy.

'A female,' she said. 'I'll train her. I'll call her . . . Amazon.'

Arimaspou smiled. 'Maybe,' he said. 'Let's see what the future brings us.'

And as soon as the Spartans left, well, there was still the plague to be fought.

Halo found out, that harsh, sick summer, what she *could* do. She could fight, she could tend wounds, she could learn from Hippias and she could care for the victims of the plague. One patient of Hippias had hired a man to take her sister's body and throw it on someone else's already-burning pyre. 'What else could I do?' the woman cried. 'I have no money, there's no wood left, it's all been burned in other pyres. There's no one left to carry her even. Everyone's dead. The mourners – all dead. What would you do?' and then she hurried away from Halo, consumed with shame.

*A year ago*, Halo thought, *I stood on the rocks at Cape Sounion making offerings to Poseidon for my parents. Nine months ago, Pericles made his beautiful oration at the splendid funeral for the men killed in the war. And now, this decent woman has to throw her sister's body on a stranger's pyre as if it were an old rag.*

Halo's heart squeezed tight inside her, as if trying to make itself small so it wouldn't have to feel the pain of this long summer of death. Everywhere she went, she took her medical kit: the tea that helped people sleep, the unguent to soothe their rashes, the needles to lance their sores, and a clay tablet on which to record how many days they spent in which combination of which types of suffering, and how exactly the plague was killing them. Word got round that she was willing to help, and many people came to the Skythian compound or to Hippias's, asking for her. Among them was Bokes, slave boy to her old music teacher, Philoctetes, who had often helped to slice the fruit and serve the picnic, back in the happy days. She could see from his face that he brought no good news.

'Master's granddaughter is sick,' he said, so very quietly.

He needed say no more. Halo picked up her bag, set her jaw firm, and followed him.

Arimaspou watched her go, his damaged face unreadable.

Everything was worse. It was as if people had no resistance, physically or mentally. As soon as eyes grew red and throats sore, everyone threw up their hands in helpless misery, and gave up, pitched into a horror which grew more dreadful every day.

Lenane, the music teacher's granddaughter, was weeping when Halo arrived. She was in the early stages. 'The Gods have deserted us,' she cried out, over and over.

Her older brother, Alexis, was there at the bedside. He was drunk, although it was only midday. 'She's right,' he said unevenly. 'Why should we live by their laws when believers and non-believers alike are dying?'

'Hush, my child,' their mother squawked. 'It's against the law to say such things!'

'Well, why obey the law?' Alexis cried. 'What, will the Skythian Guard come and take her away to prison? So what? She'll be dead by then anyway, as likely as not!'

His mother put her face in her hands.

'Halo, don't bother with being good,' he muttered. 'Good people die even quicker than bad people. Why bother? My brother inherited all our father's money when he died two weeks ago – you know it's true, Mother – and now – ha ha! – they're both dead, and Lenane is nearly dead, and soon we'll all be dead. Spend your money now, Halo, it can't help you . . .'

'You should all leave the sickroom,' Halo said calmly. 'For your own protection. If you stay near her, the sickness will pass to you.'

She said it automatically. She knew they wouldn't go. How could they? They loved Lenane. They wouldn't leave her alone.

Philoctetes, sad and silent, sat at the back, strumming his lyre quietly, and said nothing. Halo touched his shoulder lightly.

'Don't look at me like that,' Alexis mumbled. 'I'm just having fun. Might as well. We'll all be dead soon and the Gods don't care. Halo, just steal our money now, what's left of it, and just have some fun. For tomorrow we die. And nobody cares. Tra la la la la.'

Halo tried not to listen. She wiped Lenane's forehead.

'Well, Zeus and Apollo may not care,' burst out the mother, 'because we've offended them, but there are other Gods. There are foreign Gods who might help us, if we treat them right. There's the new god – we could go to the secret priest . . .'

'Who?' blurted her son. 'Why would they care about us, if Athena herself can't do anything for us, in her own city? We've had the Grand Dionysia *every year* to thank Dionysus for lifting the plague from us – and here it is back again. Does he care? Gods are nonsense, Mother.'

The mother started crying.

Lenane was coughing blood.

Alexis swore, and went to find more wine.

Halo blocked her ears, bit her lip, and cleared up the blood.

'I don't blame them for being like that,' she said to Arko later. 'What do they have to hold on to, after all? Hippias says what's happening is that the miasma has returned. The air is infected. But he doesn't know what to do about it anyway.'

'Well, all I hear is that the Gods are offended, because the country people are living in the temples, so the Gods are letting us die, and now they are more offended because people have died in the temples, and we are not providing proper funerals, and the Gods are even *more* offended because there are dead bodies lying around in the temples, because everybody who might bury them is dead. And no, Halo, it's not your job to go and bury them. You're doing enough to help.'

But Halo knew that the day before Arko had picked up a dead child from the street, wrapped it in his cloak, and laid it in a big grave that a rich man had had dug, for everyone to use, down at Kerameikos. Arko hadn't told her – Akinakes had, after a citizen had come to thank him for the Centaur's kindness.

'There is goodness out there,' Halo said. 'Even though the city is going mad.'

They were walking home to the Skythians, the same route

they had walked so often. The streets were quiet and empty. That was one good result of the plague – the Spartans had left early.

'The Gods may be killing us,' said Arimaspou, 'but at least they are protecting us from the Spartans. We should be grateful.'

Halo and Arko both laughed at that. A bitter laugh.

At least it meant the desolated land around Athens was still safe for riding out. She rode Ivy and watched how the green of spring was giving way to the dry ripe gold of high summer. Some farms had recovered well from the previous year; their vegetables were plump and their olives green and silver hanging in the heat. Others, though, stood empty and neglected. Their owners had not returned.

*They must be dead*, Halo thought. *Drowned or slaughtered in the Peloponnesian raids, ravaged by the plague.* Their vegetable patches were overgrown, tangled and desiccated; the land uncared for, the vines spreading wildly, unpruned, with stunted little bunches of grapes drying out where they grew. The olive trees were hacked about and half burnt. The occasional stray chicken clucked, scrawny and hungry as it scratched for food in the dry earth. These farms hurt Halo's heart as she rode by.

Going home that evening, a group of men, completely drunk, were shouting at a slave girl running an errand, and no one told them to behave. The chancers and con men were out on the streets of Athens too.

'Where *do* they crawl out from?' Halo wondered, seeing the rabbit-foot man hovering, still trying to sell rubbishy amulets and false hope, and a man dressed all in white telling a small group that the mysteries of Dionysiac revels were the only proven way to prevent getting the plague, so if they would just give him the money they had on them right now, he would arrange for them to be initiated . . .

'They were always there, just waiting for an opportunity,' snorted Arko. 'People cling to those false hopes like drowning men to a floating plank when they have nothing else.'

The next morning Halo went again to Philoctetes's house. Lenane was no better. She was suffering dreadfully. Looking at her, Halo remembered everything about how it felt, and she had to wrap her heart very tight not to give way to grief and sympathy for the girl. But Halo falling apart wouldn't do any good for anybody.

Alexis was there too. Today he was sober, and weeping, howling with grief for his sister's pain. His mother was trying to comfort him, and Philoctetes sat, silently as before, lightly picking at his lyre, at the back. Halo knew it wasn't even worth trying to make them leave. Alexis was right. They would probably all die now.

Later that day, she saw Alexis again, on a corner by the Leokorion, the new sanctuary built in honour of the daughters of Leos, who gave their lives to save Athens from a previous plague. Lots of these new shrines were popping up; no one had any faith any more in the shrine to Athena Hygeia, on the Acropolis, which was meant to keep disease away. A wealthy man called Telemachos – who had paid for the communal grave to be dug – was even talking about bringing Asclepius to Athens from his home in Epidaurus,

and building him a fine new temple. But until the war was
over, he couldn't even start negotiating for it.

*Religion has gone the way of law and order and common sense*,
Halo thought. *Telemachos is rare. Nobody else cares. Everyone's
so scared.*

Alexis was talking intently to the rabbit-foot man. His
face was tense and desperate.

Halo hesitated and thought of turning back through the
warren of alleys and steps on the side of the Acropolis, to
avoid him. She didn't want to talk to him – what could she
say, after all? But the alley was narrow, and she could not
help overhearing a few words of conversation.

'As soon as you can, get them to come, for the Gods'
sake,' Alexis was saying. 'For the sake of whatever God you
like, I don't care. Tonight.'

He was giving the man something – *money*, she thought.
She ducked down a side alley.

*What was that about?*

The next day, she found out.

When she went to Philoctetes's house, the slaves were
wailing, the mother was in hysterics before the family altar,
Alexis was standing white-faced as a statue by the door, and
Lenane was dead.

'But she's only in her fourth day!' Halo exclaimed. 'What
happened?' Her only sense of safety came from knowing
what the plague would do – if it didn't do what it was meant
to do, and follow the pattern, then what good were her
observations? What she had learned would mean nothing
. . . she would be lost.

'What happened?' she cried again, taking out her tablet to make notes.

'I killed her,' said Alexis.

Halo stared at him. She felt the heat of shock under her skin.

'I couldn't bear it,' he said, his eyes skittering around the room. 'I wanted to do it myself but I couldn't . . . I tried last night after you went . . . I'm not ashamed, except of not being brave enough to do it myself. But there's a man you can go to . . . everybody knows . . .'

Halo couldn't believe what she was hearing.

'There are two of them,' Alexis declared, and tears started to stream down his face. 'There's Polemides, a soldier, and another, Telamon. They've lost everything. Polemides did his mother. Telamon did his sister: he had sat by her through it all, and on the fifth day he did her. He'll do the same for anyone who gives him enough money to stay drunk for another day. The new god blesses it – he understands we are suffering too much already. His business is good.'

'Oh, sweet Athena, good Apollo,' Halo whispered. 'What is happening to us? What is happening?'

'Remember their names,' cried Alexis, wild-eyed. 'You might need them.'

Halo knew what Alexis had done was wrong. She knew that what those men were doing was wrong. But – but –

They were, in their way, trying to prevent suffering, just as she was. It was sympathy which made them do that dreadful thing.

*There's a topic for the philosophers to discuss*, she thought bitterly. *But those killers are better than people like the amulet sellers. At least they're honest about what's going to happen.*

As usual, she discussed it with Arko.

'Honest!' he said. 'Seems like honesty was the first casualty of the plague. Have you heard about the new god?'

'Alexis mentioned a new god. Is it Heracles Alexicacos? The daughters of Leos?'

'No, a *new* new one. He's called Balbo or Bolbo or something, and he's going to save us all, apparently. He comes from the east, he has horns like a bull, and he can cast out the plague. He has no temple, but he accepts sacrifice, and on the third day of your sickness this god will come and toss you on his horns until the plague is chased out, and then you recover. He has a secret priest who no one is allowed to see.'

Halo would have laughed if it hadn't been so tragic. 'They are so desperate for something to believe in that they will believe anything,' she said.

'No, really,' Arko continued, in a tone which told her he didn't believe a word of it. 'I met a man who'd met a man who swore it had happened to a man he met. He said this man had seen the god. He explained it all – the red marks on the body are where his horns gore you. Yes, they suffer, but in the end it's worth it. Sometimes, yes, the eyes or the fingertips are lost forever in the god's struggle with the plague, but it's a small price to pay for survival.'

'Any doctor could tell them that sometimes people survive,' said Halo.

'Ah, but the doctors are all dead,' said Arko. 'How is Hippias?'

'Not dead,' she said bleakly.

That night, she went out riding with the Skythians again. It was the only time she felt clean, and relieved. When she was riding Ivy the wind seemed to blow away the dark stink of the sickrooms, the cries of the dying, the filth of the deathbeds, the wails of the bereaved, the taste of death. The beautiful strong horse beneath her gave her a furious joy, a refusal to accept all the grief, a sense of life and glory and survival . . .

*I am young, I am not sick, I am not dead, I have a life to lead still . . . The almond blossom returns every year*, she thought. *Things change. Even this will change. Everything changes . . .*

## Χαπτερ 31

Over that long strange bad summer of death, the plague took Pericles's sister, and his son Xanthippus, his adopted son's three children, their grandmother Deinomache, and their old nurse, Amycla. The yoghurt seller and his wife and baby, Philoctetes's family, Alexis and Philoctetes himself . . . Gyges, and three other Skythians had died of it . . . Hippias's cousin, and the three doctors in Piraeus, the slaves next door, the stable boys, those four athletes, the teachers, all the patients she had tended who she didn't even know, what, two or three a day, dying? Everyone for whom she heard the wailing when she left the house . . . a thousand Hoplites at Potidaea . . . the sailors . . . the bodies in the temples – who were they?

She often thought of the child whose body Arko had taken to the pit.

She had thought that war was the enemy, but this plague was killing more than any war. *Perhaps*, the thought struck her, *the Gods really have had enough of Athens altogether. Perhaps they really want to wipe us all out.*

The day after she thought that, a cooler day towards the autumn equinox, a message came from Aspasia. Pericles's eyes were red, and he was coughing.

Halo knew she had been right. The Gods don't care at all for Athens. Without Pericles, Athens was helpless.

*Well, I don't care what the Gods think*, she snarled, and she picked up her kitbag, and went to Aspasia's house.

Pericles was already out of his mind when she got there. Aspasia let her in, kissed her, and allowed her to sit by him and tend to him. How strong hope is in the human heart! Everybody knew it was pointless to struggle against this demon plague, and yet they tried, because they loved Pericles, and the fear of living without him was overwhelming. He was given the best care anyone could come up with. The slaves brought everything that could possibly help; the finest doctors left alive came to him; Halo stayed by him eighteen hours a day, listening to him rant and rave. Aspasia gambled with her life to sit with him and pray for him.

One morning, after she had been up with him all night, Halo still couldn't sleep. She went back into his sickroom. There was the now-familiar smell, the same sense of Death waiting, quietly by the door, ready for when he gave up.

For once, he was quiet, calm and weak. It was the evening of his tenth day.

'Look,' he said, his voice low. 'The women have put an amulet on me. From the new god. They think it will save me. What do you think of that?'

Halo didn't dare to say what she thought – which was that if Pericles, the great man of Reason, let the women of the household put an amulet from the new god round his neck, as if that could make any difference, then he must be sick indeed.

'Are you surprised I let them do such a foolish thing?' he said.

Halo smiled but she was on the very verge of a great sea of weeping.

'It makes them feel better,' he whispered, and he smiled, and she thought, *How kind he is, to think of them, when he is dying*.

'Who *is* that?' he said, struggling a little, trying to peer through the dim light.

She didn't want to say. She didn't want to hear his anger, or to upset him.

But she wasn't going to start lying again.

'Halo,' she said, in a tiny voice.

'Oh,' he said.

Did he remember?

'Hm,' he said. He gave a funny little half-smile. 'My daughter . . .' he said.

She laid her head on the side of his bed, and after a while he gently put his hand on it, and ruffled her short hair.


When Pericles died, Halo, who hadn't wept all summer, sat in her old room at Aspasia's house and wept again. She wept without stopping for several days, and Aspasia feared for her sanity.

'My dear, my dear,' she said.

'I have now lost three fathers,' Halo said bitterly. 'Megacles is dead, Kyllarus is far far away, and now Pericles is gone . . . I will have no family again. The Gods laugh to take them away from me.'

'Child,' Aspasia said, 'I'm your family too. Aren't I? You will always have a home with me . . . and Lysicles . . .'

*Lysicles? Who is Lysicles?*

Aspasia's face was clear and blank. 'Look, Halo – you may not be a girl, but I am a woman . . . and without Pericles I am not such a special woman. You know how it is for us. I must protect myself, and Lysicles is a good man. Pericles liked him . . .'

Halo just stared. Pericles's body was hardly cold, and here was Aspasia talking of a new man.

'You don't mean it,' she said bluntly.

Aspasia snorted softly. 'Sadly,' she said, 'I do. But I mean my offer too – come back and live with me . . .' There was a plea in her eyes.

'I can't,' said Halo.

After Pericles died, the plague at last died down. There were no new cases. It just faded out, as autumn drew in.

It was hard to feel any joy. The Athenians were so battered that they could hardly even feel any relief.

'It's as if he were the final sacrifice,' Arko mused.

'Let's hope so,' said Halo. 'Let's hope so.'

## Χαπτερ 32

A few weeks later Halo, astride Ivy, was hurtling up a dust track north of the city. Arimaspou and Akinakes and Nephiles were with her, along with a hairy Skythian called Nikates and a couple of others. For sheer fun and pig-headedness, to let off steam, they were racing. Their horses' hooves pounded the track as they galloped, their blood pounded in their ears, dust flew up behind them, and they all felt wonderfully, utterly free and alive – alive the way only people who have been surrounded by death can feel. The dogs galloped alongside them, swift and loping, their big ears flapping in the wind.

Finally the riders drew in, panting and laughing, near a spring in an almond grove, so the horses could water. The nuts were ripening on the branches, and the grass was still bright and lush where the spring irrigated it. It was a cool and lovely spot, but though it was peaceful now the area had suffered badly under earlier Spartan ravaging. Farms had been seriously damaged, and the people – even if they had survived the plague – had not returned. Away from the spring, the fields were baked dry and neglected under the hot, high blue sky.

They all dismounted, each silent for now in the reverie of quiet countryside, glad to be out of the shocked and mourning city.

The dogs scattered around, to snuffle and sniff and relieve

themselves. One of them was mewling — he had found something.

'Here, boy!' called Nikates.

But the dog didn't come — just carried on whining. Grumbling, Nikates pulled himself to his feet and went to where the dog was. The other hounds had gathered, making noises half of pride in discovery, half of fear.

'What is it?' Akinakes called out, just as Nikates cried, 'Hey! You'd better come!'

The Skythians looked round. Arimaspou and Halo, livelier than the others, jumped up and went over.

In front of them, in a hollow, curled over on his front across his great bronze shield, lay the body of a young Spartan. He wore a leather cuirass, and his crimson cloak lay half across him. His crested helmet was at his side. His long black hair fell curling, hiding his face. He was motionless.

The Skythian prodded the body with the toe of his boot. 'That's recent!' he cried. 'A Spartan Hoplite!'

'Check the area!' Arimaspou said. 'There may be others.'

A shudder ran through the Hoplite's body.

'He's not dead,' Arimaspou said, and quickly drew his sword to finish him off.

'No!' Halo shouted.

Arimaspou paused.

'He's not wounded,' she said. 'There's no blood.'

'So?' said Nikates.

'So why is he lying here?' she said. 'Out here, alone? They're never alone. Who is he? What's wrong with him?'

Arimaspou put his boot under the unconscious body and tipped it over.

The Spartan's arm flung out, and his head lolled.

The Skythians saw the bloodied mouth, the rolling eyes, the waxen skin.

'Plague!' cried Arimaspou, and jumped back.

'Sweet Goetosyrus, not again,' Akinakes murmured.

'At least it's them and not us,' someone else said. 'This could turn the tide!'

But Halo saw only one thing. A great surge of something . . . something strong, something irrational . . . rushed to her heart, and to her head. It was Leonidas.

'Don't touch him,' she said harshly.

Arimaspou looked at her. 'Well no, of course not,' he said. 'He's riven with it. But what do we do with him?'

'Send him back to Sparta, and he can infect the rest of them,' cried Nikates, and the others laughed. 'It's about time they got it too . . .'

'No, Halo's right,' said Arimaspou. 'Why's he here? What's he doing here all alone?'

'It's not an ambush . . .' said Nephiles.

'But he might be a spy,' Arimaspou said thoughtfully. 'In which case we should take him back to the city, but we can't, obviously . . .'

'I'll look after him,' said Halo faintly. 'He can't travel. He'll die. If he's a spy he must be questioned, but – someone must come here. Go back to the city and get someone out here. A plague survivor. We don't want him to die before someone talks to him.' She hardly knew what she was saying.

She had just one idea in mind – they mustn't kill him. She mustn't leave him. He mustn't die.

'*We* can talk to him,' said Nikates.

'No,' she replied. 'Someone from . . . you know,' she said feebly. 'You go. I'll guard him. I'll nurse him. You should get away from here, all of you.'

They were happy to go. Nobody wanted to hang around a plague-riven man.

Except Halo.

The moment the Skythians and the dogs were out of sight she dropped to her knees beside Leonidas, and laid her head on his chest. She rested there a second. She could hear his heartbeat.

*Not dead*, she thought. There he was. Leonidas, not dead.

Halo's strength and courage were returning to her. She took his hand in hers, and she said, softly, 'Leonidas – don't die yet . . .'

She almost laughed as she remembered how he had appeared to her when Death was standing by her bed.

'Leonidas,' she whispered. 'You've never let me die – remember? I won't let you die . . .'

She stared down at him.

They couldn't stay where they were. The Skythians would be back, decisions would be made, everything would be out of her hands. She had to get him somewhere safe. Somewhere with water. Somewhere with shelter.

She looked around, and she made up her mind. She refilled her water bottle and slung it from her belt. Then she led Ivy over, pulling on the bridle to lower her to her knees. Halo rolled Leonidas and hefted him up on to the horse's back. He was heavy but Halo was strong, and she managed. She propped him in place as best she could, while Ivy carefully and ungracefully rose again to her feet for Halo to strap the helmet and shield on behind, wrapped and hidden in her cloak.

'OK, OK,' Halo muttered soothingly, to herself as much as to the animal. 'OK there . . .' and, once Ivy was properly up again, she swung her leg over the horse's back. Leonidas lay flopped on his belly. If they didn't go too fast, he'd probably stay in place. She didn't want to have to lift him again, that was for sure.

*Dear Gods, what if one of the Skythians comes back? What would they make of what I am doing? What* am *I doing?*

She grabbed tight to the leather belt at Leonidas's waist, which held his sword and his knife, and gently chirruped to Ivy. They started off. Where they were going, Halo had no idea. Away from Athens, that was for sure. Head north, take the small roads, avoid villages, find a deserted farm with a well. There'd be one. Bound to be.

She was helping him. That was all there was to it.

She saw several that would have done, but they were too close to the city. She didn't want the Skythians finding them again the very next day. They had to get further away. Beyond Acharnae, she thought. There'd been lots of ravaging up there. Things would be quiet. But she had to get him settled soon. If there were Spartans about, she couldn't risk running into any.

What would Spartan law do with one of their own, a full Spartan Hoplite, who had the plague?

Suddenly, Halo realized why Leonidas was out in the field

all alone, away from his line and his sacred brothers. Why, despite all his training, all his fierce loyalty, he'd deserted them. He'd felt the plague coming. He'd realized what he had. He had left, in order that they shouldn't catch it. Rather than risk their health, he'd die a horrible death, alone in the ruined countryside, far from home.

She held his belt a little tighter.

*He'll die anyway*, came a nasty little voice in her mind.

*I don't care*, she retorted. *He saved me three times at least – I'll do anything for him.*

After several hours, when the moon had risen over the glistening plain, touching the olive leaves with silver, she saw a dark shape looming behind a mud wall, and the black fingers of a pair of cypress trees against the starry sky. No lights, no sound. *That'll do.*

Riding in, she saw a well in the yard. All was silent, the moon-shadows black as oil. Dry round pumpkins sat like skulls in the vegetable patch; the vines wandered wildly all over the place as if searching for their owners. Abandoned, definitely.

She told Ivy to stay, as she swung down and approached the door. It opened at first kick. Inside was a mess: dusty, cobwebby, empty, burnt out, smelling of neglect and loss. A bit of roof remained in one corner. There was a bale of mildewy straw in an outhouse. She dragged the straw under the roof, and spread it flat. She laughed softly as she lugged Leonidas's heavy body off Ivy and on to the straw bed.

'Probably the most comfortable bed you've ever had, eh, Spartan?' she murmured. 'Luxurious by your standards . . .'

She propped him up, and pushed his long hair back from

his face. She didn't want to look at those hot and rolling eyes, and his bloodied mouth. She was used to him being strong. *Be a doctor*, she said to herself, and that helped her to clean his mouth and give him water. She pulled off his leather boots and his belt and weapons, and laid him down, trying to make him comfortable. He was half conscious now, disturbed by being lugged around. She laid her own cloak on top of him.

Eventually she had to look at him. *Dear Gods.* He looked older – there was stubble on his jawline; his cheeks were leaner – and he looked horribly ill. His temples were hollow, his skin sweaty and waxen beneath his tan, his lips white and moving wordlessly, with the blood constantly bubbling and seeping. But he looked like himself still. Like the confusing, amusing boy she used to know. The first human she ever knew. What a long time ago it all seemed. Delphi, Sparta, Taegetus, even Zakynthos – it was all a dream to her now.

Sitting there in the dark, watching Leonidas as the stars wheeled overhead, she began to realize the madness of what she was doing. She had tricked her dear friends the Skythians. She had given help to an enemy soldier. She had carried off an enemy spy, to keep him from being questioned. She had run away from her beloved Athens. All this was some kind of treason – and on top of it all, Arko didn't know where she was. But despite all that, and despite Leonidas's sickness, despite him being the enemy, despite everything – she was incredibly pleased to see him.

There was no sleep that night. Halo lay down beside Leonidas on the itchy straw, but just at the moment she was dropping off he became restless, fidgety, frantic, his chest sinking and sucking for breath. He was thirsty. She gave him the water from her leather bottle, but of course it did not satisfy him. She recognized this stage – she had seen it so many times before, and she had lived through it. The unquenchable thirst that had people running in parched madness from their beds, and leaping into rivers or streams or pools, anything, to get water.

She filled her bottle over and over from the rotten bucket in the well outside. She fed it to him, poured it over him. Each time, he wanted more. Each time, she gave it to him.

As far as she could judge it was the sixth or seventh day. If he survived the next twenty-four hours, he had a chance.

*My brother to the left*, she thought. *I will cover you. Dear Gods, do not forsake us. Please, do not forsake us. Asclepius, if I have ever pleased you . . . Apollo, Athena . . . Please . . .*

Leonidas cried out, in his illness, and scraps of words came through. He called on Melesippus and other men, by name. He called on Archidamus – apologizing for letting him down. He called on Pausanias. He cried to his mother and his father, and he cried in anger and pain and delirium.

Halo had nursed many people through the plague. She had watched many people die. She had learned a knack of closing off her heart to their suffering, so that her tears and her sympathy did not prevent her from washing them, changing their linen, bringing their water. She had ignored howls of suffering that would break any heart; indeed she had won a reputation for hardness, which only others who had survived the plague understood. Only they knew there was no point in weeping.

But now, in the ruined farm, in the desperate long darkness of the autumn night, helplessly pouring water for Leonidas, she wept.

She slept fitfully at dawn, too dog-tired to stay awake, her skin crawling with sleeplessness. She heard him moaning and muttering beside her, unable to sleep, unable to stay still. Stumbling in a daze across the room to the well, she brought him more water. She must try to feed him. And herself, though she felt no hunger.

He smelt dreadful. The pustules were forming on his neck. She should try to wash him. But she had no soap, no clean linen, no herbs, nothing.

*Is he going to die like everyone else?*

She brought him more water and began to run through in her mind the list of everyone who had died so far. *NO! Stop it!*

Outside, the day was growing hot, shining, beautiful with golden autumn. The scent of jasmine hung in the warm morning air. Inside, the dim room stank of the plague.

*But this will not kill me*, she thought. *I do not have that way out. I have to survive this.*

Leonidas rolled over, his lips bloodstained and cracked as he half talked in his semi-stupor.

'Help me,' he muttered. 'I don't want to die.'

'So don't die,' she said to him. She grabbed him by the shoulders, leaning over him. 'So don't die! Not everybody dies! I didn't die! You don't have to die!'

He was moaning again, with the pain and the thirst, clutching at his own skin as if trying to tear it off. She watched him for a moment. She remembered how that felt, then she lurched to her feet and went outside. Food. Sour wine-grapes, figs, last year's almonds, some plums, small and black. She found the remains of a sack of very old oats, which soaked in water would make a cold porridge for them for a few days. She couldn't risk a fire.

*Here we are again*, she thought. *Still, he's a Spartan, he's trained to live on next to nothing.* She laughed at her own stupid joke. *So what I am I going to do? Just sit here and watch and wait?*

*Yes. There's nothing else.*

He didn't die that day. *He'll go on the eleventh day, then*, she thought. Meanwhile, she got into a routine. She brought water and mopped his vomit, cleared away the dirty straw, washed his face, soothed his brow, failed to quench his thirst, brushed away the flies that settled on his eyes and mouth. She sat by him for as long as she could bear it, talking to him, holding his hand, watching his pain, as if that would help.

Then when it became unbearable, she ran out into the yard and spun in wild circles, wanting to scream, but not daring to make any noise.

Ivy would look at her kindly, and Halo would go and stroke her smooth neck, and rest her head against it, and cry, longing for her Centaur mother, for someone else's strength to help her through. When she felt a little better, she gave Ivy water from the bucket, picked some fruit, and poked around in search of anything else to eat. Then she went back into the dim and fetid farmhouse to try to feed Leonidas, and force some food down her own throat.

Then, she washed him again, and the cycle started over.

She was sitting by him, holding his hand, wondering whether it was worth trying to gather the strength to move on, because the Skythians would track them down sooner or later if they stayed still – when she heard the march and rattle of hooves on the dirt road outside.

She froze.

*Pass by*, she prayed.

The sound stopped. Shouts and the clanking of armed men replaced it.

Military men.

Her heart stopped beating for a moment, then she jumped up.

Athenians? Skythians? Spartans? Sweet Athena, which would be worse?

Leonidas's shield and helmet and crimson cloak were hidden, she'd taken care of that – they were in a dirty old sack, in the rafters, where only the rats would find them. Ivy was round the back in the old stable. Pray the Gods she wouldn't make a noise – Halo didn't want to lose Ivy. And Leonidas himself? Well, she'd challenge anyone to recognize him. He looked like a corpse.

And she hated to think what she looked liked – filthy, tattooed, with her head matted and stubbly.

She went silently to the doorway, where the old door hung crooked and heavy on its hinges, and peered out.

It was not the Skythians. It was not Athenians.

It was Spartans – a couple of strong, healthy Spartans, with a handful of Helot squires or slaves. They were laughing, and filling their water bottles at the well, talking their Doric Greek. She felt as if she hadn't seen anyone healthy in weeks. It was alarming.

*Go away, go away*, she prayed silently. She stood behind the door and she didn't even breathe.

How could they laugh and chat so easily? Didn't they know that the end of the world was going on?

And one of them turned. She could tell by the way he glanced around that he was looking for a place to relieve himself.

'Won't be a minute!' he called, and then he was lumbering towards the door – towards her.

She had a split second to decide what to do.

Just as he reached to push the door open, she jumped out.

'PLAGUE!' she shouted.

The man jumped back. Halo knew she looked strange, but she could have no idea *how* strange. The Spartan thought she was a ghost.

He cried out.

She shrieked.

The others crowded round, hands on the hilts of their knives.

'Plague!' she shouted again. 'Don't be here! Leave! There's plague here!'

And they might have left but that Ivy, disturbed, started to neigh, and the men, standing well back, started to wonder why anyone would be in a desolated farm, with a horse and the plague.

'What's the matter with her?' one called.

'Think she's mad,' said another – and that was when Ivy broke out of the old stable, and one of the Helots grabbed her by the bridle, and another grabbed Halo, and she yelled and kicked him and thought, *That's it. It's all over*.

But it wasn't – because as she kicked and yelled, a terrifying, filthy, half-dead figure lurched out of the dark of the farmhouse, clutching the door frame, at any moment about to fall . . . He laughed, a low laugh, and in a soft, harsh voice, like an owl's claws grasping at a cliff-face, he murmured, 'Phaedippidas, can't I even die of the plague in peace?'

Everyone froze. Halo gulped. The Spartans stared. Only Ivy's whinny broke the silence.

'Well?' said Leonidas.

The Spartan Phaedippidas swore quietly. 'Leonidas,' he gasped, horror and fear in his voice.

The Helots backed away.

'Leave us,' whispered Leonidas. 'Go, tell my brothers, Spartan passing by, that here, according to their laws, I die . . .' He laughed again. He was leaning – almost hanging – on the door. He was so thin. His eyes glittered with fever and death in his hollow, waxen face, and his hair hung back heavy from his brow. Halo could hardly believe he had found the strength to stand.

'We must . . .' Phaedippidas said, and Halo could almost see the process of his thoughts ticking by, as he realized that he could not help his friend, could not take him home, could not even come near him.

'No,' murmured Leonidas gently. 'You mustn't.' He lurched again, and Halo ran to him, slipping easily from the aghast Helot's grip. She caught him, and he leaned on her. 'Thank you, Halo,' he said.

*He knows it's me!*

Phaedippidas's face was full of pain. *Yes, welcome to the plague, Spartan. This is how it feels. This is what happens,* she thought. She felt sorry for him. How dreadful the pain was, at the beginning, before you got used to it. Tears sprang to her eyes. No matter how she pretended, she *wasn't* used to it. She could *never* be used to it.

Phaedippidas glanced at her. He had that strange look on his face – the look of a Spartan who isn't sure what to do.

'Go,' said Leonidas. 'Send my love to my mother. And don't steal our horse.'

'We'll come back for you,' said Phaedippidas, his face stern again, his decision made. 'We won't leave your body here unburied.'

'Give me a week or two,' murmured Leonidas. A ghastly smile lifted the skin tight over his cheekbones.

And the Spartans went.

Halo laid Leonidas down again. His breath was stuttering and tangled, and new bruises had appeared on his arms and belly. She wanted to hold him in her arms and tell him everything would be all right.

'You don't have to die,' she whispered.

But he was back in the arms of the plague. He didn't even hear her.

*Her.*

*The Spartans had said 'her'.*

She'd been careless. She hadn't been bothering to bind

her breasts under her chiton. Fool! She must do it now. What if someone else came?

The routine started up again.

Halo was too sad to try to remember anything for her notes. Why bother? She knew all too well what this illness did. Time passed, in moaning and thrashing and filth. She lay by Leonidas, still sleepless, almost as dirty as him, staring with misery and desperate exhaustion.

*Today*, she thought one morning, *is day eleven. Today he dies. Pericles died, with the very best care available. Leon will die and I've hardly been able to care for him at all.*

She didn't tie Ivy up that day. *Let her go*, she thought. *Let her go home.*

He was quieter. No vomiting – he had nothing left to vomit. No more diarrhoea. Less coughing. For a short while, he even seemed to doze off.

*Goodbye*, she thought. She had watched strangers die, or people she knew a little, new acquaintances, recent friends, poor dear Philoctetes. And Pericles. She had thought nothing could be worse than that. But watching Leonidas die was a thousand times worse. Leonidas was her own friend, part of her past. He should have been part of her future. She had always known that he would be back.

Despite herself, she fell asleep, lying beside him, tear-stained, thin and grubby.

*I love him.*

*He'll be dead when I wake.*

# Χαπτερ 33

He was not dead when she woke.

When she woke, he was sitting up, drinking water.

'I'm hungry,' he said. 'Have we any food?'

She stared at him in utter disbelief.

'Did you just ask for food?' she said.

'Yes,' he replied.

'I . . . I . . .' she said.

'Well, I haven't eaten,' he said, and he smiled, a weak smile, but the best smile she had ever seen.

She stared intently at him. 'Is this real?' she asked.

'I believe so.' He was smiling. Alive.

She sat up next to him, shoulder to shoulder, and rested her head against him. He put his arm around her, and a weight of pain washed off both of them.

'Oh,' she said.

For about thirty seconds they were both filled with joy.

Then she started thinking ahead again: *Feed him, what with? Find something — then wash him, then — we have to move on. It's a miracle the Skythians haven't found us — the Spartans might come back any time. He might want to go with them — but he isn't well enough. It's the time people lose their minds, or their sight, or their fingers. Where can we go? And will it be safe to take him among people?*

*Every minute counts.*

*North,* she was thinking. *Away from Athens, and the war — Euboea?*

*Thessaly! Of course — to Kyllarus and Chariklo! But food first. And water. And what could he wear? Not his armour . . . Ivy? Is she still —*

— and suddenly all decisions were taken from her, and all planning fell away.

Again there was a pounding of hooves outside.

The whinnying of horses.

Men's voices shouting in the yard.

*Spartans. They'll kill me.*

*Athenians. They'll kill him.*

Her heart was battering her ribcage, her breath came short and ragged, she was helpless.

It was the Skythians.

Ivy was neighing in welcome to her companions. Someone went to her.

Halo stood up, hesitating in the dim room. She didn't know what to do. Leonidas rose beside her, very carefully and slowly.

And then Arimaspou strode into the filthy room like a stormy west wind.

'Have you been here all along?' he shouted. She had never seen him so angry.

'Yes,' she said.

'We have been looking for you,' he said, with steel in his voice.

*They are going to take me back and I will die for treason. I'm going to die now after all.* She wanted to pray to Artemis but she didn't feel like a young girl any more. She wanted to pray to Athena, but Athena had deserted the Athenians . . . She was scared.

'I had to hide,' she blurted.

'Why?' said Arimaspou.

'I had to protect him,' she said, and her voice tailed away as she said it.

'Why?' snapped Arimaspou. 'Who is he?'

'My name is Leonidas,' said Leonidas. It seemed to use all his strength just to say. He was leaning against the wall. His green eyes were alive again, but still he looked terrible.

'I asked *him*,' said Arimaspou dismissively, gesturing to Halo.

'A man can give his own name,' murmured Leonidas with a little snort.

Arimaspou glanced shortly at him, then turned again to Halo.

'Listen,' he said shortly. 'Don't mess around here. No one else would even give you the opportunity to explain yourself. Why in the name of all the Gods and my sweet patience are you putting your life and your reputation and many, many other things at risk, to protect a Spartan?'

'He protected me,' she said. 'Saved my life. Three times. He saves me.'

Leonidas, leaning against the wall, looking at the floor, gave a slight smile.

Arimaspou glanced at him again, then back at Halo.

He sighed.

'Then we are in his debt,' he said curtly. 'We are in his debt.' He closed his eyes for a moment, and stood quiet. Halo looked at him curiously. Then he pulled himself together, and snapped, 'And what are you going to do with him now?'

'I was thinking,' Halo said quickly, before he changed his mind, 'when he's a bit stronger, of going north, to Thessaly, to find Chiron and Kyllarus and ask the Centaurs what we can do about the plague . . . No one else has any ideas, but maybe, maybe the Centaurs will know something, and we can bring their knowledge back to Athens.'

Captain Arimaspou looked at Leonidas, then looked at her, and rolled his one eye to heaven and then, to her amazement, he said, 'So we will come too.'

The other Skythians, who had been silent all this time, did not seem at all surprised at their Captain's words. But Halo was. She wasn't sure she'd heard him right.

'Why?' she cried.

'Because it is our duty,' Arimaspou said, without smiling.

'Surely it's your duty to take him hostage and drag me back to Athens and fling me on my knees in the dust before our leaders,' said Halo.

'No,' he said, looking at his fingernails. 'It is our duty not to risk that.'

'Why not?' she said. She didn't understand. 'You're the Athenian Guard and I have certainly broken the Athenian law . . . Why aren't you arresting me?'

Arimaspou stared deeply at his fingernails. For an oddly long time. Then he said brusquely, 'Don't any of you have any food? Feed them, for the Gods' sake, and get this Spartan cleaned up.'

'Arimaspou!' said Halo. 'What's going on?'

The Captain dropped his hand by his side, and glared round at his men. Then he grabbed Halo by the arm, and dragged her out the rotten door into the bright autumn sunshine. For a moment, she was dazzled.

'Look at me,' Arimaspou said. He took her face in his two hands. 'Look at me.'

'I can't,' said Halo, confused, trying to keep her voice steady. 'Your scarf covers half your face. Nobody can look at you.'

Arimaspou's one clear pale eye was gazing at her. Without wavering his gaze, he put his hands to the piece of silk and tried to untie the knot.

'You could just pull it off,' Halo said.

'Yes, yes I could,' he replied, but he didn't.

Very gently, Halo reached out to help. It took a moment or two.

The silk fell, and Halo looked, for the first time, at Arimaspou's face.

'What do you see?' said Arimaspou very gently.

Halo saw an ugly, twisted, empty eye socket. She saw a tangled web of shining scars. She saw, among the scars on his forehead, a few lost lines and scraps of deep turquoise tattoo. A horribly damaged face. A face that had been beautiful. A strong, determined face.

A woman's face.

Their eyes locked. Neither of them spoke. For one long moment they stared at each other in silence, while a cricket scraped its legs in a branch above them.

Halo frowned.

'Are you . . .?' she said.

'Yes,' said the woman.

'But . . .' said Halo.

'Yes,' said the woman.

'Do they . . .?' said Halo.

'No,' said the woman firmly.

'But how long . . .'

'Thirteen years,' she said. 'Since I lost my . . . since I lost you.'

Halo was shaking. The woman bent and gently, almost apologetically, with utter tenderness, kissed her cheek. 'I won't lose you again,' she said. 'I am sorry,' she whispered. 'For so many things.' Then she took the scarf, and swiftly and firmly she wrapped it back around her head.

It was Arimaspou again.

Halo fell into a dead faint.

The Captain caught her as she fell, lifted her and cradled her carefully, carrying her next to his heart.

## Χαπτερ 34

After that, everything went into a wild blur of activity. Halo came round as she was being piled on to Arimaspou's horse. 'I'm all right,' she said. 'Let me down . . . I'll be fine.'

'We're going back to Athens,' Arimaspou was saying. 'There are Spartans everywhere to the north. It's too dangerous with a sick man.'

For a second Halo thought she must have imagined the whole thing. Hunger playing tricks with her mind. That's Arimaspou. Just as he always was.

'Well, you should go somewhere,' murmured Leonidas, from against the wall where he had propped himself. 'They'll be back here for my dead body any time.'

Arimaspou said calmly, 'Then let's leave now, shall we?' and swung himself up behind Halo.

'Am I going with you?' inquired Leonidas.

'But – plague!' Halo said confusedly. 'We can't take the plague into Athens!'

'It's thirteen days since we found him,' said Arimaspou. 'And he had it then.'

'That's right,' said Halo.

'Then he's clear,' said Arimaspou.

'How do you know?' she said.

'Hippias has been studying it,' said Arimaspou. 'Basing his studies on your notes, you'll be glad to hear.'

She *was* glad to hear. 'Then yes you *are* coming,' she said to Leonidas. 'You could still die. The Spartans can't care for you – they won't come near you.' She turned to the Skythians. 'We need to get his belongings.'

'There's no time,' said Arimaspou.

Halo insisted. 'He's a Spartan, he doesn't leave his shield behind.'

'He's a Spartan, so, what, you want to advertise that to the whole of Athens? Akinakes – give him *your* clothes.'

'What'll I wear?' asked Akinakes.

'Halo's cloak. You can be a prisoner. Don't talk. You neither, Leonidas. Your lack of moustache is less than convincing, but at least your hair is long. Try and look Skythian.'

'What does a Skythian look like?' asked Leonidas.

'Like me,' said Arimaspou, with a sneer, 'only with a moustache.'

Leonidas sneered too, as he pulled on Akinakes's silk trousers.

'Akinakes and Leonidas, go in the centre of the group,' said Arimaspou.

While they were swapping clothes, Halo slid down and went to get the sack of armour from the roofbeams. She reappeared with Leonidas's heavy *hoplon* over her shoulder.

'We can tell them it's a trophy,' she said to Arimaspou.

'Oh no, you can't,' said Leonidas, and reached to take it off her.

She was glad to see these signs of life from him. But he was still so weak. She gave him a boost-up on to Ivy, to ride behind her.

'Hold tight,' she said.

'Happy to,' he murmured, flopping against her, sliding his arms round her waist. She felt the warmth of his chest on her back as they took off down the road.

Then Akinakes called, 'But Halo, where is Arko?'

'He's with you,' said Halo. 'Isn't he with you? In Athens?'

'We thought he was with you!' cried Arimaspou. 'We haven't seen him for two days – he was out looking for you – we thought he must have found you . . .'

'No . . .' said Halo.

'Then where in Hades is he?'

'Think about it in Athens,' said Akinakes. 'He can look after himself for the moment. There's dust on the horizon which says it's time we left . . .'


The Skythians on the city gate took one look at Arimaspou and didn't question for a moment that ten had ridden out, and twelve rode back, with a Spartan *hoplon*. Eight rode straight out again, to look for Arko.

Arimaspou would not let Halo go. 'You're too weak,' he said brutally. 'You'd get in the way.' He made both her and Leonidas wash and change and lie quietly on pallets by the fire; he ordered broth and fish and milk, fruit with honey and yoghurt, and cherries in syrup for them to eat, and he called for Hippias. 'You're not well,' he said to Halo. 'You should be in bed.'

Halo started laughing. He sounded like a mother.

They both ate like lions, and Leonidas slept like a dog, but Halo couldn't rest, not knowing where Arko was. The riders returned – they had been all over town, asking for him, but no one had seen him. People were very sorry to hear that he was missing. They had grown fond of him.

'Where can he be?' cried Halo. 'He wouldn't just go off. He just wouldn't. He wouldn't get lost. He was with you, looking for me, and then – what?'

'I'd gone into an old barn, to search,' said Nephiles. 'When I came out he wasn't there. I thought he'd gone back to the others, then when he hadn't, we thought maybe he'd found you, but something had happened to stop you both coming back . . .'

'So we must go back there,' said Halo.

'We did,' shrugged Akinakes. 'Twice. We thought he might have been hurt . . . nothing. He's not out there now, that's for sure. Nor any sign of what happened.'

'He might have been hurt, and the Spartans took him . . .' she said.

'Wouldn't we have heard?' said Arimaspou. 'That's just the kind of thing that is hard to keep from spies and prisoners and traitors . . . Perhaps, we thought, he might have gone back to his own people – we sent a message but we don't know yet if it got through . . .'

'He wouldn't go without saying,' Halo insisted.

It was a mystery of the worst kind.

Leonidas lay on his pallet bed, listening to the conversation, and the circling worries.

'Perhaps,' he said. His voice was still hoarse, and he paused while talking. 'Would anybody else want him? A Centaur is a rare thing.'

The Skythians stared. Halo too. Something was stirring in her mind.

'You remember,' said Leonidas, holding her gaze. 'In Delphi. Manticlas wanted him. Very disappointed by the Oracle.'

'Manticlas,' Halo whispered. Then she shouted, 'By all the Gods, Manticlas! He was here – Leon, I saw him, in Athens, it was . . . When was it, oh, before I was ill – it was just before the plague got me! That day! I saw him in the city. I never told anyone, because I fell sick that evening. I was going to warn Arko – oh, Leon, you're right . . .'

'Manticlas?' said Arimaspou. 'The boy who was threatening you, when you first arrived in Athens?'

'A seer,' said Leonidas. 'Nasty. Corrupt.'

'He was up in the Centaur lands, looking for . . .' said Halo, before realizing that none of them knew anything about this. 'He's weird-looking. Has a strange spooky way of talking. Madly pale, white hair, white skin, white eyes almost . . .'

'Small and thin? Looks like he's never been outdoors in his life? Like a plant grown in a dark cellar?' said Akinakes. 'And moons around like he's got Hermes sitting on his shoulder, taking all his thoughts direct to Zeus?'

'Yes,' said Halo and Leonidas together. 'Why?'

Akinakes and Arimaspou were looking at each other. 'Hecatores!' they said.

'And who is Hecatores?' said Halo.

'By the description, he's your Manticlas,' said Arimaspou. 'He calls himself the secret priest of the new god. He never goes out, just sits there like a spider in his secret web, but we know what he's up to.'

'And why did he want Arko?' said Akinakes. 'Do you know?'

Halo and Leonidas looked at each other again. She spoke first. 'Yes,' she said. 'He wants a Centaur's heart, because he believes it can win any battle.'

'But Arko is protected by Apollo,' said Nephiles.

'People don't believe in the Gods now . . .' said Arimaspou.

'And Apollo said he was backing the Spartans,' said Halo, trying and trying to make sense of it. 'But Manticlas is a Spartan . . .'

'No,' said Leonidas. 'He's not Spartan. He's from Persia.'

'Excuse me,' said Akinakes. 'I'll be back in ten minutes. I must just fetch something.'

'Persia?' said Arimaspou.

'Banished from Sparta,' Leonidas continued. 'Trying to get money off Persian envoys in the King's name. Chased out of town a year ago.'

'Does he want the Centaur's heart to win the war for the Persians?' asked Arimaspou. 'Or who?'

'Does it matter?' said Halo. 'He wants Arko's heart. And maybe he has Arko. Does he have any power here?'

'He has followers,' said Arimaspou. 'He promises them everything under the sun, and they believe him.'

'Then we must follow *them*, and find him,' said Leonidas.

'We?' said Arimaspou. 'You can't come . . . you're sick.'

Leonidas gave him a devilish grin. 'Well, my friend,' he said, 'that might be useful.'

It was the first time that Arimaspou got a glimpse of Leonidas's strength of character. It made Halo smile. Arimaspou glanced at her, and Halo felt suddenly weak again. It *did* happen. Arimaspou *is* . . .

'We'll make our plan when Akinakes returns,' said the Captain.

Leonidas, looking rather yellow, lay back down. He was asleep in moments.

'Halo,' said Arimaspou.

Her heart started to beat wildly. He took her elbow, and carefully led her away from the fire, out where they could be alone.

Halo didn't want to go. It was too much. She couldn't – Arko lost, Leonidas . . . it was too much.

He sat her down by the wood pile, and sat opposite her. 'It's hard to find any privacy round here,' he said, with a dry laugh. 'Believe me, I know.'

Halo stared at him. Was he going to take the scarf off again and show that female face, and those lost tattoos? She didn't want him to. She wanted him to be Arimaspou.

'Halo,' he said. 'Aiellina . . . That's your name. What we called you. Short for Aiella, after me. When I was . . . Halo, when Gyges brought you in and I saw you, saw your *tamga*, I swear I would have recognized you anyway . . .'

'What's my *tamga*?'

'Your tattoo. Tattoo of our family, only for the females – and look, here there are two of us living as men . . .'

'You always knew I was a girl?'

'They all know you're a girl,' he said. 'Oh, Halo, there is too much to tell you, and so much we have to do – I must tell you quickly . . .'

'They *all* know?'

'They all know.'

Halo reeled at that. 'Why didn't anyone say?'

Arimaspou started laughing, and shaking his head. 'They wouldn't dare,' he said.

Halo was lost. '*What?*' she said. 'Please explain what you mean!'

'Halo. To me, you are my lost and found child, from whom I will never again be parted, and for whose safety I will die or kill. To them, you are . . . well. To them, you bear the *tamga* . . .'

'Meaning . . .?' said Halo.

'They think you're their queen. They respect your royal wish to live as a boy. They discuss it, when you're not around. They realize that you don't know who you are, and they wonder what to do about it. But in fact, they're wrong. You're not their queen. I am. You are their princess.'

Halo was staring, dumbstruck. *What?*

'You are a Skythian queen,' she said finally, doubtfully.

'Actually, Amazon queen,' Arimaspou said. 'The Skythians also honour Amazon royalty . . . anyway, it's complicated . . . No, we're Amazons.' Arimaspou started to laugh again. 'Couldn't you tell?'

'I am an Amazon,' Halo whispered.

'Amazon princess,' said Arimaspou gently. 'You are Aiellina, the Amazon Princess, daughter of Megacles of the Alcmaeonids, and me.'

Halo cheeks had gone stiff. She blinked. *That's who I am.* It was too much.

But there was more.

'What happened?' she said quietly.

Arimaspou bit the inside of his cheek, and raised his chin for a moment, as if to gather strength. He closed his eye.

'A storm,' he said finally. 'There was fire on the ship. I was caught in it . . .' He gestured to his face. 'Your father had strapped you into your little cradle, he had put weights in the bottom so it wouldn't capsize . . . and as the ship went down he pushed you away towards the land, and tried to swim with you. I saw you both . . . I tried to swim to you . . .' He swallowed. 'A good family on the island took me in, helped me. After I was a little healed I searched the island for you, for him . . . I found his body on a beach in the north. I buried him by a patch of fig trees, near some beautiful blue caves. There were no people up there. I searched and searched but never found you . . .'

Tears flooded down Halo's face. The fig patch. The beach. The blue blue caves. Her father had been there all along.

Arimaspou held out his hand, and Halo took it, lightly.

'I chose then to live as a man,' he said. 'I was an Amazon, I couldn't live as a Greek widow. I couldn't bear to . . . so I took my husband's clothes, and I bound up my head, and I became a man.'

'Why didn't you tell me?' Halo whispered. 'You could have told me all this months ago!'

'If I had told you it would have come out – it always does – and Halo – I would have had to become a woman again and I *cannot* be a woman again. I am Arimaspou and I am staying Arimaspou. But *you*, Halo . . . you are going to be a woman. Do not do what I have done. Be a girl. Don't do what I did.'

'But I must be a doctor,' Halo said.

'The Skythians will never question you,' said Arimaspou. 'Among them you can live however you wish. And you told Hippias, didn't you? So you can be who are. Doctor, and girl, and Amazon Princess.'

Arimaspou was smiling at her.

*That's my mother.*

'Then you can marry that handsome Spartan and live happily ever after. Now look – here's Akinakes.'

Some kind of furore was breaking out by the fire. Halo, dizzy from Arimaspou's revelations, sat for a moment, stunned. Then: *Come on*, she told herself. *There's work to be done. First you must find Arko.*

# Χαπτερ 35

A kinakes was by the fire. Struggling in his iron grip, pinned back by the elbows, was the rabbit-foot man.

'Be quiet,' said Arimaspou, his voice like a whip, striding towards them. 'Where is Hecatores, and what is going on? Tell me, or I'll kill you and ask someone else.' He had his sword to the man's throat, its tip quivering on the skin.

'New moon tonight,' said the little man, who was so terrified he had wet himself. 'Down at Vouliagmenis, on the beach. Big sacrifice for the end of the plague. People are paying all kinds of money for the blessing, dedicating gold and everything . . .'

'And I bet if the plague came back he'd make them pay to get rid of it . . .' muttered Akinakes.

'Where exactly?' said Arimaspou.

'Big beach, to the east – there's a cave . . .'

Arimaspou shouted something in Skythian. 'We'll go ahead – all hands follow on!'

The horses were there and ready. Halo and Leonidas mounted quickly. Akinakes threw the rabbit-foot man in a ditch, and they were off.

They rode faster through the dusk that night than any of their races, any of their chasing Cretan archers or Spartan gangs. The sea on the right, Attica on the left, the moon rising, the road thudding beneath their hooves . . .

Halo was filled with fear and horror. *It can't be. It can't be.*

But it all added up.

She glanced across at Leonidas, galloping along beside her. Where he had dug out the strength from to ride with them tonight she couldn't imagine. But there he was, lean and determined, hunching forward over the neck of a horse, urging him on.

Akinakes led. He knew where the place was. Arimaspou, Halo and Leonidas followed on. They passed fishermen's villages, dark now, the men out at sea with their lamps, the wives and babies sleeping peacefully.

As they had left the city, the Skythian guards on duty had wanted to know what was up, where were they going, did they need more manpower?

Arimaspou glanced back. 'No, but if we're not back before dawn, arrest Hecatores!'

On they galloped — steady, pounding now along the wide beautiful sandy beach that flanked the coast. The sound of the horses' hooves was muffled but steady, steady, eating up the distance.

Akinakes slowed, and turned to signal for silence. They all reined in. Even the horses seemed to understand the import. Akinakes beckoned them close.

'It's round the corner,' he murmured. 'The cave is about a third of the way along the beach, before the rocks. They're gathered already on the beach . . .'

It was true. Halo could hear the murmur and soft roar of a crowd; strange to hear in so isolated a place, in the dark.

'How will we do it?' she whispered, though who she was asking she didn't know.

'We won't wait for the others,' murmured Arimaspou. 'We don't want a big fight if we can avoid it. Most of these people are innocent fools. We'll leave the horses here for the moment, and blend in.'

'Locate Arko, and get him out,' Leonidas said. 'Do they need tethering?'

'Certainly not,' snapped Arimaspou. 'They'll stay, and they'll be silent. Can everyone hoot like an owl?'

Akinakes grinned, and Halo saw white teeth flashing in the dark.

'Three hoots means you've found him. Hoot again, twice each time, so we can locate you. While you're waiting for us, figure out the escape route. Any comments?'

They were all armed. They were all ready.

'North, Leon. South, Halo. West, Akinakes. East, me,' said Arimaspou. 'All right?'

It was all right.

'Good luck,' said Arimaspou.

'Good luck,' they each said. And then they slipped off into the dark.

They were all perfectly trained for this. Spartan Leonidas, Centaur-trained Halo, the dedicated Skythians – each could run invisible through the night. Each could make themselves silent. Each could blend with a crowd, and disappear.

So they did.

Halo knew that Arimaspou had given her the south to cover because the south was the sea, and it was where Arko was least likely to be, and therefore the safest area, as he thought it. She covered it quickly. There was nothing there except the crowd of devotees of the new god. They looked strange to Halo. They were everyday Athenians, men and women, but their faces were at once bland and crazed-looking, hopeful and desperate. They were dressed in white, some wearing bull horns on their heads, some drunk, some on their knees in the surf, crying out their dreams and their fears into the night, hoping that this god at least would hear them.

*More likely Poseidon will hear you, and wash you away for your insolence*, Halo thought.

But Arko was not there.

She turned and glanced up and down the beach. Lurid orange flame torches flared weirdly against the night sky. The figures of the worshippers lit up like ghosts or demons. It felt bad. Very bad.

She knew where Arko was. She felt it in her belly.

A woman near her was wailing in the surf. She had dropped her white cloak, which she had been waving around in a trance. Halo picked it up and wrapped it, wet and salty as it was, around her upper body and head. She started wailing too, and thus disguised she began to wander up the beach, melting into the crowd, heading for the low cliff at the back. Heading for the cave.

The crowd of swaying bodies grew denser as she drew nearer. *Yes*, she thought.

She tried to wriggle between the worshippers. There was a heavy bitter smell – incense of some kind.

But she wasn't going to get through. She stopped for a moment, and looked around. There was a pile of tumbled rocks to the right of the cave, from the clifftop to the beach.

Some people were up there, gaping down at the mouth of the cave. If she could scramble up there, she'd be able to see . . .

She was a good climber, and it didn't take long. Then she found a place a little way from the worshippers, a little higher. But what she saw, when she turned and looked down, made her blood run cold.

Of course she had feared it – she had expected it – but to see it, she wanted to vomit.

The cave mouth had been decked out as a temple – garlands of ivy, swags of leaves and boughs from trees. In front of the cave, a great flat rock, like an altar, lay across the entrance. Around it flaring torches flooded the scene with jumpy, twitchy light. And behind the altar stood three masked figures in white, with bulls' horns on their heads. The priests of the new god. Manticlas stood in the middle: the smallest, the palest. He was holding a large glinting knife.

And there on the rock lay Arko, lying flat, torso twisted, arms wide, bound and gagged, ropes stretched tight to spikes hammered into the rocks on either side, as if he were caught up in a great cobweb.

*Apollo, you cannot let this be* – was her first thought. *What are they waiting for? How long do we have?*

She summed up the scene quickly. She had to release him and there had to be a way for him to escape the crowd . . . But they were so outnumbered . . . Was he still strong? Or had they drugged him? He looked strong . . .

The twelve ropes she counted were tight enough for an accurate arrow to snap.

She had twelve arrows.

She laughed. *OK then.* She raised her bow to her ear, flicked an arrow into place, and aimed for the nearest of the ropes. *Apollo, if you ever cared for me, or for Arko, guide my arrows now . . .*

But before she could start to shoot, something extraordinary happened.

A commotion started in the crowd. A frisson, a movement . . . it was following someone – she could make out a figure, the centre of the commotion, working its way to the front, leaving a widening wake behind it.

It was scrawny, half naked. Moving awkwardly, scratchily, it burst out at the front of the crowd, and jumped up on to the altar rock. It turned to face the crowd. Even from here, Halo could see the glint of the torches reflecting in its wild red eyes, and the black blood dripping from its mouth.

'Plague!' it roared. Its voice was hoarse but the words were clear. 'Plague! False gods! Plague! The anger of Apollo, the curse of Zeus – Athenians, remember your true Gods! Plague! Plague!!!'

The priests were looking round, frantic suddenly, helplessly calling for their guards.

'Take him!' one shouted – but the guards hung back in horror.

'Plague!' one yelled. 'Plague! Plague!' and panic burst out.

Terror gripped the crowd, and glee gripped Halo.

She found her aim, pulled back the string firm against the groove of her thumb-ring. She loosed her arrow and it hissed past her ear. It hit the taut rope, snapping it and sending it coiling crazily back on itself.

Arko's head snapped up. He looked right at her – and she saw the strength run through his limbs as he tried to struggle to his feet. He was alert all right, and wondering what in Hades was going on. He was OK.

She shot again.

*Yes!*

And the next.

In training, she could hit twelve bullseyes in less than a minute; from further away than this. In training in the dark, ten.

She breathed steadily. This was easy. Don't let the circumstances make it difficult.

Four – yes. She heard the rope's quick snap.

The crowd were running, mad, up and down the beach.

Don't even look.

Snap.

Snap.

Snap.

*Apollo, don't desert me now.*

Snap.

The sound of the surf behind her, her own blood in her ears, the rhythm of her shots . . .

And then, reaching back to her arrow carrier, there were none. Instead, something grabbed her hand, swung her round.

A face, a strong man's hand on her arm, higher up the rocks than her. A man's voice, swearing. His other hand held the remains of her clutch of arrows above his head. He was dressed in white – a devotee, trying to protect the sacrifice and the priests.

Without even thinking about it, Halo twisted his arm, kicked him, elbowed him in the ribs so he bent double and swung him over her shoulder and down the rocks. *Thank you, Arimaspou, for teaching me Skythian hand-to-hand combat*, she whispered.

But her arrows were gone with him. She turned back to the chaotic scene below.

The ropes were almost all released. The skinny, mad figure of Leonidas was cutting the last one with a glinting knife – Manticlas's knife! The other priests were cowering in the cave mouth, yelling at their guards. Their guards were running away. Everyone was running away.

Well, almost everyone. Two figures were heading *for* the altar, and two remained there.

Leonidas was spitting blood and laughing and sticking Manticlas's knife in his belt when Arimaspou and Akinakes reached him. Arko was rubbing his wrists and crying, 'It's the Spartan toad!' in disbelief. Halo, the last to arrive, just flung herself into Arko's arms.

She did the same to Leonidas, who held her tight for a moment, though he was still laughing with a kind of mad hysteria. Then he collapsed in a faint.

'Get him on my back,' said Arko. 'And let's get out of here.'

Arimaspou and Akinakes lifted Leonidas up, and he slumped forward against Arko's tattooed back.

'You too,' said Arko to Halo. 'Hold him in place.'

'I'll be too heavy for you,' she said, but Arko just gave her a look, so she climbed up, reaching round Leonidas's waist to hold on to Arko's.

'I suppose he and I will *have* to be friends now,' Arko said to Halo.

'Yes, you will,' she said, resting her head on Leonidas's back. She couldn't stop smiling.

'Is he your human then?' he asked. 'Like Chariklo said?'

Halo laughed, looked down. 'Shut up,' she said.

'What's happened to Manticlas?' Arimaspou shouted.

'He was in the mouth of the cave,' Halo called.

'You go on, take them back,' Arimaspou called. 'Akinakes and I will get him.' He gave a fierce whistle, and the horses came cantering up the beach.

## Χαπτερ 36

'Arko! Thank the Gods,' cried Nephiles, jumping up from the fire as they lurched into the compound. 'Is it all of you?'

'Arimaspou and Akinakes are still out there,' said Halo. 'Going after Manticlas – or rather Hecatores.' She slid from Arko's back. 'Help me with Leon.'

Nephiles was already there to help him down. They laid him on a rug by the fire.

'We saw the others on the road – told them. They've gone with them,' panted Arko, getting his breath back.

'You two should go to bed,' Halo said.

They were back, and safe. They were safe. Arko was safe.

'We'll wait for the others,' said Leonidas.

He and Arko both looked grey with exhaustion in the firelight.

*Maybe I do too*, Halo thought.

Nephiles threw blankets to them, and they pulled them round their shoulders.

'His guard had deserted,' she continued. 'The dogs will find him.'

'Get this down you,' Nephiles said, handing them each a bowl of stew, and a cup of honey tea.

Nephiles's hound came and curled up to Halo. She stroked it absently. 'I must put something on Arko's rope burns,' she said.

Nephiles handed her her bag, and held the light while she tended the wounds. Her hands were shaking with tiredness and relief.

Finally, her work done, she let herself fall on to the rug. Leaning on Arko's chestnut flank, she whispered, 'Arko, what happened?'

'They shot me,' he said, between mouthfuls of stew. 'I didn't know at the time, I worked it out later. I remember the skirmish in the morning, and heading off with Nephiles in the afternoon to look for you . . . The next thing I knew, I was in a cave by the sea, and my head was splitting with pain, and I had this wound.' He gestured to his shoulder, where the wound was still not properly healed. 'Hecate only knows what they put on that arrowhead . . .'

'I put some galbanum on it,' she murmured.

'Anyway, it knocked me out completely, and I've no idea how long I was out for. Even when I came round it was all like a fog, I couldn't tell time, or place . . . hard things were soft, soft things were hard, the sea was talking to me . . . For a while, Halo, I thought I was in our cave in Zakynthos, breathing the bubbles, do you remember . . . ?'

She smiled.

Leonidas was listening, and trying to eat, but his swollen tongue made it difficult.

'What did you do to your mouth?' asked Arko.

'Cut it,' said Leonidas.

'How?' asked Halo.

'With a knife,' said Leonidas drily.

'When you were eating?' Halo asked, puzzled.

'No! I cut it to make it bleed.'

'You cut your tongue open, on purpose,' she said.

'Of course,' he said. 'It had to look real.'

She smiled. She particularly liked how matter-of-fact he was about it.

'Gargle with salt,' she said. 'It'll help it to heal.'

It was deeply dark by now, with only the tiny horned crescent moon sailing high like a shining bow flung through the night. Nothing to do now but wait. What was taking them so long?

Leonidas and Arko fell asleep, side by side. Halo looked at them: her two wounded heroes. She'd stay awake, wait for Arimaspou. She lay back. *Oh, the beautiful beautiful stars . . .*

In moments she was asleep.

Something disturbed her. She opened one eye. The sky was high and cold and pale: early morning. She could hear Nephiles singing softly as he tended the fire, and smell the woodsmoke. *Are the others back?* It was only a half thought, as she rolled over into her blanket, warm and snug between Arko and Leonidas. *Please, don't make me wake up . . .*

But there was a clattering, a knocking, a pounding of hooves, shouting at the gates of the compound.

*No, no more excitement . . . let me sleep . . .*

Then a voice above her. Long hair that tickled her cheek. 'Halo! Are you awake?'

Halo leapt up from the rug. All sleep fell away instantly. The courtyard was full of Centaurs. There were at least forty of them milling around, their fine hooves, their long hair, their swishing tails. They were drinking honey tea, and eating warm bread. Nephiles was giving them cake and bowls of yoghurt. Other Skythians were appearing sleepily from their huts, astounded. By the gate, Arimaspou and Akinakes were clambering wearily from their horses, smiling, bleary in the first shafts of sunlight and the horses' breath rising in puffs. Slung across the back of Arimaspou's horse Halo could see a figure, bound, wrapped in a blanket, a bit of blond hair sticking out of the top.

And Chariklo was hugging her; and Kyllarus was hugging Arko.

'We got the message,' Chariklo said. 'We came at once. We were just in time – we followed the noise and the lights, we heard the ruckus and spotted Manticlas heading inland – luckily he shows up in the dark! We surrounded him and then your friends were there . . .'

Leonidas was staring at her. 'Oh dear,' he said. 'The fever's back.'

'No, actually this is real,' Halo said. 'Chariklo, Kyllarus, this is Leon . . .'

Leonidas stared. 'Hello,' he said. 'Are you sure?'

Arimaspou was approaching. His face was pale, and his expressionless eye rested on Chariklo.

'Arimaspou,' Halo said, as he drew near. She went to him and hugged him close. Soon she would be as tall as him. 'Mum, Dad – this is . . . Captain Arimaspou. Arimaspou, this is my . . . the mother and father who saved me.'

She looked from one to the other to the other. Leonidas and Arko looked on.

Suddenly her heart was so very full she could feel it like a bursting ripe fruit inside her ribcage.

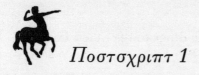

# Ποστσχριπτ 1

ater, Leonidas said, 'So what are you going to do now?'
'Everything,' she said. Then, a little hesitantly, 'How about you?' *Please don't say you're going back to Sparta.*

'I'm going to recover,' he said, 'as best I can. Then . . . who knows . . . now I can't go back to Sparta . . .'

'Why not?' she exclaimed. *Yes!!!*

He waggled his hand at her. 'I'm not perfect any more,' he said. 'My finger fell off.'

Halo stared, in horrified fascination. Then she jumped up to get a dressing.

Leonidas was laughing. Then he threw up again. Then he was laughing again.

Everybody was laughing.

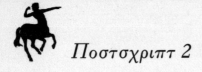

# Ποστσχριπτ 2

Later still, Nephiles, cleaning a big fish in preparation for the great feast for everybody, called out, 'Hey! Look at this!'

Halo, who was slicing onions, glanced up.

'Look what I found!' he said.

In his fingers, shining and dripping with fishgloop, was Halo's golden owl.

# Νοτεσ

1 *Agora*: literally, field; but mostly used to mean the central square, meeting place and marketplace of a Greek town. Though in the Centaurs' case, it really was more of a field.

(!) 2 How to make baklava (you must have an adult to help you with the knives and the cooking): 1) Mix lots of chopped almonds and hazelnuts with a bit of sugar and honey to make a paste. 2) Melt some butter. 3) Put a sheet of filo pastry in an oven dish and brush it with melted butter; add two more layers of filo pastry, brushing each in turn with melted butter. 4) Spread the nut and honey paste evenly on the pastry. 5) Add seven more layers of filo pastry, brushing each in turn with melted butter. Pour any leftover butter over the top. 5) Cut the whole thing carefully into diamond shapes with a pointy knife. 6) Bake for 25 minutes at 200°C (gas mark 6) or until golden brown. 7) While it's baking make a syrup in a pan from hot water, honey and rosewater if you have any. 8) Take the baklava from the oven. Let it cool a little in its dish, then pour the warm syrup over it. When it's cool, eat it.

3 Chiton: a not-very-long tunic, worn by all kinds of Greeks, male and female, usually hitched over a belt at the hips.

4 How to find north: look for the constellation called the Plough, or Great Bear – it looks like a shopping trolley or saucepan. The two stars forming the right-hand edge (opposite the handle) point up and away to a very bright star about five-times-the-distance-between-the-two-stars away. This is the North Star. Look at it, and you are facing north. South is behind you, east to your right and west to your left.

(!) 5 How to make a bow (you must have an adult to help you with the cutting): Find a strong but bendy branch of yew, elm, ash or hazel with a natural curve, a metre or so long and about 2 to 3cm in diameter. Cut a right-angled notch at each end, on the outer side of the curve, about 1.5cm deep, about halfway through the width of the wood. Make a loop in the end of a piece of string (shorter than your bow) and loop it round the top notch, press your foot or knee against the middle of the bow for leverage and loop the string round the bottom notch, tying it so the string is tight but still pullable. To make an arrow, take a straight, hard piece of wood about 30cm long. Peel off the bark to make it aerodynamic. Cut a notch in one end to hold the string in place. This bow and arrow will work, so unless you are starving in the woods. **DO NOT SHOOT, OR EVEN PRETEND TO SHOOT, AT ANY LIVING THING**.

(!) 6 How to clean a fish (you must have an adult to help you with the cutting): 1) Hold the fish firmly around its back, belly up, tail towards you. 2) Minding your fingers and aiming away, with a knife slit open the underside from the little hole at the tail end to just between the gills at the head end. 3) Stick your finger into the slit between the gills, and run it down the length of the slit, inside the fish's belly, pulling out the gloopy guts. They will come away almost in one lot. 4) Rinse the fish properly, particularly inside.

7 A hundred years before, some of the family had killed some traitors who had claimed the protection of a temple. The traitors tied a string to the altar, and tried to sneak off holding the string as the protection of the God; the string broke and the Alcmaeonids said that meant the God did not want to protect them any more, and killed them. Since then, whenever a political enemy wanted to discredit an Alcmaeonid, they cried, 'Blood guilt!' and invoked this dubious curse.

8 Unburied.

9 A short length of hollow stalk that safely carries a little bit of burning ember, which the ancient Greeks used to transport fire.

10 Bad air from which the plague was thought to come.

# Greek Alphabet

| Uppercase | Lowercase | Name | English letter |
|-----------|-----------|------|----------------|
| A | α | Alpha | a |
| B | β | Beta | b |
| Γ | γ | Gamma | g |
| Δ | δ | Delta | d |
| E | ε | Epsilon | e |
| Z | ζ | Zeta | z |
| H | η | Eta | e |
| Θ | θ | Theta | th |
| I | ι | Iota | i |
| K | κ | Kappa | k |
| Λ | λ | Lambda | l |
| M | μ | Mu | m |
| N | ν | Nu | n |
| Ξ | ξ | Xi | x |
| O | ο | Omicron | o |
| Π | π | Pi | p |
| P | ρ | Rho | r |
| Σ | σς | Sigma | s |
| T | τ | Tau | t |
| Υ | υ | Upsilon | u, y |
| Φ | φ | Phi | ph |
| X | χ | Chi | ch |
| Ψ | ψ | Psi | ps |
| Ω | ω | Omega | o |